Otherwise Engaged

a novel

lindsey j. palmer

Skyhorse Publishing

Skyhorse Publishing books may be purchased in bulk at special discounts for sales promotion, corporate gifts, fund-raising, or educational purposes. Special editions can also be created to specifications. For details, contact the Special Sales Department, Skyhorse Publishing, 307 West 36th Street, 11th Floor, New York, NY 10018 or info@skyhorsepublishing.com.

Skyhorse® and Skyhorse Publishing® are registered trademarks of Skyhorse Publishing, Inc.®, a Delaware corporation.

Visit our website at www.skyhorsepublishing.com.

10 9 8 7 6 5 4 3 2 1

Library of Congress Cataloging-in-Publication Data is available on file.

Cover design by Erin Seaward-Hiatt
Cover illustration by iStockphoto

Print ISBN: 978-1-5107-3239-1
Ebook ISBN: 978-1-5107-3242-1

Printed in the United States of America

to emilia bea

Chapter 1

FOR ONE WEEKEND this landscape is ours. It's a dewy July morning, the sun barely poking through the branches, making squinting unnecessary. But I'm wide-eyed anyway, awake since dawn, hunched over on the little porch watching sparrows flit through pine trees and ants scribble across my skin. Gabe is still asleep inside the yurt. I hear his faint snores, and I notice I've matched my breathing to his. It's like a fiber connecting our bodies through the canvas flap and ten feet of humidity, like part of the silken web I see winking in the light, flexible in the breeze. My vision darts, on the lookout for a spider. But it turns out I'm edgy for the wrong reason: A moment later, a mosquito probes my ankle, breaking skin, and by the time I smack the spot it's gone, leaving a fresh pink mound in its place.

"Oh fuck," I say, my first words of the day, voice raw.

I hear Gabe stir inside, and I can picture him waking: the long lean of him arched in stretch, a tangle of chestnut hair swooped over big sky eyes. The image makes me go weak and tingly. I know in a moment he'll call out to me—the anticipation is delicious. Until then, I savor the quiet. I spot something out past our clearing in the woods, a flare of cardinal red tucked in the bramble, a petal or a wing or a balloon fragment. It flashes in the sunlight, daring me to go explore.

But Gabe's gravelly morning voice pulls me back in to the promise of comfort and warmth: "Molly!" I hear a crescendo of wind through the leaves, the screen door's creak, and then Gabe again: "Good morning, Molly-moo. I was calling you."

I crane my neck, and there is my Gabe. Two years in, and the sight of him still floods me with feeling—how lucky I feel to have found him, how grateful I am that such a brilliant and beautiful man has chosen me, how downright giddy I get when he flashes me his half-asleep half-smile. I'm suddenly pulsing with lust. I follow Gabe back into the yurt—the mattress is a magnet—and as we intertwine ourselves, I listen to the birds trilling above us, as if they're composing a soundtrack just for Gabe and me, telling us we belong here, together.

We hike until the sun is high in the sky, and canoe until it nearly disappears again. Then we use twigs and magazine pages to build a fire, and we watch the inked art transmute into rainbow flame. All day I'm like a metronome, counting heartbeats, and steps across the trails, and oar strokes through the water. Also, Gabe's and my rotations around the sun: thirty for me, thirty-one for him, and as of today, a pair of them together. We char hot dogs and s'mores to celebrate the occasion.

"I have a surprise for you," Gabe says, his sticky smile glistening in the firelight.

"What is it?" I'm wary of surprises, preferring predictability and clear expectations. My lap is littered with graham cracker crumbs, and my mind is itchy with a sudden memory of a talk with my friend Kirsten: *Your two-year anniversary, and Gabe planned a romantic getaway? Hmm,* my friend said with a conspiratorial lilt. My own response was feigned bewilderment. Kirsten's fourth finger, dotted with diamond, dangled before me like a secret divulged. I flicked it away and said, *Stop it, silly.*

Not that I haven't thought of it, many times, stomach aflutter. Engagement and marriage excite me in the same way fairies and princesses did when I was little, for their magic and sparkle and mystery. But I was never one to don a tiara and a wand for Halloween; even as a kid, pretending at those kinds of fantasies felt over-indulgent. Similarly, now, I have trouble imagining myself married, or even admitting that I want to be. Wishing to become a wife would be an admission that my current life isn't good enough. And if there's one thing I've learned, it's to be grateful for what you have. When I explained all of this to Kirsten—marriage's most ardent proselytizer, someone who seems to have been born a wife—she smiled skeptically, and I diverted the conversation to less charged territory.

"Follow me," Gabe nudges me now. My heartbeat quickens, ringing in my ears, and I try to ignore it. "Come on, Molly-moo." He slings a tote over one shoulder, and I track its bob and dip down the path to the lake, wondering at its contents: a bottle of booze, a steno pad, and maybe something more? I imagine myself tethered to Gabe for the rest of my time, for moments wonderful and terrible and mundane. I try hard to picture it, and the image flickers like figures in the distance at dusk—here and then gone. I trudge faster to keep up, aching to stay close.

Gabe parts saplings that look like skinny arms, holding them aside for me and pointing to a clearing. Taking in the view, I make my gaze soften, like it's a Magic Eye: The sun goes melty, like eggs over easy, yolks on the brink of burst.

"Okay, I've got three things," Gabe says. He passes me sparkling wine and a joint, numbers one and two. I'm happy and a little fidgety as I guess at number three. With each sip of cool bubbles I grow happier, and with each inhale of warm smoke I get calmer. I'm amazed by my boyfriend, who couldn't have picked a more perfect way to propose.

The eggy sun soon cracks, oozing over the wavy water. I lace Gabe's fingers through my own, and together our arms invent a dance, loop-de-loops and big backstrokes and spinning undulations, Gabe following my lead. These same movements make up my earliest memories—me a wisp of a girl, hair wild, skip-skittering across a Maine shore. That was before a stony hardness took up residence inside of me, numbing out any softness. For a moment, I'm that little kid again, reckless and carefree. Then Gabe reels me in like a yo-yo, and our torsos press together, all heartbeat and pulse. The air is a ricochet of cicadas, the water a murmur of ripples. Gabe whispers in my ear, "Last but not least," and I command myself, *Remember this, Molly!*

There's a rustling of paper, and my shoulders slump. *Proposals don't usually require notes, right?* Still, I hold onto a shred of hope. Gabe's smile is sheepish as he opens a folded sheet. "I wrote you a love poem."

It's instinct; I adjust my expectations in a snap, burying my blip of disappointment under a sheet of contentment. *Everything's fine. My boyfriend wrote me a love poem!* I make a choice to bask in it—this piece of my Gabe, this gift he's sharing with me—and before I sharpen my focus to concentrate on the poem's specific contents, three or four lines are gone, faded to echoes over the lake's nervous surface. Gabe is still reciting: "Orange of my sigh, dapple of your thigh."

After he's done, Gabe bows inelegantly. I stand on tiptoes to kiss him. "Thank you, my Scrabe." "Scrabe" is a portmanteau of "scribe" and "Gabe." I coined it on one of our first dates, when Gabe took me to a bookstore and gave me a tour of all the writers who inspired his work. Gabe lit up at the new nickname, and then made sure it stuck, my sweet narcissist. I ad-lib now in the style of his poem: "Apple of my eye, capsule of my guy."

"Happy anniversary. Here's to us."

I repeat his words back to him and we clink glasses.

"To many more," Gabe says.

But exactly how many more? I wonder in a flash, before willing the question away. "I love you," I say. I kiss my boyfriend of two years and we drain our glasses.

⟋ ⟋ ⟍

As Gabe sleeps easily beside me on the lumpy mattress, my night crawls along, a steady hum of nerves punctuated by short naps. At the darkest hour, I submit to Gabe's snores and slip into sleep.

We wake to a shout of "Yooo-hoooo!" It's Carol, who steps inside our yurt like an invader, although in truth she owns the place. She holds out a roll of toilet paper like it's a gag gift.

Gabe gets up, guileless in his boxer shorts. "Thanks," he says. "We could use the reinforcements." I mumble hello from under the covers, shy in my silk shift. Carol hands me a laminated pamphlet and I feel her looking at me looking it over. There's a portrait of her in profile and, below it, bold claims in block lettering:

RELATIONSHIP COUNSELOR, SEER OF PAST AND FUTURE, GIFTED AND EXPERIENCED.

I'm intrigued, despite myself. I glance from the pamphlet to the person and back to the pamphlet; Carol's photo is un-retouched. Both versions of her have graying hippie hair and chunky turquoise earrings. It's a look I recognize from Gabe's mother, Barb.

"Eighty dollars a session," Carol says. "A real bargain." She peers back and forth between Gabe and me. "I specialize in young couples who are on a kind of precipice."

Gabe's glance at me is ironic, but then he blinks back to sincere. "Cool, we'll think about it."

Now Carol shifts to guidebook mode, advising us where in the area to find fresh eggs, thrifting, and antiques. As Gabe sees her out, she again recommends her fortunetelling: "I really think you two could use it. You're clearly lovebirds, but you both seem a bit, well, moody. A double session's one-fifty. Please consider it." She looks at us intently. "You ended up here for a reason, you know."

Her footsteps are barely beyond earshot before Gabe is reduced to fits of laughter, which prove contagious. Gabe is the better mimic. He continues Carol's sales pitch, pressing his fingers to my temples and delivering a faux-astrology reading: "Molly Stone, I sense that you possess a mercurial nature. This, of course, was fated by the celestial position of Mercury at the moment of your conception. Alas, you were born under the shadow of Uranus." Gabe's bare butt is a shock of pale skin in my face.

"Very professional," I say, swatting him away. "Where should I leave my payment? Also in the shadow of Uranus?"

Gabe flops over on the bed and flips open Carol's pamphlet. I peer over his shoulder, searching for something else to poke fun at, a misspelling or a bad clip-art logo. But Carol's branding is sparse and grammatically correct. She describes the future like it's a physical place, easily accessible to her trained mind. I, on the other hand, have always thought of the future like a magic trick, shadowy and shifty, something to be vigilant against and brace oneself for.

I glance at Gabe, who's reading Carol's bio, his lip twisted up and his eyes narrowed. I know this look well. It means he's disappeared into himself, memorizing this moment and storing it away—for a story. I'm in awe of this, how Gabe sees his surroundings not just as they are but as potential for his work, how he can mine reality for his fiction, translating and transmuting our world into new ones of his invention. It's so courageous.

"What are you, a Capricorn?" Gabe asks distractedly, a sliver of his attention returned to me.

I couldn't care less about horoscopes, and I know Gabe isn't really expecting an answer. "Can I see your poem?" I ask. He hands me the sheet and I skim at random: "candle of my pie, reason to my why," and again, "dapple of your thigh."

"What, as in, cellulite?" I ask. Gabe looks at me like I'm a puzzle, so I point to the line, and then run his fingers along the dimpled flesh below my butt, my steadfast companion since adolescence.

Gabe's laugh is all chest. "Oops, I didn't realize." It's a relief when he can laugh at his writing, and I giggle too as he tickles me inward toward smoother skin. "I was thinking of this part right here."

• • •

Driving back to the city, zipping past cows and barns and freshly mown fields, Gabe and I collaborate on an ode to cellulite, and then another to stretch lines and crow's feet and thinning hair, all the lovely indicators of age. It's a pleasant way to pass the time. Early on between us, I remember Gabe noting how much he liked driving because it was one of the few times he wasn't staring zombie-like at a screen; so, when he found himself behind the wheel, he made a point not to just tune out to the radio, but instead to tune in to his thoughts. I liked this. The two of us have had some of our best conversations in cars, plus long stretches of serene silence.

I spread my palms across the dashboard, inspecting my smooth skin and bare nails (and bare fingers, too, I think, before banishing the observation). I imagine my hands mottled and lined, knuckles gnarled. I wonder how the decades will change my insides, too. And when I'm forty then fifty then sixty, will Gabe still be by my side? I let myself wish for it, for just a moment.

There's a beep of sudden cell service, and my phone displays four missed calls: Mom, Mom, Mom, Mom. Annoyed, I click the screen dark, although my mother's persistence remains roiling inside of me.

"Ode to dark spots?" Gabe suggests. But I shake my head. I'm now picturing my own body aged, mutated to become my mother's, my future life a copy of hers, all alone in a big, echoey house. The two of us are like twins, people always exclaim, as if that's clearly a cause for celebration. Even our names are near-doubles—Molly and Emily—a fact I find equal parts comforting and unsettling.

Halfway home, Gabe and I stop at a farm stand. We buy blueberries, realizing too late that they're actually from New Zealand. This makes us laugh, and still, we gobble them by the handful. "Open wide," Gabe says through a full mouth, and I bare my bruise-colored tongue. "Here it comes, imported all the way from down *undah*." He tosses me a berry, underhand. It takes five until I catch one—I swallow it whole in shock.

Gabe lifts his arms in victory, then nearly shouts, "I have something to tell you. It's important!"

"Oh?" *Oh!* I think, dutifully taking in the panorama—farmland until the horizon, sky a clean sheet. I go damp under my t-shirt. Of course Gabe would choose broad daylight to mark a milestone, I realize now. He thrives on sun and space. I remember my phone filled with my mother, and I soften toward her and her surfeit of attention. Gabe drapes an arm over my shoulder, and my mood soars. How I adore his paper-light touch, how I appreciate his affection that's ardent but only in bouts.

He scoots to face me head-on. *Here we go,* I think, *this is it.* I'm nervous, but excited, too—I can admit that to myself.

"Molly," Gabe says, staring me square in the eye, "I finished my novel."

"Wow!" I swallow sharply, as the news settles like a stone in my stomach. My eyelids drop, eclipsing the world into darkness. Part of me wants to crumble to the ground into a fetal curl. But I don't give in to the urge. Instead, I force my eyes open and spread my mouth into a smile. With effort, I bury my previous expectations. With focus, I say to Gabe, "I'm so proud of you! Congratulations, my Scrabe."

I *am* proud of him, very, very, very. I picture Gabe's novel like an Athena sprung from his head by axe and computer keys, emerged in full armor. How strong and brave he's been to birth it.

"I'm still tweaking it here and there, but I'm almost ready for you to read it," Gabe says. His eyes have turned timid and hopeful, and I think, *Oh, precious boy, how lucky I am that you are mine.*

"I'd love to," I say, meaning it. Water pools in my eyes, that's how thrilled I am for Gabe.

A breeze sends a rustle through the trees, and I'm suddenly chilly. "Should we head back?" I say. Gabe helps me up, and I wipe dirt from my shorts and stamp my feet to rid them of pins and needles.

Trudging to the car, aware of the muddy sink of each step, I consider Gabe's offer for me to read his work. As far back as our first date, he told me about his novel; back then, he'd just begun writing it. I remember leaning in like an accomplice, coaxing out details over our second and third drinks. In those early days, I begged for chapters, synopses, even single sentences, so eager was I to get glimpses into my new boyfriend's thoughts metamorphosed to the page. Gabe was kind but firm: *Not yet. No. Still not yet.* He did show me a short story once. It was a history of a man's regrets told over the course of his whoosh down a waterslide, two decades condensed into the two-minute ride. I found it really moving. But I was also distracted by the misplaced modifiers and run-on sentences, so I marked the errors, then handed the pages back to Gabe. He was quiet, before pointing out that he hadn't asked for notes. True. Fair. But didn't he want his work to be grammatically correct? I ventured. I was focused on the wrong things, Gabe replied, nostrils flared. He never showed me another piece of his writing, and his accusation haunted me: *I was focused on the wrong things.*

I haven't asked Gabe about his novel since. On mornings when he's writing, I've made a habit of becoming quiet and still, and I've grown to covet that time. It's felt like meditation, evanescent and gauzy. It's sometimes easy to forget that during that same time, Gabe has been working toward something concrete, a pile-up of pages, a record. *But, of what?* I wonder now, curious and a little excited.

I let my mind drift over the highway until I realize we're back on the BQE, back in Brooklyn. "That yurt was all right," Gabe says. "Like camping but without the sore back and having to dig a hole to do your business."

"They call it glamping," I say. "Glamorous camping."

"Who calls it that? Surely not our magical soothsayer, Carol. Anyway, I'd say we're champion glampers. We should go back. We could start an annual tradition—a yurt a year."

"I'd like that," I say. I picture the trip as a refrain to look forward to, next year, next decade, and so on. It feels like a promise.

Gabe offers to drop me off at home and return the rental car on his own, but I'm eager to keep him by my side. I slip into this clingy mood sometimes on Sunday nights, anticipating a week of days spent apart. When we're both finally back home, unpacked and in pajamas, I flop myself across Gabe on the couch. We relax into our routine: wine, laptops, and reliable Wi-Fi. At some point I must have fallen asleep, because I wake with a jolt from a dream: I'd followed that scrap of red back in the woods, and discovered a cherry Ring Pop. I sucked it to its nub, and then Gabe appeared, in a panic about a lost engagement ring. I pressed my sticky lips to his, the sugary syrup swirling in my belly, and told him not to worry, the ring was safe inside of me.

I sit upright. I'm in bed—I guess Gabe carried me here. I hear something—snatches of song through the cracked window. I get up to peek down at the street, and I see three girls in slip dresses standing under the streetlight. They're holding hands, entertaining each other with a manic rendition of Taylor Swift's "Shake it Off." My mind goes to Kirsten and Sam, my best friends of more than a decade, the longest relationships of my adult life. Why are anniversaries reserved for romantic relationships, I wonder; why don't we celebrate *friend-iversaries?* It's a fleeting middle-of-the-night thought. So is the urge to fling open the front door, run outside, and join those happy drunken girls in song. The bedside clock blinks 4:11, less than two hours until my alarm will signal the start of the workweek. I know I need to sleep. I turn over, place a pillow over my ear, and nuzzle up to Gabe.

"Hello, my good girl," he murmurs in his sleep, and tucks me snug under his arm, where I feel safe and happy.

Chapter 2

IF IT WEREN'T for her steady barrage of calls, I'd say my mom has a sixth sense for when I'm free to talk; in truth, she's just persistent. I'm circling Bryant Park, a midday break from the computer screen and canned office air, weighing my lunch options, when my phone rings again. "Hi Mom." To a background hum of her concern—no word from me all weekend, she worried a bear might've smelled my menstrual blood and eaten me alive, et cetera—I decide on a burrito, and order via pantomime from a man in a truck. "I didn't have cell service, remember? I'm fine. We had fun!"

My mother barrels ahead into her run-on commentary of news and non-sequiturs, which I let wash over me, soothed by her voice but only half-listening: "You should switch to Verizon. And please talk to your brother about his birthday plans. Find out what he wants, or I'll assume it's train tickets to visit me, ha! Did you brown-bag your lunch, or are you treating yourself to one of those clever new grain bowls, or—what do they call it?—pokey? poke-eye? I can tell whatever you're eating is messy—I hope you're not wearing silk." I chew more quietly, and dab my mouth with a napkin. "I'll send you some Shout wipes. Costco practically paid me for a tub of them."

"Not necessary, Mom" I reply, flicking a black bean from my sleeve that is indeed silk, and noting with annoyance the oval of grease left behind.

"The woods must've been a nice break from the city's concrete and filth," she says. I don't respond. Since the moment my NYU diploma was in hand, my mom has alternated between demonizing New York and evangelizing the bliss of my hometown, trying not so subtly to lure me back home. She's right, though; the trip was a nice break, and I happily relate little moments from the weekend—picking wild blackberries, cannonballing off the dock into the lake, stargazing at night.

Then she's on to neighbor gossip, and I'm interested enough to hear about the people I grew up with moving on to new life stages, to promotions and home ownership and marriage and babies. As my mom tells it, her life is a constant stream of wishing *Mazel Tov* to friends on becoming mothers-of-the-bride and grandmothers. "But what a pain to have to slim down for a wedding," she says. "Or to baby-proof a house—the den alone with all those sharp edges!" I almost laugh at how clearly she's trying *not* to pressure me to marry or reproduce; it sends a stronger message than if she were direct about her wishes. Mostly I'm just relieved to hear that my mom is seeing enough friends for her to stack up her life (and mine) against theirs.

I pitch my burrito ends into the trash, and park myself on a bench. The sun is seductive, and the park sparse for summertime, and I'm not eager to return to my office.

The shift in our phone call is inevitable, occurring when my mom mentions Carol: "That yurt owner, she calls herself a 'life coach fortune teller.' Tell me, what on earth is that? Her web site mentions no professional training. She's a snake oil salesman, if you ask me, convincing vulnerable people that she can predict their futures. Shameful!"

Rice and beans churn in my stomach, along with a blend of pity and pique. I picture my mother, alone late at night in the house that's far too big for her but that she refuses to sell. She's straight-backed at the computer, clutching a mug of Splenda-spiked tea as she deep-dives into

Internet research about my trip—every detail of where we stayed, all the local amenities, perhaps even the traffic patterns back to Brooklyn. "I have to go," I snap, cutting her off.

I'm left pondering Carol's prognosis, wondering if she really could intuit something significant about Gabe and me. But I quickly excise the thought from my head. As much as my mom irritates me for being the world's most determined busybody, she's right: It's this kind of irrational musing that lets Carol prey on people for profit. I get up and hurry back to work.

It's a relief to be back in my office, with its cool air and sleek lines, and the clean slab of my desk. I text Gabe a heart. No response—he turns off his phone while he writes. But what if there was an emergency? I once asked him. Like what, he wanted to know, a lackluster rebranding of one of my company's products? He wore his irresistible smile; otherwise I would've clocked him. "Ah, a dig at my ignoble job," I replied, donning my own charming smile, "the one that so handily pays all of our bills." Not heat or cable, Gabe pointed out. True, although Gabe is the one at home all day using said heat, and how should I have known if "writing" didn't really mean binge-watching *Game of Thrones*? I'm reminded with a jolt: Gabe finished his novel. Three hours later, he texts me back:

Kiss kiss. Off to the grind.

Most days, our schedules barely overlap. Gabe starts prepping at four for the Nonno dinner rush, and I'm freed from my office by five-thirty. Which means dinner for one, if I'm staying in, or waiting until midnight to eat whatever Gabe doggie-bags—spaghetti carbonara, eggplant parmesan, Caesar salad and garlic bread. Nonno specializes in comfort food made with big blocks of butter and cream, which then sits brick-like in the stomach.

Entering our apartment tonight, I sense a strange presence. In a snap, I'm transported back to being six years old, in the months after my father's death, when I suddenly grew terrified of monsters. I sensed them everywhere—under the bed, behind shower curtains, in the backs of closets. My mother would dial up the monsters' mommies to tattle on them for being out past their bedtimes, then she'd shoo them away from our home and back to their own. I never really got over that fear of monsters, I'm ashamed to admit; I just buried it under a will to be brave. "Hello!" I holler now to the bedroom, "Hello!" to the bathroom, and the kitchen galley, and the closet. I finally spot it on the coffee table. I approach it timidly. Gabe's novel.

I pick up the bulk of it, and run my fingers over the cover page, a sea of white with several small words stamped in the center: "*The Charms of Dahlia,* by Gabriel Dover." Curiosity courses through me. Here is physical evidence of Gabe's inner thoughts, and I realize I have absolutely no idea what they might be. My heart starts pounding, my skin grows goosebumps. I replace the manuscript on the table and carefully straighten its pages. I make myself grilled cheese, drink a glass of wine, and immerse myself in a bubble bath, until I hear Gabe's key in the lock.

We trade our Monday run-downs over more wine and penne with vodka sauce, the slippery noodles a salve down my throat. Gabe impersonates his patrons table by table, a variety show that still entertains me months into its run, and I describe an interview with a job candidate who mispronounced every brand she mentioned: Uniqlo, LaCroix, Fage, even Adobe. (I don't admit that I echoed the mispronunciations back to her so she wouldn't feel bad.) When we finally slip into bed, it's past one a.m. I'm half-asleep as Gabe nudges me and, with a tentative voice, asks, "So, did you start reading my novel?"

"Not yet," I say. "Too much work tonight." The lie slips out easily, and I roll over, pulsing with guilt. "Good night, love."

But I do start reading, the next evening.

The Charms of Dahlia, by Gabriel Dover
CHAPTER 1

It had been five weeks, six days, and nine hours since Russell had kissed a girl. *[Not a bad first line.]* He knew this because it was the longest he'd gone in years without that kind of human contact. And because the moment Colleen confessed she'd slept with her lab partner and then kissed Russell goodbye was still replaying on a loop in his head, causing a thrumming ache in his chest. It was a point of pride for Russell that he and Colleen had dated for five full years, surviving even the supposedly impossible transition from high school to separate colleges. Colleen had stuck with Russell through regrettable haircuts and gruesome bouts of acne. Less to Russell's credit, he'd witnessed Colleen grow from a gawky high school freshman to a full-fledged woman, her pancake-flat chest transforming to a C-cup, a topographical miracle in his teenage mind.

Yuck. I can't help it, I roll my eyes.

Russell knew how lucky he'd been.

He hadn't cared that his frat brothers all heckled him about his relationship with Colleen. They pointed at his framed photo of her in a collared shirt and hair ribbons and asked how much she put out (not at all until senior prom, plenty since then). And when Colleen broke it off, Russell wasn't ashamed of his heartache, of skipping class for a week to wallow in video games and Bud Light. His buddies' insistence that now he could finally enjoy college without the dead weight of a long-distance girlfriend didn't move Russell. He knew they'd simply never been in love the way he had been. They didn't know what it meant to have a partner and a best friend whom you trusted and respected to the core of your being.

The prose is just like Gabe talking in my ear, fluent and mellow. It's sort of fun observing him observe this Russell character, who I guess might be a version of himself. The first shock comes on page two:

> When Russell first laid eyes on Dahlia, he didn't feel trust *or* respect. He felt lust (something which, if he were being honest with himself, he hadn't felt towards Colleen, not really, for months). The party Russell's friends dragged him to was shoulder to shoulder with bodies. Dahlia was in the kitchen doorway, moving her body to a song that, like Dahlia herself, Russell recognized but couldn't have named. She was blocking the way to the keg, although no one was complaining. Her jet-black hair tumbled over narrow shoulders, and when she spun around, she fixed Russell with glinting almond eyes.

Jesus, I think, *he barely even changed the name.* Because Dahlia is so obviously a version of Gabe's ex, Talia. Talia with the long dark hair, small frame, and hazel eyes. A flighty sprite, a so-called creative spirit, a vegan with a minor cocaine habit, perennial couch-crasher, all potential but... I've heard plenty about Talia over the past two years. "You, Molly, are the polar opposite of Talia, thank god," Gabe once said, kissing me chastely on the nose, and then praising my reliability and well-adjustedness. I may as well have been a small child or a pet.

I met Talia just once, when Gabe and I were newly dating and she appeared beside me at his friend's book launch, wrapped in an intoxicating perfume of white wine and lilac shampoo. She introduced herself, and I complimented her shoes: glitter pink jellies, despite the chilly night. I admired the boldness of the choice. My own feet were clad in scuffed Mary Janes. I marveled at how Talia held herself with total confidence. She looked luminous, almost electric, even with a constellation of zits spread across her cheek; I remember thinking she could've modeled if she were half a foot taller. But then Gabe spotted us. He marched over, grunted at Talia, and then yanked me to a faraway row of seats, filling me in on who she was with a furious whisper. He insisted we leave right after the reading, skipping the reception. *What could be so threatening about an ex-girlfriend?* I wondered at the time. *How could a casual catch-up pose such a threat?*

I keep reading, breath now held:

"What?" As Dahlia said it, her lips' parting revealed a sliver of a scar on her cheek, a faint comma catching the light. She led with it, which was maybe what possessed Russell to walk right up to her and press the pad of his finger against that scar. It was rough, the one snag in her creamy-white complexion. Russell wanted desperately to know its origins, some past hurt that had stamped itself onto her face, which she now wore bravely for all the world to see. But Dahlia swatted his hand away, her reflexes fleet. "How dare you touch me?" she said, challenge flashing in her eyes. A second later she kissed him, her lips as soft as her tone was fierce. When she pulled away, she poked a finger hard into his chest. "*I* touch *you*."

Ugh. I actually groan aloud.

By the end of the night, Russell had a sense that he would never trust Dahlia. He would never consider her a partner or a best friend. But he was already a little in love, and he knew this was only the beginning.

Dahlia is without a doubt Talia. Only, Talia's acne has been replaced by Dahlia's little scar—much cooler, much sexier. *Wait.* Mining my memory, I recall a news report about a massive fire in a nearby apartment complex. I was so moved by the victims' burn scars, and the courage it must've taken them to face the world each day wearing their traumas right on the surface of their skin. Unlike most of us, they didn't have the choice to hide their hurts away. I remember noting all of this to Gabe. But I wasn't talking about a cute little half-moon on the face of an otherwise beautiful girl at a party. And I certainly wasn't giving him permission to co-opt my observation into his novel—as a way to ogle a fictionalized version of his ex-girlfriend, no less.

I can hear my heartbeat. I can feel my hands shaking. Just a few pages in, and already I'm worn out.

I make sure to be asleep by the time Gabe comes home from work tonight, and in the morning, I'm gone before he's up. He's packed me chicken cacciatore for lunch, plus a tea bag whose label contains a question in his miniature handwriting: **How do chickens dance?** I think about it on and off all morning, before giving up and texting him from my lunch break:

I dunno, how?

Hours later, Gabe responds: **Chick to chick!**

But by this point, I've forgotten the setup to the joke, and I wonder if his message is some oblique attempt at a sext, or a reference to some inside joke I've long since forgotten.

*   *   *

That evening, I flip ahead in *The Charms of Dahlia*, wondering and worrying about the range of this Dahlia character's so-called charms. In other words, I'm looking for sex. I come across a few choice phrases: "parting of firm thighs," "sweet dew," "cooing." *Jackpot.* I scan the scene through a squint, thinking, *awful, awful, awful.* It's somehow both treacle and pornographic, our smitten narrator worshipful of Dahlia's lithe limbs, her—I can barely read it—"honeypot." *Blech.* Is this what sex between Gabe and Talia was like, or has Gabe just done a horrendous job of capturing it? I'm not sure which option is worse.

I don't know how to broach the subject of the novel with Gabe. But it just sort of slips out the next night, at my company's happy hour. Gabe, who has the night off from Nonno, is a hit at parties, and with the Funhouse Branding crowd in particular. As soon as we enter the bar, my boss, Natalie, makes a beeline for him and claps him on the back. "How the hell are you? How's the creative life treating you?"

"Oh, it's humming along," Gabe says. "Most days I marinate in my pajamas till the sun goes down. Then my beautiful patron, Ms. Molly Stone,"—he kisses me on the forehead—"comes home after a day of adulting, and I proudly read aloud the four or five sentences I've managed to scribble down in the past eight hours."

Natalie laughs. "That sounds blissful. Can a corporate sell-out treat a struggling artist to a beer?"

It's fun to watch Gabe enchant my coworkers with his witty self-deprecation (even if the truth is, never once have I returned home to him proudly reading aloud his day's work to me). They can bask in his noble dedication to his art while feeling reassured by their own steady paychecks. His intrigue also happens to reflect well on me.

On my way to the bar, I'm ambushed by Melinda Lowe, our grating assistant designer. "Molly," she squeals, her voice several decibels louder than necessary. "You must tell me about your weekend upstate. My Hamptons share has been a total bust. Mobbed beaches, crazy drama with the girls, and the bars have turned full-on bridge-and-tunnel. It's been such a nightmare, I feel like I need a vacation from my vacation!"

I'm nodding politely, as a Human Resources associate does. I recount a few details from the yurt trip, to which Melinda responds as if I'm revealing the true meaning of life: Her eyes pop and she gestures with her glass of wine, at one point sloshing a quarter of its contents onto her shirt. "Oops," she says, examining the patch of fuchsia that's now stained a deep purple. Her laugh is a honk, but only I seem embarrassed.

"Excuse me," I say, spotting Gabe across the room. Regrettably, he's chatting with someone only slightly more tolerable than Melinda. Jonathan Wexler is the type to introduce himself with a bone-crushing handshake and both his first and last names; he's Funhouse Branding's self-proclaimed "focus-group guru." At some point I must've mentioned to Gabe that Jonathan is a published author. I approach and drape an arm over Gabe's shoulder.

"You know what Grace Paley said," Jonathan pontificates, ignoring me. "You write *from* what you know. You write *into* what you don't know."

Gabe nods heartily. "That rings so true, I can't even tell you."

I'm still feeling sullied by my encounter with Melinda, and stunted by my professional responsibility to play nice. Also, my stomach rumbles with hunger. Naturally, I take all of this out on Gabe: "So, do Dahlia and Russell end up married with a minivan full of kids?" I regret the words as soon as they leave my mouth.

Gabe's eyes widen, and he turns to me, forgetting about Jonathan. "Wait, you read my novel?"

"Part of it. It's intriguing." I say this breezily, feeling anything but. "So it's about Talia, right?"

Gabe suddenly doesn't look like himself. He cocks his head and wrinkles his forehead, assuming a pose that could be named "The Thoughtful Author." "Well, it's inspired by her, yeah. I mean, sort of. It's more about . . . how can I put it?" I wonder how many times he's practiced this speech in his head, consciously deciding on the length of each pause, the number of verbal tics to insert in order to sound most off the cuff. "If I had to sum it up, well, I'd say it's about the relationships so many of us seem to find irresistible, even if they're not the healthiest, and how what strikes us as sexy and seductive is often at odds with, um—"

"I told Gabe I'd love to read his book," Jonathan cuts him off, oblivious. "It seems to have a lot in common with *The Story of Maya Z*."

Right, Jonathan's novel. *The Story of Maya Z* is the stream-of-conscious musings of a twenty-something nymphet with a sex addiction. Male critics adored it, praising its authenticity of voice—one even called it a modern-day *Mrs. Dalloway*—whereas female critics used phrases like "misguided at best," "reductive and misogynistic," and

"400 pages of mansplaining." I myself couldn't get through the first chapter. Still, I realize Jonathan is in a position to help Gabe, so I do what Gabe would never stoop to: "Hey Jonathan," I say, "would you be willing to introduce Gabe to your agent? He's helped you achieve such success, and it would mean so much." Flattery goes everywhere with Jonathan.

"Of course," Jonathan says, voice soggy with patronage.

On the subway home, Gabe and I talk about my boss' insistence on doing a shot with him, and my brother's upcoming birthday party, and an ad for a movie we both want to see. Finally, I venture, "Gabe, I have to say, I'm finding it hard to read your book." I take a breath. "It's basically a love letter from you to this other girl, a girl who couldn't be more different from me, by the way."

Gabe's face is at once hurt and understanding. After a pause, he says softly, "I see what you're saying. But you know it's just a story, right?" I nod, although I've never heard Gabe talk so dismissively about his writing; the way he describes novels he's read, they sound more real than real life. Gabe seems to want to add something else, but decides against it.

"I'd find it reassuring to know that, in the end, Russell meets a girl named Dolly or Holly and they live happily ever after. Is that what happens? I don't mind spoilers." I poke Gabe under his ribs, where I know he's ticklish.

"That's an idea." But he says it halfheartedly. He's distracted, examining the card Jonathan gave him like it's a golden ticket. I see him lip-reading its contents: "Bill Matherstein, literary agent."

• • •

Friday morning, I'm touring around a candidate for a copywriter position, the short tour since I'm leaning toward no. She pauses in front of the conference room and asks what's going on in there. Jonathan Wexler condescending to a group of suburban moms, is what's going on, since some energy bar brand wants to break into the after-school snack market. Even through the soundproof glass, I can detect his false chumminess—*As I look at this group, it's crystal-clear that your children's health is your number-one priority. Seeing as how you're the experts, what do the words "healthy" and "natural" mean to you?* I was the one who hired Jonathan. Because I knew that to a certain type of person—the type who'd sign up for a product rebranding focus group—he's irresistible. I see it now on the moms' faces, and also on the face of this candidate, who's blushing. "Market research," I say, deciding definitively not to ask her back for a second interview. "Jonathan is our focus-group guru."

Spotting us through the glass, Jonathan ducks out of the conference room and extends his hand. He's not one to miss an opportunity to meet a pretty girl. "Oh, Molly," he says, like an afterthought. "I read your man's book. I found it completely captivating. That Dahlia—so luminous, so sensuous. Tell Gabe I passed it on to Billy Boy, my agent, this a.m." *Gabe sent his novel to Jonathan? And what the hell kind of a review is that?* I'm too stunned to respond.

I continue the candidate's tour, but twice I have to ask her to repeat her questions. I answer on autopilot, detailing our company benefits and office culture, wishing I could say instead, *Forget it, we're done here.* Meanwhile, Jonathan's words ricochet through my head like boomerangs, fast and hard.

Chapter 3

As THE 7 train careens through the tunnel, Leo's birthday cake sits precariously on my lap. The thing is six-layered, and has the heft of an infant, although my mom was definitely copied on the email from Lana, saying my brother wanted a small, low-key party for his thirty-third birthday: bowling and beer. My mom, clearly bereft to miss the affair, has overcompensated with dessert ordered from a specialty bakery in Queens. How many calories and grams of sugar must the cake contain, I wonder idly. Lana will cut a sliver for each guest, truly savor her three bites, maybe split another piece with Leo tomorrow, and then box up the rest for him to take to the hospital for the nurses. It's always a marvel sharing a meal with my sister-in-law: Lana eats happily and heartily precisely until the point of satiation, then puts down her fork with a satisfied smile, the epitome of health and sanguinity. I doubt she's ever once dieted or felt uncomfortable in her skin.

When I arrive on her doorstep, Lana's eyes go wide at the cake box. "Come in, come in," she says. "Gee, your arms must be sore. Here, put that down there. I just knew Emily would go over-the-top."

"My mother? Not a chance! It's German chocolate, by the way, though she made sure to mention that it was baked right here on American soil."

Lana has been part of the family long enough to be allowed to make fun of my mom. "So, it's not imported from Germany? No Nazis got their hands on it? Phew."

I am a careful tip-toer in this apartment, which is curated like the Met, and immaculate as a showroom. I don't know how Lana has kept in check my brother's natural messiness, but it's typical Leo to have found the one woman who's not only willing to put up with his filth but who manages it so expertly that he comes off like the picture of tidiness. I'm worried about the stack of frosted slabs now perched upon the side table; I can imagine the disaster of chocolate all over their Persian rug.

Lana distracts me with an assignment to mix drinks. I'm set up kindergarten-style with a row of supplies: vodka, limes, ginger beer, and copper mugs. "Moscow Mules, to complement the German chocolate cake," Lana says, tossing me an apron that matches her own. "Apparently the party will be Eastern-European themed. Did I tell you the mail-order brides are on their way from Lithuania?" She giggles. "Sorry, not funny. I'm just a teensy bit stressed. Leo got paged and he's been at the hospital since six. He said it would be quick, but what is it now—7:45? Thanks for coming early to help, by the way. You're a lifesaver."

"Classic my brother to disappear and leave you with all the work. He's probably at the bar across the street watching baseball."

"No, no, it's one of his patients, this kid Jasper," she says, suddenly solemn. "Leo says he can't seem to kick a bad flu. It's scary stuff." Lana is always serious about the sanctity of Leo's work. He's a third-year resident, training to be a pediatric surgeon—I know it's a very important job, but my brother also loves to be the hero. It's one reason he and Lana are so compatible; he's happiest being admired, and she's an earnest admirer.

I rub what I hope are soothing circles against Lana's back. She points to the pitcher of drinks. "Pour me some of that, a tall one." I fill glasses for us both.

"Well, Leo will definitely beat Gabe here. His shift's not over until ten."

"How is Gabe?" Lana asks.

"Good." I report on our vacation the way you do after several tellings—a capsule version of three highlights—editing out the hopes I harbored about returning home engaged.

"And his writing?"

"Actually, he finished his novel."

"Good for him. I won't ask what it's about—I know writers hate that." *They do?* I'm relieved not to have to recount the little I know about the plot. Realizing I've been holding my breath, I inhale sharply. "Well, I look forward to reading it."

Lana starts telling me about a new line of dresses, all intricate beading and lace for winter. My sister-in-law is a shopper and client consultant for Bella So, a high-end bridal boutique in SoHo. She landed the position back when she was shopping for her own wedding gown and ended up matching several other women with their dream dresses; Bella So gave her a commission for the sales along with a job offer.

Lana pauses to show me a text from Leo:

Complications. Stuck here for now.

Groaning, she gestures for a drink refill. "Everyone'll be here in twenty minutes. I know it's just a party, but the guest of honor isn't supposed to be missing at his own party, darn it." I can't help but laugh; this is the closest Lana comes to cursing.

So, no Leo. The guests arrive and drink up my Moscow Mules, even though they've ended up too gingery. There are jokes about Godot and fashionable lateness and the possibility of a grand surprise, like Leo bursting out of that monstrous cake in the corner. Leo's doctor friends intimidate me for one reason, and Lana's fashion friends for another, so I mill about drinking too fast and reapplying lip gloss every five minutes. The apartment grows crowded, and there start to be calls to cut the cake, despite the missing birthday boy. But then the doorbell rings, and someone shouts, *Hurrah, he's here!* and several others cheer. It makes no sense, like, why would Leo not have keys to his own apartment? But people are chanting, "Leo! Leo!" the doctors and designers united by the drama. So, when Lana opens the door and it is decidedly not Leo, most everyone sighs in disappointment, and then returns to their private pockets of conversation.

Everyone except me. Because instead of my squat older brother with his perpetually wrinkled pants, and instead of my boyfriend, off of work early and smelling of tomato sauce and garlic bread, there is a vision before me that quite literally makes my knees go weak, so that I have to steady myself against the side table.

It's Charlie Ashbury.

Lana is all polite hostess babble—"I wasn't sure you'd make it . . . Drinks and snacks are over there . . . Let me introduce you around"—but Charlie is paying her no attention at all. Not out of rudeness, although I imagine that's what Lana assumes. Rather, because even though I am way over here on the far end of the room, blocked four guests deep, and even though my hair is three shades darker than the last time Charlie and I were in the same room together, he sees me. I see him see me. I start babbling silently to myself: *Oh, my Lone Ranger, mystery mountain man, defier of every expectation, my poison and tonic, upper and downer, salve and shot in the heart, the one I swore I was done with, the drug I quit years ago, quit, quit, quit.*

The magnetism is palpable between us. As Charlie walks my way, stepping on toes and clunking past shoulders, I'm so frightened, I think I might pee my pants.

"Hey, it's Molly."

That tobacco baritone stirs up my insides, and my response is a reflex: "Gee golly."

Charlie's laugh spans his whole face, making him look like the Joker. I laugh too, feeling a little loopy: "What the hey is a yokel like you doin' in the big ol' city?"

I have no idea why I'm talking like this. Something has loosened inside of me, relaxing muscles and tendons and a thousand little fibers that I had no idea were so tense. I feel simultaneously like I've occupied a stranger's body and like I'm rooted deeply in my own.

We stare and stare at each other. It's been nearly five years, but Charlie looks the same. I remember how he can hold a gaze forever, how he's perfectly at ease in quiet, and how perfectly at ease he can make me. I break the silence first. "Well?"

"My oldest friend in the world turning thirty-three? I wouldn't miss it for the world." Yeah, right—Charlie didn't even make it to his own high school graduation. (I know because I searched for him like a hawk.) "Also, I'm contemplating transferring my occupational post, hoping to fraternize with different breeds of fauna and flora, know what I mean?"

I snort. "So, what, they released you from the Badlands?" This isn't even a joke. Charlie is a forest ranger in the Badlands, the national park in South Dakota. Last I knew, he lived in a primitive cabin and was responsible for patrolling a section of the prairie so isolated that weeks could pass without a single visitor—the perfect gig for a misanthrope like him, so long as he had access to a steady supply of whiskey. Charlie, the amiable (or, amiable enough) recluse. Yet here he is like a mirage on Manhattan's Upper East Side, room dense with perfume and conversation.

"I guess I've grown too bad for those birds," Charlie says, eyebrows raised, eyes like magma.

"Meaning?"

"My contract's up next month."

I'm silent. Not because I've run out of things to say—that's never happened in the history of Charlie and me—but because no words seem adequate to the freight train of feelings barreling through me. "I made cocktails" is all I can finally manage.

Charlie repeats my words like they're razors on his tongue: "You made cocktails." His face turns mischievous and a little snide. It's a look I know well—from high school when he'd catch me eavesdropping on his campaigns to convince Leo to skip school and join him instead to get high down by the lake, from the dance floor at Leo's wedding when we clasped hands and clumsily grapevined our legs to the hora, and from various tangles of bedsheets over the years. "I don't think so, Molly." Charlie pulls a flask from his back pocket and drinks until it's empty. Spotting the liquor cabinet (although probably he spotted it the moment he arrived, right after he spotted me), he sidles up to it, grabs a bottle of Maker's Mark, and refills his flask in one well-practiced swoop.

Lana appears at his side. "I can get you a glass, Charlie. You don't have to steal our alcohol like some Prohibition-era bandit." Or like a teenager, I think, remembering how we used to plunder his parents' booze back in high school. That was half a lifetime ago, I remind myself.

I pretend not to see the apologetic look that Lana intends for me. I will her to walk away. But she yanks my sleeve and leans in, a tad teetery. "Leo's not coming home, Molly. Little Jasper needs emergency surgery."

I only really pay attention when she slurs "surgery," and I realize how upset she is, plus drunk. It takes Lana two light beers to get blotto, and the Moscow Mules are stiffer than their sweetness suggests. "How can I help?" I ask, trying to concentrate on her and not Charlie. "Do you want me to get rid of everyone?"

Lana's eyes are glassy and unfocused, which I interpret as assent. The sensible thing is to cut the evening short—yes, I nod, trying to convince myself—and that's definitely what Lana wants, too. "Attention, everyone," I announce to the room, a little embarrassed. "Leo is officially a no-show. Sorry to say, but the party's over."

Charlie pipes up: "You don't have to stay here, but you can't go home." He must know he's inverted the line. I feel his eyes on me, and I don't dare look his way.

Lana flashes me a look of gratitude, then forces upon me paper plates and tin foil, and insists I pack up cake for everyone. As I dutifully slice and wrap, licking gobs of rich chocolate icing from my fingers, I'm aware with every sensor in my body of Charlie circling me.

But then Lana drags me in to the bedroom. "Come lounge with me, Molly," she says, flopping onto her bed. Her satiny dress rides up and she rubs at her eyes, smearing her mascara so she looks like a vampy burlesque star, an artist's still life, frameable. Even wasted, my sister-in-law is stunning. "God, we're getting so old," she moans, ruining the portrait.

"Lana, it's not your birthday, remember?" I say it gently, covering her with a blanket.

"I know, but . . ." Her words fade out and she hums the first few bars of "Here comes the bride." "Down at the store, it's bride after bride after bride. A conveyer belt of brides, all of them off to walk down the aisle."

"Uh huh." I'm stroking Lana's hair, hoping I can soothe her to sleep.

"And then there's me, standing still, watching it all from the sidelines."

"Well, that's your job," I say, and I can't help adding, a little resentfully given my own recent hopes, "And you had your turn to be a bride." It's hard to tell if this is just drunk talk, standard work griping, or a larger existential thing. My job is sort of like Lana's—only instead of a conveyer belt of brides, it's job candidates, heading toward new positions, not new marriages. But, personally, I *like* standing on the sidelines, shaking the candidates' hands and welcoming them to the team. For them, everything is unfamiliar and uncertain, whereas I get to remain where I am, steady, solid, secure.

"It's just . . ." Lana faces me, and for a flash her eyes grow from slits to normal size. "Wouldn't it be wonderful to *always* be the bride? To have that wedding ecstasy last on and on, to be the center of attention forever?"

This sounds like the polar opposite of wonderful to me, but still I nod in support.

Lana motors her lips, releasing an audible puff of air. "If it were up to Leo, my career would be dunzo and I'd be home taking care of a litter of kids. But I've told him, that's not for me. Mothers couldn't be more different than brides, you know? All that drudgery, day after day after day. No glamour. No fun at all."

Lana nods off, which is lucky because I'm speechless. She and I have never discussed these things before. I'm scared she'll remember this exchange in the morning and be mortified; I'm mortified on her behalf. Although who knows if she means any of it? I feel a pang for Leo—I'm close to my brother, but I had no idea he was so eager to be a dad. There's so much none of us knows about anyone else. The thought sends a shiver down my spine.

"Molly." Lana wakes up, her eyelids fluttering. "I'm sorry about Charlie. I never thought he'd show. When we sent out the invite, he wrote saying he might be in town, and asked if you'd be there—can you believe the nerve?"

"Oh yeah?" I'm tempted to say there's nothing for her to be sorry about, that in fact a part of me feels there's no one I would rather see than Charlie. Especially since there's little chance Lana is recording this conversation to memory. But personal confession is not my style. I stay prudently quiet as I tuck her in. Lana cajoles me into taking home the rest of the cake, I kiss her on the cheek, and then I'm gone. Leo can deal with the mess of the party he missed in the morning.

The elevator is a box of mini-mirrors, and seeing my reflection from so many angles returns me to practicalities. I text Gabe:

Abort mission. Birthday boy MIA (stuck at hospital). Be home soon! XO.
Then I step outside warily, bracing myself for Charlie to skulk out from the scaffolding and croon, "You don't have to stay here, but you can't go home." But, save for a far-away taxi horn and the scamper of rodents

among trashcans, the street is quiet. Then I remember, another shiver running down my spine: Charlie Ashbury is patient; he bides his time.

◆ ◆ ◆

I return home to a twirl of colored lights. Gabe has fished out the disco ball from the closet, and is arranging seltzer bottles in a triangle formation at one end of our apartment. Taped to the wall is a sheet with two labeled columns: "Molly in the Alley" and "No-Gutter Gabe."

"I was really in the mood to bowl," Gabe says, and for the second time tonight I'm handed tin foil, this time a round wad of it. Gabe performs deep lunges and slow swings of his arm, practicing his form like he's game for a serious competition. It's sweet.

"What are the stakes?" I ask, half-masking my smile behind my best cutthroat sneer.

"Loser makes breakfast tomorrow?"

"Deal." We shake on it.

But we only manage a few frames before Gabe grabs the bowling ball (i.e. tinfoil) from my grip, storms up the alley (i.e. hallway), and with a single pelt topples all the bottles. "Strike!" he declares. "We did it, Molly-moo, you and me!" He lifts me into the air and spins me around the apartment. "We are the champions! Shout it out from the rooftops!"

I go for it, yelling like a maniac: "We are the champions! We're the best! We're amazing!" I believe it, too, confidence filling me like helium inflating a balloon. Gabe urges me on as he whisks me off to bed.

What follows is so fun that I almost forget about everything that happened earlier in the night—almost.

Chapter 4

GABE'S LAPTOP IS a thud on my prostrate body. "Look!" he says.

The screen sharpens to focus as I blink awake. It's an email, one short line: **love dahlia lets chat**. It's some kind of cryptogram that I'm trying to puzzle out through a sleepy haze. Then I notice the signature: **Bill Matherstein, literary agent**. *Ah, right: Billy Boy.* My chest goes tight, and I'm struck by how hard it can be sometimes to distinguish between excitement and anxiety.

"Wow, that was fast," I say. I try again: "That's wonderful, babe!" I can't help adding, "But what kind of literary agent doesn't capitalize or punctuate his emails?"

I see Gabe deciding to ignore my comment. He's pulling on shorts, and then lacing up sneakers. "I've got so much energy, I feel like I could run a marathon."

I, on the other hand, feel like my insides have turned to lead. When Gabe is gone, I return to bed, taking his manuscript with me. I start again from the start, determined to love it, to get swept up in the story and embrace Russell's enchantment with the supremely confident Dahlia. I speed through several chapters, wondering, despite my resolve, if things might ever turn sour between Russell and Dahlia. A hint comes in Chapter Four:

It started like so many of their nights—with pleasure Russell hadn't even known was possible. He walked through Dahlia's doors into a last-minute party. Dahlia took his hands in hers and they pressed their bodies close on the slapdash dance floor, dancing until it seemed like their limbs might give out. Then she led him up the stairs, through a window, and up the fire escape to the roof. They collapsed into lawn chairs and peered through the interlacing of leaves down to campus, busy with late-night comings and goings. It felt like they were on top of the world.

They fucked out there in the open air, twice, Dahlia's skirt hiked up above her hips, Russell not even caring about her full-throated screams of rapture, or the concrete scraping at his knees. Eventually they fell asleep, and when Dahlia's stirring nudged Russell awake, the sky was heavy with almost-dawn, the darkness just starting to thin. Dahlia led Russell downstairs, through the party's wreckage and back outside, where the grass was wet between their toes. She mounted her bike and began tracing figure eights around Russell. "Hop on for the ride of your life."

Dahlia coaxed him onto her handlebars, then pedaled them across campus, over the bridge, and into the heart of downtown, where the streets were magically deserted. "Close your eyes," Dahlia whispered in his ear. "Let the motion wash over you." So Russell did, listening to her off-key whistling, and when he opened his eyes again they were back at Dahlia's place. They dismounted, shivered, and yawned all in unison, like they'd choreographed it, which made them both laugh in unison, too. Retreating inside towards Dahlia's bed, Russell felt he'd never been more in synch with another person.

I'm imagining myself in the scene, biking in tandem through a sleepy morning, and I'm surprised to catch myself momentarily rooting for Russell and Dahlia.

But when they next woke up—it must have been past noon, the sun aggressive through the blinds—Russell felt tremors beside him, like a tiny earthquake exploding from inside his new girlfriend. "Hi," Dahlia squeaked, the strange sound even more alarming because of the word's ordinariness.

And then everything came to pieces—the strange, magical night dissolving into a big, confusing mess. Dahlia clutched at Russell, and he rocked her overheated body and called her "Love" for the first time. They made it to the bathroom, where Dahlia leaned over the sink and emitted a low whine, then emptied her stomach. Russell stood next to her, oaf-like, pressing hard into his heels and not knowing where to look.

When Dahlia was done, Russell carried her back to bed. She gazed up at him, her eyes blinking lucid, and in a raspy voice, said, "You're what keeps me going, you know." Terror flashed through Russell, paralyzing his thoughts. Dahlia ran her fingers through his hair and for a moment she was the one comforting him, saying, "I'm sorry. I know. I'm sorry." Then their roles reversed again, and Russell was once again the comforter.

I get panic attacks, Dahlia would explain later. By which point Russell would've started to find pill bottles strewn around her room and in the pockets of her purses and jeans; he would have a vague idea that the two things were related. Although he wouldn't have admitted it then, Russell soon discovered that there was something incredibly thrilling about being so needed. He matched her growing need with his own, until they were entwined into the sexiest symbiosis, and he felt perfectly ecstatic.

I'm startled by Gabe's appearance in the doorway. He's watching me, wearing a nervous look. "Well?"

My response is a reflex: "It's great. I love it."

"You do?" Gabe's smile is so bright it's contagious. I try out a fantasy of Gabe's grand literary success, of having a successful author for a boyfriend, or—dare I dream—husband. Gabe wouldn't have to come home from work with garlic screaming from his pores, he could pay off his college loans, and maybe he'd even let me offer notes. He'd have fulfilled his big dream. I really am proud of him.

"I didn't mean to interrupt you," Gabe says.

"That's okay. I was about to take a break." I want to hang on to this feeling of happiness for Gabe about his novel. "Wanna hit the park?"

We pack baseball mitts, and fall into the rhythm of catch, the wind-ups and releases and thuds into mitts. It requires all of my focus, rendering my inner monologue blessedly mute. After several back-and-forths, Gabe lobs one high above my reach. Chasing after it, I'm led to the blanket of two women, lying prone with legs pretzeled amid a tangle of flowy skirts. The ball rolls to a stop inches short of a bottle of wine. I say "Sorry" and "Cheers" in the same breath, then retrieve the ball and hurl it back to Gabe. The women watch with me as it arcs gorgeously across the sky and lands with a pow right in Gabe's glove. "Good arm," one says, and I thank her and run back to my spot.

Back at our blanket, Gabe and I feed each other forkfuls of Leo's birthday cake. The chocolate is rich and velvety on my tongue, taking me back to last night. Gabe interrupts my reverie: "Look," he says, pointing to the two women. One is squatting, her palm open to reveal a little gaping box. The other woman's mouth gapes, too. They slip rings onto each other's fingers (the box contained two), then they kiss, collapsing onto one another in the grass. Gabe squeezes my hand and whistles, and other onlookers whoop and call out congrats. Our pocket of the park turns magical as everyone collectively delights in the pair's joy. Eventually, I tell myself it's rude to keep eavesdropping, though really I'm fighting pangs of envy. I close my eyes.

Mistaking this for a romantic overture, Gabe leans in for a kiss. When I open my eyes, he's staring lovingly into them. "I'm so relieved you're liking my book," he says. "I know I used some details from my time with Talia, but all writers mine their past for material. It doesn't mean I'm any less into the present."

He runs his hands through my hair, and I decide to believe him. Because of course it makes sense that our past might occasionally bleed into our present; like if our ex happened to appear out of the blue at a party, of course it would bring back a flood of old feelings. That's just common sense.

"The present is pretty great, right?" I say, meaning it rhetorically, but it comes out like an actual question. Gabe doesn't seem to notice, though, so maybe I'm being paranoid. I snuggle against him and he wraps his arms around me. We stay that way, watching the sun fade from the sky. All is quiet and peaceful, except for a low rumbling in my stomach from too much cake, my satiation cut through with a faint tinge of queasiness.

*   *   *

I'm brushing my teeth the next morning when I see Sam's text:

Bailing on brunch, stayed out til 4 and barfed twice already.

Kirsten's reply comes within seconds:

Sorry you're sick :(though kinda relieved. Buried under mountains of work, probably best to tackle it in lieu of mimosas.

I, for one, am not relieved. I've been looking forward to meeting my friends for our Netflix-and-Spill Club. It's the second iteration of our book club, since according to Sam, bingeing on television is the new reading. (Gabe was decidedly unimpressed with our revised club ethos.) A morning with Sam and Kirsten would've been a balm for all that's happened in the last couple of days. I text the group,

Skype instead?

Even pixilated versions of my friends' faces cheer me up, and I raise my coffee cup in greeting. "So nice of you to dress up for us, Molly,"

Sam says. I'm still in my pajamas and I may have forgotten to brush my hair.

"Ignore her," Kirsten says. Of course, she's wearing a cardigan and matching earrings, plus full make-up; she's likely been up since seven. "So, what's up?"

With both of them blinking at me through the screen, I freeze up, a blockage surfacing in my lungs. I can't tell them about seeing Charlie and the torrent of feelings it dredged up. I can't share that Gabe's novel is all about him and Talia, and how hard it feels to know that every single day of our relationship he's sat at his computer paying tribute to his ex. I can't say any of it.

"Molly?" Kirsten is leaning so far forward that I can spot the tiny pores of her nose under her foundation. "Are you all right?"

"I think her screen froze," Sam says. "Or her love for us, her dearest friends, has led to permanent paralysis."

"I'm fine, sorry," I say. "I was just bummed about no brunch. I wanted to hang out with you guys. And I have a lot to say about Season Two of *Insecure*."

"Let me guess—you took a dozen pages of notes, with discussion questions and everything?" Sam's smirk morphs into a frown. "Shit, hold on." There's a jostling of her on-screen window, and then she's gone, replaced by distant guttural noises.

"I guess she really is sick," Kirsten says. She shouts out "We love you" to Sam, and I add, "We're virtually holding your hair back!"

Kirsten's voice softens: "Hey, what's really going on, Molly? Is this about your father? I know the anniversary's coming up."

My heart swells. She's right—as of tomorrow, it'll be twenty-four years since I lost my dad. "It's so sweet for you to remember that, Kirsten. That must be why I've been feeling down." I feel terrible for the lie. And for the fact that it took Kirsten's mentioning it for me to recall the significance of the date. "But I'm okay, I promise. Tell me about your crazy workload."

Sam is back, wiping at her mouth. "Pardon my interlude. What did I miss?"

"Nothing. Kirsten was just going to fill us in on her clients." Our friend is a public defender in East Harlem, carrying a caseload fit for three attorneys.

Sam groans. "I can't handle stories of human heartbreak on top of this epic hangover. Sorry, Kirsten."

"That's all right. Plus, talking about all my work instead of doing it will just stress me out. I gotta get back to the grind."

After my friends sign off, I stay seated, staring into the middle distance. I start mulling what Kirsten brought up. It's hard to believe nearly a quarter-century has passed without my dad. I try to rewind all that time. It's a tic of mine, this effort to remember the period right after he died; all I can ever conjure up is a fuzzy haze of anger. My mom has often related how strong and brave I was—she says I stood in the receiving line at the funeral like a little lady, politely greeting every guest and wowing everyone with my poise. And I was only years old. My mom always describes this with pride, in contrast to Leo's behavior: Apparently he was a wild, bawling mess. He stormed out of the chapel in the middle of the service, and was found later in the bathroom beside a kicked-in stall door. My brother barely made it through the fourth grade, whereas I ended that school year with an embarrassment of accolades: most books read in my class, most gold stars for random acts of kindness, and a report card extolling my astonishing self-control and empathy. I've heard these stories countless times, and I'm always left baffled, trying to square my mother's version of events with my own dim memories of that time. All I recall is a fury so big it smothered everything else.

I'm startled from my stupor by the distinct aroma of Gabe after a run—earthy sweat, plus the espresso he's inevitably downed at our corner coffee shop. It's comforting how precisely I can conjure up Gabe's routine, down to the calf stretches he performs while waiting at the counter for his cup. I blink at my screen, noticing that my Skype call ended half an hour ago.

"Hey, Molly-moo," Gabe says, bending down to kiss me. "I thought you were meeting up with the girls."

"Change of plans," I say.

"Lucky me. Now we can spend our whole Sunday together."

"Yep." I kiss him back. "Just let me change and then I'm all yours."

Chapter 5

I'M NOT REALLY surprised when, scrolling through the workweek's first emails, a message pings in from Charlie. I read it through a squint.

Hey. I'm leaving for Bear Mountain in the afternoon. Free for lunch?

I swig the rest of my coffee and chalk up my body's buzzing to the caffeine. My thoughts flit to the two interviews I have to prep for and the job listings I need to post, and yet, with fingers hovering over the keyboard, I keep coming back to Charlie. I first developed this habit in high school, pushing aside everything in favor of Charlie, letting all my senses surrender to his pull. Succumbing to it again half a lifetime later is disorienting, and a little exciting—I can't remember the last time I felt like a teenager.

At age fourteen, I knew Charlie Ashbury only as my brother's cipher of a friend, the guy I watched from afar to distract me from the drudgery of freshman year. I'd anticipated high school to be a relief from middle school's petty dramas, tedious classes, and my mother's nervous watch over my every move. But it was proving to be the same old. That is, until the first time Charlie went from assuming I was part of the background to registering my actual personhood (*woman*hood, I hoped desperately). Charlie had dropped by the house to pick up my brother for a party, forgetting that Leo was out of town on a college visit; like an afterthought, he invited me instead. My mother must've been away, too, because there was no one stopping me from saying yes.

From then on, my formerly dull life became painted over with a neon sheen, even brighter for the fact that Charlie and I were a secret. Leo would've been furious if he'd known, and my mother—*forget it*. I began wandering through my days limp and stupefied that I could experience feelings so intensely. My concentration was wrecked for anything but my clandestine boyfriend. For a dozen weekends, the lies about movies with friends rolled off my tongue, and I hurdled across town as if in a trance toward the object of my obsession. Prudent, practical Molly was replaced by her bold, carefree double, and it felt like a revelation.

On the last of those nights, there was an early winter chill in the air, and I remember Charlie's silly smile as he appeared in front of his house and framed my cold cheeks with his warm hands. "Hey, it's Molly," he said. "Gee golly." As he looked at me intently, I felt high already. Charlie touched his toasty lips to my chilled ones, and then, as if I were just a pit stop to something else, he was off, spinning in circles, bounding around the lawn, lifting his face to the sky. His dark curls peeked out from under a cowboy hat. He wore no shoes.

"Whatcha doing?" I yelled out. With Charlie, I could never predict what would come next, which was a major part of his appeal.

"It's a rain dance. It's Incan, or Mayan." Or maybe he said "mine."

"It's not raining, you know."

"That, my dear, is precisely the point. Rain, currently, exists only as *desiiire*." He dragged out the last word to match his undulations. His laugh was almost a cackle, and I wasn't sure what to make of it. I tried to recall how he might laugh, but couldn't. I'd already grown accustomed to feeling thrown off by Charlie—his chatter ambled easily between mathematical proof and *Alice and Wonderland*-style ramble, and his body was an instrument, always in play. But I was becoming uneasy, the trance thinning. I shivered and dug my hands into my coat pockets. And then, as if Charlie's reeling had willed it, the sky opened and the drops descended, heavy and frigid.

I escaped to the front steps and sat slumped, sheltered by the house's awning. But Charlie didn't seem to notice, and he didn't stop dancing. I followed his maddening movements, watched his toes muddy and his t-shirt mat against his skin. He was oblivious to the couple crossing the sidewalk in front of his house, umbrellas fanned out in taut bursts of blue. His dancing was like a separate entity, on some other plane of existence far away from our boring little town; the fact that I was a part of it, if only tangentially, sent a spike of thrill through me. The rain grew denser, and I called out: "Hey, Charlie."

He was beside me then, his arms wet and cold around my waist. "Let's go play inside." His parents weren't home—they never were—and up in his room I warmed up, wrapped in a towel and then Charlie's limbs. I felt cocooned, and in a comforting refrain I surveyed his things: pack of cigarettes, bag of sunflower seeds, book of crosswords. Then I saw, too, the empty bottle of cough syrup. *Hmm.* I recalled the off-kilter smile of Charlie's hello, and the scene snapped into focus: He was Robo-tripping, something I'd overheard being discussed by some older girls in the locker room after gym class, a high you could buy for cheap right at Walgreen's, no ID required. Charlie was probably seeing me in pretty, swirling colors. I regarded him with interest, even as my insides churned.

At some point he added music—a treasure of a tune, slow and wistful—and I was being lifted up and waltzed with. I'd never waltzed before, so how did I know that's what we were doing? A mystery. Charlie began humming. He fixed me with dark, steady eyes, and I gazed back with my light ones, and it took me a minute to remember who this was I was dancing with. This was a look I was sure was not Charlie's. He was reeling and almost smiling and maybe dreaming, staring at the tip of my ear or my jawbone. "How're you doing?" I asked.

"Hmm, happy." I considered this, wondering what the word "happy" encompassed for Charlie, what exactly was bumping around his head. He ran his fingers through my frizzing hair and told me I was beautiful, which was the first time any boy had said that to me. That was the moment I decided I would sleep with Charlie, another first for me, and soon he led me to his bed. Charlie was sweet and gentle with me, and I fell asleep feeling like the definition of happy. Unlike my usual night thrashings, I rested easily by Charlie's side.

Until the middle of the night, when my mother somehow figured out where I was—I suspect she installed a GPS tracker in me before they were invented—and bore down on the doorbell with such persistence that at first the series of buzzes was a melody in my dream. I was dragged from the house with no chance to grab my sweater or say a word to Charlie. My mom had a few words for him, though. I remember the conclusion: "It's one thing for my son to waste his time with someone like you, but my daughter is all potential, and I refuse to let her throw it away on you!" She punctuated this with a door slam, and a final point for me: "If there's one thing I've learned, Molly, it's that life throws you enough obstacles without having to go seek them out on your own." She fumed the whole way home.

I was grounded for what felt like years. Charlie kept his distance at school, and at some point he and Leo had a falling out, not connecting again until years later. So, save for a few glances across endless school corridors, it would be nearly a decade before I'd see Charlie Ashbury again.

Now at my desk, I type a reply to Charlie's email:

I can't.

Several times I delete it and retype it and delete it again. I think how excitement isn't all that Charlie kicks up in me; there's tumult and turmoil, too, those hallmarks of teenage life that I would prefer to leave in the past. He's like fireworks—dazzling but dangerous, and if a particular mood strikes, irresistible. I stare at my feet, as if they might provide a solution. And they do, sort of: I notice that my boots are scuffed, their heels worn down. They're unprofessional, frankly, and I need new ones. Knowing that Charlie is allergic to shopping, and particularly shoe shopping, after his brief stint as a shoe salesman, I type quickly:

Hey Charlie, Good to see you this weekend. I have to spend my lunch break buying shoes, sorry. Good luck upstate! Best, Molly.

Innocuous, dry—but with the teeniest-tiniest opening . . .

At 12:15, I'm navigating Macy's shoe racks, with Charlie at my side. I never expected he'd show, but of course, Charlie often does the thing you expect least of him. I'm so hopped up on adrenaline that I can barely hold a thought in my head, never mind consider how I feel about this turn of events. So, I shop: I try on a dozen varieties of the same black booties.

Meanwhile, Charlie keeps his promise to say not one word, offering no snide commentary or cutting critique, although I'm sure he's brimming with both. I appreciate this quality in him, the ability to stay quiet. I remember it from our museum outings, during those six months following Leo's wedding, the period Charlie dubbed our "reunion tour." Most people keep up a running commentary as they stroll through the exhibits, just to fill the space or to sound smart or sophisticated. But not Charlie—he'd take it all in in silence, and he'd let me be to do the same. I remember standing in quiet communion with Degas' dancers at the Met, imagining they might pirouette off the canvas and sweep me away with them, feeling blissful at the thought of it. No way did I want to chit-chat about that.

The boots I buy are too expensive with too-high heels. Even Charlie's presence beside me makes me act recklessly. Only when I suggest that while I'm here maybe I'll also look at dresses do I spot a crack in his blithe façade. I laugh and mention a pizza place with the only edible food in a three-block radius. Charlie leads me out of the store like we're escaping disaster. Over pepperoni slices, he asks me what I think of Leo and Lana. I think they're a great couple, a perfect match, and I tell him so. "Why do you ask?"

He shrugs, chewing. "No reason." But apparently this is just a prelude. "And how about that Gabriel guy? That's his name, right?"

"My boyfriend? I think you know that's his name."

Charlie nods slowly, staring at me in a fierce way that eventually yields to smirk. It feels involuntary, how I mirror his expression. He pries from me that Gabe is a writer and that he's finished a novel, but I refuse to give in and tell him the premise. "Then how about I guess?" Charlie's tone is edged with sarcasm, but I'm too curious to stop him. "Let's see, it's probably a privileged man's take on the search for meaning in the modern age, an exploration of love and lust, a quest for happiness and all the ambivalence and self-loathing that goes along with that—that sort of thing. It's written in a style that's aiming for really sensitive but also masculine in that urbane, hipster, pseudo-literary way." Charlie locks eyes with me, his face ugly with smugness. "You're a clever one, Molly. You know exactly the crock of you-know-what I'm talking about."

My face is hot; I feel like I might cry.

Charlie cocks his head to one side. "What, am I so far off the mark?" His eyes bore into me.

"Well, this was obviously a mistake," I say, gathering up the remains of my lunch. "Now I remember why I slammed the door on you and me the last time. You're spiteful and obnoxious and completely unconcerned with anyone's feelings but your own."

Charlie makes a fist and pounds it against his chest. "Now that hurt my feelings." I'm pretty sure he's mocking me.

"What exactly are you doing here, anyway?" I ask.

Charlie toys with his pizza crusts. "I think the real question, Molly, is what exactly are *you* doing here?"

"Good question. Nothing." I toss my trash and head for the exit. Half a block away, I remember the boots. I debate: my pride versus my pricey purchase. I cave and slink back to the pizza place, where Charlie is still sitting, the picture of calm, my Macy's bag perched on the table in front of him. I reach for it, but Charlie grabs hold of its handles.

"Just let me say one more thing, then I promise I'll leave you alone." I could easily wrest the bag from Charlie's grip, but part of me wants to hear him out, so I wait.

"When I'm out there in the wilderness, it's just the tall grass and the occasional bison and me. And every once in a while, I get the urge to light a match and let it drop. Just to see the flames, you know? Just to watch them leap up and spread." *Of course Charlie makes me feel the way he does,* I think, *because he's still the same reckless teenager, with a compulsion to destroy simply for the sake of destroying. He hasn't grown up one bit.* He shrugs. "I won't ever do it, probably. But the thing is, wildfire isn't always dangerous, contrary to what Smokey the Bear claims. It's important. It's restorative. It clears out the dead stuff, the weeds and the muck. It makes way for new growth." Charlie takes my hand, our first physical contact. "Do you see what I'm getting at, Molly?"

I wrest my hand from his, sighing with annoyance. "I suppose you consider yourself some kind of wildfire?"

He smiles wide, his dimples deep; he must think he's adorable.

"My god, Charlie, your ego. How dare you imply that my life is weeds and muck." I snatch up the shopping bag.

"Fine. But I think you should know that those shoes are stupid. They'll destroy your feet." It's so typical, for him to come on to me, only to lash out a moment later; I can't believe I let myself get sucked into his dumb game again.

"*Your* shoes are stupid," I say. He's got on hiking boots caked an inch thick with mud. "You don't belong here, Charlie. Go back to the Badlands."

Chapter 6

I'M SO ANXIOUS to hear how Gabe's meeting with the literary agent is going that I keep glancing at my phone as the prospective marketing associate answers my questions. I tune back in and hear her say it took an entire stick of eyeliner to create her Halloween costume. "Sorry, what were you again?"

"A Seurat painting. It was super-labor-intensive, drawing all those dots."

Right, and it's a good answer for her best costume: creative and clever, but recognizable, within the zeitgeist. My last interviewee said she dressed as Catherine of Aragon—too esoteric—and the one before convolutedly explained her feminist take on a Playboy bunny, whose main difference from the classic get-up was apparently motive. I move on, asking this woman first how she'd describe Coca-Cola to a visitor from outer space, and then to design tattoos for the last three presidents. Next, I instruct her to come up with names for a nail polish to appeal to different consumers: a K-pop-obsessed teen, an aspiring Instagram influencer, and a twenty-something artist with a trust fund. And who would be the most viable customer for the color?

I realize how silly these questions can sound. But I learn a lot about someone based on whether their description of Coca-Cola focuses on the sweet, citrusy, fizzy taste, or on the insidious dangers of sugar and caffeine, or on the brand's iconic design and messaging that a can of Coke equals joy and refreshment. I'm a pro at predicting who'll be a match for Funhouse Branding, good at the job, and satisfied doing it.

"How about you?" asks my interviewee. "How would you describe Coke to E.T.?"

Caught off guard, I laugh a little. "I'm the one interviewing you, right?"

But I'm left rattled. Because the truth is, I'd have to admit to the alien that I don't really care for soda; I'd reason that no savvy politician should risk his reputation with a tattoo; and the last time I dressed up for Halloween I was in elementary school. In other words, I'd fail my own little tests; I'd never hire myself to work at Funhouse. It's no wonder that when I started off here, I was a pretty lousy copywriter. I had trouble getting behind the idea that a product is not essentially the thing itself but rather consumers' perception of the thing. So schooled was I in the art of denying my own wants that I found it difficult to try to convince others to want. Despite this, I'd majored in Marketing in college—I was more interested in Anthropology and Sociology, but I worried that focusing on those fuzzier subjects would never lead to gainful employment. This fear was validated when, a few months before my graduation, the economy collapsed. Suddenly, any type of employment seemed like a long shot, no matter what you'd studied. Every day I read the headlines about mass layoffs and a deepening recession, and willed myself not to succumb to debilitating panic. So, when against all odds, as someone with zero experience who was entering the worst job market in decades, I was offered a job at Funhouse Branding, I knew how lucky I was. And if I ever forgot it, I had everyone else around to remind me.

But all my peers' unemployment—or *fun*-employment, as some defiantly dubbed it—didn't seem so bad to me. For my part, I struggled to get up each morning and go sit under fluorescent lights and stare at a screen for eight or nine hours straight, my eyes pulsing with ache. I frequently became overcome with a powerful dread, wondering if this would be my existence for the next fifty years: day after day spent strategizing how to exploit consumers' desires in order to meet bottom lines, punctuated with dull chatter over weak coffee, capped off with the small relief of six p.m. I sometimes daydreamed about an alternate life—running my own business, something that would help people realize their passions and maybe do some good in the world—but I'd quickly remind myself to be grateful for my good fortune and reliable paycheck.

I couldn't share these feelings with my friends. Kirsten, who'd put herself through college with a string of waitressing jobs while still managing to volunteer as a Big Sister, and who'd graduated with six figures of debt, couldn't find a job despite a perfect GPA and a Political Science degree; she eventually enrolled in law school just to defer her staggering student loan payments. Sam claimed she was so disgusted by American capitalist greed that she wouldn't take a corporate job if it were the only thing standing between her and homelessness. Only someone who came from money could afford to say such a thing, although, to be fair, Sam would never accept a cent from her family. She got by with a series of side hustles: cocktail hostess, rich kid tutor, purveyor of the occasional dime bag of marijuana.

I couldn't talk about it with my family, either. Leo was busy learning how to heal the ill, pulling all-nighters in medical school; my concerns felt frivolous in comparison. And every time I spoke to my mother, she'd go on about how incredible it was that I'd landed such a great job, with a decent salary and benefits to boot. This would inevitably lead to her recalling how my father's passing had left her destitute, deep in debt from the exorbitant medical bills, a stay-at-home mom with nothing to put on her résumé and two kids to feed and clothe. Throughout my childhood, she ran an ongoing lecture series (for an audience of two—Leo and me) on the importance of security and self-reliance. I can still recite parts of her favorite orations.

I suppose this is why I've stayed at Funhouse Branding for so many years. I've felt grateful, and guilty. Also, eventually I realized I have a real aptitude for figuring out who would thrive here. Ironically, this is the opposite of a talent for branding: It means I can perceive who people really are, behind the pretty façades they project in interviews. So, after a mediocre run as a copywriter, I leveraged this newly discovered skill into a Human Resources role, quickly proved myself, and worked my way up to Associate Director. I know that being good at my job isn't the same as loving it, but it isn't nothing, either.

*   *   *

Huzzah!

Gabe's text reads, so I hurry my interviewee to a conference room for the follow-up questionnaire, then race back to my office to call Gabe. "Tell me!" I demand after he answers.

"Billy was wooing me from moment one, a kind of nonsexual courtship," he says. I make noises of encouragement, noting Gabe's use of the agent's nickname. "He loves the book—he already called it a *book*, Molly! And he has a great editor in mind."

"That's wonderful." My heart is a yo-yo inside my chest.

"He wants to get the manuscript in this guy's hands right after Labor Day, so I have to get a headshot and write up my bio and—"

"Wait, that's next week. Did you already sign with the agent?"

"Well, I have the contract and I'm on my way to Jack's,"—Gabe's lawyer friend—"and hopefully I'll have it back to Billy by end-of-day."

"Wow, it's all happening!" I say. I'm struck with a frantic wish for Gabe to rush over to my office so I can scrutinize the contract syllable by syllable, as if acute attention to detail will give me control over any of this.

"I'm a little nervous," Gabe says. "It's strange to finally be on the verge of something I've been hoping for, for so long. There's no way the reality can stack up to the fantasy, you know?" I feel a surge of love for Gabe. Despite my hesitations about his novel, I'm in awe of his courage—he believed in himself enough to spend years pursuing this dream, and now it's finally paying off. I'm basking in second-hand satisfaction. "Anyway, Billy said this kind of writing has been flying off the shelves. How did he put it?" I hold my breath as Gabe searches for the right description. "A modern man's quest for love and meaning, with a style that's fresh and male, but sensitive, too." A lump materializes in my throat, begging to be swallowed. I leave it be, as if in self-punishment.

Spotting my interviewee idling outside my office, I'm relieved to have an excuse to hurry Gabe off the phone. "Congrats again," I tell him.

I escort the woman back to the elevator bank, where she shakes my hand and thanks me. "I've always wanted to work at a place like this. I'm so fascinated by what makes people want the things they want."

This conjures up a memory of Gabe standing in the same spot a little more than two years ago. His words were a warped version of this woman's: "I don't think this is the job for me," he told me back then. "I'm not up for the business of convincing people of what they should want." I was disappointed; he'd been so funny and clever in his interview, not to mention attractive in a rugged and easygoing way. But he wasn't done: "However, if you want to give *me* a try, as in outside of your office, here I am, brand-free." Even at the time I saw through this little speech—claiming you're without branding is of course its own kind of branding; no one is brand-free. Plus, it seemed imprudent to end an interview by taking a candidate's number. Luckily, Gabe got back in touch a few weeks later—when the job had been filled—and I agreed to a date.

Back in my office, I peruse the candidate's answers about the mannequin challenge, that video meme of groups of people staying totally still, as if someone hit a pause button on life. *Why do you think it went viral? How might you use it to create a branding opportunity?* I think back to Gabe's questionnaire, its similar questions about an earlier meme, the Harlem Shake. He'd clearly already decided the job was a poor fit, and his answers were just messing around (or, I barely dared to hope, an attempt to impress me). He'd deconstructed the dance, the delight and surprise of it and its ability to bring people together, and went on to argue the cynicism inherent in trying to monetize that spirit of fellowship and conviviality. But, in parentheses at the bottom of the page, he detailed a marketing plan much savvier than the one cooked up by the guy we eventually hired. I was already smitten.

I get a text from Gabe:

If you need to reach me, kindly contact my agent!!!

Attached is an image of the signed contract.

I'm mid-response when I receive another text, this one from my mom:

Happy Labor Day to my hard-laboring daughter. Here's a little treat for the long weekend, for spending, not saving! <3, Mom.

I see she's Venmo-ed me $100. A knot of emotions tangles up in my gut: gratitude and anxiety and pleasure and unease. I know it gives my mom pleasure to send me cash in celebration of a random holiday. It's like she's making up for my lack of childhood allowance, which we could never afford. I also know how much time and effort has gone into her adopting this breezy outlook on money, which says you never know when your good fortune might end, so you may as well indulge in small pleasures while you have the chance. I, meanwhile, can't help clinging to our family's former ethos, which shared a similar premise but drew the opposite conclusion: Disaster is probably imminent, so you better prepare yourself by being as frugal and careful as possible.

As I refill my coffee, I overhear Melinda Lowe's voice carrying high over the white noise. She's sharing her Labor Day plans: "I'm so over my Hamptons share, so I said screw it and splurged on a lodge in the Catskills. The mountain vibe will be so much chiller."

"Good for you," her cube-mate replies. "You totally deserve that!" This is a girl who once told me with a straight face that her dream was to live in a loft in TriBeCa, but tragically, her parents would only shell out enough rent money for a studio in SoHo.

Screw it, I think. *I can be indulgent, too.* I text Gabe:

Let's celebrate! A night out in honor of you!

Chapter 7

OUR JOURNEY ON the Q train may as well have transported us all the way to Russia, and a century back in time, too. Gabe has chosen Ludmilla's for our big night out, one of those dinner-and-a-show extravaganzas in the deep Brooklyn enclave of Brighton Beach. It's all-you-can-eat caviar and borscht, all-you-can-drink vodka, and as many hours as you can handle of full on bombardment of the senses. Gabe doesn't enjoy eating at most restaurants—it's his job, he says, the equivalent of my spending my time off touring another company's HR department—but Ludmilla's is the polar opposite of Nonno.

I sit at our table sipping vodka and trying to embrace the overstimulation. Our fellow guests are hair-sprayed, deep-cleavaged women who look like instead of removing their makeup each day they simply add new layers on top and men in shiny shirts gaped to reveal tanned chests with tufts of dark hair. I weather crosswinds of perfume and cologne, and eavesdrop futilely on the roars and guttural thrusts of the unfamiliar Russian. It's only when I tilt my head up to the gilded ceiling that I realize I'm a little tipsy: The chandelier is like a plaza fountain tipped upside down, spraying not water but sparkling crystal and glass. I stare and stare, thinking it's a miracle such a structure can stay suspended. Perhaps I'm more than a little tipsy.

"Molly, look." Gabe, equally spellbound by the scene, directs my attention to the stage, where a dozen dancers have taken formation. The music picks up, pulsing in my ears like a physical presence, and I watch, transfixed, as the costumes' bells and tassels swing along with the dancers' gyrations. Colors flash and blur, making me feel like I've been caught up in a peacock's seduction.

As Gabe sweeps me up into the stream toward the dance floor, I'm unsteady on my feet. Spinning away from him, I feel like a breezy child; back in the cocoon of his arms, I'm a sensual woman. I lock eyes with a nearby dancer, and she winks at me, before shimmying back to her own private revelry with her partner, same as I do with Gabe. Something about this foreign, faraway place is letting me let go and drop in to what feels like a realer version of myself. Or who knows, maybe it's just the vodka.

Back at our table, glasses topped off, I propose a toast: "To Gabe, my Scrabe!" My tongue is like rubber. "And to Bill Matherstein! To getting an agent! To having agency!" Every utterance is an exclamation.

"And to you, Molly-moo," Gabe says.

There's a clink of glasses, glug-glugs, then a swish of refills.

A drama is now unfolding up on stage, and I force my swimmy vision to focus. A woman in a glittery two-piece undulates around the space like a mermaid goddess, her rope of hair pendulating a beat behind. Two men circle her seriously, one stocky and fair, the other wiry and dark. Our star begins spinning from man to man, singing out in a powerful chest voice. I can't understand her words, but in her kohl-lined eyes I read pain and confusion—she doesn't know which suitor to pick. The men echo her song, both full of desire and anguish: *Pick me, pick me.* The mermaid goddess flings herself wildly from one set of arms to the other, from dark to light and back, and I hear in her song a duality of loyalties, of longings, of possible futures.

Soon the stage grows crowded with performers, a grand fete of movement that folds the three lovers into its fray, overtaking their passions.

But I stay with the mermaid goddess, hypnotized by her movements. Her light feet and flitting arms belie what lurks beneath, that torrent of doubt and fear and conflict. When the song ends, nearly all the dancers retire to the wings. Only our star is left on stage, and her twinned paramours crouch in shadow behind.

Her next song is like a dirge, slow and low and regretful. But something shifts in its final notes; she seems to be shoring herself up, like she's finally come to a decision. One lover drops back and disappears, while the other comes forward to meet our star. The music turns buoyant, and the couple's dance is a triumph of love.

I'm startled by the swell of applause, sloppy claps and cheers and clanging of glasses. There's a flourish of bows, and then the show sweeps along to the next act. I shift my attention to Gabe, who's pouring us fresh shots. I notice the bottle is more empty than full. "When in Odessa," he says. "Bottoms up!"

I again don't realize quite how drunk I am until I'm in the bathroom blinking at myself in the mirror through sludgy eyes. Women on both sides of me apply lipstick to impossibly pillowy lips. One sees me staring and holds out the tube. A few swipes and my own lips transform to a rose blooming out of my face. I twist up my pout and it looks like a bloodstain. I make a kissy face, and it's back to the rose. All three of us are laughing. I feel like I'm made entirely of kinetic energy, or soda bubbles, or sex. Streams of Russian tumble out from between the women's red, red lips. I sense I can almost understand them, like if I wanted to I could pluck up a fluency in the language like fishing keys from my purse. As I strut back to my table, I'm aware of the clicks of my new heeled booties against the linoleum, and of the gazes clinging to me— men's, women's, Gabe's. I feel I could do anything, be anyone.

"Let's get some air," I say, grabbing Gabe's hand.

It's balmy outside, and as we stroll along the boardwalk, the sea is a black void in the distance. I tell Gabe I'd like to have a getup like the mermaid goddess', along with a body to pull it off. "I'd pull it off for you," Gabe says in a silly voice, one arm slung around my shoulders. "I thought the show would be pure schlock, but that dance actually moved me."

"I know, right?" I nod like a marionette, like there's an invisible string connecting me to Gabe.

"You could see how love overtook that lady, almost like a tide," he says, "how she couldn't help giving in to it and falling for that dude with the gold tassels."

"A tide?" I thought the very opposite; I feel the string between Gabe and me snap. "No, she had to muster up all her strength and courage to choose which version of love to pursue." A gull caws in the distance, emphasizing my point. "It's like anything in life: You take stock of your circumstances, you weigh your options, and you pick a path. You hope for the best, but whatever the outcome, you're responsible for what you decide to do."

Gabe is shaking his head. "You've got it backwards. Love chose *her*, and she was powerless to resist it. Just like how it is for everyone: We listen for our calling and we do our best to heed it." The sea is noisy against the shore. "To ride the wave of what's meant to be."

"Did we just watch the same show?" I ask. What I really mean is, *Do we have totally different understandings of how life works?* I feel the vodka pulsing through me, warping the edges of my thoughts and limbs. I can't quite gauge how big of a deal this is—Gabe believes in something that sounds a lot like fate. Here I've been thinking we've been building a life together, whereas all along Gabe has just been riding a wave, believing he's following someone else's plan. No wonder he hasn't proposed—if he's waiting for some mysterious sign from the universe, who knows when it'll happen? I narrow my eyes at Gabe, trying to decide to whether this new information qualifies as merely curious or cause for despair. I wonder what other bizarre discoveries about him are in store for me. "I think maybe you left Russia and crossed over the border to the Ukraine."

"Or Mongolia," Gabe says.

"Maybe Poland," I respond.

"Kazakhstan?"

I giggle and repeat the word under my breath, unsure whether it's a real country or just a made-up territory from a board game. That's the extent of my knowledge of Russia's bordering nations, so I pull Gabe down to a bench. "How about right here in the U. S. of A.?" I press my lips to his.

"I love you, Molly-moo," Gabe says, just as a giant wave crashes thunderously to shore. "And I have an idea."

I'm expecting a hand up my skirt, or a suggestion that we strip and run buck-naked into the sea. But instead there's a whisper in my ear, ticklish like static: "Let's get married. What do you say, wanna be my wife?"

I look at Gabe: his mouth now stained the same red as mine, his eyelids at half-mast, his cheeks dabbed with dimple. I try to capture a clear snapshot, a solid souvenir to take away from this moment. But I can only see Gabe through the hazy lens of love. I couldn't even describe what he looks like, beyond sweet and beautiful and mine. Lingering in the air is the question I've spent hours upon hours turning over in my head, hoping to hear, even as I simultaneously tried not to hope too hard. Finally, what I've wished for is happening, as natural as the tides, the words dashed off so easily—vibrations carried up through Gabe's throat, forming sound, becoming voice. The world around me wavers between real and surreal.

"Molly?" Gabe says.

"Yes?" His smile is contagious, then I remember that a question requires an answer: "Yes!"

Gabe lifts me in the air, his hands steady around my waist, and he whoops and hollers. The ocean whooshes and froths. Two women stumble by, laughing, enhancing our cheer.

Through some series of steps, we end up back on the Q, the two of us alone on what feels like the last train out of Brighton Beach.

Gabe pinches my thigh and drops his head onto my shoulder. "Hey, fiancée."

I've sobered up slightly, and it occurs to me that in all my imagining of a proposal, I didn't let myself wish for more than the question. Now an image forms in my mind: Gabe on bended knee, a ring, a little speech. I'm embarrassed by how traditional it all is.

"What's on your mind?" Gabe asks.

"Oh." I inhale deeply, shoring up my courage, and then I confess my hopes for all the rituals of engagement. "I know it sounds silly and old-fashioned."

"Hey," says Gabe. "Never apologize for what you want."

I consider this as we ride several stops in silence, moving up the alphabet of avenues, from U to M to J to H. Suddenly Gabe is crouching down, kneeling before me on the grimy subway floor. He's holding a circle of twisty-ties between two fingers, wrangled from who knows where. I fixate on it like it might disappear. "Just a stand-in, of course," he says.

"You don't really have to do this—"

But Gabe cuts me off: "Molly, I really do believe love chooses us. Falling in love with you felt inevitable. Every day I've asked myself how I got so lucky." A jerk of the train totters Gabe's balance and I reach out to steady him. "So, will you, Molly Stone, do me the honor of joining me not just for the rest of this subway ride"—he can't help a smirk—"but for the rest of my life?"

"Yes, I will," I say, just as the overhead speaker blares, "Next stop, Beverley Road."

"How's that for romance?" Gabe says, joining me back on the seat, both of us laughing. I rest my head on his shoulder and nod off for the remainder of the ride, content.

Not until we're home in bed, long after we've undressed and "engaged" with each other (Gabe's dumb joke), does a crack of curiosity pierce my joy. It's about Gabe's take on the mermaid goddess, and fate. "Psst," I say, poking through the thin skin of his sleep. "Is that what you think about your writing, too—that it chose you? Like it was destined?"

Gabe's eyes are still shut. "Uh-huh," he murmurs.

"The topic, too?"

"Mm," he says, rolling over directly into snore.

I sit up. I picture the character of Dahlia floating around in the ether and then finding her way into Gabe's brain, Gabe apparently just a vessel. I'm wary of this belief in a bigger system of forces at work. It seems like an awfully convenient way to shirk responsibility for your own choices.

To my mind, everyone's situations are a nexus of happenstance and a million deliberate decisions. So much is chance (I feel a pang, thinking of my father, a shadow figure I know mainly from my mother and brother's stories). But the rest is how we choose to act in the face of all that randomness. We have *agency*.

Although, of course, Gabe now has a different kind of agency: He has an actual agent, one Bill Mathcrstcin, a.k.a. Billy Boy. Is that what getting an agent means—outsourcing your own agency to someone else? In other words, is the future of Gabe's novel now out of Gabe's control? It's an unnerving thought. But then I consider my own agency, and I remember Gabe's words on the train: "Never apologize for what you want." Apologizing for what I want is what comes most naturally to me. And if I can't even admit what I want, can I truly have agency either? Gabe turns over, his snores fizzling out, and I'm happy to realize I admitted to wanting at least this one thing: Gabe and me. I kiss my fiancé and whisper to his sleeping form, "I choose you."

Chapter 8

GABE AND I attempt to blunt the blades of our hangovers with runny eggs and buttery toast. It doesn't work, but we're in good spirits anyway. We lay sprawled across the living room rug like seals at low tide, and I'm content simply to be still beside the person I've decided to tether myself to for good. I rub my cheek against the rug's soft fibers and my hand against Gabe's muscled calf.

"So," says Gabe, "ready to share our news? Whose family first?"

The thought of talking to my mom at the moment adds aches to my chills. "Yours."

Joe answers and Barb picks up the extension. Using their modulated post-meditation voices, they trade off telling us about a new natural pesticide they've been trying in their garden, and how they've cracked the best carrot-to-ginger juicing ratio. They would go on like this, speaking at us without pause, no detail about their lives too minor to share, if Gabe didn't interrupt to say we have news. I'm so relieved that I blurt it out: "We're getting married!"

I don't know what I expected from the Dovers. But it wasn't a tepid "That's cool" from Barb, as if I'd suggested, say, that she top her carrot juice with a sprinkle of turmeric. Joe follows up with "So what inspired this turn of events?"

I gape at Gabe, wanting to delight together in their ridiculous response. But Gabe avoids my eyes, and his mouth is set in a line. It's a look I know well, from whenever his parents are forcing upon him their ideas of what has value and what doesn't. The Dovers reject anything that smacks of societal norm. "Tradition is hogwash" is practically their mantra, although notably, only in reference to other people's traditions. It drives Gabe crazy, but personally I'm fascinated by how sure they are of their own way of being. Barb starts in on the familiar story of her wedding day, how she and Joe "just swung on over to the courthouse one morning to sign some papers." Moments before Barb says the same sentence aloud, I whisper to Gabe, "I wore exactly what I had on—culottes and an old blouse." Gabe barely cracks a smile.

"So, are you happy for us?" he says, cutting off his mom. "Are you happy that Molly's joining the family?" This breaks my heart a little.

His parents are offended and defensive. "Gabriel, yes!" Joe insists, then Barb takes over: "Silly boy, of course we're happy! But Molly already *is* part of the family. We're simply surprised that such a retrograde institution would interest—"

"Oh Barb," Joe interrupts, but I can hear the amusement in his voice. "You crazy kids should be yourselves and feel free to do your thing. More power to you!" Gabe rolls his eyes, as now his dad has swung to the other extreme—treating an engagement like it's a radical act. "We love you, son!"

"And you too, Molly!" Barb chimes in.

I squeeze Gabe's hand. Because of course his parents love him, in their way. I mouth the words "Literary agent?" but Gabe shakes his head. As we're saying our goodbyes, Barb promises to send us a batch of their pickled beets.

"Pickled beets!" I exclaim to Gabe after we hang up. He manages a chuckle, but his distress is apparent. It's much easier to have a sense of humor about difficult family members who aren't your own—for the first time, the notion of "in-laws" is a flicker in my mind.

Gabe perks up: "Next up, ladies and gentlemen, Emily Stone!"

But as I go to dial my mom, my brother's name pops up on the phone screen. Leo has a rare break from the hospital for Labor Day weekend, so he and Lana have rented a cottage up in the Finger Lakes. I'm expecting a text about champagne cocktails on a yacht, or a snapshot of a stunning sunrise over their private dock. Leo and Lana's life tends to be picture-perfect, and I can't help steeling myself for the stab of envy I'm sure to feel at their paragon of a vacation.

A swipe of my phone reveals a different kind of update:

Lana had a water-skiing accident, 3 slipped discs in her lower back, immobile. At ER up here, returning in a.m. for transfer to Lenox Hill. Visiting hours 2-4 tomorrow.

Icy panic runs through me. I can hear my heartbeat, dull throbs of guilt at my recent thoughts. I picture Lana moaning in agony. Or worse, completely numb. I force myself to banish the image from my head. I ping back a flurry of messages to Leo, filling his phone with every question and condolence I can conjure. But his end has gone silent. Soon my mom calls, already in full-on mobilization mode she's drafted a threatening letter on her law firm's stationery to the water-ski company, she's researching treatments for spinal disc herniation, and she's coming to New York in the morning. We make a plan to visit Lana, and then hang up.

Gabe clears his throat. "You didn't mention the engagement." He sounds hurt.

I look at him like he's nuts. "Of course not. Lana's laid up in the hospital seriously hurt. It would be pretty obnoxious to flaunt our good news."

"No one said anything about flaunting," Gabe says. "There'll always be bad stuff going on. The good news would probably be a nice distraction."

I scoff at his insensitivity. "The important thing right now is to do all we can for Lana. Postponing our own celebration is a small price to pay to be there for her."

"I guess," Gabe says. "It's just . . . never mind, you're probably right." His unsaid retort hangs in the air like humidity, and his nod seems to signal the opposite of assent.

"What?" I snap.

"It's just, fixating on Lana's suffering isn't actually helpful to her. You know that, right?"

Irritation rises in my throat like bile. I echo Gabe's belittling tone: "If by fixating on her suffering you mean offering our sympathy, actually, I think that's the most helpful thing we can do."

"Fine, okay." Gabe raises his palms in surrender.

Feeling pricks of regret for having pushed him into an argument, I try to lighten the mood: "Anyway, the real reason I want to keep our engagement under wraps is for an excuse to take off this ring. I think I'm allergic."

Gabe brightens. "You're still wearing that thing?" He takes my finger, removes the circle of twisty-ties, and kisses the little red bumps that have formed there. "I'll get some Neosporin."

"Mr. Florence Nightingale," I say, touched.

"Here's an idea," Gabe says. "Instead of wedding rings, we get tattoos."

I laugh. Gabe knows that tattoos are my worst nightmare: a permanent stamp on your skin to remind you of a decision you'll inevitably come to regret. Not that I think I'll regret marrying Gabe, but I still don't want to be branded.

● ● ●

When Gabe leaves for his shift at Nonno, I remain in my little burrow on the couch, my mind on tomorrow's hospital visit. I'm both dreading it and wanting it to hurry up and happen already. To distract myself, I grab Gabe's manuscript and flip to where I last left off:

"Baby," Russell typed, then quickly deleted it, unsure if Dahlia still *was* his baby. They'd agreed on an open relationship during his semester abroad in Spain.

Already I'm annoyed—*I* studied abroad in Spain, not Gabe. I scan down and recognize every description: the bidet in the bathroom, the home-stay *Señora* who summons her charge every time the Pope appears on TV, the split-second red-to-green traffic lights that send pedestrians scuttling toward the safety of sidewalks. All these details of my experience appear like stolen souvenirs on Gabe's pages. Next will he appropriate my homesickness? Will he attribute to "Russell" a sudden patriotic passion for Bruce Springsteen and apple pie while in the land of flamenco and *tortilla española*? Will he detail *Russell*'s inability to adapt to a schedule that splits sleep between nighttime and siesta, so that he feels stuck in a foggy fugue state (not ideal for those impulsive traffic lights)?

But no, I discover; apparently Russell is adjusting just fine to Spain, and he's been quite busy, too:

Russell didn't know how to explain to Dahlia that although he'd been with a different girl nearly every night, although he'd learned all the private corners of the local parks since the girls all lived at home under the watchful eyes of their *padres*, it only made him more desperate for Dahlia. The Spanish girls, with their caramel skin and ample asses and tongues well practiced in rolling their Rs,

Seriously? I myself am becoming well practiced in rolling my eyes.

—they only made Russell yearn to squeeze Dahlia's taut body until she squealed, and to breathe in her intoxicating scent. No, Russell couldn't say any of that. Anyway, Dahlia wasn't good with email. She was distractible, her messages strings of half-thoughts, often missing connections and conjunctions. Dahlia was hard to keep track of, especially from across an entire ocean.

Russell clicked out of his email and logged on to Expedia, where, on a whim, he bought a roundtrip ticket from Philly to Madrid for Thanksgiving. He probably had enough in his bank account to cover it. He typed, "Dahlia Freid" in the space for passenger name, then forwarded the flight confirmation to his girlfriend.

This strikes me as equal parts romantic and stupid. Never would I want Gabe to deplete his bank account to surprise me with international plane tickets . . . but I also happen to know that he never would do that, which gives me pause—why is Dahlia worthy of such an extravagant gesture, but not me?

Russell refreshed and re-refreshed his email, and soon he received his reward—a record full paragraph from Dahlia:

"is this for real? if so, wahoooooo! i feel like charlie in the choc factory with my own golden ticket... can't wait to reconvene . . . miss you. kiss kiss, dahlia."

Russell bounded out of the Internet café. The run-down street now appeared bathed in a luminous glow, and Russell basked in it, imagining that the sunbeams were Dahlia's limbs swaddling him.

Jesus, what a tortured image! I can't help it, I've started reading through a squint.

The day before Dahlia's scheduled take-off, Russell received another email, subject: "salutations from america." A trickle of acid rose in his throat.

"rrrrussell! the sun's up and smiling, the sky's bright. is it sunny over there across the world thousands of miles away? tho not for long, baby.

7 hours on a plane and i'm there. i practically forget what you taste like. strange, right? daahling, i. will. see. you. soon. –d."

A fear took root in Russell's gut. His head dropped onto the keyboard, and when he lifted it, he blinked hopelessly at the muddle of letters on the screen. Something was very wrong, and Russell realized he'd been dreading it all along.

~

Oh no, here comes something I've been dreading all along: Dahlia's point-of-view.

Dahlia wanted a lot of things very badly and all the time. Sometimes it surprised her that she wasn't just a massive kinetic ball of want but instead attached to a body, to hips and lips and tits.

Lord.

One of the things she wanted was Russell. She was so fired up to see him and to get away from this crappy campus that she'd skipped class all week—presumably to pack, although she hadn't gotten around to that yet. Her excitement ballooned; she felt giddy and giddier; she had energy for days.

To celebrate the imminent reunion, Dahlia went out—on her bike around campus, then to a string of parties, then to the roof of the athletic center via a hidden ladder that a pair of soccer players showed her. By the time she made it home, the sky was lightening and Dahlia made for her pill supply. She wasn't sure how long had passed—the sun was soon gone again—when she felt her roommate, Natasha's, hands heavy on her shoulders and heard, "Girl, get a grip." Only then did Dahlia wince at the blare from her speakers. Only then did she wonder when she'd last eaten.

"What day is it?" she asked.

"It's still November 23rd," Natasha said, "and your flight's still at 11. It's 8 now." Dahlia nodded, feeling like only a thread attached her head to her neck. "You have three hours, okay?"

"Yes, ma'am." Dahlia saluted Natasha. She pulled out her duffel bag, an empty vessel, all potential, to be filled with shirts and jeans and bras and panties, toothbrush and makeup, and . . . ? She added her flask and a smattering of pills, then zipped it shut with satisfaction.

It was chilly in the cab, conditioned air gusting at Dahlia from what must've been a dozen vents. She tried to alert the driver, but the man jabbered into his phone without pause in a foreign language. Dahlia fumbled with every switch and button, but still, the frigid wind. No matter where she slid to on the seat, the jets pointed vengefully at her. She settled for warming swigs of rum.

Curbside, 9:35. Dahlia gave the driver exact change, no tip, *arctic asshole*. Confirmation number in the machine, ticket printed. Oh, she should get a gift for Russell, who'd summoned her from halfway around the world, all expenses paid. At the newsstand, she found mini Liberty Bells and Ben Franklin stamps and triangle prisms of Toblerone. "No, no, no," she said. She turned to a fellow customer. "Will you help me?" but the woman recoiled and strode away. Dahlia made herself think of Russell—his wavy hair, muscled shoulders, gentle eyes. She should get him an award. Yes, he'd love that! "Which aisle are the prize ribbons in?" she asked the clerk.

"What's that?"

Dahlia repeated herself, but the clerk's face stayed slack, staring. Dahlia had an urge to slap her, to hear the smack of her palm against that dumb, fleshy cheek.

"Never mind," she said, "Stupid store."

"Excuse me, miss, please lower your voice. There's no need to get riled up."

"Riled up?" Dahlia laughed. "You only don't have the most import-ant thing." Her arm reached out and, as if it were an entity separate from her body, swiped at a row of candy bars. They went soaring, thuds and smacks of Kit Kats and Snickers against shelves and calves. Dahlia strutted out.

She scanned the signs for Terminal B. She marveled at the orderly lines of people, all waiting patiently for their turn to shed their shoes and succumb to security. They were sheep, lemmings, soldiers blindly following orders. When it was her turn, Dahlia high-fived the TSA agent and glided through the metal frame. *Beep.* She was instructed to try again—and again she triggered the menacing *beep.* "Miss, please step aside," someone said, then Dahlia noticed a team of TSA agents approaching her like she was magnetized for it. They closed in on her with their bloc of beige uniforms and stern stares. Dahlia felt all the energy seep out of her body. She could picture it frame by frame: all the fucking bullshit that would follow.

Thankfully, the chapter ends there. Gabe has spared us a slog through some plaintive explanation of the insidiousness of addiction or unbal-anced brain chemistry or whatever's underlying this debacle. Dahlia is her own unique hot mess. Bearing witness to it has made me squirm and sweat and read at double-speed just to be done. But it isn't just what Dahlia does that's so cringe-worthy, I realize; it's that she's entirely unashamed of it. Even while getting detained by airport security, Dahlia is wholeheart-edly, unapologetically herself. It's horrifying, yes, but also a little heroic.

The next chapter is back to Russell, and I speed through it: the check-ing and re-checking on Dahlia's flight, the familiar dread "slick and dark as obsidian," the disappointment giving way to resignation, the bulk box of condoms woefully observed *[ugh]*, the lonely night wander-ing the city, and the inevitable finale in the arms of *una chica muy guapa* as Russell pines away for his elusive true love.

My jaw is clenched and my hands are fists. I want to shake Russell for letting himself be seduced by the desire to save Dahlia, for confusing that impulse with love. For not getting himself a different girlfriend, someone practical and good-natured who at minimum knows how to navigate airport security drama-free ... someone like me. Of course, really I want to shake Gabe for having once felt this way about Talia— and, I fear, for still feeling it, despite recent proclamations implying otherwise. I glance at my hands, fingers bare save for the lingering rash from my faux ring. What a chump I am, to have settled for a drunken, do-over subway proposal with twisty-ties in place of a real ring. Dahlia would never stand for such a lame counterfeit of what she wanted. No doubt Talia wouldn't either. So, what, then, is my problem?

Chapter 9

I HATE HOSPITALS. In the face of bodily fluids, smells of sick, and people who need help and for whom I can do nothing, I pretty much shut down. (This despite my insistence to Gabe of the healing power of sympathy; really that was just wishful thinking.) Ever since I was a kid and my family spent those six long months practically living at Maine Medical, I've done all I can to avoid the places. My only coping mechanism is the cafeteria staple of warm sugar water known as Swiss Miss. Which is why, after a glimpse of the usually exquisite Lana now laid out on a hospital bed writhing in pain, face splotchy and eyelids droopy with drugs, I offer to make a beverage run.

My mother narrows her eyes at me. "Molly, you just got here. Spend some time with your poor sister-in-law."

But Gabe knows my feelings about hospitals. "I'll take a latte."

"Leo? Double espresso?" My brother nods, and I pat him on the back. I haven't seen him in such rough shape since I used to bring him egg-and-cheeses after his all-nighters in med school.

"Fine, I'll take a mint tea, two Splendas." My mom holds out a twenty, which I wave away.

I take my time moseying down to the cafeteria. When I return, Lana is passed out, tongue lolling from a slack mouth; Gabe is uncovering the tin vats of food we brought from Nonno; Leo is rattling off medical jargon to a nurse; and my mom is nodding along, unable to hide her pride in her son, the doctor. I half-listen, hitting idly at a Mylar balloon whose cheerful font demands, "Get well soon!"

When the nurse leaves, Leo's eyes find the floor. "Her prognosis is not good. She's either high on Oxycontin or in acute pain. She'll get an epidural tomorrow, and then her doctor will decide about surgery."

No one responds—what can we say? I know that ordinarily Leo's outlook on hospitals is the opposite of mine: Faced with the fragility of life, he wants to know all there is to know and do all he can do to fend off the inevitable. But right now, it's clear he can't do anything for his wife, and he looks bereft. My mom strokes his head like he's a child.

I'm glad when Gabe presses plates of pastas into everyone's hands. We all mechanically chew and swallow. I pick at a piece of garlic bread, my fingers growing slick with butter.

A moan from Lana rouses her from semi-slumber, and she blinks at her guests. "Molly. Emily. Gabe." Her voice sounds coated in phlegm. "Exciting news: I'm thinking of training to become a professional water skier." Gabe is the only one to respond, with a half-hearted "Heh." Leo murmurs that she's made this joke three times in the past twenty-four hours.

I take her hand. "How are you, Lana?"

"Eh." She shrugs, then tries to hide her wince. "Hey, I'm sorry I was such a mess at our party." She slurs the last word, and I can't help but smile; she's much more of a mess now. "Also, guess what? Two bottles of bourbon disappeared along with Charlie. Typical, right? I could use some bourbon right now."

"The doctors must have you on some pretty strong stuff here, right? You'll be better in no time, I just know it." I don't know what I'm saying. I plaster a grin over my anxiety, relaxing my facial muscles only when Lana drifts off to sleep again.

I monitor the minutes in anticipation of when it would be not totally inappropriate for Gabe and me to leave. At the one-hour mark, I announce that we have to go. Leo pulls me into a hug, his shoulders heavy as boulders. "Lana will be okay, right?" I ask. He mumbles something indecipherable. "We'll be back on Tuesday." Gabe is working the Labor Day brunch shift tomorrow, and I don't think I can handle this scene without him. Plus, maybe after her epidural Lana will get discharged, and then we won't have to return at all. I picture my sister-in-law up on her feet again, in four-inch heels, her former happy and healthy self—for the briefest moment, I imagine I can will this picture into existence, and then I chide myself for the fantasy.

My mother escorts Gabe and me back to the elevator bank. "Leo puts up a good front," she says, "but underneath, he's suffering most of all. It's worse to understand it all medically."

"You think so?" I would've thought the opposite.

"Back when Dad was sick, I kept convincing myself that if I just learned everything there was to know about his condition, I could somehow control it." She shakes her head. "Well, our Leo will do all he can for his wife."

I'm struck by a memory: "Do you remember how Leo would take Dad's temperature and feed him juice through a straw?"

"A very good doctor, even as a child. And you'd crawl into Dad's bed and wouldn't budge for whole afternoons. I couldn't drag you outside that summer, even to go to the beach. You'd been such a water baby before." I can feel it in my gut, the fear of leaving my dad's side tied to a sudden fear of the ocean.

"Anyway," my mom says, turning to Gabe. "Thank god, or should I say 'Thank Gabe,' we have good, hearty food to eat until the cows come home. If only worrying burned calories, right?"

"I'll bring reinforcements on Tuesday," Gabe says.

I wonder, is Gabe actually right about good news mitigating the bad? Maybe this would be a nice time to tell my mom about our engagement.

But when I nudge Gabe, he seems irritated, so I let it go. My mom kisses us as the elevator doors open.

On our descent, I notice Gabe has gone quiet. "What's up?" I ask.

He doesn't look up as he responds: "You didn't tell me Charlie was at Leo's party. You know, the party you told me I shouldn't bother coming to."

"Oh, Gabe, come on." I take his hand. It remains limp in my grasp, but he doesn't pull it away. How can I explain that these two things are unrelated? I'm not sure I can, I realize. So instead, because I'm overwhelmed by Lana and the hospital, or irritable from the heavy food, or anxious to turn the tables on Gabe, or perhaps all of the above, I say, "*I'm* the one who studied abroad in Spain."

"Excuse me?"

Already I regret my words. With less conviction, I add, "What I mean is, you can't just steal my stories and spin them into your own."

Gabe guffaws. "Oh, is studying abroad in Spain your intellectual property, as if about a million other people haven't done the same thing?" His tone is harsh. "Are you also planning to copyright living in Brooklyn and working in an office? Sorry, ladies and gentlemen, it's off-limits to write about your monotonous desk job. The rights belong to one Molly Stone!"

Gabe's words are unfair and ridiculous, not to mention mean. I decide to wait for him to cool off. But when I attempt a joke ten minutes later—"Aw, our first fight as an engaged couple!"—Gabe doesn't even crack a smile.

I toss and turn that night, and wake up with my mother's voice in my head: "Life is short. Just apologize." It's a refrain she's repeated to me my whole life. So, I write Gabe a note: I'm sorry I didn't tell you about seeing Charlie. It was inconsiderate. I love you. I doodle a cartoon of a girl who looks a lot like me, only bustier and with hearts for eyes, next to a boy who looks a lot like Gabe, only taller and with more muscle tone. I fold up the note and tuck it into Gabe's shoe.

When I reach for my Metrocard on my way to Netflix-and-Spill Club the next morning, I find a paper folded around it with Gabe's chicken scratch: **Sorry for being a jerk yesterday. I love you.** It's a relief that we can both come back to kindness.

Still, I have a nagging feeling that neither of us is really sorry for the things the other accused us of: Gabe didn't apologize for co-opting my life events, only for defending doing so in such an obnoxious way. And although I apologized for omitting the fact that I saw Charlie, I didn't reassure Gabe that he has nothing to worry about. He doesn't, but for some reason I didn't want to commit to that in writing. It occurs to me that my mom's oft-repeated advice is sweeping: If someone believes they've been wronged by you, you should apologize, period. There's no consideration of whether you really mean it, or who's truly at fault, or whether there's more to the story. The important thing, my mom drilled into me, is just to say you're sorry.

All day long, my hand keeps returning to my pocket to find the evidence of Gabe's apology and his love. I imagine Gabe's hand doing the same, reaching again and again for reassurance that everything is all right.

Chapter 10

KIRSTEN IS ALREADY settled in when I arrive at the restaurant. She's spreading jam on a popover and cooing at a nearby baby, who's making a valiant effort to propel himself out of his mother's grip and over to my friend. Kirsten is a magnet for the under-two set. "Sorry to interrupt the courtship," I say, pecking her on the cheek.

"I've missed you," she says, passing me half a popover.

"Me too." I see Kirsten quickly scan my hand, I assume for a ring; she'd guessed that my anniversary trip would come with a proposal. Kirsten and her husband, Caleb, got hitched fresh out of college, and she's been waiting ever since for the rest of us to join the married club. I don't like withholding my news, but I'd feel bad telling my friends before my mother.

Sam shows up at the same moment as our waitress, who says, "I'm Felicity, and I'll be taking care of you today."

The three of us erupt into laughter, leaving poor Felicity bewildered. Kirsten, Sam, and I met in the back row of our freshman Psych seminar during our first week at NYU. We became instant best friends, and since then, we've bonded over having three out of four of the names of the original American Girl dolls; Felicity is our missing fourth.

"Did you by any chance grow up in Virginia and rescue a horse named Penny?" Sam asks the waitress, citing the origin story of Felicity the American Girl.

"Should we warn her the British are coming?" I add.

"Please ignore my friends," says Kirsten. "We'll take three coffees, milk and two sugars in each."

As a kid, I was more interested in the American Girl books than the dolls. I raced to read them one after another. The Molly series was my favorite, naturally, especially since the fictional Molly's father wasn't around, either—although in her case, he was off fighting in World War II. Sometimes I secretly pretended my dad was away at war, too. Kirsten, who, like her American Girl counterpart, grew up in a family with little money for extras, longed futilely for both the books and the dolls. Sam, who had all the books and all the dolls, plus enough clothes to change all their outfits for a week, rewrote the books into sci-fi thrillers and restyled the dolls' hair into mohawks and mullets.

"All right," says Kirsten in her down-to-business voice. We've met up to discuss *The Americans,* our most recent pick for Netflix-and-Spill. "What'd you guys think of the husband and wife? They, like, murder people and then just take off their spy wigs and go home to make dinner for their kids? Totally chilling, right?"

"It's so fun," says Sam. "They come off as so boring and picket-fence, but really they're working to take down our whole country. *Mwa-ha-ha.*" Her evil laughter makes the baby at the next table giggle; Sam scowls back.

"The real question is, how does the Keri Russell character look so amazing?" I ask. "She must be at least forty." Ever since our club abandoned books for TV, I've wholeheartedly embraced its lowbrow-ness.

"It's because she's carrying around all that guilt for being a cold-blooded killer, probably too anxious to eat," says Kirsten.

"No," says Sam. "It's because she's in an open marriage, having loads of thrilling sex on her secret spy missions. It's an ideal situation: companionship, but also wild flings; love and devotion, but freedom, too."

"Well, I think it's tragic," Kirsten says, "and I wouldn't call that love and devotion, unless you mean for Mother Russia. Their marriage is basically a business arrangement."

"Whatever it is, it's hot," Sam says. "It's exciting, not monotonous—I mean, *monogamous*."

I jump in: "It's funny how supposedly we all share one definition of marriage, but in practice everyone defines it differently."

"Yeah, think about *The Good Wife* or *The Crown*," says Kirsten. Both shows were previous club picks. "One marriage is a front for friendship with co-parenting duties, and the other's this complicated bond that's as much about a commitment to their country as to each other."

"I wonder," I say, "if behind closed doors, most marriages aren't at all how they appear to be." I can't help wondering what my own marriage will be like.

"Eh," Sam says, "I just don't think most people are that interesting."

Kirsten snorts. "I think you'd be surprised."

"Oh really?" Sam leans in. "Do reveal to us the inner workings of matrimony, oh wise married one."

She swats Sam away. "I meant what I see in court." As a public defender, Kirsten spends her workdays witnessing private dramas turned public. But my mind goes to what she's told me about her own private drama: her struggles to get pregnant. The oldest of six kids, Kirsten has been anticipating motherhood since before I knew how to do my own laundry. For years, she and Caleb have been on a merry-go-round of fertility specialists, hormone injections, and false starts ending in miscarriage. But she doesn't like to talk about it; I'm guessing she's told nothing to Sam, who isn't exactly shy about expressing her dislike of kids.

"Anyway, if you find the right person, monogamy doesn't have to mean monotony." Kirsten smiles mysteriously, and Sam and I both laugh at our sweet friend. "Right, Molly?"

I feel myself turning red, and now both of them are laughing at me. Discussing fictional TV relationships is one thing, but my friends know how uncomfortable it makes me to talk about myself.

Sam shakes her head. She and her boyfriend, Tom, have dated for years, on and off, the offs usually prompted by Sam's extracurricular activities. "I'd happily get hitched if Tom said, 'Sure, baby, you go out and fuck whomever you please, and I'll do the same.' If he didn't throw fits about random sex like he was a goddamn twelve-year-old."

The woman with the baby at the next table glares at Sam. Kirsten smiles back, apologetic on our friend's behalf, but Sam's look is hostile as she meets the woman's gaze. "Is there a problem?" she demands.

"Could you please watch your language? There are children here."

Sam scoffs, and I touch her shoulder. "Sam, chill."

Ignoring me, she says, "I just don't think that because you've procreated, you get to be the fucking language police. Last I checked, this is a public restaurant and I'm a paying customer." Her volume is rising. "Speaking of which, where the fuck is Felicity with our goddamn omelets?"

Kirsten and I are silenced by this display, but the baby has the opposite reaction: His face wrinkles in distress, a split-second preview to an ear-splitting wail. His mother leaps up and whisks him toward the door, away from the dirty look Sam is burning into her back.

"Some people!" Sam says.

Kirsten and I exchange a look. "Sam," I say. "Did someone slip cyanide in your coffee? You talked to that woman like she murdered your mother."

I expect her to brush me off, but instead, something unprecedented happens: Water begins pooling in her eyes.

"Hey, it's okay," Kirsten says. "What on earth is the matter?"

I'm mesmerized. After a decade of friendship, I'm finally seeing how Sam cries—and it involves plenty of sniveling and wheezing. "I'll tell you what's going on," she says, wiping at her nose. "I'm fucking pregnant."

"Holy shit." It just slips out of mouth. I point my focus at Sam like an arrow; I can't bear to glance at Kirsten. "Like, *pregnant* pregnant?"

Sam rolls her eyes at me; it's a relief that she's no longer blubbering. "Yes, and spare me the birth control speech. The condom broke, okay? The worst part is, Tom wants me to keep it."

"Okay," I say, "so you don't want to keep it?"

Sam is tearing her napkin to shreds. "I don't fucking know. I mean, I want a kid, eventually, I guess. Probably with Tom. But like, *years* from now. On the other hand, I'm a grown-ass woman, not some desti- tute teenage idiot. Did you know that, on average, American women have their first baby at twenty-six? That's a full four years younger than we are!"

Sam continues this debate with herself, making no effort to lower her voice, and people around us start sneaking glances. My heart aches for Kirsten, and I realize how imperative it is that she not be subjected to any more of this, so I cut off Sam's rambling: "Let's get out of here. No one has an appetite anymore, right?"

Outside, Kirsten stutters, "Um, I just realized I'm late for an appointment."

Sam barely hears her, quarantined as she is in her own distress.

"I'll call you later," I say to Kirsten, meaning "I hope you're okay" and "I love you," and then I watch her walk away.

·   ·   ·

Sam and I end up by the Gowanus Canal, leaning over the bridge, star- ing down at the muck. The sulfur stink is particularly strong today. "What a hole," Sam says. "Do you think breathing in this garbage is hurting the embryo?"

"Yep, it'll probably grow twelve toes."

"If it ever gets to grow *any* toes," Sam says idly.

To distract her, I tell her about my run-in with Charlie. I play up the sight of him in Leo's refined apartment wearing his muddy ranger gear. Soon she's chortling—unlike Kirsten, Sam has always indulged my soft spot for Charlie. She respects him for being one of the few people who can drink her under the table.

"That Charlie is so sexy," she says. "I mean, a total alcoholic, but a very hot one. Good thing you found Gabe."

"Can I tell you a secret?" I suddenly feel desperate to share my news. "Gabe and I got engaged."

"No shit!" Sam's clap on my back knocks me off-balance. "That's fantastic!"

"I haven't told my family yet, so don't say anything."

Sam makes the sign of zipped lips. "Can I tell *you* a secret?" She balances herself on the bridge's guardrail and tees out her arms. "I think I'm going to have this baby, become a mom, the whole freaking shebang."

I feel tears form in my eyes. I'm about to say something sappy, but Sam preempts me: "Look at us, all grown up and shit. Let's go for a celebratory swim!"

She grabs my arm, counts to three, and right at the moment I think she might actually be crazy enough to propel us over the bridge and into the rank, polluted water—I feel proud to have such a brave friend, even as I'm bracing myself, pleading to stay on solid ground—Sam lets go.

Chapter 11

UPON ENTERING THE office Tuesday morning, I hear squeals. I'm unsurprised to discover that they're coming from Melinda Lowe's cubicle. The junior copywriters and assistant designers are all clumped around, reacting to what I assume is some celebrity Twitter feud or Snapchat scandal.

The diamond's glint catches my eye from several feet away—for a moment I think I've gone blind—and subsequently I notice that all the gazes are focused on Melinda's fourth finger. "My fiancé worked with Larissa Laraby's jewelry designer," I hear her boast. What a strange point of pride, to share a ring designer with a reality TV star. I congratulate Melinda as I pass by, and she beams, like she's achieved something grand.

I'm halfway down the hall when I overhear, "You must be so excited to start wedding planning!" Rapid-fire questions follow: "Who'll design your gown?" "What's your vision for flowers arrangements?" "Where will you register?" "How would you describe your bridal style?" "Which color palette will you pick? What kind of ceremony?" "Big or small reception?" The words get warped on the way to my brain, so it all sounds like a foreign language. I'm rattled, but I chalk it up to needing coffee. I hurry to my office, thankful for the door I can close.

Not until now has it hit me that, unless I want to go the route of Gabe's parents and commemorate a major life event at a depressing municipal office, I too will be planning a wedding. I've never been one to fantasize about my wedding day. It's not just the unsavory indulgence of imagining an entire event set up just for me, but also the daunting prospect of having to consider exactly how I'd hope the event to unfold. Planning such an affair will require a thousand different decisions—just thinking about it overwhelms me.

I've never liked weddings anyway.

I was first introduced to the ritual at age ten, as a junior bridesmaid in a cousin's wedding party. I remember the spaciousness of the reception ballroom, its cathedral ceilings and views of a garden that seemed to stretch to the ends of the earth. It was the most beautiful place I'd ever been, surrounded by such beautiful people, the women in long dresses, the men in tuxedos. My mother was so glamorous in her blue gown with the silver sash and her hair piled up onto her head—for the first time I noticed that she was beautiful.

I felt pretty, too. I got to wear heels and have my makeup done, despite my mom's grumbling that it was inappropriate for a girl my age. I danced and danced, and my brother and I took turns with the disposable camera at our table, documenting the dinner roll pyramid, a tissue stamped with a perfect pink kiss, and a piece of cake smashed into a toilet bowl. As the night crept along, way past my bedtime, I became aware of the adults acting strange, their laughs too loud, their bodies bent at odd angles. I was under no one's supervision—I was free. I opened a door in search of my next snapshot, and was startled to hear a fragment of my mom's voice. There was her long back and silver sash. A man's hand was pressed against it, and his mouth was mushed into her neck. He noticed me and looked up. His face was puffy, and he had a hook nose and bushy eyebrows. I stuck out my tongue and ran away.

The band was packing up their equipment when my mom finally found Leo and me. I wouldn't meet her gaze. I told her that her makeup was smeared and that she looked disgusting. "Well, you're not looking so hot yourself, kiddo," she replied, laughing a little. The insult stung. It felt unforgivable. Since then, I've never fully shaken the impression that weddings are events that make people do ugly, illicit things.

The next real wedding I attended—not counting Kirsten's, a casual afternoon barbeque in her parents' backyard—was Leo and Lana's. I was twenty-four, a bridesmaid once again, which at the time meant to me only that I was forced to wear a dress not of my choosing. For six months leading up to the event, I obsessed over its unflattering mermaid cut, and of course what Charlie would think. I hadn't seen him since high school. Even as I stood by the altar and teared up watching my brother take the hand of his new wife, I was fully aware of Charlie sitting in the middle of the fifth row. He was like a planet exerting his gravity on me. We orbited each other through cocktail hour, as one by one my relatives demanded an accounting of my new post-college life. Not wanting to expose how lost I felt, floundering in a soulless job that I knew I was supposed to be grateful for and crammed into a crappy apartment I could barely afford, I downed glass after glass of pinot grigio. This gave me the courage to make things up. I sensed Charlie's eyes on me, his ears attuned to my voice. When my great-aunt Rose asked what I was doing for work, I invented a gig as a chorus member in *Hair*. I heard Charlie chortle—he knew the actors stripped naked in that play, and also that I was tone-deaf. Within moments, he was by my side, delivering a fresh glass of wine into my hand.

The rest of the night was a blur. I was sharing a hotel room with my mom, but I didn't make it back there until morning, when I arrived to find one bed untouched and the other containing my sleeping mother. I braced myself for the same fury she'd hurled at fourteen-year-old me after dragging me from Charlie's bedroom. But her only commentary on my night was a quip: "At least you're consistent."

As she stood and stretched, I noticed how small and vulnerable my mom seemed in her pop-art pajamas, two Campbell's soup cans printed suggestively across the chest. Later, I wished I'd asked her about her night; I hoped she'd snuck off with some new iteration of the man with the hook nose. But in the moment, I said nothing, silently accepting the bottle of aspirin she handed me like a peace offering. She tucked my hair behind my ears and said, "Let's get you cleaned up for brunch." I followed her into the bathroom and we brushed our teeth together, side by side. Had my mother known then that I'd spend the next six months in Charlie's thralls, I don't think she would've been so kind.

• • •

Gabe swings by my office after work and we head up to the hospital. He's more affectionate than usual on the subway, gripping my waist rather than the pole. I ask him what's up. "Just in a good mood," he says, nuzzling his nose into my hair. "Billy said it's looking promising for my book. He's getting really positive reactions. We'll know more later this week."

"Great!" I lean into Gabe, happy that he's happy.

I spot my mother by the hospital's entrance, pacing like she's on a smoke break, minus the cigarette. She hugs me hello, her muscles like taut ropes, then she pins me with an accusatory glare. "So, when exactly were you going to tell me that you two are engaged to be married?"

"What?" I say, at the same time Gabe that says, "Today—we were going to tell you today!" He sounds delighted, like it's a funny coincidence. My mother confirms the source of the spoiler: Gabe's parents.

"Apparently Joe and Barb were informed days ago."

I try to explain—Lana's accident, the inappropriateness—but I can't cut through my mother's hurt. "I'm sorry, Mom."

"What do you think of their plan, then?" She pauses dramatically, basking in our ignorance. "I mean, to have the wedding on their *estate*." This is said ironically, although "estate" is probably my mom's word, not the Dovers'; their yard would fit about fifteen people max. "And to cater it from their garden?"

"Believe me, Emily," says Gabe, "we knew nothing about this."

I add, "No way are we serving pickled beets and carrot juice at our wedding."

My mom laughs, a sign that we're back on the same side. "I didn't think so. Well, the Dovers wanted to make it very clear that they'd happily host, or otherwise they could offer"—she makes air quotes—"an abundance of love and good energy." She adds unnecessarily, "As in, I believe, not any money."

I steal a glance at Gabe, who's fidgeting his feet. For all their "all of us are one" vibe, Joe and Barb are cheap. Their real estate business is definitely more lucrative than my mom's paralegal work.

"Anyway, I'm thrilled for you two. Gabe, my dear,"—my mom pinches his cheeks, making him look like a child—"welcome to the family! Wait until you tell Leo and Lana! We'll bring up a cake. I'm sure you've always dreamed of having an engagement party in a hospital!"

"How is Lana?" I ask.

My mom's reply is a manic whisper: "The epidural didn't help. Leo's going nuts because the residents are all new this month, so it's a terrible time to have surgery. Who knew? Labor Day means stop wearing white, and don't have surgery! But it can't be postponed, so it's scheduled for next week."

On the elevator, I try to soothe myself by counting along as each ascending floor lights up. It's disconcerting that there's no 13th floor— that even a hospital would bow to superstition, acknowledging that science isn't always enough to ward off the worst. I stand very still, careful not to lean against the germ-ridden walls.

The flowers and fruit baskets have multiplied in Lana's room, somehow making it feel more rather than less depressing, like an overprotestation of cheer. Lana is dozing, whereas Leo looks like he hasn't slept since last week. I still feel uneasy sharing our happy news when

92 . lindsey j. palmer

their situation is so grim, but I'm overruled by my mom's insistence. She nudges Lana awake, and then steals our thunder: "Molly and Gabe got engaged!"

Leo's exclamations are so loud that a nurse pops her head in to ask if everything's okay. In her out-of-it voice, Lana says, "This calls for champagne." I free a bottle from the gift baskets, and we all share a toast, even Lana, despite Leo's chastising. "It complements the Oxy," she says, smile loose.

As it turns out, a little bubbly goes a long way toward tempering my hospital phobia. I top off my cup, and start to feel at ease. That is, until a familiar voice pierces through the feeling: "What are we celebrating?"

Charlie. I watch him take in the room—the bottle first, then the get-well display (he's shown up empty-handed), then my family, and lastly of course, Gabe. The two of them have never stood in the same room together, although I'm sure each recognizes the other. I'm a statue. My mom, whose insistence on civility prevails even over her distaste for Charlie, pats him on the shoulder and says, "How have you been, dear?" and then excuses herself for the powder room.

"Fancy hospital," Charlie says, "with a powder room and everything."

Gabe stands to introduce himself, presumably to show his maturity and lack of ill will toward my ex. I imagine Charlie privately ridiculing him for his overly hearty handshake. Leo, in his haze of exhaustion, is slow on the uptake, but after a moment he approaches the doorway, and thankfully inserts himself between my current and former partners. "Hey man," he says to Charlie. "I thought you were coming by tomorrow."

"Change of plans. I wanted to bring Lana some special meds before hitting the road." Ah, so then he has brought something: a baggie of joints, which he's now showing off to the room.

Leo eyes it warily. "You can't have that stuff in here."

Charlie ignores him and tucks the baggie between two pineapple daisies in an Edible Arrangement. I giggle, despite myself, at the updated arrangement, at which point Charlie pretends to notice me for the first time. "Oh hey, Molly. I bet Lana will share if you ask nicely." He pats Gabe on the back, and adds in a patronizing tone, "You too, buddy, if you're into that sort of thing." Wisely, Gabe doesn't respond. Surely Charlie must realize he's unwanted here, but he goes ahead and helps himself to a cup of champagne anyway. "So, what are we celebrating?" he asks again.

"Molly and me—we're engaged," Gabe says. His tone is hostile, which annoys me. I wish everyone would all just go away, including myself.

"Ah." Charlie's expression is inscrutable. "To the happy couple, then!" He drains his cup, then reaches for a refill. Only Lana drinks along with him. I reach for her hand.

The next half hour is stupid as we all sit around and pretend one of us isn't high on Oxycontin and the rest of us aren't way too sober, despite the champagne. I try not to notice how attractive Charlie looks, his shirt for once not rumpled, his pants well fitting, his footwear loafers that not only lack a coating of mud but also seem to have been buffed and shined. I keep willing him to get the hell out, but he stays stubbornly put. When he starts in on a lecture about the etymology of the word "fiancé," I cut him off to say it's getting late. Gabe and I stand to go, and I aim for a neutral voice while wishing Charlie safe travels home.

"Thanks, Moll," he responds, and I feel Gabe bristle at the nickname. "By the way, I got that job upstate. So maybe I'll be seeing more of you."

On the elevator down, I'm counting floors again, from 15th to 14th to 12th, trying to dial down my head's pounding from Charlie's news. I'm bracing myself for Gabe's reaction, too. But he seems distracted, swiping at his phone, and when he exclaims, it's with joy: "There's a bidding war on my book!"

"Oh, babe, my Scrabe." I kiss him. My enthusiasm is compounded with a rush of relief that we've moved on from the scene in Lana's room. "It must feel fantastic to feel so wanted."

But then Gabe's expression shifts, his face a flash of irony. "I guess you know a little something about that." It's his only reference to the previous hour, and a moment later he's beaming again. He picks me up and presses me against the elevator wall, and I'm so thrilled to be kissing my happy fiancé, I don't even care about the gross hospital germs.

Chapter 12

KIRSTEN HAS CAJOLED me into lunch hour yoga, and the middle of our sun salutations seems as good a time as any to tell her that I'm getting married. She silently squeals.

"That's right, work out those facial muscles," the instructor says.

Kirsten looks particularly strong in her Warrior Two, so I whisper-ask how she's feeling about Sam's pregnancy. "Good," she whispers back, her face fierce. "I'm going to be the best auntie to that little one." It must've taken her a lot of yogic breathing to get there.

"Sam'll need a ton of help," I say. Kirsten nods as we tip forward into Half Moon. "She might actually give up on the whole motherhood thing and then you can swoop in and take over."

Kirsten stumbles from the balance, letting out a guffaw. "Shh!" scolds the woman beside us, and I sigh loudly, like I'm in mindful ecstasy.

During handstands, an upside-down Kirsten says, "I know I'm supposed to wait for you to ask, but can I please be a bridesmaid? I want to throw you a shower and a bachelorette party, and help plan everything—the cake, the favors, the guest book."

Blood rushes to my head; woozy, I come down from the inversion. "I don't know if I'm even going to have bridesmaids," I say, shuddering at the word and its implied servitude. "Let's talk about it sometime when I'm two drinks in, okay?"

Kirsten's cheeks go blotchy, and I can tell she's wounded. "I'm sorry," I say. I don't know how to explain that talk of all these wedding rites freaks me out, that the very idea of a wedding, of making a big show of my good fortune and compelling everyone I know to participate in that show, feels both garish and risky to me. Or that weddings, in my experience, invite stupid behavior and poor decisions. Kirsten, who revels in all of life's little celebrations, would never understand. As we settle into corpse pose, I pour all my effort into clearing my head.

Later I will look back on this hour with nostalgia. It'll be the last time someone congratulates me on my engagement without in the same breath wanting to discuss Gabe's book deal. When Kirsten and I return to the locker room, I have four missed calls: Gabe, Mom, Gabe, Mom.

• • •

I call my mother back first. Within two minutes she's told me about three wedding venues in my hometown—a hotel ballroom, a seafood shack, and a raw event space. "I toured them on my lunch break," she says breezily, even though she's been back in Maine for less than twenty-four hours, and I happen to know she never takes a lunch break. It makes me wonder how much other wedding planning she did before I even got engaged. "I don't want to stress you out," she says, "but all the summer dates are booked already. A couple of places had a few open slots for spring."

"Noted," I say, regretting the call. I hurry her off the phone, and try Gabe next.

"My book sold!" he says straightaway.

"Oh babe!"

He barrels ahead with a flurry of information. I take in every second or third detail: the imprint, which Gabe says is respectable if modestly sized; and the advance payment, which is also apparently respectable if modestly sized, although it sounds like a lot to me. I wonder fleetingly how much a wedding will cost. "The publisher is rushing the book, since they think it'll do well in the current literary climate," Gabe says. "All the summer slots were full, so it'll come out in the spring."

"Wow," I say, struck by the echo of my mom's wedding venue talk.

"As of March 15th, *The Charms of Dahlia* will be a real, actual book!"

"Seriously, the Ides of March?"

"Ha, I guess so. I was thinking more like, what's that expression about March? 'In like a lamb and out like a lion.'"

I don't correct him that he has it flipped, because who knows what it'll be like, everyone we know reading Gabe's novel? My happiness for Gabe is punctuated with panic as I picture a mash-up of metaphors: a lion tearing into a lamb, Brutus standing by wielding a knife.

"There's so much good stuff going on," Gabe says, his voice an echo of the little-boy version I've heard in old Dover family videos. He's probably been dreaming about publishing a book since he was that young. "I mean, besides Lana. And my shift, which starts in an hour. And the book edits I'll have less than two weeks to turn around. And your unhinged ex-boyfriend showing up at the hospital. Okay, I've gotta run."

I ignore the reference to Charlie, and fixate on the mention of book edits. It calms me to know that Russell and Dahlia's relationship isn't fixed, that there's still time for changes.

That night, I pick up Gabe's manuscript and skip ahead at random— past Dahlia's pathetic attempts to solicit a TSA agent, past her manic meanderings after the botched Spain trip, past her anonymous (and very detailed) sexual encounters in which she imagines Russell's face onto various men she meets in bars (*yeah, right*). It's the start of a new semester, and the pair is reunited. Russell is at Dahlia's place smoking pot with her and her roommate, Natasha. I brace myself for a description of Natasha as some voluptuous sexpot, followed by pages of *ménage a trois*. But it turns out Natasha is one of those fade-into-the-background types that Dahlia keeps around to make herself seem shinier, a type I've sometimes worried people pin on me.

Natasha was bogarting the pipe. "It's cashed," she said apologetically, and Dahlia sighed in annoyance. Natasha was like a piece of old furniture, neither exciting nor offensive, just inevitable. Russell settled back into his girlfriend's lap, his head pleasantly abuzz. He pictured the semester laid out before him, the classes where he could again speak in English, where he could again prove himself confident and wise.

Ugh, I can just imagine Russell's insufferable mansplaining.

"Dahlia, you should set up your schedule so we have Fridays off together."

"Yes, it's generally advisable for college students to avoid Friday classes," Natasha said snarkily. "Right, Dahlia?"

"Shut up, Nat," Dahlia spat.

Sometimes Natasha was the kind of furniture whose edges splintered against your skin. She was clearly jealous of Dahlia; most girls were. Dahlia's thighs tensed under Russell's head. He sat up, looked from face to face, and realized he was out of the loop. "Dahlia?" But she wouldn't meet his gaze.

Natasha, however, was staring right at him, smirking. She lit a cigarette and began blowing smoke circles—Russell had never before noticed how full her lips were.

Uh-oh . . .

Dahlia shot her roommate a look, which prompted her to stand up and, with a sigh, leave the room. Her ass looked enormous in her jeans.

"Dahlia?" he said again. No response. "Are you taking classes this semester?"

"I don't think so," her voice a third its normal volume.

It was a familiar feeling: the crush on his chest. "When were you going to tell me?"

"Uh, I hadn't really decided."

"How can—" Russell stopped and sucked in a breath. He tried again: "Why are you going all college drop-out on me?"

"Come on, Russell, only a quarter of people in this country graduate from college." She'd been ready with the stat.

"Yeah? And what's the graduation rate for people with full scholarships to the country's top universities?"

I roll my eyes. Gabe's ex Talia went to City College. Nothing wrong with City College, but it's certainly not one of the country's top universities. Somehow it rankles me both when Dahlia is a clone of Talia and when she's her own unique character.

Dahlia shook her head, freeing tendrils from her ponytail, which framed her face in a sexy hippie kind of way. Russell tried to stifle his desire. "The scholarship was grade-dependent. I got the ax after my stellar record last year." Russell didn't even want to know what that meant. "There's no way I can afford this stupid place."

This was clearly a copout—surely she could go on financial aid like almost everyone else. But Dahlia stood up and stretched, making it clear that she was done discussing this.

Russell could have left. Dahlia wasn't just a mess, she'd lied to him.

Well, she'd withheld information, which isn't the same . . . although I don't know why I'm defending Dahlia. Russell should get the hell out of there and get rid of her already.

But as Dahlia reached her arms over her head, it made her tank top ride up just so, and Russell felt helpless against that sliver of stomach. He followed her into her bedroom, knowing full well how pathetic he was.

Soon Dahlia's hot breath was on his neck, on his chest, then lower and lower. As Dahlia eased off Russell's pants and boxers, he felt his whole body relax. He kept his eyes clamped shut, and didn't open them again until the very last moment, when he shivered all over and let out a soft, satisfied groan. Dahlia was peering up at him with a half-smile.

These final lines have a strange effect on me. When Gabe comes home from Nonno, I push him down onto the couch and slide off his pants. He's gazing at me with a mix of desire and curiosity, like I'm a delicious delicacy. "What's gotten into you?" he asks. I tell him to shut up and close his eyes.

Afterward, my skin is warm and tingly all over. I feel as if I've been replaced with a sexier, more powerful version of myself. That night, I dream of Dahlia, long hair mussed around flushed cheeks, smile languid as she lounges, skin bare against silk sheets. Then she's morphed into Lana, drugged and dazed, propped up in a hospital bed, starched white sheets tucked tightly around her. Then it's a composite of the two of them, loopy and enigmatic, cotton gown hanging off one shoulder. I myself am unsure of my place in all this—I'm a gauzy presence on the sidelines, then I blink and it's me in the bed, then I blink again and I'm gone.

Gabe and I make love again in the morning. My body is still vibrating, contours fuzzy, as I stumble into the shower. I imagine myself in a shampoo ad, the warm water cascading through my hair and caressing my shoulders and back like the gentlest of fingers. I imagine it's Gabe touching me as I close my eyes, breathe in the steam, and luxuriate in the soothing sound of running water.

A loud jingle jars me from my bliss. It's coming from the other side of the curtain. I peek out and see Gabe's phone by the sink. I'm about to return to my shower when the name on the screen catches my eye: **TALIA.** I'm frozen, watching the device sing and shake, blinking **TALIA, TALIA, TALIA.** When it finally goes still and silent, a notification pops up, flashing like a warning: **MISSED CALLS FROM TALIA: 17.**

I stay in the shower until my fingers are raisins, willing the water to wash away what I've seen. By the time I'm out, the bedroom clock scolds me. I'm never late to work. I race to get ready, throwing on the first dress I find and grabbing a granola bar, chewing and swallowing so fast I nearly choke on a shard of almond.

* * *

I attempt to sneak discreetly into my office, but Jonathan spots me and plays welcome committee, ushering me through the entrance like he's the proprietor and I his guest. "Now that Gabe's getting published, and you guys are getting married, no wonder you're strolling in half an hour late. Who gives a shit, right?" He wears a self-satisfied grin; he's proud to know all of my personal news. I walk more quickly, but Jonathan keeps up, hounding me about Gabe's book deal. He asks about the print run, the marketing plan, and the promotion tour, clearly angling to measure it all against his own success. "I don't know, Jonathan," I say, trying to dismiss him. At the moment, I couldn't care less about the details of Gabe's book deal.

It's an echo in my head: **MISSED CALLS FROM TALIA: 17.**

"I bet they'll want him to pose with a smoldering, sexy look in his author photo," Jonathan says, "It'll be good practice for your engagement shoot." Trying to annoy me is a sport for him.

"Jonathan, I've got work to do. Please excuse me." I speed ahead.

He calls after me: "I've got work, too, you know. This men's margarita mix won't rebrand itself."

MISSED CALLS FROM TALIA: 17. I do have work to do, but I don't have any plans to do it. Instead, I shut myself in my office with Gabe's manuscript, which even in my mad dash this morning I managed to slip into my bag. I place a stack of résumés on my desk for decoy, then I open to where I left off.

Dahlia got a job waiting tables. Now when Russell saw couples holding hands outside classrooms or tucked together into library stacks, he couldn't picture himself as part of that. Not that Dahlia had ever been one to play the college co-ed, to sling a backpack over her shoulder and walk hand in hand with him across campus.

As usual, the two of them created their own world, more dazzling than everyone else's. Now Dahlia returned home with take-out containers of food that they gorged on while she told tales of all her crazy customers.

I feel a pang, thinking of Gabe's and my post-Nonno ritual.

Now Dahlia had money in her pocket, which she spent on what she called her cultural enlightenment—museum passes and fat philosophy books and (Russell guessed but didn't have hard proof of) an array of mind-altering substances. What did college lectures have on this kind of learning? Dahlia challenged him. Russell knew her logic was flawed, but her days did sometimes seem more enriching than the drudgery of his classwork. And without the stress of school for her, their time together expanded deliciously. Dahlia seemed almost happy, almost satisfied.

After she'd been working for a few weeks, Russell decided to surprise her with a visit. Dahlia had described Meridian as a family diner, but it turned out to be more like a lounge, with mirrored panels and high leather booths whose cracked edges were visible even under the low lighting. Russell hadn't expected the seedy décor, or the smell, a pungent mix of fried food and artificial vanilla. Almost all the patrons were men. Russell didn't see his girlfriend anywhere.

"Dining solo?" He was startled by the hostess' eyebrows, painted into pert arcs. Everything about her appearance seemed intended to shock: dark hair highlighted into frosted chunks, a catalog of gold hoops snaking up one ear, a mini-tee stretched tight over full breasts, which Russell had to stare at in order to read the pink lettering of "MERIDIAN." "Sir?"

"Yeah, it's just me. Could you seat me in Dahlia's section?"

The girl fiddled with her tongue ring. "Who?"

Rescanning the room, Russell spotted Dahlia taking the orders of two men. She also wore a "MERIDIAN" shirt, cut low and cropped high. No bra.

Of course no bra.

Leaning over one of the men's menu, she was giving him an eyeful. She touched his arm, and something he said made her laugh—the cheeks-dimpled, full-throttle release that Russell was always trying to elicit with his stupid jokes. Russell felt equal parts turned-on and disgusted. But as Dahlia walked away, the men's eyes inevitably ogling the back of her skirt, Russell caught a glimpse of her face: It was empty, a total blank. For a moment he wondered if it was even Dahlia.

The hostess noticed Russell's glance. "Oh, *Dede?* Follow me, right this way."

But he didn't; instead, he fled. Outside, he took one last look at Meridian, its ugly sign blazing neon, then he returned to campus, to its stately architecture and manicured greens. If the hostess said something to Dahlia about Russell coming by, Dahlia didn't ever mention it. Russell stayed at his own place that night, churning out a research paper, and by the next day he found he could pretend the visit had never happened. He could erase from his head the fact of how his girlfriend spent her nights. He didn't feel bad about it; he assumed Dahlia, too, employed a whole litany of her own similar mind tricks

"Molly?" My boss, Natalie, interrupts my reading. "Have you narrowed down those candidates?"

"Almost," I say. "Give me ten more minutes."

As I flip through the résumés, searching for project management experience, I'm attuned to all the euphemisms—how "results-oriented" is a mushy cover for not having any hard data on said results, and how banal phrases like "out-of-the-box thinker" and "creative innovator" usually indicate their opposites.

MISSED CALLS FROM TALIA: 17.

I wonder if Talia worked somewhere like Meridian, if she wore a teensy tank top and a short skirt and served wings and fries to a bunch of sleazy drunk bros—and if Gabe was one of them. I wonder if she might still work there, and if Gabe might still be her customer.

I glance down and am shocked to discover the state of the résumés: pen-holes punched scattershot through the pages, edges torn to fringe, a few crumpled into balls. It looks like a trash can has been overturned onto my desk. A little scared of myself, I quickly pull up the résumé files on my computer and print out a new batch, pretending the first batch never existed. As I grab them from the printer, I realize my hands are trembling.

Chapter 13

GABE INSISTS I come with him to cash his book advance check, and then he whisks me uptown and won't say a word about where we're headed. I suspect a museum, but when we turn from Sixth Avenue onto 47th Street, the flashing signs announce our entrance to the Diamond District. My stomach flips and I'm embarrassed to sense a smile spread across my face. "I figured it was time to replace those twisty-ties," Gabe says, squeezing my hand. We navigate the crush of people, one half in suits and furs, the other in the tourist uniform of jeans and sneakers.

The scene both fascinates and repels me; the atmosphere feels both enchanting and illicit. Gabe claims he got a tip about a jeweler, but I grow nervous as we're led through a store that feels more flea market than Tiffany, then down a steep concrete staircase and through a maze of unfinished hallways. We're greeted by a man whose stomach spills over his pants, and whose stubby fingers are rough against my palm as we shake. I decline his offers of both Stoli and Godiva. I whisper to Gabe, "Where are we?" Gabe accepts a truffle and shrugs. I flash back to Brighton Beach, another pocket of another world, and think maybe everything about this engagement will feel otherworldly, perhaps in preparation for the uncharted world of marriage.

The jeweler lays out a handful of worn baggies, and starts pulling out diamonds—some specks, others rocks. Even in this dingy room, they shine and twinkle and catch the light like magic. The jeweler gestures for me to peer into the microscope, and I get lost in the sparkle. I barely listen as he catalogs karats and clarity and impurities. Instead, I picture walking through the city with one of these treasures strapped to my finger. I fantasize that arming myself with the strongest material in the world would give me superpowers, that owning an unbreakable substance would make me, and my bond with Gabe, unbreakable.

This fantasy is snuffed out by the sudden clamor of Gabe's parents' voices in my head: *How archaic, capitalist, wasteful! The diamond industry invented engagement rings as a marketing scam! And don't get us started on the horrors of the diamond mining business!* I've heard Joe and Barb orate on this subject on more than one occasion. Now, when the talk turns to our budget, I get edgy, wishing I'd accepted the Stoli. Suddenly, I can hear my mother's voice, too: *Count your blessings! And remember, all that glitters isn't gold! And what's so special about gold anyway?* The noise of everyone else's opinions discombobulates me. The display of diamonds transforms in a blink before my eyes from grandiose to garish; then, blink—gorgeous; blink—gaudy. My vision goes blurry with vertigo, and my stomach gurgles with anxiety. I need to get out.

I nudge Gabe. "Hey, let's come back later, okay?" Gabe takes his time unwrapping another chocolate, and I think he might protest. But he nods and follows me out.

It takes us several tries to maneuver our way back through the hallways to the stairwell. My panic has subsided somewhat by the time we've rejoined the throngs on the street, but now we're both irritable. We dodge the solicitors and duck into a pizza joint. Our slices come out greasy and lukewarm, and I'm not even hungry. What I am is anxious, feeling pressured to justify my actions back at the jeweler. I start to ramble: "It just makes a lot more sense to use your book money to pay off your student loans, right? Or for rent, or utilities, or a vacation, or"—I try for irony—"a donation to combat fatal diamond mining?" That came out wrong. Gabe looks annoyed. "There are just so many things we could buy that would be so much more practical than an engagement ring."

"It's not 'we,'" Gabe says, his voice edged with anger, and I feel suddenly scared, thinking of his flashing phone: **MISSED CALLS FROM TALIA: 17.** I've been trying to bring that up for days, but I keep chickening out, dreading Gabe's explanation. "You said, so many things *we* could buy. It's not our money; it's mine."

"I know, but—"

"No, don't interrupt me. It's not even about the money. People in every culture all around the world decorate themselves with jewelry or pendants or body paint or whatever. But only you, Molly—it's like you're pathologically incapable of forgetting about the practical and letting yourself be treated. When in fact, I think you want to be treated—I think you want it so fucking badly—but for some reason a desire like that disgusts you. So, instead of admitting it, you pretend to feel the opposite. Do you know how frustrating that is for me, your fiancé? I just wanted to buy you something nice. That's it, okay? You always have to overcomplicate everything."

I have no response. At first, I'm furious. How dare Gabe dictate to me what I want? But after a moment, I wonder if he's maybe a tiny bit right. Why hadn't I considered that a ring could simply be something nice, a gift from Gabe to me? I feel sad and foolish. Everyone talks about relationship milestones like they're all celebration and joy, and maybe they are for everyone else. Something must be very wrong with me.

Gabe spends the train ride home hunched over his notebook. I assume he's recording the details of this morning's appointment, although hopefully not also its aftermath. I picture him on the phone with Talia, relating the back-and-forth of our tiff. To force the image from my mind, I survey the ring fingers of the women around me on the train. I observe naked digits and digits bearing all kinds of rocks: tiny, modest, hulking. Who gave these women their rings, I wonder, and how do they feel about the givers? What meaning, if any, do they attach to wearing or not wearing a ring? I think of Kirsten, who inherited her grand-mother's rose-gold band with a fleck of diamond. And Lana, with her three-karat yellow diamond that Leo spent months saving up for; he was so excited to give it to her that he ended up proposing early, a week before their big Brazil trip. I think of my mother who, nearly twenty-five years after she last swatted away my father's hand after one of his corny puns, still wears the princess-cut diamond he gave her the night they graduated college. I wonder, has she ever thought of taking it off? I bury my own bare hands in my pockets, feeling small and alone.

* * *

A week later, I wake up to a tickle on my foot. There's something caught on my big toe. It sparkles aqua, now cerulean, now the same shade of Gabe's eyes as he crouches by the foot of the bed, a look of anticipation flashing across his face. "After more thought, I decided you might be more of a blue sapphire kind of girl," he says. "Diamonds are forever, but sapphires . . ."

I finish for him, feeling giddy and grateful for my second chance at this moment: "say desire?"

Gabe nods and tickles the ring up my leg, compiling a list of other things that are my favorite color: "Blue moon, blueberries, blue sky, blue jeans, blue mood, bluebell, Blue Man Group."

The ring hangs loose on my fourth finger, but it fits my middle one just right. I admire its place at the center of my hand, my new blue adornment and armor. A sapphire feels so much less loaded than a dia-mond. Now I could flip someone the bird in style, that is, if I ever had the guts. At the moment, I only want to spread my hand across Gabe's chest. "It's perfect. Thank you. I'm sorry about the other day."

Gabe leans in to kiss me, but we're interrupted by the doorbell, and despite Gabe's protests, I scurry to answer it. A UPS guy deposits a box at my feet with a thud. I note the return address—South Dakota—and my mouth goes dry. "Am I allowed to decline the delivery?" I ask, only half-kidding.

The man shrugs impassively. Gabe is soon at my side, signing for the package and carrying it inside. I eye it warily.

My pulse races as Gabe cuts the thing open, and a pile of soil and sand spills out onto the floor, a tumble of deep reds and rich browns, nothing at all like the black dust that populates the parks here in the city. Buried like roots in the soil is a card, which I reach for and read:

> Congrats on your engagement. May your marriage be multi-layered, like the sand and silt and clay of sedimentary rock.
> Love, Charlie.

It's funny in a Charlie kind of way. Gabe, however, is not amused. "What kind of present is a box of dirt?" He snatches up the card, then answers his own question: "He's saying he hopes our relationship is like dirt—you realize that, right?"

"Well, Charlie is a dirt-bag, so what do you expect?" I'm entertained by my retort, but Gabe still isn't smiling. My mother has been hinting for me to start a wedding registry, but I much prefer the idea of an odd gift like this to a set of flatware or a stand mixer. I dig my fingers into the dirt because, well, why not? I close my eyes, enjoying the damp cool of it, imagining I'm in a nature preserve somewhere far from Brooklyn. When I open my eyes, Gabe is observing me with suspicion. I free my hands and go to the sink. "Anyway," I say, shouting over the running faucet, "we should be thankful, because he could've sent us a ferret. There's an endangered breed of them in the Badlands that are apparently highly revered."

I can tell it bothers Gabe that I know this fact. So, I don't mention something else that Charlie once told me about the park, how the water is eating away at the rock at an impressive rate of one inch per year. In a few hundred thousand years—a snap of the fingers, geologically speaking—the park will have disappeared entirely.

As I take a broom and dustpan to the mess, I think about the time I made a visit to the Badlands, a few weeks after my brother's wedding, when Charlie was still new to his ranger gig. Our tent looked out onto a panorama of rock formations. According to Charlie, their strange, otherworldly lines had been sculpted by erosion. Charlie spent much of that trip teaching me about the park. The rest of the time we spent rolling around in the same dirt that I'm currently sweeping up from my hardwood floor; I remember it was impossible to get it out from under my fingernails. I survey my fingers now and see that that's still the case. The dirt is incongruous with the winking sapphire on my finger, and I experience a wave of profound unease.

"Maybe we should start composting," Gabe says. "I bet this would be great soil for it. Add a few worms and we can dump in all our rotting food and garbage." He cackles, obviously thrilled at the poetic justice of the idea.

"Good plan," I say. Composting is regenerative. It transforms something bad into something good. At least, that's what people claim; I have no idea how or even if it really works. For now, I relegate Charlie's box to the cabinet under the sink, deciding I'll deal with it later.

Chapter 14

MY MOM'S EMAILS about additional wedding venues read like chapters of a long-winded memoir, with a title like *Adventures in Wedding Planning: A Mother's Journey*. I'm skimming one of her screeds, about her partiality for rustic charm and original detailing, when I spot a familiar vista in an embedded image: a little inn abutting the Marginal Way, the seaside cliff walk in Ogunquit. When I was a kid, my family would drive out to the vacation town on summer weekends. We'd spend the day on the white sand beach, and then amble along the Marginal Way to Perkin's Cove. We'd all eat lobster rolls, except for my dad, who preferred oysters; I can almost hear the slurp of them. After dinner, we'd walk down to the harbor and wait for a tall boat so we could watch the drawbridge split. "Will you look at that," my dad would say, voice full of wonder, as the bridge bisected and the boat passed through. I'd marvel alongside him, squeezing his hand and feeling utterly happy; I wonder if I've ever felt as happy since. According to my mom's email about the inn, we'd have the run of the place for the reception, and we could hold the ceremony out on the cliffs.

I took Gabe to Ogunquit once, last spring. We hiked out onto the cliffs with a thermos of vodka-tonics and a bag of Tootsie Rolls, and

Gabe listened attentively as I told him all my childhood memories of the place. Then we fooled around to the soundtrack of lapping waves. That night, back in my childhood bedroom, we surveyed the nicks and cuts our fumblings had left across our bodies and we tended to each other's wounds. Then we stood naked, laughing at our Band-Aid-pocked skin. At first it felt wrong to add this new memory to the vault I'd reserved for my childhood vacationland, from back when our family was a foursome—but ultimately it was a relief. Now I picture returning there for our wedding day, a major moment overlaid onto all that bittersweet history, the ocean spray against the rocks the closest thing I can imagine to my father watching over me. It feels just right.

"What do you think?" I ask Gabe later, clicking through the inn's virtual tour. I can't help thinking how far away the spot is—literally and figuratively—from Talia and Charlie and the rest of the noise of our lives here. We're soon on the phone with the innkeeper, a good-natured man named John, and then zeroing in on the last weekend of May. As Gabe reads off his credit card number, I do the math: a quarter of his book advance forfeited in exchange for our reservation.

Eager to share the news, I type out a save-the-date email, subject "Married by Memorial Day!" I CC close friends and family, hit "Send," and then sit back and wait for the good tidings to roll in.

The first response comes from Gabe's college friend, a reply-all: **Congrats on the engagement . . . and the press!** He's pasted in a link, which I click to discover is a *Publishers Weekly* roundup of the most anticipated novels of spring. *The Charms of Dahlia* appears at number thirteen, along with a blurb:

WHEN AN EARNEST COLLEGE BOY FALLS INTO THE CRAZY-GIRL TRAP IN THE ALLURING GUISE OF DAHLIA FREID, THE RESULTS ARE EQUAL PARTS THRILLING AND DISASTROUS.

This dispiriting summary is accompanied by an equally dispiriting cover image; it's my first glimpse of it. The main illustration is a neon pin-up girl, the kind you see on strip club signage. The title tracks along the girl's curves in a fanciful, looping font. A guy's silhouette—his profile shockingly similar to Gabe's—appears on the bottom, tilted longingly up at the girl. Just below that, stamped in all-caps, "By Gabriel M. Dover."

"I didn't know there was press already," I say to Gabe, "or a cover."

"Me neither," Gabe says, hijacking my laptop. "The publisher sent me three image options, and this was definitely not my pick. It's tacky, right?" The distress on Gabe's face makes me understand something worrying: Not only is this book out of my control, it's out of Gabe's, too.

By the time I return to my inbox, there are dozens of new messages: congrats on the wedding and the book, or on the book and the wedding, plus the inevitable jokes comparing the two: "Molly, it's a good thing you've managed to trap Gabe with your allure!" "Hopefully your relationship is more thrilling than disastrous!" "Molly must've been the model for that cover, right?"

A text from Sam interrupts my reading:

Please tell me this is just marketing BS and Gabe's book isn't SEXIST SMUT?!

This cheers me up, and an entertaining exchange of emojis follows. Sam's words remind me of what I should already know, given my job: A thing's branding is separate from the thing itself. It's a reassuring thought—*The Charms of Dahlia* shouldn't be judged by its cover, or by one write-up announcing its publication. Although a queasy flutter in my gut is the knowledge that even the most outrageous of Funhouse Branding's campaigns are rooted in at least a kernel of truth. Plus, I've read Gabe's book, or at least parts of it, and maybe it is sexist smut.

Tucked among the emails from well-wishers is one from someone called "Wendy the Wedding Wizard." It includes a "What's your bridal personality?" quiz, plus a planning timeline that indicates I'm already three months behind, and a budget calculator whose price ranges seem more fitting for a house purchase than a party. To quell my rising panic, I close my laptop. I notice there are still traces of Badlands dirt under my fingernails. I tell Gabe I'm going to get a manicure, happy for an excuse to go out.

I welcome the nail salon's anesthetizing fumes. I pick a color called Film Noir and delight in watching the manicurist muddy my nails with it. I'm admiring the pop of my sapphire against the black backdrop, when two women sit down on either side of me, each clutching a bridal magazine. Flipping pages as steadily as metronomes, they volley commentary over my head about appetizers and hairdos and invitations. I'm trapped. When one holds up a page of what she describes as "the most stunning gown ever," I brace myself for some monstrosity of lace and poof. But a peek reveals that it's a tasteful design from Bella So, Lana's store.

Lana. I must've said it aloud because both women start, as if they only just noticed they've been conversing across another person. Here I am stressing over trivial wedding stuff when today's the day of my sister-in-law's back surgery. I wonder how she's doing, and Leo too. Nails still tacky, I dash off a text to my brother saying I'm thinking of them.

Down the block, my eye catches on a mannequin in a store window: It's draped in a dusty rose sheath, long and flowy silk with an asymmetrical neckline and hem. It's bold and unconventional, not at all my style, but something pulls me into the shop to try it on. Taking in my likeness in the dressing room mirror, I feel transformed. The dress is like nothing I've ever worn or even seen, and as I shimmy and then spin in circles, I imagine all the stressors of the past two months vanished. I picture another setting: the cliffs of Ogunquit, Gabe by my side reciting some silly little poem, and all the people we love standing around. The dress feels like it's already mine.

I'm back home hanging it carefully in my closet, in the back where I hope to keep it hidden from Gabe, when I finally hear back from Leo:

Lana's in rough shape, but surgeon says today went well. Now we hold our breaths . . .

For some reason, I take this literally: I hold my breath, thinking of Lana in pain and Leo helpless at her side. I think of Gabe writing a 300-page tribute to his ex-girlfriend, which will soon be published for all the world to read. I think of Talia, who is apparently back in the picture, or maybe has been in it all along. And Charlie, trying his darnedest to be back in the picture, too, as usual knowing exactly where my tender spots are to probe at. And me, falling for the fantasy that a wedding dress can be some kind of chrysalis, metamorphosing me from a regular person with all my regular person problems into a beautiful butterfly, fit to fly away from it all. How naïve I am, how stupid.

I realize I'm still holding my breath when the edges of my vision blur and I start to feel dizzy. I inhale a deep gulp of air and slide down to the ground. I'm trembling and queasy, and for a while it feels as if I'll never, ever catch my breath again.

* * *

Leo, who can't take any more time off from work, warned me that Lana was on a lot of painkillers, and that it would be a while before the surgery's benefits outweighed the pain of recovery. Still, I'm not fully prepared when I enter their apartment, which, without Lana's careful attention, has been overrun by Leo's messiness. Surrounded by a sea of clutter and medicine bottles is my sister-in-law dozing in a hospital bed. I decide that while she sleeps I'll tidy up. I'm halfway through mopping, wearing plastic gloves and a t-shirt I picked up off the floor, when I hear Lana's laugh. "Leo's going to kill you," she says. "He loves that shirt."

Okay, I think, so maybe she's feeling better, or at least drugged enough to joke around. As if reading my mind, she adds, "Ask me literally anything but how I'm feeling."

All right, then. I show her my engagement ring, and she spends a full five minutes turning it this way and that in admiration; she seems to find it trippy how the sapphire hits the light, which I find a little unnerving.

"So, have you started wedding planning?" she asks. I groan. "Oh, it'll be worth it in the end. Weddings are so romantic—didn't you reunite with Charlie at ours?" I give her a look. "His pot is fan-friggin-tastic, by the way."

"If there's anything Charlie's good for, it's that."

"Molly," she says, not quite pulling off the pronunciation of my name, "as soon as I'm a functional person again, we're going on a field trip to Bella So to pick out your gown. It'll be half-price with my discount!"

She looks too happy for me to tell her I already found a dress. "Sure, that sounds great."

When Lana stretches, I can hear her joints crack; she looks so fragile. Within twenty minutes of waking up, she yawns and drifts off again. I wonder if this might be kind of nice for her, to check out of real life for a few weeks just to rest.

I soon regret the thought. When Lana wakes up again, her cries are shrill and agonizing, sounds I've only ever heard from the mouth of an infant. She's writhing like a rabid animal. Her meds schedule instructs me to administer her next pill in an hour, but Lana insists she needs it immediately. "Please," she begs, "please, please," her voice growing direr. Panicked, I give her half a pill. It's twenty long minutes before her anguish gives way to a strange stupor.

Only then do I ask her, "So what does it feel like?"

At first I think she hasn't heard me, but after two or three minutes, she says, "Like pins and needles. But, *actual* pins and needles, twisting around and sending little electric shocks right into my spine."

"That sounds unbearable."

Lana doesn't contradict me. "Honestly, I don't think the surgery worked," she says. "I'm terrified I'll be stuck like this forever, always with the *zap, zap, zaps* into my back. I never realized how terrible it could be to feel so much."

I don't know how to respond. I can't reassure her that she'll be fine, or say I know what she means. Even though I think I do know, a little, pain being pain, that awful, profound awareness of the body and mind. I often tell myself I don't remember anything from the aftermath of my father's death, but it's not totally true: For blips, I never felt more aware, every thought and sensation like a live wire to my skin. Going numb was the only way to cope.

I consider the half-pill tucked in my pocket. "Here," I say, handing it to Lana. Within seconds, it's been swallowed. Soon Lana's limbs go slack and her eyes turn drowsy. I assume she'll want to rest, but she asks me to stay and read her something.

"Okay." I scan the bookshelf by the bed—the rows of medical text-books, coffee table books on design, and a few paperback mysteries. Then I remember, *The Charms of Dahlia* is in my purse. Something about Lana's vulnerability makes me want to share it, so I fetch the manuscript and bring her up to speed. Opening to the next chapter, I see the story is back to Dahlia's point-of-view. I clear my throat and begin:

Midnight. Dahlia's shift was finally over. By the end of a night at Meridian, everything stunk of fries and beer—her clothes, her hair, even her skin. Back in the staff room, she couldn't shimmy out of her uniform fast enough, shirt first, then panties and skirt. She was free.

Eye roll.

She glanced in the mirror, admiring her naked form.

Oh, come on.

Full breasts, pert pink nipples, cute curve of a belly, freckles crawling their way from her hips to the meeting of her thighs.

My jaw is clenched, my mouth goes dry.

She had a nice, firm ass, decent legs, although she wished they were longer, and stupid flat feet. Overall, Dahlia would rate her body an A-minus.

My voice cracks at the grade. I feel simultaneously furious at Gabe and mortified to be reading this aloud—so, why do I continue? Because it feels like a train that's derailed with no way to get back on track, and because I wouldn't know what to say to Lana if I stopped.

She could lay off the cocktails her customers regularly treated her to, maybe start running. Oh, who was she kidding? Dahlia wasn't going to cut back on drinking any more than she was going to start a workout routine. It didn't matter, anyway. She knew she was hot as fuck, and most every guy she encountered made sure she knew that he knew it, too. Content, Dahlia pulled on her favorite halter dress—black, tight, short. She was going out.

Lana starts giggling, and I look up, relieved to be interrupted. "Sorry." She's covering her mouth, but I tell her it's fine. "It's just, how long have I worked at Bella So? Never once have I seen a woman check herself out in the mirror like that. Can you even imagine?"

Her giggling turns contagious. My sister-in-law and I are soon joined in a laughing fit—it's such a release, I feel manic with it.

"So that's the Gabe gaze, huh?" she says. I look at her, confused. "You know, like the male gaze, but in this case it's Gabe specifically." She's right. It's Gabe's admiring Dahlia admiring herself in the mirror. How creepy. My heart pounds furiously, adrenaline coursing through me, as I picture my fiancé mentally undressing every woman he encounters, cataloging each as a collection of body parts, doling out letter grades.

"It's bad, isn't it?"

"Well, who knows, Dahlia could be the exception," Lana says. "Maybe, unlike the rest of us women, Dahlia really does hang around in the nude in front of mirrors, lusting after herself. Maybe she's the woman of men's fantasies—the one any guy would leave his wife or girlfriend for. What do they call her? Right, the manic pixie dream girl."

My mouth floods with saliva and I feel like I might throw up.

"Oh, don't worry," Lana says, laughing lightly. "Those girls don't really exist. Thank god, right?"

"Right." I force myself to smile. "Thank god."

"Anyway, I'm spent." She yawns widely and starts to drift off. I prop up her pillow, tuck her in tight, and tiptoe from the room.

Alone now, I turn back to the manuscript like a rubbernecker at a crash. I race through the rest of the scene: After getting dressed, Dahlia paints her nails—it's an odd plot point, and I swear it's included only because Gabe couldn't be bothered to research the undoubtedly complicated makeup routine of a girl like Dahlia. As she primps, she describes the generosity of her customers, the tips they leave her in the form of money (twenty-five, thirty, fifty percent of their bills), plus various pills and things. This drags on for pages and pages, and—despite everything that's come before, this still shocks me—the scene concludes with Dahlia sitting on the floor of the break room getting herself off while fantasizing about one of her regulars. What a climax, I quip to myself, picturing (as I'm sure any other woman reading this would, too) Dahlia's nails tacky with nail polish rubbing against her most sensitive parts. Not sexy, not sexy at all.

I return to Lana's words, turning them over in my head—Dahlia doesn't exist, of course not, I know . . . but Talia does. And, unless she's recently moved, she exists locally, somewhere in this city. I can't believe I didn't think of it before. I pull out my phone, open a web browser, and type in her full name.

Chapter 15

IT TAKES ME until the check arrives to admit to Sam and Kirsten why I suggested this particular brunch spot in a pocket of Brooklyn that's convenient to none of us. I take a deep breath: "Gabe's novel is about his ex-girlfriend. I did some digging and found out she lives across the street, right there." I point to a brick building opposite the restaurant. "Also, she's been calling Gabe. A lot."

Kirsten's eyes go wide with concern, but Sam yelps with glee. "Well, this is an interesting turn of events—Molly the Internet stalker! Come on, guys." She ushers us outside to a bench, which she dubs our stake-out spot, then makes us strap on sunglasses for cover, despite the overcast sky.

Sam's gaze is fixed forward, but Kirsten is looking askance and fidgeting, clearly uncomfortable. "Hey," she says, pointing to my bag, "Is that Gabe's book?"

Before I can respond, Sam has snatched up the pages. "'*The Charms of Dahlia,* by Gabriel Dover,'" she announces like a cheesy voiceover. "Ooh, can we read it? Pretty please?"

I shrug, feeling resigned to the inevitable; once Sam wants something, she'll get it. A moment later, she and Kirsten are hunched together over Page One. I take the second half of the manuscript and pick up where I left off, mostly to avoid seeing my friends' reactions to what they're reading. I flip to the next chapter—a return to Russell, thankfully.

The eviction happened the night of the awards ceremony. Each spring, all the Poly-Sci majors submitted their best work, competing for the $1,000 prize. A junior now, Russell thought he might finally have a shot.

He'd splurged on a suit for the occasion, patronizing one of those dusty shops downtown where an old Italian man took a shaky tape measure to his inseam. It made Russell squirm, but the result fit him like a second skin. He pictured wearing the suit to his first day of some yet-to-be-determined job. The image was hazy, but Russell still had plenty of time to sharpen it—graduation felt far off.

Knotting his tie, Russell saw Dahlia's name flash onto his phone screen. He picked up. "Hey babe, I'll swing by in fifteen."

"You need to come now."

"I just threw a pizza in the oven."

"Just come over."

When Russell arrived, Dahlia was slumped onto her stoop, sur-rounded by a pile of clothes and her desktop computer. Her room-mate, Natasha, burst through the front door, silently dumped a bucket of toiletries at Dahlia's feet, then reversed back inside. Russell recog-nized the vanilla lotion he'd given Dahlia for her birthday, and her Chanel No.5.

No way would Dahlia wear Chanel No. 5—too classic, too old. Gabe must've Googled "perfume" and picked the first result.

"What the hell is going on?"

Natasha reappeared, this time with an armful of bras and panties. "I'll tell you what's going on," she said. "Dahlia hasn't paid rent in three fucking months."

"Babe, is that true?" Even as he waited for Dahlia's response, Russell knew. She'd quit Meridian over a disagreement with her boss (so she said), and since then she'd been working up the motivation to start another job-hunt (so she claimed). A few times she'd mentioned moving in together, which thrilled Russell even as he knew he should've been suspicious. Dahlia, the free spirit. Dahlia, who bristled at the words "girlfriend" and "relationship." Dahlia, who was now a squatter on her own stoop, and still not saying a word.

Natasha turned to go inside. "Wait," Russell said. "Three months' rent. How much is that? $1,500? $2,000? I'll get my checkbook. Who's the landlord? Or hold on, can I pay with a card?" He took out his wallet. He wasn't sure how much he had in his bank account, but he'd figure it out.

Russell's desperation disgusts me. Stop, I will him. Go home, rescue your burning pizza from the oven, and go to your event. Leave Dahlia to fend for herself.

"Too late, Justin Timberlake," Natasha said. She was eyeing his outfit, and Russell touched his lapels, feeling suddenly stupid in the suit he'd been so proud of minutes earlier. "I've been telling her for weeks to get her shit together or she's out. A new tenant moves in tomorrow. Dahlia, I'm done with your bullshit."

"Cunt," Dahlia spat.

"Oh, *I'm* the cunt? You're fucking unbelievable." Natasha lobbed a sneaker at the computer monitor; it made a dull thud.

"Let's all calm down," Russell said. "Natasha, don't you have anything better to do than haul all of Dahlia's things outside? We'll take it from here."

Natasha scoffed. "What about you, Russell? Don't you have anything better to do than take on all of Dahlia's debts?"

My thoughts, exactly.

Russell realized he was still clutching his wallet. *"And* all her bullshit? You know she cheats on you, like, twice a week. You must've realized by now that your girlfriend is a lying slut." Natasha chucked a second sneaker at the computer.

Natasha was the liar, of course. She was angry, and worked up, and jealous of Dahlia. Ignoring her, Russell set to work moving out the rest of his girlfriend's stuff. It took three trips to transfer her things over to his place.

Dahlia refused to step back inside her now-former apartment, so Russell did the final inspection of her room. He examined the space where they'd spent hours and hours together, exploring every inch of each other's bodies. It seemed smaller now—just four walls and a worn carpet—and tomorrow it would belong to someone else. Russell closed the door behind him, flashed a middle finger at Natasha, who was on the couch slurping ramen, then went home.

"Russell." Dahlia was sitting on his bed, looking impossibly sexy in a tank top and short shorts. "I was scared to tell you."

"We'll talk about it later. I'm an hour late. You stay here and settle in." He kissed her on the head, not wanting to get sucked in for more, and jogged to the Poly-Sci building.

Like some kind of miracle, just as he walked inside, he heard his name being called from the front of the room. Russell felt shaky as he walked to the podium to shake his professor's hand. *Had he won?* Almost—he'd gotten runner-up. Here he was, being showered with the praise he'd craved for years, and he could barely take it in. He tried to reciprocate the professor's smile. It was a relief when she handed him his certificate and he could return to the crowd.

At the bar, Russell spotted a welcome face: Chrissy, his study partner from freshman Econ. They'd pulled all-nighters together before exams, then unwound at the campus bar that was laxest on IDs. Back then, he'd only dared to think of Chrissy as a friend, but as Russell hugged her now, he noticed her backless sundress and warm skin. The hair that had always been pulled into a ponytail now tumbled over her shoulders. She looked amazing, and he told her so.

Chrissy didn't blush. "Well, you're looking quite dapper in that suit. Congrats on the award."

"Thanks, though they say runner-up is the first loser." Russell hoped he sounded humble rather than idiotic.

"I kind of wanted to save you up there. Rough day?" Chrissy placed a hand on his arm, and Russell couldn't tell if he wanted to kiss her or bury his head into her hair and sob. Instead, he rolled his eyes, trying to make it look lighthearted.

Huh, this Chrissy seems normal and nice. I let myself get my hopes up a bit.

They talked summer plans. Chrissy had an internship in New York, where she'd be subletting a studio with her boyfriend. (Russell's heart fell a little.) Russell told her he was staying put—to take classes, he said, although in truth he hadn't thought of any plan beyond being with Dahlia. As they reminisced, Russell wondered why he and Chrissy hadn't kept in touch. Who was this boyfriend and how serious were they? Could Russell ask Chrissy out for a drink, for old time's sake? But he felt guilty, thinking of Dahlia, who'd just nearly became homeless. "I've gotta run," he said.

I feel my hopes fall.

"Let's hang sometime."

"Definitely," Chrissy said in that vague way that meant the opposite.

Back home, Russell found Dahlia parked in front of the TV, volume cranked up on some reality trash. She was wrist-deep in a bag of

Cheetos, the couch cushion next to her stamped with florescent orange fingerprints. Russell's exhaustion caught up with him all in a rush; his body ached and his head pounded. "I'm turning in," he said.

Dahlia's smile was almost shy as she followed him to bed, and Russell couldn't help but anticipate all the ways she would soothe and heal him.

Sam interrupts my reading: "So this Russell dude pays for the chick's textbooks *and* her lab fees? What a chump." I must've skipped over the section she's referring to—I can't picture Dahlia taking a Science course. "Let me guess: Next he becomes her sugar daddy and by the end she's scammed him out of everything?" I glance at her page—she's not even close to the part where Russell treats Dahlia to international plane tickets (or where he offers to pay several months of her rent).

"Well, I think it's great," says Kirsten. "Who knew Gabe was such a talented writer?"

Sam ignores her: "Or does Dahlia turn out to be a vampire with a taste for the blood of misogynistic frat boys?"

"I don't think Russell's misogynistic," Kirsten says. "He's love-sick and maybe a little confused, but—"

"Enough." I cut them off and snatch up their pages. "This was clearly a bad idea."

"Molly! Hey, Molly." Sam yanks my arm and points not at all discreetly across the street. Exiting the building is a trio of girls, all in the uniform of petit twenty-something hipsters: layered thrift store threads, oversized sunglasses, and greasy hair pulled into complicated knots. Any one of them could be Talia.

"Hey Talia!" Sam calls out, her voice booming across the concrete, arms flailing. My body tenses, heart pounding, and when the girls swivel to face us, I'm relieved to discover that none of them is Gabe's ex. They continue on their way.

I grab Sam's arm. "What the hell was that, you crazy person?" My voice is a shriek.

Sam jerks back her arm and gives me a withering look. "Seriously, you think I'm the crazy one? I was just being a good friend, going along with your crackpot little plan. I mean, what *was* the plan anyway? Besides making Kirsten and me take two trains each to meet you here?"

The question, so matter-of-fact, has a way of crumbling my half-baked imaginings for today, of making me realize my foolishness. Here I was reading about Dahlia's eviction from her home, feeling exasperated at Russell for being so pathetic, and meanwhile I'm the one loitering outside Talia's home, half-hoping for a dramatic scene of my own. What I wanted was for Talia to see me, engagement ring and all, and to understand that whatever she had with Gabe is over and done with—that she was evicted from his life long ago. That's the irony, it occurs to me now: I don't really want to see Talia; what I want is the opposite, for her to disappear.

Mercifully, Kirsten breaks the tense silence: "I think it's time for us all to head home."

"Yeah, you can't get me out of here fast enough," Sam says.

On the walk to the subway, I barely register it when Sam stops to throw up in a trash can. I'm irritable and angry—at Sam for her pushiness, at Kirsten for silently standing by, at Dahlia for being so irresponsible, at Russell for enabling her, at Gabe for writing these characters into existence, at Talia for existing, and most of all at myself, for thinking that confronting Talia on her home turf would solve anything at all. The sun has emerged, and along with it a shadow on the sidewalk in front of me: a squat, rudimentary version of my body, which I hardly recognize as my own, which Gabe would probably grade a D-minus, I think bitterly. Of course, no matter how much I quicken my steps, my shadow self stays with me. Talia, too, feels like a shadow I can't shake.

*   *   *

I remain agitated long after brunch. When I spot Gabe's credit card bill in our mail stack, Sam's plot predictions return to mind. Gabe has been upfront with me about his past money struggles. "I went through a bad stretch," was how he explained it, back before we moved in together, and he showed me the evidence of having paid off most of his debt. At the time, I was sympathetic, impressed at his discipline to get himself back on track. But now I wonder, how did Gabe sink into such deep debt in the first place? And why, back then, didn't I push him for the details? An image of Talia surfaces in my mind, pockets empty, lips pursed in a pathetic pout, peering out the window of her brick apartment building. Did Gabe pay for her schoolbooks, her lab fees, plane tickets to Europe, three months' rent, more?

It takes me a full day to get up the nerve to confront him about it. "Of course not," Gabe responds. Only when I push does he add, "I gave her my credit card number, but only for emergencies."

"Emergencies," I repeat. "Meaning what exactly?" I picture shopping sprees, resort vacations, drug benders—or some hedonistic orgy combining all three.

"Molly, are we really doing this?" Gabe doesn't say that it's none of my business, and I don't say that he chose to write a book about it so actually it is my business. Instead, we're both silent, until finally Gabe relents: "Fine, I paid for a hospital bill when she dislocated her shoulder. And groceries a few times towards the end of her pay periods. And a couple other things here and there."

"Is it the same credit card you have now?"

"Talia hasn't used it in years, since before we broke up."

"So, that's a yes?"

"Everyone knows closing a card hurts your credit score, and with my history—" He catches sight of my face and stops short.

"That is really fucked up, Gabe." Adrenaline floods my nervous system, which gives me the momentum to get out what I've been trying to say for days: "I know Talia's been calling you." I wait for an explanation, my pulse racing.

Gabe's posture collapses. "She wants to meet up."

"She does, huh?" I sound braver than I feel. A sludge of ugly thoughts churns in my belly, and for some reason what gurgles up into speech is a taunt: "Well, maybe you should, then."

"I know you don't mean that," Gabe says. The words fill me with relief. "Come here." He begins massaging the knots in my neck, and I close my eyes. It feels nice, even though I consider him to be the one responsible for the knots, and even though no matter how long he rubs, I can't imagine the tension ever disappearing.

That night, it's like I've never heard of sleep. I get up for water and there's Gabe's open credit card statement on the table. I freeze, blinking at it like it's a wild animal that might pounce. *I'll just peek,* I decide. *I won't even touch it.* I scan the month's purchases: Uniqlo, Falafel Spot, CVS, Gabe's time-stamped wants and needs mapped out across the city. A trickle of remorse creeps into me, but it halts when I read, "Pretty Horizons," a charge of $422. *What in the hell?* I envision a boutique filled with stupid trinkets, or some new-agey church, or an unlicensed plastic surgery clinic. Whatever it is, Pretty Horizons has Talia written all over it. I rescan the other charges with a new skepticism: When has Gabe ever worn clothes from Uniqlo? Does he even like Middle Eastern food? Why is he shopping at CVS when there's a Duane Reade right down the street? Everything is contaminated by Talia—I picture her gallivanting around town, buying color-block sweaters and shawarma and drugstore makeup, all on Gabe's dime.

I stew all through the night. At dawn, I poke Gabe until he stirs. Bracing myself, I ask, "What's Pretty Horizons?" impressed with my directness.

Gabe's eyes adjust to awareness and then light up. "Did you find the package?"

"Huh?"

He hops out of bed and returns with what looks like a shoebox. "I wanted it to be a surprise, but I guess now's as good a time as any to show you." I still have no idea what's in the box, but already I feel terrible for mistrusting Gabe, for assuming he was still bankrolling his ex's life.

Gabe removes the lid, revealing a pile of cards, five-by-seven in sturdy stock, edges elegantly curved. I pull one out. The image is an illustrated version of a view I know well: rocky cliffs overlooking the sea. The waves are swirls of blue and white, the cliffs purplish-gray, the sun a fuzzy orange ball. It's simple and sweet. Our names and our wedding date hover in the sky, above a web site URL. Gabe pulls his laptop into bed and loads the site, which features the same design as the card. He scrolls through information about the inn and the town of Ogunquit. He turns up the volume, and I hear waves crashing, a seagull's caw, and then Gabe's low voice: "I will give Molly and Gabe a thousand dollars." On repeat.

"Subliminal messaging?" I ask. Gabe grins. "Nice. Very classy. With this brilliant plan, we'll be able to retire directly after the wedding."

"Honeymoon for life!" Gabe says, kissing my cheek. "Don't worry," he adds, "we can make it just the ocean sounds. Or, Abba or whatever."

"Phew. Definitely Abba."

"Hey, if you didn't see the package, how did you know about Pretty Horizons?"

"Huh?" I try to hop out of bed but I get tangled up in the sheets. "Uh, I'm going to make eggs. Want some?"

"Sure. But not so fast." Gabe grabs my foot and tortures me with tickles. I barely hear him over my cries for mercy: "So, I have to tell you something," he says. I hold my breath, scared. "*Maxim* asked me to write an article."

"*Maxim*?" I say, exhaling, confused at Gabe's solemn tone. "That magazine still exists?"

"They've got two million readers."

"What's the topic—five ways to annoy your fiancée? First, tickle her till she screams." I grin and bat my eyes at Gabe, feeling a little loopy from having been up all night. "No, first, write a 300-page ode to your ex."

"Actually, there's a working title." Gabe mumbles it so low that I have to ask him to repeat it. "Um, 'Ten signs your girlfriend is a psychopath.'"

A heaviness descends upon my chest. Just so I won't scream, I arch an eyebrow and attempt to remain lighthearted: "So I was right, it *is* a listicle." The term "listicle" is so dumb. The subject is so dumb, too, and it makes Gabe seem dumb to be writing it. I think of the first time I met Gabe, when he was too principled to take a job convincing people that they needed more stuff. I think of his belief that writing is his fate, the little speech he delivered with such conviction. This *Maxim* article can't be what he meant. Then again, I guess, good for Gabe for getting his name in front of two million readers, even if they're all—to borrow Sam's phrase—misogynistic frat boys. It's probably important for Gabe to write this kind of thing to promote his book. I try to believe this.

And yet . . . *Ten signs your girlfriend is a psychopath.* Dahlia is flighty and irresponsible and aggravating, sure, but *a psychopath?* It seems harsh. And what about Talia? For the first time, it occurs to me that maybe she won't find it flattering to have her past relationship memorialized in fiction from her ex-boyfriend's point-of-view. Maybe Talia's been trying to reach Gabe to vent her anger and, dare I dream, to stand up for me and my anger, too. It must feel infuriating for her to be ignored by Gabe. And how will she feel when she finds out Gabe is implying she's a psychopath in the pages of a magazine with two million readers? "You know, maybe you really should get together with Talia," I say.

"You think so?" Gabe eyes me warily, searching for a hidden agenda.

"It just seems like the right thing to do."

"Okay."

"Anyway, I'm starving."

As I stand at the stove whisking together yolks and whites, listening to the ocean sounds streaming from the web site dedicated to Gabe's and my wedding, I'm satisfied with my new sympathy for the person who until now has felt like my number-one rival. I stir and stir, watching the eggs fluff up velvety and bright—a perfect specimen of an omelet—then I add a generous swirl of Sriracha, and plate it. I eat with relish, delighting in each bite, as somewhere in the back of my head I hear that old adage, about keeping your friends close...

Chapter 16

CONFIDENCE CARRIES ME through the next couple of weeks, even spilling over into wedding planning. It's fun to tally up the people in our lives and imagine them all in a room together mingling and getting tipsy. Gabe and I divide and conquer: He stuffs envelopes with save-the-dates, and I address them and affix starfish stamps. As the two of us release them into the mailbox, I feel a welling up of excitement.

I even decide I'll have a bridal party. I invite Sam to dinner to pop the big question: "I know it's a silly tradition," I say, "but I'd love to have you by my side at the altar. Will you be my maid-of-honor?" (I'll include Kirsten, too, but I wouldn't be able to handle her intensity in the top gig.)

Sam tears up, a shocking sight. "Sorry, hormones. Everything makes me cry these days."

"It's pretty fun to see the least sentimental person I know get weepy over wedding rituals."

Sam rolls her misty eyes and groans. "Anyway, yes, obviously I'll do it. And speaking of things that make me bawl . . ." She swipes to an image on her phone, a swirl of black and white and a misshapen suggestion of a head. "I know, it looks like every ultrasound you've ever seen. But it's mine, which makes it rad."

"Totally." I'm thrilled for Sam. But then I catch sight of the due date stamped at the top. "Wait, May 27th? Is that a joke?"

"No, dodo. That's how long it takes to cook up a human baby in a womb."

I brought a save-the-date to deliver in person to Sam—I hand it to her now. Hovering among the cartoon-y clouds, in a font I now decide is all wrong, is my wedding date: May 27th. I point to it. "What? No." Sam starts sniffling again. "Well, maybe the baby will come early, so I can make it, all bloated and leaky."

"Sure," I say half-heartedly, thinking, why gather a hundred people together for us if Sam won't be among them? "Why didn't we realize this before?" But I remember: Back when I sent out the email with the date, I was preoccupied with Gabe's book write-up, and Sam was probably preoccupied with trying to dismiss the reality of this baby.

The mix-up feels sinister, like I'm being punished for having let down my guard and taken pleasure in something as silly as party planning.

This suspicion deepens over the course of the next week. The RSVP tally on our web site remains at zero. The page views are in the single digits. I would've predicted several hundred from my mother alone. "Something's wrong," I say to Gabe.

"Yeah, I thought we'd have at least 10k siphoned into our bank accounts by now. I guess I need to work on my subliminal messaging skills." He smiles, but I'm genuinely concerned.

The answer comes to me via a calendar from Gabe's parents, mailed cross-country thanks to six forever stamps, each one featuring a different pose from the sun salutation yoga sequence. The Dovers are militant in their refusal to switch over to a digital schedule, and dedicated in their recruitment to the resistance.

"We needed more postage," I say. Gabe looks confused, so I clarify: "On the save-the-dates. That heavy card stock. We were short on stamps."

"Ah, Lady MacGyver cracks the case! The cards are probably stuck in post office purgatory." Gabe looks amused, but I feel the opposite. I picture the starfish-dotted envelopes languishing in a broken bin in some musty back room, fraternizing with mislabeled credit card offers and blacklisted hate mail. It gives me the chills. I think of Gabe's belief in fate: Is this a sign from the universe that our wedding date will not in fact be saved? My best friend will be howling through labor contractions, and the rest of our loved ones will be brunching or erranding or cleaning their bathrooms, or whatever. I start whimpering, which makes me feel stupid on top of the stupid I already feel for the thing that's caused me to whimper in the first place.

"Oh, Molly-moo." Gabe pulls me onto his lap, and I whimper even more.

For some reason, my mind goes to my annoying coworker Melinda: "She's engaged too, and she was blabbing about her homemade save-the-dates." I can hear myself whining, giving in to my misery. "Each one has a little string, and when you open the fold it ties into a knot. Cuz they're tying the knot—get it? One of her socialite friends tipped off Papyrus, and now she's in talks to design a line of cards for them."

"Come on," soothes Gabe, "what does that have to do with us? We emailed the date to most people anyway. We'll just write to them again with a link to the site."

"Yeah." I start paging idly through the calendar from Barb and Joe. I'm horrified to learn that each month is dedicated to a different humanitarian crisis: January for Syrian refugees, February for child brides in India, March for gun violence fatalities. Meanwhile, here I am bereft about lost party invitations; my self-respect nosedives farther.

My mother's call feels inevitable, and when I pick up, she opens with, "Molly, I need answers from you yesterday on the caterer and the florist and the band." I vaguely recall a flurry of unopened emails, which I planned to deal with later. "If we don't secure the vendors right away, all the best options will get snatched up by other spring brides."

Everything about this irritates me—my mom's strident tone, her use of the word "vendors," her implicating my membership in a group called "spring brides." So, I snap back: "God forbid we end up with appetizers that score under five stars on The Knot." I hear myself morphing into the snotty teenage version of myself, but I feel powerless to stop it: "What will people say if our flowers aren't the loveliest arrangements in the history of wedding bouquets? How will we ever live down the shame?"

My mother sighs. "Molly, do you want my help with this wedding or not?"

What I want is to demand that she stop pestering me. But I know I can't trust what might come out of my mouth next, so I say I have to go. After I hang up, my gut is a tornado of regret and irritation.

From the other room, Gabe calls out, "Hey, I made plans with Talia, like you suggested."

"What's that?" I must've misheard.

"Talia. She pushed for drinks, but I held firm on coffee."

"Okay," I say brightly, feeling like an insane person. *Did I really suggest this idea to Gabe? What was I possibly thinking? Why can't I come up with the right reaction to any situation?* I idly flip the calendar to May, our wedding month—the image is of Nepalese earthquake victims. I feel a kinship with them, their eyes wide with panic and fear. It makes me pulse with shame. Obviously Gabe meeting up with his ex does not qualify as a humanitarian crisis. Talia's power wouldn't even register on the Richter scale, or only just barely. And really, I try to reassure myself, what could possibly happen over a cup of coffee?

•   •   •

Gabe's meet-up with Talia is scheduled for the following Saturday, and my corresponding plan is to stay occupied, to be so engaged in my own thing that I don't even remember that my fiancé is off doing who-knows-what with his ex. Since Lana is now up and about with the help of a cane, I take her up on her offer to go wedding gown shopping at Bella So. She opens her apartment door wearing a velour sweat suit, her hair oily and her face bare, so I assume she's running behind. But as I settle into the sofa, she says, "Ready?" and with much fumbling pulls on a coat. In the cab, my sister-in-law rolls her window all the way down. "Just a little lightheaded," she explains, sticking her entire head outside, like a dog, the thirty-degree wind rushing in. Her hair soon resembles Einstein's.

I start wondering if Lana is well enough to visit her place of employ-ment—it's her first time back since her accident. My unease deepens as we loiter outside (Bella So is a doorbell type of establishment). A woman who introduces herself to me as Ingrid lets us in. She's wearing a cham-bray jumpsuit and stands a willowy six feet tall in ballet flats. I watch uncomfortably as Lana, all giggly waves, goes in for a full-body hug, in contrast to Ingrid, who waits a short beat before extracting herself from the embrace. She takes a step back, like Lana might be contagious. "How have you been?" Ingrid asks, expression neutral.

"Oh, just fine, thanks," Lana says brightly. Ingrid barely nods, not even bothering to fake interest.

Equally as off-putting is the shop itself. The other customers seem to belong to an elite species, *Homo supermodeliens*. Their long, slender limbs are draped delicately in expensive, silky fabrics; their engagement rings are veritable rocks, visible from across the room. No one acknowl-edges our entrance. I'm reminded of high school, when I'd emerge from the bathroom stall to find myself an accidental crasher of a popular-girl meeting at the sinks. Not a girl would move aside to let me wash my hands; I'd try to meet my eyes in the tinny mirror, attempting to con-firm that I did in fact exist.

But Lana doesn't seem to register the other customers, or doesn't care—after all, until she devolved into her current state of cripple, she herself was a member of this elite echelon. She walks me through the racks, stopping at each gown to orate on cut and material and style, the litany of jargon washing over me like a foreign language. I feel like I'm on a museum tour, like it's forbidden to touch the displays.

Lana pushes a dress on me. I catch a glimpse of the price tag. Even with her fifty percent off, there's just no way. Not to mention that I already have a dress. But I humor my sister-in-law by taking it into the dressing room. "Usually wedding sample sizes are eights," Lana tells me through the curtain, "but our clients tend to be smaller, so we carry mostly fours and twos. Don't worry, anything can be let out."

The zipper stalls halfway up my back, and I can barely move my hips. There's no mirror, so in order to see how I look, I'm made to leave the privacy of the stall and stand on a public platform. Lana has told me this setup is supposed to make clients feel like a figurine on a wedding cake, but I stand there feeling more like an exhibit in a freak show.

"Gorgeous!" squawks Lana. I have an absurd thought that "gorgeous" is one of those words that also means its opposite, like how "sanction" means both "approve" and "penalize," and "left" means both "remaining" and "gone." Because the truth is, I look like a marshmallow squeezed into an organza tube. Meanwhile, the woman on the platform beside me is the quintessential bride, the one featured on magazine covers and in venue brochures: tall and swan-like, her pale skin and auburn curls striking against the ivory damask cocooning her feminine curves. Lana is captivated—I can see the old Lana in her gaze, longing to go adjust the gown's straps and smooth out the train. Of course, Ingrid steps forward to do these things.

Turning her attention back to me, Lana narrows her eyes. Then she goes to get another gown. "Try this one. Duponi will suit you better." *One more,* I think, *and then I'm out of here.*

But Lana's right. This one's also too tight, but when I emerge to check myself out in the mirror, I can see why people spring for wedding gowns that cost several months' paychecks. Now I feel like the cake figurine, like I fit in in this rarefied world, like I'm the person Gabe would want to marry, no matter how he's spending his afternoon. Ingrid approaches the platform and pats me on the butt. "Cut out carbs for a few months, start hitting the gym, and this would be stunning on you."

I watch myself blush in the mirror. I nearly trip stepping down from the platform. I can't get the dress off fast enough. As I stand in my underwear in the dressing room, hearing giggles through the curtain, I scrutinize my body: the sloping curve of stomach, the thighs that rub, the slight jiggle under my arms. I think of Talia and her narrow, child-like form. I think of Dahlia and her generous self-admiration. It's all mortifying. I pull on my jeans and sweater, eager to escape from my own sight and my own thoughts, and of course also the store.

But where's Lana? I weave through rack after rack. I finally find her up front behind the register with Ingrid. Her back is to me, but I can sense her agitation. I ask if everything's all right. She whips around, looking startled, her face red.

Ignoring me, Ingrid addresses Lana: "We'll discuss it later. For now, you just focus on getting well." Her voice is calm and firm.

I have to scurry to catch up with Lana's exit—it feels like we've been banished. Lana doesn't speak until we're in a Lyft heading uptown. Her voice is a snarl: "That bitch won't put me on next month's schedule."

"And it was pretty rude how she suggested I go on a diet, right?" I'm genuinely offended, but mostly hoping to distract Lana from her rage.

But she doesn't seem to hear me. "We'll go back another time. You can find your dress when I'm working. *Next month.*"

"I don't know, Lana. I might go with something a little more low-key, less pricey."

She shrugs, moody. "If that's what you want."

Since Sam is a no-go for the wedding, I planned to ask Lana to be my maid-of-honor; I was going to do it today. But she's picking at her nails, and her eyes are bugged, and it makes me feel a little scared of her. She chugs half a bottle of water, then nearly chokes asking the driver to make a pit-stop at CVS. "I'll just be a minute," she tells me. When she returns, she's chewing a big wad of gum.

Entering Lana's apartment, I'm spooked by its shadowy stillness—all the curtains are drawn, and it's freezing. As I crank up the heat and let in some light, I have an impulse to run around buck-wild speaking in tongues. "Where's Leo?" I ask, realizing I haven't seen my brother in weeks.

"Working, as usual." My sister-in-law starts fiddling with her bracelet, and the little twangs echo through the quiet like alarms. I notice the smallness of Lana's wrist attached to an arm so twiggy it looks like it might snap off. I decide to make her a sandwich. She ignores it. So, I set her up with a blanket on the couch, flip on a *Friends* rerun to give her some company, and then guiltily say I have to go. But Lana doesn't even hear me; she's already nodded off.

*   *   *

My edginess follows me home. Gabe is nowhere to be found. No texts or emails, either. How long can one conceivably stretch out a coffee meet-up? To comfort myself, I try on the decidedly un-Bella So sheath I bought to wear to my wedding. But after a month hibernating in the back of my closet, it seems like an entirely different dress. The asymmetrical cut looks haphazard instead of interesting, the thin fabric shoddy not sleek, and whereas before I appreciated its curve-hugging shape, now I picture Ingrid at my side pointing out how it pulls there, there, and especially *there*. Scrutinizing myself in the mirror, I can hardly stand how much space I'm taking up. I feel like a fraud, thinking I could pull off this look. Frantically, with shaky fingers, I wrest the thing off and fling it on the floor.

I'm still in my underwear when Gabe returns home, bringing with him the aromas of Thai takeout. It turns my stomach. I can't remember if I've eaten today, but my lack of appetite feels like a physical presence.

"So how did it go?" I ask, aiming for casual, although it's belied by the anxious tremor in my voice.

"Predictably," Gabe says. He kisses the top of my head, and I sniff something burnt and sour. "Talia made us sit outside in the cold so she could chain-smoke. She told an endless story about her supposedly psycho roommate who stole all her shit and took off. Also, she's thinking of quitting her job. In other words, same old Talia."

"Cool," I say. "I mean, I'm sorry." I can't figure out how to respond. Is Gabe charmed by Talia's drama? Is he exaggerating for my benefit? Is he simply recounting a scene he wrote about Russell and Dahlia that I could've sworn I read?

"I kept trying to leave," Gabe says, "but she kept ordering more drinks. She was practically shoving shots down my throat."

My stomach clenches. "I thought you guys were meeting for coffee."

"The coffee place was closed."

"Oh." It's a strange excuse, considering Brooklyn boasts at least one coffee shop per block.

"And Talia was thrilled about the novel," Gabe says, his voice inflected with irony. "She tried to hide it, pretending she was far above giving a shit, but I could tell it made her feel supremely important. Her take is that my writing a book quote-on-quote 'about her' implies that I'm clearly not over her." Gabe's look is one of incredulity. I swallow a lump in my throat. "She said she sort of got it, since after we broke up she wrote reams of poetry. But the difference, according to Talia, is that she would never stoop to publish those poems. Of course, the *real* difference"—Gabe cackles—"is that she would never find anyone willing to publish them!"

"Ha," I say limply.

"Anyway, her unsolicited advice was for me to do some serious soul searching about why I would feel the need to write this book." He scoffs. "Can you believe her nerve?"

"Well, why *did* you feel the need to write it?" I ask—but only under my breath. I can't summon the courage for a confrontation that might lead to strife. I recall Lana, and our exile from Bella So, and how she looked so lost in her eerily stark apartment. I'm desperate to feel at home here with Gabe.

"What's that?" Gabe asks.

"Nothing," I say, frustrated at my cowardliness. "Good for you for facing Talia. I'm proud of you." I smile stupidly, feeling all wobbly, like the floor beneath my feet has turned to quicksand.

"Thanks. Well, I'm famished. You?"

I nod. But as much as I yearn to sit and eat dinner together with my fiancé, when Gabe unseals the plastic tubs of Pad Thai, releasing a stink of wet dog into the room, my body rebels. My vision goes swimmy, and I careen across the apartment just in time to lunge for the toilet.

I heave and heave, long after my stomach has emptied. It seems like an hour later when I finally have the strength to pull myself up from the tile floor. I retreat to bed, drawing my knees tight into my chest. Gabe calls out to me, and it sounds like it's coming from very far away. I may as well be underwater.

"I'm here," I respond. But it sounds like a lie.

*　*　*

Somehow, the rest of November slips away. I'm getting up, going to work, coming home, doing it all again the next day, but if pressed, I couldn't relate much more beyond that. It all blurs together; I may as well be sleepwalking. Gabe seems to have double shifts nearly every day—he even works Thanksgiving, and when Leo texts to cancel our holiday gathering, saying Lana isn't up for it, I'm relieved. I can barely get myself to call my mother, who's decided to spend the long weekend with an old college friend.

When Gabe finally has a Saturday off, it seems like the first time in weeks we're having more than a two-sentence conversation. Our buzzer rings—it's a delivery of a box so heavy I nearly throw out my back carrying it inside (I think of Lana—poor Lana). It's from Gabe's publisher, and he gleefully tears open the lid, revealing stacks of advanced editions of his book. He cracks a copy's spine to show me the dedication:

Molly-moo, this is for you.

I feel the same welling up that I feel whenever Gabe signs a card this way or whispers the nickname in my ear. I snatch the book away to examine it further. But its weight in my hands reminds me that this isn't some private love note; it's a public declaration, the opener to a story that's all about Gabe's ex-girlfriend. In what way is this "for me"? How is it a gift? And what will Talia think when she reads the dedication? How about everyone else?

"You know what would be hot?" Gabe says. Before I can answer, he's unbuttoning my shirt, and then laying me back onto a pile of his books, my own half-nude body sprawled across the many illustrated outlines of Dahlia's form. It feels like a choice to not become outraged, to instead leave my head and occupy my body, to feel Gabe's gaze drink me in. The recent disappearance of my appetite has flattened my stomach and slimmed my thighs; in place of hunger, I've felt a heady high that's been strangely centering. I feel empty and clear. Our maneuverings disturb the pile of books, and one flips open to a page I can tell I haven't read; the word "caught" catches my eye. From then on, with each of Gabe's movements, I can't help hearing his voice on repeat: "Molly-moo, this is for you." Tenderly at first. Then indifferently. Next, aggressively, sweetly, ironically, dismissively, ecstatically. I can't catch ahold of who this person is moving inside of me; I can't catch ahold of how I feel. After we finish, Gabe goes to the bathroom, and I sit on the floor carefully restacking the books. I try to excise the dedication from my head.

The next morning, I wade through the packages of books that Gabe has prepared to mail out. I'm searching for Talia's name, half-bracing myself for it. It appears on the very last mailer, along with the familiar address. I grip the package and consider chucking it. Wouldn't that solve so much—severing Gabe's connection to his ex, preventing her from weighing in with more unsettling insights about the book, and preserving my peace of mind (or whatever scraps of it remain)? I'd like to believe I reject the idea out of virtue, but really I know I'm too much of a coward. It's one thing for me to investigate where Gabe's ex-girlfriend lives and to take two trains to go there and stare at the building from across the street; it's quite another to commit mail fraud, which I'm pretty sure is a felony. I loosen my grip and reluctantly return the package to the stack.

In three to five business days, Talia will be able to read all about her fictional alter ego, dreamed up by the guy who once held her (but supposedly no longer does) in his heart.

Chapter 17

GABE AND I barely have time for goodbyes. He's rushing to pack for his flight to San Francisco to spend the holidays with his folks, and I'm racing to the office for back-to-back interviews, trying to squeeze in two new hires before I'm off to Maine in the morning.

My first three candidates are three shades of mediocre, and I skip lunch to review the rest of the day's contenders, powering through on coffee. I scan the next applicant's résumé: Tufts undergrad, Stern MBA, experience at both a big corporation and a start-up, amateur chess league member, and coach to a kids' ultimate Frisbee team. She seems ideal for the role, and interesting too. As she walks in, my first thought is, *A little frail for ultimate Frisbee.* Then I take in her face and stutter hello. Her acne is as angry as ever.

"Hey, Molly."

"You're not here for—"

"I had to see you." Talia doesn't wait for me to invite her in; she settles right in to the empty chair, crisscrossing her legs on the seat. I've spent so much time pondering Gabe's ex from afar, feeling scared of her and angry at her and in awe of her, that she's grown larger than life in my mind. But here in the flesh, Talia is surprisingly small. She's as beautiful as I remember, even with un-brushed hair and smeared mascara. "So, any holiday plans?" she asks, then she points to the wall. "I like that print—is it an O'Keefe?"

It may seem strategic for me to stay quiet, like I'm biding my time to figure out Talia's end game. But really I'm just tongue-tied, stunned into silence.

Talia, on the other hand, seems completely at ease. Inevitably, she takes out her advanced copy of *The Charms of Dahlia*. When she places it on my desk, I have an urge to swat at it, like it's a poisonous insect. With much effort, I keep my hands in my lap. "You should know," Talia says, "it didn't happen like this, not at all. The drinking, the drugs"—she manages an epic adolescent eye roll—"the stupid, mundane relationship problems."

She flips through the book, whose pages are dog-eared and highlighted and annotated. It's like she's been prepping for an exam on herself. "What Gabriel and I had was powerful and pure—too pure, ultimately, for this shitty, corrupt world. The kind of passion we shared,"—Talia shakes her head, pausing for emphasis—"it was dangerous. It nearly killed the both of us."

I'm trying desperately to stay calm and to dismiss Talia's words as the melodramatic prattle of a deliberate provocateur. It should be so easy to shut her up and show her the door—this is *my* turf, she has no right to be here—but I can't help wanting to keep her in my sights and hear her out. And Talia keeps talking: "You know, Gabriel wanted to dedicate the book to me. But it wouldn't have looked right, because of you. How did he put it? That you were sensitive. Or no. *Fragile*—he said you were fragile." Talia makes eye contact, and I feel her registering my reaction. Inside I'm fuming—although whether at Talia or Gabe is unclear—but I work to arrange my face as neutrally as possible.

Talia shrugs. "I told Gabriel I'd do any press he wanted. I'm happy to help, especially since I'll be earning ten percent of the royalties."

My fury dials up, filling my ears with buzz. It takes all of my effort to remain calm and cool and seated behind my desk. She must be lying, right? This is Talia's modus operandi: Manipulation 101.

Her laugh is surprisingly raspy. "You know, when I asked Gabriel what he saw in you, he said he likes how steady you are, how rational, how calm." She pronounces each adjective like it's a terminable disease. "He claimed it was a relief after dating me. But my god, Gabriel must not know you at all. I've never seen someone so angry. You look like you're seconds away from punching me in the face." She laughs again, and I hate that she can read my exact impulse. "Listen, I get it. I think you have every reason on the planet to be fucking furious."

The profanity snaps me back to the here and now: We're in my office, at my place of work, supposedly in the middle of a job interview. I inhale deeply, trying to eradicate any waver from my voice: "Talia, how can I help you? Why are you here?"

She shrugs. "For the job."

"You must be joking. For starters, this résumé is completely fabricated. And . . ." I don't even know how to summarize what's transpired so far during our "interview."

"Not completely—I'm a champ at chess. I play with those pro dudes down in the park. I even win sometimes. Anyway, I read the job description, and it seems like an easy gig. I'm free immediately. Plus, I need something to tide me over until all those royalty checks start rolling in." She winks. I have no idea whether she's trolling me or totally delusional. Maybe she actually is a psychopath. My mind flashes to Gabe's credit card, the string of numbers that has definitely been burned into her brain.

My mother's always said, when you don't know what to do, opt for courtesy. "Well, thank you for coming in," I say, adding absurdly, "I'll be in touch."

I stand. But Talia doesn't budge. Her facial features make a stunning transformation—what was delicate and pretty turns fierce and ugly.

"Don't bullshit me, *Molly-moo*." She makes the pet name sound pathetic. She reaches idly for one of my business cards, and I resist the urge to snatch it back. I'm still standing; I feel like I'm a server in a restaurant waiting on her as she mulls over her order.

"Funhouse Branding," Talia reads aloud. "So, it's all about smoke and mirrors, huh? Never mind, I wouldn't want to work here anyway. I want to do something real." Her combination of deranged chatter and possible insight is dizzying.

"Then I guess we're done here," I say. Talia stretches leisurely, arching her whole body like a cat, then gets up, slow as she pleases. I watch her, transfixed, wondering how she can simultaneously look like a homeless person and an Instagram model. On her way out, she knocks a stapler off my shelf.

*   *   *

I don't even pretend to pay attention to the day's final candidate. My thoughts are pinballs: Have I ever purposely knocked anything off a shelf? Or spotted a knocked-over item and not immediately picked it up to replace it to its rightful spot? And yet, Talia's words echo in my head: *I've never seen someone so angry. Gabe must not know you at all.*

Of course Gabe knows me. Of course when I talk to him he'll reassure me that Talia has invented all of his supposed promises to her, and probably the entire exchange.

"Excuse me?" I say, realizing that the man across my desk is waiting on an answer.

"I said, I wondered if Funhouse offers flextime?"

"Right." I will the interview to end. It finally does. But by then I've missed my window—Gabe's flight has taken off. He's soaring above the clouds headed west, unreachable until eleven tonight.

Unable to pick his brain in real time, I do the next best thing: I lock my office door and settle in with a copy of his book. I flip toward the end and force myself to read a Dahlia passage. Apparently she's headed on a trip:

They'd spent hours yelling and crying and screaming the worst insults they could up with at each other, then Dahlia had taken off and driven straight through the night. She'd stopped twice—once for gas, and once to walk fifty feet beyond the breakdown lane, hike up her skirt, and let go. She drip-dried, legs spread and feet planted firm, mesmerized at her liquid's path into the cracked earth. In this moment of stillness after hours of motion, Dahlia felt a powerful wave of everything catching up to her; it threatened to knock her over. She steadied her feet, shook herself furiously, smoothed out her skirt, and sprinted back to the car.

I can't help imagining Talia's annotations on the scene—does she find it poignant? Pathetic? Heartbreaking? Phony?

Now the sun was rising over the side of the road. Dahlia gunned the gas, trying to tune out the techno blaring from the stereo. It reminded her of the crap they played at Meridian. But it was the only thing keeping her awake. Dahlia hated driving. Sitting still and staring into so much of the same, she forgot to pay attention. When she and Russell had gone camping, he'd driven while she sat in the passenger bucket seat of his old Volvo, singing along to oldies on the radio and spreading peanut butter onto crackers and, when he stopped to take a piss, doing lines on the dash. She'd gotten a crick in her neck giving him road head as they crossed the Pennsylvania border.

My hands are fists. Gabe and I took a camping trip in the Poconos. We had the oldies singalong and the peanut butter crackers, but no cocaine, and certainly no en-route blowjobs. We spent most of the drive playing Twenty Questions. Now I wonder, was our trip an attempt to re-create a more exciting trip Gabe had taken with Talia, or is this scene Gabe's reimaging of how much more thrilling it would've been with her instead of me by his side? Either option stings.

When the day's brightness began cutting horizontally at the dash, Dahlia found a rest stop. A ping announced her entrance to the mini-mart, and she spun the sunglasses carousel three times before picking out big round pink ones with rhinestones.

Even I know Talia wouldn't pick pink.

They made her look like a rock star, invincible. At the register, she added a pack of Hostess cupcakes. She pushed her new sunglasses down her nose to check out the clerk, a pimply teenager who was probably picturing her naked. "Birthday candles and matches?" she asked with a wink. "Thanks, champ." She guessed he wouldn't charge her, and he didn't.

As Dahlia returned to her car, she recalled last night's fight. Russell had accused her of wanting to ruin his life.

This makes me smile.

Dahlia knew he was just stressed about other stuff, taking it out on her. What the two of them had was powerful and pure—too pure, maybe, for this shitty, corrupt world.

Incredulous, I re-read the sentence several times. I hear it being read in Talia's voice, along with echoes of her nearly identical words from earlier today. So, did Talia steal that little speech from the book? Or did Gabe take it from Talia to insert in his book, attributing it to Dahlia? Or did Gabe put into words something that Talia had felt, and then Talia borrowed Dahlia's words to describe it back to me? The possibilities spin out like anagrams in my mind, making me dizzy. The more I deliberate, the less of a grip I feel I have on what's real and true. So, I push it all away and return to the story.

> A wave of exhaustion rushed over Dahlia. She reclined her seat nearly flat, then tore open the cupcake wrapper, placed one on top of her stomach, stabbed a candle into its center, and lit the wick. As a kid, whenever she'd felt low and lonely, Dahlia would imagine it was her birthday: She'd lock herself in her room, dress up in a tiara and a silver top hat, then stand before her mirror and belt out a booming rendition of the birthday song to her reflection. It had been a neat feel-better trick—

I stop mid-sentence, cheeks burning, jaw a vise. What I'm reading is a warped version of my own secret childhood ritual. After my father died, once a year, on his birthday, I'd lock myself in my room, stare into the mirror, and sing happy birthday to him. It was my most private moment, the only time I'd allow myself to cry—deep, choking sobs that had built up over the past twelve months. I'd think, if I just stood there long enough, exposing my true self to the mirror, my dad might magically emerge from inside the reflection; I was half-convinced of it even when I grew too old to believe in magic. I always found this exercise enormously comforting—at least, in the moment; afterward, it mortified me. I swore to myself I'd never tell a soul about it. But I did tell someone, eventually, because I finally found a person I trusted: Gabe. I touch my cheeks; they're hot and wet. I speed-read to the end of the chapter:

> —and Dahlia attempted it now in the car with the cupcake atop her belly. When she reached the penultimate line, the silly self-dedication—*Happy birthday, dear Dahlia!*—she sang it at the top of her lungs. What should she wish for? Money? Pills? A decent job? For Russell to stop being such an uptight prick? For a new guy, hotter and smarter and

all-around better than Russell—or, better yet, several guys? Dahlia wanted all of it. She inhaled deeply and, with one forceful breath, extinguished the flame and wished for the world. Then she ate the cupcake, melted wax and all.

I fling the book on the floor, thinking, *Utter blasphemy. What next? Dahlia finds some sexy trucker with my late father's name and we're treated to pages of their disgusting groping?* My office doorknob turns, and I rush to unlock the door. My boss, Natalie, stands on the threshold. "Everything okay in here?"

I nod profusely, hoping I don't look as deranged as I feel. "I was just reviewing today's interviews."

"Any luck? How about that candidate you said seemed really promising?"

I don't know how to explain, so I just shake my head.

"Rats. Well, we'll find someone great in the New Year. In the meantime, have a wonderful break."

"Thanks, you too." It feels like a miracle that I can pull off participating in such a mundane exchange.

That night, instead of eating dinner and packing, I drink a bottle of wine, stare at who-knows-what on TV, and mull over Talia's description of her relationship with "Gabriel": *a passion so powerful and pure it nearly killed them.* It's the language of soap operas, melodramatic and maybe meaningless. But, I can't shake it. The moment Gabe's plane is scheduled to land, I text him, **Did you tell Talia you'd pay her royalties?**

He pings back: **Deplaning, will call you in a minute.**

I text back: **Yes or no?**

He responds: **Complicated.**

I take that as a yes. Unbelievable. I ignore his call in favor of a second bottle of wine and a private dance party to music turned up so loud I can't hear myself think. I flail my limbs and bang my head until I can no longer feel a thing.

• • •

The sun eventually stirs me. My phone flashes with three more missed calls from Gabe. I splash water on my face to fight the sludgy feeling behind my forehead. I blink to see couch-cushion creases decorating my cheeks like river tributaries. I race to pack, and I manage to get myself to midtown just in time for my bus home to Maine.

The stop-and-start traffic out of Manhattan leaves my stomach jiggly like undercooked egg. It worsens when I consult my email. Gabe's note is a lengthy explanation about how earning any royalties from the book is unlikely considering his advance, and how he only told Talia he'd *think* about giving her a cut, and how he only did *that* to calm her down so she'd stop making threats. Threats of what nature, he doesn't specify, but since he doesn't ask how I know about any of this, I imagine at least some of them concern me. At this point, I don't know what to believe.

My response is terse:

Glad you landed safely. And what about the dedication? Was it supposed to be to Talia?

Eleven minutes pass before Gabe's call. I don't pick up; I can't bear the idea of having this conversation aloud right now, especially with the rest of the bus listening on. I text back:

On bus, can't talk. Courtesy counts.

I laugh at my little joke, as if that's all Gabe needs—a little lesson on courtesy.

He responds, Dedication for what?

Unbelievable. I write back: And what about Talia singing happy birthday in front of the mirror as a kid? Is stealing the story I told you in confidence supposed to be another touching tribute? I thought this was FICTION!!!

Huh? Gabe responds.

I mean Dahlia.

Gabe's text window fills with bouncing ellipses—they disappear and then reappear and then disappear again.

But I'm suddenly sick of talking about Talia and Dahlia and Gabe's book, and sick of weighing and evaluating and trying to rationalize away my many worries and suspicions. I shut off my phone, chuck it in my bag, and close my eyes. It's hours before I see Gabe's reply:

Are you okay, Molly-moo?

Chapter 18

I'M BACK IN my hometown, pedaling the familiar streets, the frigid air whipping at my ears and numbing my fingertips. I find it refreshing. The snow is like fairy dust, the lightest blanket settling on my hair and the sidewalks. It's just my mom and me for these two days, since Leo and Lana aren't scheduled to arrive until Christmas Eve. I came home to her doing the dishes and botching up the lyrics to "Little Drummer Boy," and it took just fifteen minutes for me to grow antsy and claustrophobic, and to go fetch my old bike from the garage. I can't tell if I'm breathing especially hard or if seeing my breath in the air just makes it seem that way. Muscle memory leads me on the familiar path across town.

And then I'm on the street, and then I'm in front of the house. I'm not even sure his parents still live there, until I spot the green Subaru in the driveway. My stomach seizes. I run my fingers across the "Save the Dolphins!" sticker peeling off the back windshield, the same one I used to touch as a good-luck charm. I walk to the backyard, stand below his bedroom window, and look up—even this particular angle of neck crane is a potent memory. The lamplight is a beacon. I stay very still, steeling myself for movement above, hoping. And then it happens: I catch a glimpse of the back of Charlie's head. My heart leaps. I find a pebble on the frozen ground and wind up to lob it. I'm trembling, my fingers like icicles. It's a perfect shot, pinging against the glass. Charlie turns to look outside, and I dart out of his sight.

I bike home so fast my heart feels like it'll pounce free of my chest, but my legs are spinning so ferociously they wouldn't even notice.

*   *   *

Christmas was my father's holiday, and for a long time my mother did her best to keep up the celebration in his memory. But we've slacked off in recent years, half-heartedly stringing up tinsel, then ordering Chinese food with the rest of the Jews.

My mom and I are many pours into the eggnog, weepily pitying Charlie Brown and his tree, when the doorbell rings. Leo stands alone in the doorframe, shouldering a small duffel and a take-out bag that steams with smells of sesame oil and soy sauce.

"Where's Lana?" my mother asks.

"Greetings to you, too, Mom," Leo says. "With her recovery, it was too much to travel here and then to her parents' place." So, it's just us, the original three.

I spend the meal drinking wine and pushing broccoli around on my plate, then the three of us move to the couch and I open a new bottle of wine. My mom turns to me: "Molly, since you're now *affianced*"—she uses an exaggerated French accent—"I wanted to share something your father and I did on our wedding night, in case you and Gabe want to steal it." At the mention of Gabe, my missing him becomes a physical ache; it makes me feel pathetic to be so mad at him and also still long for him.

Leo groans. "Mom, I think I speak for both of us when I say we don't need to hear the details of your wedding night."

My mom slaps his wrist. "Not sexual intercourse, silly. Your dad and I wrote letters about our hopes and dreams. His was about building his own firm, and mine was about wanting two kids, a boy and a girl."

"You both got what you wanted," I say.

My mom's eyes turn liquid. "It's true." She squeezes Leo's and my hands. "Your father always worked so much, and I was always with you kids, elbows-deep in diapers and Play-Doh. I assumed things would change when you both got a little older." Things did change, of course, though none of us says so.

"Oh, Mom." Leo hugs her from one side, and I tilt her head onto my shoulder from the other. It's a relief to focus on someone else's emotions for a change. My mother dips into sleep for a minute, before jolting upright and exclaiming, "What? Where's Santa?" Leo and I burst into laughter.

"Okay, Mom," Leo says, "It's past your bedtime." He helps her upstairs, and I help myself to more wine.

"Let's stay out of Mom's way in the morning," I say when Leo returns.

"Yeah, that's not going to be a pretty picture. Hey, wanna take a walk, see if we can spot Santa's sleigh?"

My insides feel toasty enough to manage it. "Sure."

Outside, the air is crisp. It's stopped snowing, and the moon is a sliver. As Leo and I trudge down the block, the only sounds are our footsteps' muffled crunches in the snow. I kick a chunk of snow in his direction. "It feels like months since we've hung out." I think about all that's happened, how nice it is to be so far away from it, up here in my sleepy hometown.

"I know," Leo says. "I've been working nonstop. After Lana's accident, I used up all my time off and called in every favor so I could stay home with her. Now I'm making up for lost time." I think of Lana alone in that hushed museum of an apartment. "It's been rough. Lana can't go more than a few hours without pain meds. She barely sleeps. I hate to say it, but I'm looking forward to a few nights without her tossing and turning next to me."

"So, you're not joining her in Chicago?"

"I couldn't get the days off. Don't tell Mom, okay? I don't want her to worry." I nod, though it's too dark for Leo to see. "What about you? Did you stop eating or something?"

"What?" I'm not used to my brother noticing how I look. "I'm getting married, remember? Every bride diets." Leo's snort is skeptical. I add, "I've been stressed, okay? Did I tell you Gabe's novel is all about his total nut of an ex-girlfriend, Talia?"

"Yeah, but it's fictional, right? Gabe is marrying you, Molly, not this Talia person." He makes it sound so simple.

Leo pulls out his phone, so I check mine, too. There's a "Merry Christmas" text from Sam, but predictably, no word from Gabe; he and his folks are up in the mountains, with no cell service or Internet.

"Charlie just invited me over for a nightcap," Leo says. "Wanna come?"

I start panicking—did Charlie see me the other day outside his window? Did he tell Leo? Did Leo tell Gabe? Is this some sort of a test? I suddenly wonder if I'm being watched. I feel desperate to be back in the house. "I'm tired," I tell Leo.

Back in my childhood bedroom, I text Sam back: Merry Christmas. I hesitate, before adding: **Not so merry for me, actually. Gabe's being a total prick, and it just took all my restraint to say no to drinks with Charlie.**

Sam responds immediately: **WHAT?! Tell me exactly what's going on! Are you ok? I demand details!**

Over the course of the next ten minutes, Sam sends missive after missive, begging me to fill her in on what's happening, encouraging me to talk to Gabe, insisting that I cut off all contact with Charlie, and then scolding me for ignoring her. But I'm too tired to respond to any of it. I silence my phone and fling it aside.

I'm on the blurry edges of sleep when Santa Claus appears in my mind's eye. "What do you want for Christmas, Molly?" he asks. I'm paralyzed and mute. He asks again: "What do you want?" Someone else appears beside him—it's my father—and now he's asking me too: "Molly, what do you want?" Others soon join in, a whole cast of characters from my life—Gabe, Charlie, my mother, Talia, Sam, Kirsten, Leo, Lana. They start closing in on me as they chant more and more urgently: "What do you want? Molly? Molly, what do you want? Molly!" The chorus of questions grows louder and louder, until I fear my eardrums will rupture. My eyes fly open and I scream, and only then does everyone disappear. I take a breath, finally alone.

* * *

Christmas is a wash—a whitewash, actually, the biggest Nor'easter in years. Leo hits the road early, hoping to make it out of New England before conditions become un-driveable. My mother remains in bed, referring to her hangover as a head cold. I spend the day battling the snow's enthusiasm. Minutes after I clear the sidewalks of snow, they re-carpet in white. But I'm enjoying the focus on a simple, straightforward task, the Sisyphean pattern of working up a sweat shoveling, retreating inside to rest, then getting sweaty shoveling again. I picture Gabe, warming himself by a flickering fire. His family celebrates the winter solstice, not Christmas. His mother once explained to me the tribute to the light, warning me that if you're not vigilant, you could get dragged down into the belly of winter's darkness. At the time, I dismissed it as hippy nonsense, but now I reconsider her words. Maybe that's my main problem: the season.

I send Gabe a text: **Hi**. It bounces back undelivered—no service. I scroll through his Instagram feed, whose most recent photo is of me holding *The Charms of Dahlia*, a big, stupid grin on my face; I "heart" it. I swipe to his Facebook wall, and there at the top is a thumbnail of Talia, skin airbrushed smooth, her fatuous duck face like a personal taunt. Maybe this was part of her deal with Gabe, too—a reinstatement of their Facebook friendship, which I thought had been terminated over a year ago. Her post reads, "Merry Xmas, Gabriel! Here's to a kickass new year and to our book! XOXO." *Our book*. It could be a typo, omitting the "y" at the start; it likely isn't. The post has twelve likes— none of the names are familiar to me. I want to track down all dozen likers and berate them for affirming Talia and her B.S. I want to comment in all caps. I want to scream—I do scream. Surely if Gabe had Internet access, he would delete the post. If only a click of the mouse could delete Talia from our lives, too.

I set my phone down, eyeing it like it's toxic. When it beeps a moment later, I know in my bones who the text is from.

Meet me at the lake.

*   *   *

Charlie is waiting at our old spot, and it feels perfectly natural when he braids his fingers into a foothold and hoists me up onto the fence. I cling to the top, just as I used to do half a lifetime ago, waiting for Charlie to fling himself over and help me down. Our boots crunch through the crusted-over snow. We leave footprints like evidence.

It's only five o'clock, but it might as well be midnight for how dark it is. I take in Charlie under the moonlight. His coat is open, the zipper busted, and his shaggy hair is tucked under a wool hat with a pompom, probably his mother's. I wonder if he'll always look like a sexy, disheveled teenager, or if only I see him this way.

Charlie squirms under my scrutiny. "Look up," he says. When I tilt my head, I see luminous white dots spread across the sky, an infinite Van Gogh. It's as if I've never seen a night sky before. It's as if I'm high on a powerful drug.

"That doesn't exist in New York City, does it?" Charlie says.

"What, the sky?" I say it like he's crazy, but actually he's right.

Now Charlie's gaze bores into me. "You look underfed," he says. I feel exposed, despite my big coat. "You're still beautiful, but . . ." His voice fades out, and my heart pounds. I don't respond. "Well, should we go skating, or what?"

"I don't think the ice is thick enough yet."

But Charlie is already gliding out onto the surface. I'm vigilant, tracking his every tic, which I'm sure he knows and is relishing. If I told him to be careful, he'd start performing cartwheels.

"Uh-oh," he says, freezing long enough for me to imagine I hear the ice crack, and then play out the whole sequence of nightmarish events. Just when I feel my pulse might explode from panic, Charlie whips around, grins, and says, "Just kidding," then scurries back from lake to land. My fear gives way to relief, then anger, then relief again.

We don't talk about our jobs or the holidays or the last time we saw each other. Being with Charlie is like being outside of time. But then Charlie says, "Let's make New Year's resolutions."

"You're kidding." There's no way Charlie has ever set a single personal goal.

"Come on. You first."

"Fine." My life unquestionably has room for improvement, but I can't take this seriously: "I resolve to live each day like it's a gift, to dance like nobody's watching, to stop and smell the—"

And then Charlie kisses me. His lips are impossibly warm and soft, and they melt my own frozen ones. The moment is at once a revelation and as familiar as my left elbow. Charlie's touch is like a treasure chest that's remained buried inside of me; rediscovering it makes me feel rich and lucky all over again. Still, I stand like a statue, too stunned and scared to kiss back. Charlie tries again, longer this time, and I give in. We kiss and kiss and kiss. The whole world is our kissing. When he finally pulls away, he says, "I resolved to do that."

My legs are numb with cold, but I stride away as fast as I can, the long way around so I don't have to navigate the fence on my own.

Charlie's calls to me echo over the lake: "Molly! Wait! Hey!" I speed up. Somewhere beneath my frozen exterior is a swirling chaos of emotion. I ignore it as I run the rest of the way home.

* * *

I'm bundled in my coat and scarf under the covers in bed, unable to stop shivering. I'm trying to erase what just happened, but it's like my thoughts are being held hostage. I'm thinking how it was even better than what I'd remembered. I'm thinking, when's the last time Gabe kissed me like that? I'm thinking, this is too big for me to think about alone—I need to share it with someone. Maybe I should text Sam. But no, she'd just berate me like she did last night, telling me I'm being a stupid, selfish asshole. But, what if this is actually a good thing, a turn in the right direction, a new beginning? Even as I form the thoughts, I feel disgusted with myself, like I've smeared sewage all over my mouth. But what if Gabe deserves what happened, if it's just an evening of the score, a readjustment that'll set things right? Really, who's to say he didn't kiss Talia during their coffee-turned-drinks meet-up? Who's to say he hasn't been sleeping with her through our whole relationship— or that she's not in San Francisco with him right now, cozying up to him this very moment before a crackling fire, while I'm here in bed, alone, freezing as all fuck? I'm working myself up into a fit of outrage, but it quickly dissolves into a pool of sadness. I ran away from the lake, at least there's that; I didn't follow Charlie home. Although, if I *had* gone home with him, I'd be a whole lot warmer than I am right now. I press my frigid lips together—the kiss remains like a stain.

I'm startled from my ruminations by a noise coming from the kitchen—is it a giggle or a shriek of pain? Both options are unnerving, and it doesn't sound like my mother, either. I go downstairs to investigate. I register my mom's presence first—one hand clutching a glass of wine, the other toying with a curl of her hair—but my gaze is like a laser to a spot on her shoulder, upon which rests the hand of a man. I wonder if it's a mirage, this man in the kitchen. Besides Leo and Gabe, I can't recall the presence of a man here in either recent or not so recent memory. He's stout with a full head of white hair. He is not unattractive.

"But what does one even wear to a bingo and bluegrass night?" my mom exclaims, voice frothy with flirtation. Only when she twirls around does she notice me. "Molly!" She sounds caught.

I wave and make a move to leave, my stomach a pit. Her voice changes registers, now all business: "This is John, the owner of the inn where you're getting married."

"So nice to finally meet you, Molly." The man has a serious handshake. He smells of coffee and pine.

"Hi," I say.

"John came over to discuss wedding logistics."

This lie, or half-truth, or whatever it is, stabs at me. Since when does my mother keep secrets? But I want to convey how it's no big deal, how of course she deserves to have a crush, or more, and how ridiculous it would be for me, a full-blown grown-up, to be disturbed by her romantic involvement with someone other than my father nearly a quarter-century later. So, I raise my eyebrows and try for coy: "Wedding logistics? As in, what, who you'll slow-dance with at the reception?"

"Oh, Molly," my mom says. "Honey, are you okay? You're white as a sheet."

Her attention grates on me. "I'm just cold," I snap. "It's fucking freezing out." She winces. "Anyway, I'm sorry to interrupt your important logistics meeting. Nice to meet you, John. I'm turning in." My mom kisses me goodnight, and despite myself, I savor the feel of her warm cheeks against my chilled ones. Her flush brings out the blueness of her eyes. She's very pretty, my mother.

Up in my room, I can still hear their conversation, and my mom's bright laugh. I pull up the web site for John's inn and click on the "About Us" page. A photo captioned "Meet John the Innkeeper!"

shows the man downstairs posed with a wide smile. He seems like someone who gardens and bird-watches and bakes a signature pie that wins prizes at block parties. He seems nothing at all like my father. Though who knows? He could be an ax murderer, or Maine's next governor, or anyone. I wonder what my mom sees in him, and what he sees in her, and how long she's been hiding secret romances from me. I shiver, pulling my coat tighter.

I click back to the home page. Pictured is the Atlantic, waves mid-crash over the Ogunquit rocks, spray like liquid fireworks, a rainbow arcing low over the water. It's the spot where Gabe and I will recite our vows. The same image is featured on our wedding web site. It strikes me that tonight's sky over the lake has nothing on this panorama. Stars are just dead light, after all; the ocean is alive. I shut my laptop, pulsing with guilt.

I can't warm up, no matter how many blankets I pile onto the bed. My feet are ice. I wish someone were next to me radiating heat—I wish *Gabe* were next to me, I revise. I curl into a fetal ball, trembling. At some point I hear my mom creep in, and then the anxious whir of a space heater. I feel the weight of her head nestle next to mine on the pillow, and her hands through my hair, a sensation so comforting it soothes me back to sleep.

When I wake up, I'm sweating, my throat dry as dust. The blankets are in mayhem across the floor. Minutes pass before I remember where I am.

Chapter 19

OUR APARTMENT BUZZER is about as pleasant as a police siren. I jolt up from my cocoon on the couch, and crane my neck out the window. But instead of Gabe with his luggage, I spot Kirsten idling on the stoop. The last thing I want is visitors, but it's New Year's Eve and she looks distressed, so I buzz her up. A moment later, my friend strides through the door and shrugs off her coat with a sigh.

"Caleb got me a puppy for Christmas," she says flatly.

"Oh, cute," I say, trying to sound interested.

Kirsten shakes her head. "He named her Jennifer, as if that's any kind of name for a dog." I'm unsure of why this is such a grave offense. "Did you know that a pet is much more cost-efficient than a child? Caleb actually said that, like it was an insightful point!"

She's clearly angry, but I'm not following why; I wonder if this is who I've become: someone who can no longer communicate with her friends. Kirsten must notice my confusion, because she explains, "We've been talking about adoption. But Caleb's having second thoughts." She swallows a sob.

"Oh, Kirsten." I pull her in for a hug and do my best to say some comforting things, but my friend remains unmoved. "It sounds like Caleb's trying," I add, but Kirsten wiggles away from me and twists up her face in disgust. I don't have the energy to keep trying to figure out how to be a good friend right now. So, I go for the next best thing: wine. I pour us each a generous glass, and we both drain them in several gulps. Only then does Kirsten seem to realize that she's shown up uninvited on New Year's Eve: "Sorry to barge in on you like this. Where's Gabe?"

"Heading back from California. His flight was delayed."

"Ah. Then it's a good thing that I'm here to keep you company." She extends her glass for a refill. "Also, I called Sam. She's on her way." I'm too tired to protest.

When the buzzer again convulses the apartment, I expect Sam to swoop in, armed with an inventive solution to lift Kirsten's spirits. But it's my brother who steps over the threshold, looking fidgety and distracted, like he has no solutions to anything.

"Did someone forget to tell me I was hosting a party?" I say, not bothering to hide my annoyance. "What are *you* doing here?"

"Happy New Year to you, too," Leo says, and then kisses my cheek.

"I thought you and Lana had tickets to some black-tie benefit thing."

Leo shakes his head as he plops himself onto the couch beside Kirsten; I can't tell if he's drunk or just burnt-out. "Lana pushed back her return. She needs more rest, which apparently can only happen in Chicago. Also, she's going back to work next week, which is a terrible idea. Not that I know what I'm talking about! I'm not a doctor or anything!" This makes Kirsten laugh, which alerts Leo to her presence. "Oh, hey."

Sam shows up twenty minutes later, sporting flannel pajamas and a glittery cardboard hat. "You're lucky I made it out," she says. "I bailed on a party with Tom. Me and this energy-sucking parasite who's taken up residence inside of me were planning on hitting the hay at ten o'clock." She removes a bottle of Prosecco from her purse, and pops the cork. "Don't worry, I'll just have a taste. Where's Gabe?"

"Flight delay," Kirsten says.

Sam hooks up her '90s R&B playlist to the speakers, then presses my hand to her stomach. I feel pitter-patters. "She's already got rhythm, right?" Sam says.

"She?!" Kirsten exclaims.

"Uh-huh," Sam says.

Leo proposes a toast and holds out his glass to clink with hers, but Sam gives him a withering look. "Obviously I wanted a boy. Can you imagine what the sexting situation will be like by the time she hits puberty?"

"And the selfie situation," I say, thinking of Talia's social media pages.

"I like to call them solipselfies," Kirsten says to Leo, drunkenly pleased with herself; she has definitely never once called them that.

"Lord help me," Sam says. "Maybe when she turns twelve I can trade her in for a pet, one of those cute little labradoodles." Kirsten darkens at the mention of dogs. I top off both of our glasses with Sam's Prosecco.

"Well, people always say there are more options for girl names," Leo says.

"Yeah," Kirsten says sharply. "You could call her Flower, or Cloud, or even Jennifer. The sky's the limit!" She looks like she's about to murder someone.

"Um, Molly, I need your help with something in the other room," Sam says. I try to pretend I don't hear her, but she grabs my wrist and drags me into the bedroom, closing the door behind us. She lowers her voice to a whisper: "What is up with Kirsten?"

I shrug. "Caleb got her a thoughtless Christmas present, and now she's drunk."

"Okay." Sam is nodding. "And what is up with you? You seem . . . off. Did you ever end up seeing Charlie?"

I hesitate, trying to decide whether or not to lie, but there's no lying to Sam—she can already read the truth on my face. She grabs a hairbrush and smacks my arm. "You moron. What happened?"

"Nothing. Well, barely. We just made out." She smacks me again. "Hey, that hurt!"

"Well, you deserve it. You better make this right, Molly Stone. I'm not going to stand by while you blow up your life. All this acting out stops now. It's time to sit down and talk to your fiancé. Promise me you'll talk to Gabe."

She threatens me with the brush again, and I wince. "Fine, I promise. Just let me go, you psycho hairbrush hitter."

When we return to the living room, I see that Kirsten has found the box of Gabe's books. I watch warily as she picks up a copy. "Dahlia would be the perfect name for a baby girl, don't you guys think?" Her tone is hostile.

"I didn't know Gabe's book was already in print!" Leo says. "May I?" He takes the book from Kirsten and starts paging through it.

"Ooh, I have an idea," Kirsten says. "Let's read it aloud, like a play!" She grabs more books from the box, and distributes them to the room.

I start to protest, and Sam backs me up: "Let's play a board game instead. Monopoly? Trivial Pursuit?"

But Kirsten is insistent, bullying: "Come on, it'll be fun." She's flipping pages, apparently searching for a suitable passage. "Ooh, here we go, a sex scene!"

It's at this moment that Gabe walks through the front door, face weary with a day of travel. During the past week, I envisioned our reunion a hundred different ways, all the possibilities of how we'd work our way back to each other. But this scenario—the motley crew in our living room, copies of *The Charms of Dahlia* in everyone's hands—was not among them. Gabe's eyes meet mine for a flicker—so fast I can't detect the emotion behind them—then he blinks and averts his gaze.

"Gabe, you're just in time!" Kirsten stumbles over to him and presses a book into his hand. "Okay, we need four readers. Gabe is the guy, obviously—what's his name, Russell? I'll be the narrator. Molly, who do you want, Chrissy or, um, Natasha?" I recall those characters—Russell's Econ friend and Dahlia's old roommate—and wonder, *What are they doing in a sex scene?*

"I don't want to read," I say, hoping Kirsten will take the hint to shut down the show, and Gabe will realize this wasn't my idea.

But Gabe is still avoiding my eye. "I'm going to unpack," he says.

Sam shoots me a pointed look, like I should go follow Gabe into the bedroom. But Kirsten is barreling ahead with her terrible idea, and obviously I have to be on hand to supervise: "Fine, Sam, you play Russell. And Leo, you can be Chrissy. You're blonde and lithe." She cackles in a way that makes me want to hurl a book at her head. "We'll figure out Natasha later.

"Page 238, everyone," she demands, standing up and stumbling a little. "I'll set the scene. Our pal Russell has just run into an old crush, and she's invited him back to her apartment. Okay, here goes." She clears her throat, and I start gathering up glasses to bring to the kitchen, trying in vain not to listen.

"'Russell ran his fingers over the boobs,' *oh, 'books!'*" Kirsten squeals. "I thought it said 'boobs'! I'll start over. 'Russell ran his fingers over the *books* on Chrissy's shelf: Pynchon and DeLillo and Gibson. She must've been in a post-modern lit class. Russell could imagine Dahlia dismissing her as a show-off, as if liking serious literature were a capital offense. *Good riddance,* he thought.'"

Leo reads Chrissy's part: "'You didn't come over here to judge my taste in novels, did you?'" His take is comic and high-pitched, and he bats his eyelashes at Sam, who laughs, clearly out of discomfort.

Kirsten continues: "'Chrissy handed him a Coors Light, and Russell took a long swig and winced.'"

Sam reads for Russell: "'Nah, just your taste in beer.'" She sounds bored, which actually works for the character. I can't believe I'm getting drawn into this.

"'Touché. Cheers,'" Leo reads.

Kirsten has settled into a grating, over-emotive narration: "'The crappiness of the beer didn't stop them from drinking more, three cans each on the beat-up loveseat while they chatted through half an airing of *Fargo*.'" She harrumphs and then calls out to the other room, "Hey Gabe, do you mean the movie *Fargo* or the TV series? You should really clarify." She laughs at her own cleverness, before returning to the book: "'Then, matter-of-factly, Chrissy leaned over and kissed Russell on the lips.'" She stops to whistle, sounding more desperate than joyful.

I wonder why Gabe remains in the bedroom, why he isn't interceding to stop this horror show. As for me, I sit by helplessly bearing witness, suspecting it might feel something like this to witness your own funeral. If I believed in fate, I might think this was punishment for my recent transgression.

Kirsten goes on: "'Russell went along with the kiss. It was both the same as with Dahlia and different. Nibbling on Chrissy's neck, Russell caught a whiff of her hair, that intoxicating strawberry, and he became his freshman self all over again, drunk in lust at their late-night study sessions. Now Russell dared to run his fingers through that hair. Next, he made his way over to her end of the couch. Chrissy let him lay his whole weight on top of her.'"

Leo chimes in as Chrissy: "'My roommate will be home soon. Come on.'" He purrs the line at Sam, who recoils.

Kirsten: "'Chrissy led him to her room. As Russell pulled off her t-shirt and her panties, taking in what he'd only previously imagined, it was as if a part of him was watching from above. His fingers on her pointy little nipples, her smooth belly, her plump inner thigh. Suddenly he was naked on top of her, skin against skin.'"

"Oh my god," says Sam. "I am *not* reading this." But Kirsten shoots her a look of death, so she sighs and continues as Russell: "'So, where do you keep your condoms?'"

Kirsten reads, "'Russell felt like a moron for not having any, but Chrissy just smiled.'"

"'Russell, you surprise me,'" Leo says, as Chrissy. "'After all this time.'"

Kirsten narrates, "'Chrissy reached into her bedside drawer and handed him a foil packet. The strangest part was that Russell couldn't shake the thought of Dahlia. Or maybe it was that he knew Dahlia would've found it irresistibly hot to know that he was picturing her as he fucked another girl. Or maybe it was that Russell had an urge to call Dahlia right then and there to tell her all of this, in addition to all the things he had a sudden urge to do to her.'"

"Okay everyone, I think that's enough," Sam says, clapping her book shut. "Good for Russell for getting some action. Shots all around, and a big old swig of water for me." Sam, my savior. I want to hug her. One more page of that, and I might've chucked the whole box of books out the window, along with one certain guest.

"That was getting a little hot and heavy," Leo says. "But good job, bro," he calls out to Gabe in the bedroom, and then follows me back to the kitchen, whispering, "Is the whole book like that?"

"Not really. Or, kind of. I don't know. Kirsten certainly managed to find a scene that would make everyone incredibly uncomfortable."

I pour myself another glass of wine and down it in two long gulps. Leo's phone rings, and a moment later, Charlie's voice is here, right in my kitchen. Is this some sick joke? I can't make out his words, but the sound is enough to make me feel like I might pass out. It's suddenly about a thousand degrees in here. I brace myself against the sink and motion to Leo, putting a finger to my lips. He nods and says into the phone, "At a colleague's party."

I mouth, *Thank you,* before retreating to the bathroom, where the fan isn't as strong or as loud as I wish it were. I hear my brother say he'll have to make a visit upstate. I hear Kirsten's shrill laugh. I hear Sam announce that the year is officially drawing to a close. I splash water on my face, but it's not enough. The evening's events swirl like contaminated whirlpools under my skin, threatening to spout up, slosh over, and leave me drenched in mess. So, I turn on the shower, crank up the

172 · lindsey j. palmer

cold, and slip out of my clothes. A couple minutes later I hear a knock on the door, and Gabe's voice asking if I'm okay. "Fine," I shout out. I stand under the freezing stream until I notice my fingers turning blue. I don't feel anything. There's another knock on the door, and then Sam is shouting out that I better get the hell out of the shower and join my guests since it's two minutes to midnight.

When I emerge from the bathroom, clutching a towel around my body, I spot Gabe. He comes and stands next to me. "Hey," he says tentatively.

"Hey," I reply.

I notice the TV is on. I stare at the screen, watching the glittering ball hover over Times Square as swarms of people count down in unison. *Three, two, one* . . . The ball plummets to the ground, and everyone cheers. Gabe tucks my dripping hair behind my ear and kisses me gently on the lips. It's over before I think to reciprocate.

I look around at the people gathered in our living room: Sam does a rat-a-tat on her swollen belly, cooing, "Happy New Year, little lady." Leo high-fives Kirsten, quipping that he'll have to wait an hour to wish his wife a happy new year in Chicago. Kirsten starts in on a sloppy rendition of Auld Lang Syne, and everyone else joins in. The bittersweet melody makes me feel clammy and claustrophobic. I'm desperate for everyone to get out.

Sam eyes me. "Well, when your hostess is standing around in a towel, I guess it's time to hit the road. It's way past my bedtime anyway." She pulls herself up with effort, and I hand her her coat. "I love you, you pain in the ass," she says, leaning in for a hug.

"You're the pain in the ass, but I love you too."

She wags a finger at me. "Talk to Gabe, okay? Also, take care of our drunken pal." We glance at Kirsten; she's nodded off on the couch, her gaping mouth leaking a string of drool.

Leo heads out, too. At the door, I wish him luck with Lana's return and silently thank him for not asking about Charlie.

With everyone either gone or unconscious, Gabe says he's turning in. He asks if I'm coming. "Soon," I reply.

I take in my friend, passed out on the couch—I'm tempted to leave her be, knowing she'll wake up not only mortified but also with a killer crick in the neck, payback for tonight. But my humanitarian instinct kicks in, and I ease her onto her side and tuck her under a blanket. I text Caleb to say his wife is safe and sound.

As it turns out, the stupid staging of Gabe's book has piqued my interest—did Russell and Dahlia break up, or has he started cheating on her? The latter seems highly unlikely—but then again, until a few days ago, I would've said it was highly unlikely for me to kiss someone other than my fiancé. I pick up one of the discarded books and skim past the sex scene with Chrissy. On the next page, I spot Natasha's name:

> Russell hadn't meant to hook up with Natasha. It's just that after the night with Chrissy, the electricity that hummed through him just kept on humming, like the opening of a floodgate.

The mixed metaphor doesn't even bother me, so relieved am I to be reading the page silently and without an audience.

> When Russell remembered sex with Dahlia,

So then, it's in the past, over? I can hardly believe my eyes.

> he thought of magnets locking together with a powerful attraction, a fundamental force of nature. But there'd also been the flip side, when the fields reversed and they'd repelled each other just as intensely. Then they couldn't get close, even if they'd wanted to. A few drunken nights after their fight, after Dahlia skipped town, Russell had called her hoping for phone sex or least some comforting words, for old time's sake. Dahlia had hung up on him. She called back a few hours later, but

by then Russell had sobered up enough to come to his senses. Their timing was off, thankfully.

It was a revelation to Russell that the magnetism worked with all these other girls, too. And now the timing was perfect. College was over, he was single, and he was riding out his lease until September, at which point he'd turn his attention to adulthood. For now, he was in sweet limbo. At the moment that meant snaking through the aisles of 7–11 just past dawn, still warm from the bed sheets of the girl he'd met last night. He was filling a jumbo cup with coffee when he noticed a familiar figure at the next spigot: Dahlia's old roommate, Natasha. "Hey," he said.

They eyed each other suspiciously. Natasha ragged on Russell for using the fake vanilla creamer. But then they laughed a little, and Natasha told him about her new roommate, a Math major on the autism spectrum, whose flat affect and stringent routines were a welcome change from the high dramas of Dahlia.

Russell paid for Natasha's coffee, one cup at 7-11, followed by another at the snooty pour-over shop around the corner. Then they had brunch, which turned into happy hour, and before Russell knew it, the whole day had passed and he and Natasha were headed back to the old apartment. He hadn't returned since the day he'd rescued Dahlia's belongings from the porch. It smelled and looked the same, and an old twinge of lust overtook Russell. He touched Natasha on the arm. In less than ten minutes, they were horizontal.

The sex was rough, almost hostile, but also cleansing, like they were both pounding away at their anger at Dahlia, working together to work it out of their systems. Natasha told Russell to slap her ass, which he did, and then to slap her across the face, and when he hesitated, she growled and bit him on the shoulder, hard. He tugged at her hair and she raked jagged fingernails down his back. The scratches and bruises across Russell's body would take days to fade.

When they finished, both panting, Natasha collapsed into Russell's lap. She was wearing a single sock stamped with the logo of the college both of them (but not Dahlia) had just graduated from. Russell felt desiccated, spent. When he finally stood up, oxygen rushed to his head, along with a realization: It was time to leave this town. And so he did, the very next day, and he never returned.

At one point, I would have cheered. I would have felt filled with optimism—thinking now that Russell has left Dahlia behind, maybe I could too. But now I don't even care. I retreat to the bedroom, hoping Gabe will be asleep.

He's not. He turns over in bed to face me. "Hey."

I wave, then walk past him to go pick out pajamas, but Gabe stops me. "Molly." He gestures for me to sit. I position myself on the very edge of the bed, feeling like I've been summoned to the principal's office. Gabe clears his throat. "I know we've had some misunderstandings, and it hasn't been easy, especially being separated by thousands of miles. I want to try to explain the royalties thing. I only agreed to give Talia a cut because she was saying crazy stuff. Back when she and I were together, we made a sex tape."

"Seriously?" I scoff. "This is your apology?"

"Just hear me out, okay? I swear we erased the tape, but Talia was claiming she still had a copy, and if I didn't promise to pay her part of my book money, then she would post it on her social media. I'm sure it was an empty threat—she was really worked up—but I had to say something to calm her down. I assumed she'd forget about it once she cooled off. I didn't tell you at the time because I was hoping I wouldn't have to. I'm really sorry."

None of this makes me feel better. "It just keeps getting worse, huh? What other fun facts about you and Talia are going to be dredged up and paraded before me next?"

A flash of frustration passes over Gabe's face. "To be fair, Molly, you were the one who suggested she and I meet up."

"Oh, so this is my fault?"

"No, I didn't mean it like that. It's just, I can't change the fact that I dated Talia, or that I wrote this book, and now it's getting published. But please, let's talk about this stuff. A new year is supposed to be a fresh start, a time to clear the air. Will you do that with me? Please." Gabe reaches out a hand.

But I can't. I'm too furious. I grab a pillow and storm out of the room.

Out in the living room, I settle myself onto the rug. Kirsten is on the couch above me, her snores like an old junker's engine. I lie awake, burbling with anxiety, watching the clock's progress. At 4:30, I can still hear people reveling outside on the street, so I stand up, open the window, and shout down, "Shut up and go home already!"

A girl peers upward, spots me, and shouts back, "You shut up, you fucking party pooper!"

I'm outraged at this insult from this complete stranger. I lean my whole head out the window, take in a big gulp of air, and yell out at the top of my lungs, "Fuck you!" Then, for probably the first time in my life, I stick up my middle finger and jut it out toward the girl. My sapphire ring winks in the night, making me feel powerful and dangerous.

Chapter 20

WHEN MY BOSS schedules a New Year's check-in, I assume she wants to chat about our holidays over K-cup coffee. But after asking me to close the door behind me, Natalie hands me a progress report showing three of my recent hires that didn't pan out, and two positions still unfilled long after deadline. I shrink in my seat. She may as well have stamped me with a fat red F. I can barely tolerate A-minuses.

"I promise I'll do better," I say, voice cracking. "These last few months have just been . . ." I falter, unsure how to explain.

"Everyone has ups and downs," Natalie says. I anticipate a reassuring smile, but her lips stay pursed. "And if it were just this . . ." Now she's the one to trail off, looking down at her lap. I feel my mouth go dry and the back of my neck dampen.

"A candidate you met with in December contacted me," she says. A knot of fear tightens in my gut. "This young woman claims that during her interview you accused her of falsifying information and demanded she discuss details of her romantic life. She says that when she refused, you dismissed her out of hand. She also claims you showed up outside her home."

Talia saw me that day? I start to stutter, fumbling to defend myself.

178 · lindsey j. palmer

But I know Natalie is allergic to melodrama—and it would only damage my credibility further to explain the story of my fiancé's crazy ex-girlfriend posing as a job candidate in order to confront me and screw with my relationship, and my getting sucked into her whole game. I settle on a simple "I'm sorry."

"I'll give you the benefit of the doubt," my boss says. "I've always known you to be a consummate professional. But consider this a serious warning. I'll ask that you leave your door open during interviews for the foreseeable future."

I nod sturdily, trying to revive my reputation as a consummate professional. I repeat my promise to do better in an earnest speech that's halted by Natalie's *Okay, enough* palm.

● ● ●

The last person I want to see right now is Jonathan Wexler. His gait is even jauntier than usual, and I try to pass with just a nod, but he blocks my path. "I've been meaning to thank you." I wait out his pause, which is clearly meant to tantalize me. "You're the reason I met the girl I'm seeing."

"Me?" I try not to notice the hint of sex in Jonathan's smug smile, or the strain of hysteria in my voice. I have a feeling I know where this is going.

"We met outside the office after she interviewed with you. She bummed a smoke and we hit it off. Maybe you remember her—short-ish, dark hair, golden eyes, stunning."

"Talia?" I ask, desperate to be wrong.

Jonathan claps me on the back. "Yes! Man, is she a firecracker!"

"Excuse me." I retreat to my office, suddenly spent, my limbs like spaghetti. The first thing I do after promising my boss I'll improve at my job is curl up under my desk for a nap.

*　*　*

I'm woken by a call from Lana. Her voice is oddly low, though when it comes to her these days, I've tossed out all expectations. "Why are you whispering?" I ask. "I can barely hear you."

"I'm in the dressing room. You'll never guess who just walked in to Bella So. LaLa!"

"Who?"

"Larissa *freaking* Laraby!"

"Oh, cool," I say. The Larabys are those tabloid celebrities famous for being famous; I don't quite understand people's obsession with them. "So, you're back at work. How is it?"

"Fine. It's only been an hour."

"And already you're hiding out in a dressing room making covert phone calls?" But I'm not really one to talk—I brush off my skirt and get up from my office floor.

"Listen, Molly, I have Gabe's book in my purse, the copy Leo brought home. I'm going to give it to LaLa. How cool would it be for the world's most popular reality TV star to read Gabe's book?"

My skin starts prickling with nerves. "Lana, don't you think that on your first day back you should just do your job? Like, give this woman dresses to try on, not unsolicited reading material?"

"Don't you follow the news, Molly? LaLa's not the one getting married. She's here with her friend. LaLa's just sitting around picking at her manicure. Which is fierce, by the way. I happen to think she would really identify with a strong female character like Dahlia."

"Lana—"

"Okay, I'm gonna do it. Wish me luck! Bye."

I'm left with a foreboding thrum in my chest. Fingers shaky on the keyboard, I manage to confirm an interview for tomorrow morning, and that's it, work-wise. I pace my office, imagining Larissa Laraby's security detail pouncing on Lana, handcuffs and cries of protest, a stark jail cell, Leo arriving to bail her out, and the ensuing tabloid headline: "Shop girl turns nutso celeb stalker." I decide to cut out of work early.

The next morning, the normally reticent coffee cart guy by the subway wishes me a happy new year. Suspicious, I fumble my quarters onto the pavement, then spill half my coffee, scalding my palm. That's when I notice I'm wearing two different shoes: one black, one navy blue. I stride up Fifth Avenue self-consciously, and I'm several blocks north of my office before I realize I've overshot it. Backtracking, I'm bumped left and right by other commuters; I wonder if I've suddenly turned invisible. When I reach into my purse, I discover that my water bottle has opened, soggying everything inside, and also that I've forgotten my office key card. I miss an elevator, its closing doors nearly severing my fingertips. *Fuck*.

Late for my first interview, frantically scanning the candidate's résumé, I'm infected with an eerie sense of déjà vu. Bachelor's degree from Tufts, Stern Business School, interests in chess and ultimate Frisbee—all the stats are familiar. Even the name sounds fishy: Summer Rose Lee. *Talia,* I think. *What does that psycho have up her sleeve now?*

My computer dings to notify me of a new email. It's from Lana, subject "LaLa!" and, to the soundtrack of my racing heart, I click the link in the body. It loads slowly: First the splashy TMZ.com header, then a close-up photo of Larissa Laraby clutching—yep, there it is now—Gabe's novel. The caption reads:

LaLa a lover of literature? Reality star caught red-handed with racy new novel The Charms of Dahlia.

After staring for a long minute at the shot, half disbelieving, I speed-read the article, a shoddy, judge-a-book-by-its-cover analysis. The final paragraph makes me want to take a hammer to my hard drive:

NO WONDER LALA COUNTS HERSELF A FAN OF THE SEXY AND SCANDALOUS READ. ITS LEADING LADY IS A LOT LIKE HER: GORGEOUS AND GALLING, SHARP AND SEDUCTIVE, A TEENSY BIT CRAZY BUT TOTALLY IRRESISTIBLE. LARISSA LARABY IS ON TEAM DAHLIA AND SOON THE REST OF AMERICA WILL BE, TOO.

I'm startled by a knock. Jonathan is hanging on my doorframe. "What do you want?" I snap.

"They've been paging you out front for ten minutes. Your candidate is here." As Jonathan ushers the woman into my office, I swear I see him touch the small of her back. She's model-gorgeous, but in a scrappy hipster way—Talia's precise kind of pretty. I'm flooded with paranoia. *Who is this woman? Talia's coconspirator? Her detective? Is Jonathan in on it, too?* Panicky theories zip through my head like deranged comets.

The woman doesn't wait to be invited in. "I'm Summer Rose Lee," she says, her voice a babyish purr.

I suppress a shudder and shake her hand. "Nice to meet you."

It's all downhill from there. I go through the motions of the interview, but all of Summer Rose Lee's answers strike me as suspicious: A friend tipped her off about the job, she's heard incredible things about Funhouse Branding, she's been looking for this kind of role for a while, it's her dream job. I keep up a polite front for five minutes before I can't take it anymore. I cut the crap and change my line of questioning: "So why are you really here? What's your end game? Who sent you?"

She's a terrible actress, pretending that she has no idea what I'm talking about. Her face goes pale through a thick layer of foundation. *Good.*

I'm on a roll, adrenaline pumping: "Listen, I know you're Talia's little pawn, and she's trying to intimidate me or threaten me or whatever. But I'm telling you, her plan won't work. No, siree, not this time around. No way, José."

"Is Talia the recruiter?" Already the girl's voice has changed, syrupy with faux-fear; already she's cracking. An actual tear hovers on her lashes. Her acting is pathetic. "If there's something going on between you two, I swear I don't know anything—"

"Oh, come off it, Summer Rose Lee, if that's even your real name. And we both know it's not." I grab her so-called "résumé," and tear it to scraps, relishing the sound of the ripping. Her eyes bulge fake-naively as bits of the paper flutter confetti-like to the carpet.

"I think I should leave," she says. It's at this point, as I sit surrounded by the detritus of the résumé, my insides feeling as if they might explode through my skin, and all color drained from the face of the woman sitting across from me, that I feel the tiniest inkling that maybe I've got it wrong, maybe this is a genuine candidate who has nothing to do with Talia, maybe I'm losing a hold on what's clear and true—but it's just a flicker of a thought, barely there and then gone. I watch as the woman lifts both hands in surrender, and the melodrama of the gesture is just too much.

I snap. I zero in on the brooch on her lapel, silk petals looped to a wire pistil. It's the kind of thing you'd find at a stoop sale, chintzy and cheap. I take it as another sign of her imposterism. I don't seriously think that the brooch contains a hidden camera, but the fact that it *could* contain one is reason enough for me to lunge across the desk and grab at it, ripping it free from her shirt. My trembling fingers work furiously to dismantle the petals from the wiring. Anger pulses through me. It's invigorating. I feel strong and in charge, brimming with purpose. The shrieks and howls coming from across the room barely register.

And then Natalie is there. She doesn't even glance in my direction. She's laser-focused on the fraud sitting across from me, apologizing, asking if she's all right. Before I can explain that no, Natalie's got it backwards, my boss is ushering the woman away with a protective arm, as if she's the one who needs to be shielded from me and not the other way around.

I remain seated, floor around me littered with résumé bits and lap a mess of broken brooch pieces. My face is on fire, my palms glued to my desk with sweat. I'm fuming. Incredulous. Indignant. Natalie soon returns, and even before she starts speaking, I know she'll deliver the carefully worded speech that I've recited so many times I could do it in my sleep. She'll touch briefly on my years of good work, move on to the section about actions and their consequences, and cap things off with the details of my severance package.

I look around my office, at all the artifacts I've collected over the course of my professional career. So much junk. None of it seems to have anything to do with me. I grab the ficus tree and a photo collage Gabe made for me for our first anniversary, and abandon the rest.

On the way out, Security parades me past the rows of cubicles, and I spot Melinda Lowe craning her neck to watch. "Why don't you snap a picture?" I holler. The loud, brash voice doesn't sound like me; it emboldens me to keep going: "Post it to Instagram for your bazillion followers. Hashtag crazy coworker, hashtag meltdown, hashtag dunzo." Melinda just gapes. I overhear someone say, "I read about her fiancé on TMZ. He wrote a book about a psycho girlfriend, and I hear it's totally based on Molly."

I wheel around. "Fuck you. Fuck all of you."

I don't wait for the elevator with the guard. I push past him to shove open the stairwell door, and practically fly down the flights, feeling high. For the very last time, I'm leaving the place where I've spent most of my waking hours for the past decade, and for the first time in a very long time, I feel free.

Chapter 21

I BURST INTO Bella So, plunk down my plant and my picture frame, and breeze past the model-y clientele and through to the back room. I find Lana's torso hanging halfway out a window as she blows cigarette smoke into the alley. Instead of asking what I'm doing there, she says, "Are you hungry, perchance?"

"Fucking starving."

"Good, me too. I could eat an entire cow."

But we don't end up eating. We go to a trendy cocktail bar for a liquid lunch—three martinis apiece, followed by straight shots of vodka—after which I feel like a hero for my performance back at the office. Lana cheers me on. "Now that I don't have to go to work each day," I say, "I'll have plenty of time to confront Talia and get to the bottom of who this Summer Rose Lee is."

"Wait, did you say *Talia*?" Lana asks, eyes growing wide. "Hold on."

On her phone, she pulls up another TMZ post about Larissa Laraby. In this one, the reality star is quoted as saying, "I was totally a Dahlia in my early twenties. I had guys wrapped around my finger." Lana scrolls down to a section labeled, "Who's the *real* Dahlia Freid?" Below an airbrushed photo of Talia, the same one from her Facebook profile, is the quote, "My years with the author were the most intense romantic rollercoaster you can imagine. It doesn't surprise me that a love so passionate and pure inspired Gabriel to write a book."

"So juicy, right?" Lana says. "Gabe's book is probably blowing up in pre-sales. Have you checked the numbers?"

But Gabe's book sales are the last thing on my mind. I shove the phone back to Lana. "I feel like I'm going to be sick."

My sister-in-law studies me seriously. "I have just the thing for that." She pulls an orange pill bottle from her purse, pops it open, and presses a round white tablet into my palm.

"What is this?"

"Just take it, trust me." So, I do. Lana tosses back a few of the tablets, too.

Soon, my insides go warm and tingly. By the time the check appears, I'm pulsing with joy, basking in this patch of sunlight in the bar's window seat with my lovely sister-in-law. How lucky we are to be right here, right now, together.

The rest of the afternoon is a joyful blur of frolicking through the cityscape. The weekday sidewalks are sparse and the fresh air is languid against my skin. Hours later, as I stand gaping at the fading sunlight framing the skyline in a magical orange glow, I think, *I am so, so happy.*

Soon the world tips into darkness, and Lana and I end up back at Bella So. It feels like days, or even weeks, since we were last here. Ingrid approaches, wearing a pursed expression. She asks to speak to Lana privately.

Left alone, I grab an armful of gowns and make for a dressing room. I shimmy into what I realize is the same gown I tried on before. Only now it doesn't pull at my hips or butt; now my stomach is a smooth line and my waist a genuine gathering. I emerge from the room and stand on the platform. I spin around, and the silk plays like gentle fingers against my body. The mirror reflects my image like an illustration in a fairytale. The other clients flock around. "That's beautiful on you," one girl coos. "You absolutely must get it," another says. I find the price tag and remember the severance package coming my way; it'll be a bargain with Lana's discount.

"Sold," I say, delighting in my decisiveness and the squeals surrounding me. And then the dress is being cocooned in layers of stiff tissue, slid into a plush carrying case, and handed off to me by a dour Ingrid. Her mood can't touch my own. The gown is mine!

"First day back, and already I'm making commission," Lana says, hanging on the counter. "How about that?" She winks at Ingrid, who remains unmoved.

Lana agrees that my ficus tree would add a special something to Bella So's window display, so I decide to donate it. She has to stay to close the store. I hug her and leave to hail a cab. I lie down across the back seat, laying out the dress bag on top of me. The sounds of car horns and sirens are welcome reminders of how loud and bold and gutsy this city is. For once, I feel a part of it, totally in synch with my surroundings.

* * *

When Gabe returns from Nonno, I still haven't moved from the living room rug, although at some point the fuzzy purr of its bristles against my back has gone dull.

"Hey, Molly-moo." Gabe sounds excited. "You'll never guess what happened today."

I'm deadpan to the ceiling: "A reality star got an advanced copy of your book and now it's blowing up in pre-sales."

"Oh, you already know." Gabe crouches down, peering at me like I have superpowers. He starts spouting details—the press, the expanded print run, his editor's talk of a sequel—but I can't quite follow. I'm distracted by the sparks boomeranging between our bodies. I can practically see them. I start stripping off Gabe's layers of uniform. I push him onto his back, straddle him, and restrain his wrists behind his head.

Gabe laughs. "Um, who are you and what have you done with my fiancée?"

"Good question."

Afterward, Gabe brings two glasses of wine and a doggie bag of garlic knots down to the rug. The buttery dough melts on my tongue, delivering bright bursts of spice and salt. My stomach sings. I can't remember the last time I ate.

"Look at this, the two of us picnicking naked together at one a.m.," Gabe says, "On a work night, no less. Whatever's gotten into you, I think I like it."

I tilt back the rest of my wine, drowning the flutter of nerves in my gut.

*   *   *

When I wake up the next morning, there's a blanket draped over me, and the rug is scratchy against my cheek. My breath is rank with garlic, and my head throbs like it's been hit with a two-by-four. *How much did I drink last night?* I wonder. And then a recollection of the whole previous day whooshes over me like a tidal wave, my stomach lurches, and I crawl over to the trash can to vomit.

Nestled back in my spot on the rug, I feel a crumpled paper under my hip. It's a note from Gabe: Molly-moo, couldn't wake you. Off to early meeting with my editor. Love you.

My phone's ringing seems to originate from inside of my eardrums. "Hello?" My voice is thick.

"Molly?" It's Gabe, sounding alarmed. "Are you okay? Were you still asleep?"

The wall clock comes into focus: eleven a.m. "What? No, I'm up."

"Listen, the publisher's extending my book tour to the West coast, and we're hammering out a deal for the sequel. They want a reunion with Talia, but we'll see."

"Talia?"

"What?"

"*Talia.* You said they want a reunion with *Talia.*"

"Oh!" Gabe's laugh is light. "I meant, they want Russell to reunite with *Dahlia.* Also, they're adding me to these meet-and-greets at malls across the Midwest, with reality stars who've written books." He goes on about how this wasn't his intended niche, how he's always pictured himself as kind of a 21st century Burroughs or Exley, but how his editor advised him to recognize his luck and ride the wave of buzz and *blah blah blah* . . . I've stopped listening.

I take a deep breath and cut him off mid-sentence: "I was fired yesterday."

"Wait, what? I could've sworn you just said—."

"I did. And actually, I've got to go." I hang up. Then I don't move for minutes. I'm paralyzed with guilt for cutting through Gabe's good news with my own crap. But I'm also furious at him for having good news when I seem to have nothing but a nasty hangover; it feels profoundly unfair.

◆ ◆ ◆

I never thought I would miss rush-hour crowds, but an empty subway car at noon on a Wednesday is a bleak sight. I hook the Bella So dress bag on the overhead bar and stand next to it protectively. The only other woman on the train eyes me skeptically, like no way do I look like the kind of person to own a Bella So gown. She's right.

In the shop, an unfamiliar saleswoman greets me, and I ask for Lana. She called in sick, apparently—this woman is filling in. I hoist the dress bag onto the counter and hold out my credit card. "I need to return this."

The saleswoman looks confused. "Our gowns aren't refundable. Did Lana not tell you that?" A well of panic rises past my ears as I try to remember if during yesterday's haze Lana mentioned a refund policy. "I can give you store credit?"

I'm picturing my credit card statement: It'll be mid five figures, and take more than my whole severance package to pay off. I feel my cheeks go hot and my eyes go damp, and I implore my body to keep it together. I lean over the counter and I beg: "Could you make an exception? Lana is my sister-in-law. I lost my job yesterday. Please."

"Um, hang on a moment."

She turns her back to me and picks up the phone. Amidst her murmuring, I hear Lana's name. It only now occurs to me that being associated with Lana might not help my case. The saleswoman returns with a pinched, pitying look. "I'm very sorry."

Chapter 22

I HEAR GABE shuffling around, and I open my eyes just long enough to see the bedside clock blink from 7:27 to 7:28 a.m. Lately I haven't even bothered trying to keep track of his schedule—the interviews, the book tour prep, the dozens of promo pieces he's writing, the brand marketing sessions (yes, Gabriel Dover is a personal brand now, and the irony is, as Gabe earnestly describes the strategy specifics to me, I can't even recognize who I'm talking to). When he's not doing book stuff, he's at Nonno. Time has become a precious commodity for my fiancé. As for me, I've become unmoored from it: Days formerly jammed with appointments and responsibilities have been replaced with stretches of nothing, punctuated by an outing to buy a tube of toothpaste or, more frequently, a bottle of booze.

I feel Gabe pause, calculating whether or not to nudge me awake and ask me how I'm doing—a calculation I've felt him make every morning for weeks. I hold my breath and stay perfectly still. Gabe doesn't even know the half of how I'm doing—how I squandered my severance on a stupid dress (before discovering that due to the nature of my "departure" I wouldn't actually be getting any severance), how said departure wasn't in fact a routine lay-off but a firing, how getting fired rather than laid off is apparently a disqualifier for unemployment benefits, and how I've already maxed out several credit cards. The longer I've gone without sharing these things with Gabe, the less capable I feel of doing so. I sense Gabe decide against disturbing me, and a moment later I'm alone.

I awake hours later with an image in my mind: the missing photo collage, the gift from Gabe that I kept at my desk. It suddenly feels imperative that I get it back, each of its photos an essential part of our history: Gabe and me waiting out a rain delay at Yankee Stadium, my damp hair draped onto his shoulder; the two of us leaping into the air at the top of Mount Greylock, our eyes squinty with sun; a close-up of our flushed cheeks pressed together, Ogunquit's low tide stretching long behind us; a portrait of us toasting flutes of champagne, celebrating my promotion; an out-of-focus pale sliver that's impossible to tell is Gabe's ass, from that time we exchanged nude selfies in increasingly absurd positions, a silly escalation that eventually turned sexy for real.

Where is that damn photo collage? I ransack my apartment, rifling through dresser drawers, overturning boxes, and shoving heavy furniture aside to examine crevices where there's no way it could be. I call Bella So and ask if they've come across a framed collage. I can tell it's Ingrid on the line, her tone implying that I'm an imbecile. I ask to speak to Lana. "Lana is no longer employed here," she responds coolly, before hanging up. *What?* It feels like yesterday that I was in the store watching Lana pull gowns for clients—although the truth hits me: More than a month has passed.

Continuing my search, I catch a glance of myself in the mirror: I haven't changed my shirt in days, my hair is an oil slick, and I realize my most recent meal was three grape popsicles. All of this is exacerbated by the sense that a shape-shifting monster is nipping at my heels, making my heart race and my breath shallow. I need to go out—now.

The corner shop charges a criminal three-fifty for a small coffee, but I cough it up just to temporarily feel like a functional member of society. All around me people are tap-tap-tapping at laptops, perhaps

writing books that will betray their loved ones or emailing inappropriate missives to their exes or their exes' new partners. I can be one of the
tap-tap-tappers, too. I take out my phone and, first, I apply for a new
credit card. Then, I scroll through pages of unopened emails and unan-
swered texts. They're mostly from my mother. There's one surprisingly
tasteful note from my old coworker Melinda Lowe, expressing regret at
how things ended between us. Kirsten, bless her, has called and left me
messages every day, undeterred by my lack of response. I text her now:

Should we throw Sam a baby shower?

Within moments she responds: **YES! And a wedding shower for you!**

Sam, on the other hand, has reached out just a handful of times since
I told her about my firing. At first she seemed worried, but then quickly
slipped into annoyance when I clearly wasn't following her step-by-step
plan for how to get my life back together. The last text she sent was a
couple of weeks ago: **I guess you'll be in touch when you're ready . . .**

I share the shower idea with her now, and she replies, **Welcome back,
asshole. I've put on 10 pounds since I saw you last. Ixnay on the shower.
Let's do a trip instead.**

I text Leo a simple, **Hey.**

He pings back, **Sorry I've been MIA, sis.** I haven't noticed, just as he
clearly hasn't noticed my absence. **Life has been crazy since Lana
returned to work.** I remember Ingrid's curt dismissal on the phone. *Hm.*
Leo texts again: **Hang soon?** I propose a few times, but Leo's end goes
silent.

Then there's my mother, whom I've been trying to tell about my firing for weeks, but it's like there's cotton stuffed down my throat. Her
emails about wedding plans have become practically breezy, mentioning John this and John that, to which I've barely responded. I brace
myself and dial her number.

"Molly!" she exclaims. "I was just digging my skates out of the base-
ment. John's taking me down to the lake, now that the ice is thick
enough. Romantic, right?" For a moment I forget to breathe, but my

mom doesn't seem to notice. "If you get a call from the E.R., you'll know I'm in a full-body cast. Also, we got a waffle maker and I've been experimenting with different fillings. Today we had strawberry-ricotta. It's a kick!"

"You two are already investing in appliances together?" I snap. I'm irrationally furious at my mother for going on about herself and not asking about me, for not intuiting that I've lost my way, that I'm falling deeper and deeper into debt, and that Gabe and I are on seriously shaky ground. So, I lash out more: "My god, has John already proposed? Should we be planning a joint wedding?"

I can hear my heart pounding through my mom's long pause. My jaw is a vise. "Molly, I know it's new for me to be dating." She's speaking to me like I'm a child, which both irritates me and loosens something ropey inside of me. "It doesn't mean I don't care about Daddy just as much as I always have."

At the mention of the name only I used for my father, tears spring from my eyes and trickle down my cheeks. I attempt a blasé sigh. "Whatever, I have bigger things to worry about than who you're eating waffles with." My nonchalance is unconvincing even to me.

"Molly, are you okay? Please tell me. Please."

The words spill out of me: "Oh Mom, Gabe's becoming this big hotshot with his book, and he doesn't have any time for me, and everyone thinks his relationship with his ex is the most fascinating thing ever, and meanwhile, I'm at home all day in my sweatpants."

"Honey, slow down. What's going on?"

I tell her I lost my job. The knot inside me slackens another notch. (Though I can't tell her I've run out of money and am deep in debt—she'd want to swoop in and save me, even if it meant cutting off her gas and living on ramen for a month.) "And something bad is going on with Leo and Lana." I realize I've been angry about this too, another problem I half-believe my mother should have discovered and solved already. "And all you seem to give a shit about is screwing John the jolly innkeeper!"

"Molly, my love. First of all, John and I have only made love once."

"*Mom!*" I cry.

She starts giggling, and it makes me giggle, too. Suddenly it all seems so ridiculous. I know I'm being a brat. I apologize, and when we hang up I email her a peace offering: Gabe's recipe for chocolate-chip waffles.

•   •   •

The next morning, I will myself to wake up with Gabe at the crack of dawn. He's leaving for the Los Angeles Book Festival, followed by a visit to his parents. He asked me a couple of weeks ago if I wanted to come with him, now that I wouldn't have to take time off work for the trip. But I felt sure the offer wasn't sincere, so I declined. I obviously shouldn't be spending money on airfare, anyway.

I help Gabe by rolling his clothes into tight coils and packing them into his suitcase like pencils in a case. He's looking on skeptically. "Hey, Molly."

"It's more efficient, I swear." I start stuffing balls of socks into his shoes.

"Forget the packing for a minute, okay?" I look up. Gabe is fidgeting his fingers. "I'm worried about you. It seems like you've been having a really hard time." I hear a note of pity underlying his concern, and it makes me defensive.

"Yeah, I'm unemployed, remember? I think that's the definition of a hard time."

"I know. It's just . . ." As I watch him search for what to say, there's a flutter in my stomach—I feel myself wishing for him to recognize how lost I feel, even as I'm terrified by the same thing. "I don't know, never mind." Gabe shakes his head, and I'm flooded with both relief and disappointment. "Are you sure you don't want to come to L.A.? A last-minute ticket would be expensive, but we could figure it out." Surely, he can't mean this.

"No, I should really be job hunting," I say. I swear I detect relief on his face.

"And you're really all right with my going?" Gabe asks.

Of course I don't want to admit how freaked out I am by ten days on my own, without a job to escape to each day. "I'll be fine." I smile to prove it. Gabe smiles back. When he kisses me goodbye, I realize I've never felt farther apart from him.

On his way out the door, Gabe grabs last week's *New Yorker*, an action that triggers a pulse of panic inside me, although I can't pinpoint its source.

• • •

While Gabe is gone, I know I should be scanning job boards, networking, reaching out to recruiters, and doing all the other things that until recently landed people on the other side of my desk for job interviews. But halfway through reading a single posting for a Human Resources manager, I'm already exhausted. The notion that I'd be qualified to handle either humans or resources at the moment seems like a sick joke.

So, instead, I Google "LA Book Festival Gala." The capstone event was last night, co-hosted by the major publishing houses and rumored to bring out both literary and actual stars. Gabe brought three potential outfits for the occasion. I find a slideshow of the gala's red carpet. I click, click, click until the faces become a flipbook and the gowns firework flashes of color.

My finger twitches, freezing above the mouse. There, at the side of a shot, is someone who looks a lot like Gabe—only, this guy's hair is slicked back with gel and he's wearing a slim-fitting suit that's not one of the outfits I watched my fiancé add to his garment bag. But, there's the fountain-pen-patterned tie I gave him last Christmas—so it must be Gabe. Posed at his side is that reality TV star, Larissa "LaLa" Laraby. Somehow this doesn't surprise me. I'm scrutinizing the placement of their arms, hers draped around Gabe's shoulder like they're best buds, his disappearing behind the small of her back, like they're more than buds. So it takes me a moment to register the other two people in the huddle: my coworker Jonathan Wexler, grasping the hand of—*wait, is it really her? yes, it is*—Talia.

Her hair is an ebony sculpture ascending from her head, and she's in a floor-length getup that, were it white and not lilac, and if it showed a little less side boob, could be a Bella So wedding gown. She looks radiant, and I feel contemptuous: How much time and money did she invest in this ensemble? Did she hire a stylist, for Christ's sake? Gabe stands on the opposite end of the shot, separated from Talia by two whole people. But as I zoom in on Talia's face, I swear her gaze is directed at him, her expression lustful and possessive. Gabe looks aware that he's being looked at; he's practically basking in it. I zoom in until I can see Gabe's second-day stubble and Talia's pimples, despite her makeup (this makes me unduly gleeful). I keep zooming in until everything becomes a blur of pixels, then I slam my laptop shut.

I want to believe I'm being paranoid, that my eyes have deceived me. I also want Gabe to fess up on his own. I don't want to have to pry it out of him that while he's 3,000 miles away he's been hobnobbing with his ex, a proven crazy person and the muse for his hot new book. So, when I connect with him over Skype, I start off innocuously: "What is it, seventy-five and sunny there?"

Gabe's grin fills my computer screen. "Yep, it's pretty much paradise," he says. I glance out my window at the gray sky and sleet, then I close my eyes and try to imagine golden California sunshine warming my skin. I don't care about the panels Gabe has attended, or the press he's done, or the impressive people he's met, but I let him go on and on about all of it anyway. I'm the picture of restraint, practicing a trick I picked up as a child, shrugging a coat of numbness over my feelings.

"Wasn't last night the big gala?" I finally venture.

"Yeah, it was incredible." Gabe describes the classic literature-themed tables—he was seated at Manderley—and how he ended up next to his literary idol in the bathroom, and the delicious shrimp appetizers that he has the nerve to suggest we serve at our wedding. My coat of numbness starts to grow threadbare.

"So, did you get a plus-one?" I ask.

"To the gala? No. I guess if I'd asked they might've given me one."

"Ah." I silently will him, *Come on, tell me about Talia. Don't make me force it out of you.*

Gabe forges ahead: "Larissa Laraby was there, too. It took about a minute of conversation for me to realize she hasn't actually read my book. She thought Dahlia was a stripper! Because of that one strip-tease scene, which apparently was her favorite." It's the first I'm hearing of a strip-tease scene; maybe Larissa Laraby has read all the parts of the book that I haven't, and vice versa. "Why would she go on the record saying how much she loved the book if she didn't even read it?"

"Maybe it's part of an elaborate cover-up of her secret illiteracy," I say. I'm growing impatient—who cares whether or not some random celebrity has read Gabe's book?

"It's just bizarre, how a star's whole persona could be founded on lies." *Lies*—the word reverberates in my head.

"And who else did you hang out with last night?" I ask.

"Let's see. My agent, and my editor for a minute, and Jonathan Wexler."

"Jonathan, huh? Anyone else?" When Gabe doesn't answer immediately, I inhale sharply: "Talia?"

"Well, yeah, sort of."

I wait for an apology or an explanation, but neither comes. "It's pretty weird that you didn't mention her," I say.

"Molly, what can I say?" He sounds impatient. "It's pretty weird that your old coworker is dating her, and that she's here. It's pretty weird that she introduced herself to my publicist, and then befriended a reporter from *People,* and now there's going to be a profile on the two of us, a stupid behind-the-scenes look at the so-called story behind my book. Do you think I want any of that?"

I laugh in disbelief. "I don't know, Gabe, do you? It sounds like pretty great publicity—an excellent opportunity to build your personal brand."

"Come on, Molly-moo. All of this is totally phony. Just silly titillation for people who don't have any excitement in their own lives. Meaningless gossip for dumb people."

"Your readers, you mean."

"Christ, Molly, you should understand this better than anyone, the illusions invented to sell something. It's all smoke and mirrors."

That phrase "smoke and mirrors," it's the same one Talia used to describe my company—my *former* company. Did she feed that line to Gabe, or maybe vice versa? And why was she at the gala, but not me? Is anything Gabe's saying genuine? I fear I'm losing hold of my rational self, and my ability to judge fact from fiction. Not knowing what to say, I settle on sarcasm: "Well, I bet all of this must be excellent fodder for your sequel."

I hold my breath, waiting for Gabe to backtrack and say that he knows this must be hard on me, and that he'll talk to Talia about butting out of his life—*our* life. But what comes out of his mouth isn't any of that: "You know, Molly, sometimes I wish you were more supportive of me. Anyway, I'm running late for a lunch."

"Screw you, screw Talia, and screw the whole book publishing industry!" I scream it as loud as my lungs can manage . . . only, I wait until after Gabe has logged off to do so. He doesn't hear a word of it.

All my numbness has disappeared; now I'm roiling with rage. It's unfamiliar to me to acknowledge this, but as soon as I do, I realize just how familiar of a feeling it is. It's pathetic how I can't be straight with Gabe. And yet, I think of all the times I've been rewarded for my restraint, ever since I was a little girl. The last time I expressed such strong feelings to another person's face, I was fired from my job. Despite everything, I don't want to be fired from my relationship, too. So, I'm left panting with fury, staring at a blank screen, alone.

· · ·

I'm prepared to hate-read the striptease section of Gabe's book, to wield it as further evidence of everyone's idiocy: Gabe's for writing it, Talia's for inspiring it, Gabe's editor for publishing it, and Larissa Laraby's for admiring it. I find the scene about a third of the way in, long before Dahlia has missed her flight to Spain, dropped out of school, and been evicted first from her apartment and then from her relationship. At this point the charms of Dahlia are still at peak allure *(gag)*.

Since the first night he met her, Russell loved to watch Dahlia dance. She'd thrust herself into the middle of party crowds and invite every pair of eyes to follow her. Sometimes Dahlia indulged the oglers, showing off with sexy undulations, and sometimes she didn't—in a flash she'd shrink back to her petit self and slip away. Dahlia had no patience for the college co-ed uniform of black pants, flimsy tank top, and stiletto boots. She wore whatever she had on. She could've danced in sweatpants and a t-shirt and still had every guy and girl dying to go home with her. Dahlia was the only person Russell knew who didn't have to follow any of the rules.

As someone who follows all the rules, I find it particularly dispiriting to read Gabe's description that equates sexiness with rule-breaking.

On that particular night, they'd wandered into a random house party where Dahila seemed to know everyone. They certainly all knew her. The dance floor was dense with bodies, and Dahlia gravitated to the center, grinding up against girls and guys and couples, too. Russell remained a spectator, sipping at a beer, half turned-on, half nervous.

Dahlia began using her hands—stroking cheeks, hair, hips. Soon she was kissing people, and they were kissing her back. Watching strangers grope at his girlfriend, Russell was transfixed.

I am too, I'm surprised to discover. I think with a pang of the night Gabe and I got engaged, our dancing to that strange, otherworldly music. I'd never loved Gabe as much as I did then, the two of us swaying together, buzzing with each other's warmth, alone in the crowd. I wonder now if dancing with me that night moved Gabe as much as the sight of his ex dancing.

When Dahlia caught Russell's eye, she smiled, a warm private look that assured him all was fine, all was good. She turned back to the girl she'd just been making out with and eased off her sweater. The girl mirrored the movement, pulling off Dahlia's sweatshirt. She was left in just her blue bra, the only one she owned, which she wore only occasionally. Russell wanted to run his fingers along its lace, but something kept his shoes glued to the grimy floor. He finished his beer and squeezed the can until it crunched.

Two guys approached Dahlia and tried to sandwich her, but she shrugged them off to clear a space around herself. Russell watched as she bounced and spun and practically floated off the ground, all the while peeling off pieces of clothing until they formed a puddle at her feet. She was a marvel, feisty and sensual and teetering on magic. Russell observed her take in her surroundings, something sinister sparking in her eyes. He couldn't imagine anything sexier. She was taunting and shaming her spectators all at once, in one look both daring them to see her and crying out, *How dare you watch me?* She reveled in her power and pitied all of them who believed they were the source of it.

I feel Dahlia's gaze on me, too, taunting and shaming and challenging me, asking me why I'm bearing witness to her strip-tease, why I'm reading any of this at all. I don't know. Maybe to torture myself. Or maybe it's because I want to be the kind of person who can dance alone, half-naked, in public; because—I'm surprised to discover—I yearn to be more like Dahlia.

Only later would Russell recall snippets of what he'd overheard at the party, one girl whispering that Dahlia had been in the bathroom every ten minutes, another whispering back, *Of course, she's a total addict.* Someone accusing her of being an attention whore, a guy responding, *Just a whore, period.* A girl saying she wished she had that kind of confidence, or at least those tits. Another: *I hear she has a boyfriend.* A third: *How embarrassing, what a slut.* One guy calling her a train wreck. One saying he would kill to get inside of her. His friend replying, *No need to kill, I hear she'll fuck anyone for decent coke.* Another one telling them all to shut up and just enjoy the show. Everyone's opinions blaring like sirens through Russell's head.

But in the moment, Russell didn't hear any of it. Because here was his girlfriend—wild, sexy, alive—dancing in her panties in the middle of a party. He was gripped by desire, pure and simple.

When the song ended, the spell broke and Dahlia called out to Russell. He flew to her side. "Carry me home," she said, a tickle in his ear. Russell picked her up, warm skin abuzz in his arms. Back at his place, he tucked the two of them into bed, the place where they belonged most in the world.

"I feel like my skin could speak," Dahlia purred, "like my muscles could think." Russell knew just what she meant. They spent hours exploring each other's dips and curves and sinews, reaching peak after peak of satisfaction.

It occurs to me queasily that since I lost my job, Gabe and I have slept together just a single time.

Afterward, Russell wrapped Dahlia in his arms, pulsing with the belief that their love was epic and everlasting, that it would survive no matter what. He knew it was cheesy, but he didn't care. The truth was, the only thing in the world he cared about was Dahlia.

~

Years in the future, eons and seeming lifetimes later, when Russell would live in another city, when he'd have a wife who was different in every way from Dahlia, and a life that had nothing at all to do with the one he'd spent with Dahlia,

My hopes soar, my nerves calm, and for a moment I breathe. But then I read on . . .

he would still think back to the night of Dahlia's striptease. He'd remember it as the pinnacle of a kind of love irretrievable except in memory.

I drop the book and step away warily, like it's a feral animal. I throw a pillow at it so I don't have to see its cover. I was prepared to hate the passage—and I do, sort of. But what I wasn't prepared for was to be so overcome by it, too, to feel charged with Dahlia's pull, to come away with an understanding of her power. And it's too much.

So, I pop a sleeping pill and wash it down with a big sloshing glass of wine. But the effects of the drug and the alcohol are weak compared to the effects of Dahlia. For hours, I lie in bed wide-eyed and trembling, sick with the fear that Talia's power over Gabe is like this—that it's epic and everlasting, that it will survive no matter what.

Chapter 23

FOUR MISSED CALLS from Gabe, zero texts. When I call him back, he doesn't say hello. Just: "I finally read that *New Yorker*." His tone is curt, accusing.

"Okay?" Even as I respond, I remember: I read that issue while on hold with the credit card companies, trying to talk down the interest rates for my maxed-out cards. After the calls, I tucked the damning statements into the magazine.

"When were you planning on telling me that you've racked up tens of thousands of dollars in debt in a couple of months? And that you've stopped paying your bills?"

My mouth goes dry. The truth is I wasn't planning on telling him. I assumed I would figure out a way to pay what I owed, and then it would all just go away. "I was figuring out how to pay them off," I say, "I swear."

"It's not the money that's so upsetting, Molly. Or not only that. It's the lying."

"But I didn't lie to you. I—"

"Hiding this is the same thing as lying. It's a betrayal. A total breach of trust!" Gabe's volume escalates as he rails on about responsibility and maturity and respect, and how apparently I lack all three of them.

But I can't focus. *This* is a betrayal, a breach of trust? No, I think. This is my own problem—and there's nothing wrong with having kept it to myself. "Answer me, Molly," Gabe says. "What do you have to say for yourself?"

"I'm ashamed," I say, and it's true. "I feel like a moron for blowing off the whole savings thing, and for losing my job, and for feeling like a failure of a grownup." (And for blowing half a year's rent on a single dress, I don't say.) I feel terrible; I'm not faking it. "But . . ."

"But what?" Gabe barks.

What I want to say is, but I'm also furious. How dare Gabe accuse me so sanctimoniously, as if he himself is without blame or blemish. As if he didn't give his ex-girlfriend his credit card number so she could spend however much of his money she pleased. The same ex he's been shamelessly posing for pictures with on the red carpet, the one whom he may or may not have agreed to pay book royalties to, and whom he'll soon be featured alongside in a national magazine profile.

What I actually say is, "But I'm not Talia."

"Excuse me?" Gabe says. "What does any of this have to do with Talia?"

"I'm not going to manipulate you into giving me money or beg you for a cut of your royalties." I know how dumb this sounds. Gabe and I are engaged, after all; soon our money will be legally combined. "My point is, you can trust me, Gabe. The question is, can I trust you?"

Even before Gabe scoffs, I realize it was the wrong thing to say. "You're actually serious?" he snaps.

I'm desperately trying to figure out how to dig myself out of this hole and make things right. Meanwhile, the silence on the line gapes. It doesn't feel fair, all of this getting sprung upon me. I wish I could call for a time out. But before I can come up with the right words, Gabe says, "You're damn right, you're not Talia. Because when Talia and I were together, she'd actually talk to me. We'd scream and yell and say stupid things, sure, but at least I knew what she was thinking and where we stood. With you, I feel like I have no idea anymore. I've been trying to get through to you, but I can't even tell if you want me to try. You asking me whether you can trust me—it's like you're looking for reasons to *not* trust me, as if you want to prove yourself right that I'm some shitty guy. But it's just me—Gabe, your Scrabe, remember? Anyway, I have to go." His voice is terse and final.

"Gabe, please." But he's already gone.

* * *

The bar where I meet Sam and Kirsten is dense with a post-work crowd, and I try not to reveal how overwhelmed I am by the thrum of conversation after a day spent alone in my apartment. I slap down the latest issue of *People* and sigh. "While you guys have been contributing to society all day, I've been rotting my brain reading about my boyfriend in a tabloid." I'm not proud of the fact that I practiced this delivery ahead of time. But I wanted to strike the right note of gossipy with a touch of irritation, rather than dumping upon my friends the full weight of how I really feel, which is utterly despaired.

"Your fiancé," says Kirsten.

"What?"

"You said your *boyfriend*. Gabe is your fiancé."

"Oh, right. Anyway, look: It's two whole pages." Together we scrutinize the spread, which includes an old photo of Talia and Gabe wrapped in a loving embrace (provided by Talia, no doubt), and a quote from Talia in giant font: "Women like Dahlia and me nestle into your heart and soul and stay there forever." Gabe's quotes are milder: "I'm humbled my book has gotten so much attention," and "Anyone who's been unlucky in love, or made a decision with their heart instead of their head, will identify with this story."

"Talia sounds like an imbecile," Sam snaps. "And she's not even that pretty."

"Definitely not as pretty as you," Kirsten adds. "But who cares anyway, since you're the one with the ring on your finger?"

Sam nods. "So, what did Gabe say when you told him how upset you were?"

But I barely hear her. I'm fixated on Gabe's quote, parsing his phrasing in an obsessive loop: "unlucky" shores me up, "in love" sends me spiraling down, then "unlucky" shores me up again. I'm wondering when Gabe did the interview—before or after our Skype call, before or after he opened that *New Yorker?* I'm wondering if his words are his own, or if they've been filtered and warped through a publicist's strategic branding lens or tinged with Talia's influence. And, surprisingly, I'm wondering what Dahlia would do in this situation—laugh it all off or take off and never look back?

"You haven't told him, have you?" Sam says. When I don't respond, she scoffs.

"Molly, are you all right?" Kirsten's hand on my wrist startles me.

I snatch up the magazine. "I'm fine. Let's take that trip we talked about."

"Sure, it seems like we could all use a breather," says Sam. "Next weekend?"

"Works for me," says Kirsten.

"Perfect," I say.

"I know of these cute little cabins upstate, with no Internet or cell service," Kirsten says. "Totally off the grid." When she names the campground, I nod, knowing exactly where it is. I feel my heartbeat quicken. Whatever, it's probably a big park—just because Charlie works there doesn't mean I'll see him. I just want a break from my life.

Sam turns to me: "So is it just this article that's bothering you? Because you seem pretty pissed off." She won't let me off with just a shrug. "Come on, if you won't talk to Gabe, at least talk to us."

I take a deep breath, then deliver the play-by-play: Talia's appearance at the book gala, my credit card mess, Gabe finding the statements, our confrontation, his ridiculous accusation that I betrayed him. My friends listen without interruption, and when I'm done, I expect support and reassurance.

"Well," Kirsten says, "the only thing to do is make things right with Gabe. You have to apologize, and you have to mean it. Then you have to promise not to lie to him again."

I start to protest, assuming Sam will back me up, but she cuts me off: "Molly, like it or not, that *was* lying to him. And it's no excuse that you find it hard to open up about this stuff. You're a grown-ass woman! You might think Gabe's up on his high horse. You might be resentful that you were the one paying the bills for most of your relationship. But you can't just sit around stewing. You've got to hash this shit out."

"You know, I *am* resentful." This didn't occur to me until Sam said it. While Gabe was busy plumbing the depths of his soul to relive his relationship with his ex, I was the one earning the income to shoulder most of our expenses. "And what about Talia pretty much following Gabe to California?"

"That has nothing to do with you," says Kirsten. "And neither does the *People* article."

Sam chimes in: "It was one thing when you dragged us along on your little stakeout of that girl's apartment. But now you're really letting all this shit drive you crazy."

"If you care about your relationship with Gabe," Kirsten adds, "you have to set aside all the noise and fight for it. Together, as a team." Sam nods.

They're both staring at me accusingly, my two best friends ganged up against me, on Gabe's side. I'm on the verge of tears. "I have to go," I say, and then I'm gone.

• • •

My emotions are a gloppy stew in my gut. I'm angry. I'm sad. I feel stubborn with pride. I feel like an idiot. Sam has been texting me every five minutes, pestering me about my disappearance from the bar, and Kirsten's left me a longwinded voicemail gently encouraging me to talk to Gabe. But I can't bring my fingers to push the buttons to dial him.

I'll do it later, I decide. In the meantime, I open my laptop and I surprise myself by loading Word and typing, "Dear Diary." I kept a journal as a teenager, and I remember finding it comforting. My palms hover over the keyboard, then I surprise myself again: I erase "Diary" and type, "Daddy."

My fingers start tapping at the keys as if of their own volition: **Do you remember swimming in the ocean together? We'd paddle out past the breakers, then bodysurf to shore. You'd cover yourself with seaweed, becoming a sea monster, then chase me down the beach, and I'd sprint ahead, frightened and delighted. I can still hear my squeals like echoes in my mind. I miss that. I miss you.**

I stop typing, thinking about how after my dad died, I quit ocean swimming. My mom would spread out a blanket far back from shore, issuing warnings of wild waves, a vicious undertow, possible riptides. I'd spend the day quietly reading chapter books, bathing suit bone-dry, and my mom would stroke my hair and tell me I was such a good girl. "Your father would be so proud," she'd say like a tic, between tsk-tsking at other kids who were throwing sand or fighting over snacks. Leo, who hated sitting still, quit coming to the beach altogether.

A different memory of my father surfaces. I type it out as I recall it: **Remember when you brought me in to work and I sat on your lap at the head of the table in that big meeting? It was all men in suits, talking for what felt like hours. I filled an entire notepad with doodles, and still they droned on. When I couldn't stand it anymore, I blurted out, "When is everyone going to shut up already?" You laughed and laughed, and told me you were so proud of me.**

So why, after my dad was gone, did I become the picture of courtesy and obedience? Why did I think that was the way to honor his memory? What he'd really been proud of was my boldness and my willingness to say what I felt and do what I wanted. What happened to that version of me?

I keep typing: **There's only so long you can bury your feelings before they start corroding your insides like poison, and you inevitably melt down, right? I was so scared to confront Gabe that I took out my anger on a random interviewee. And Daddy, I'm still scared. I want to feel over the moon for Gabe and his success. But I'm terrified he wants to be with Talia instead of me. I'm frightened that our decent, quiet life pales in comparison to the thrilling tornado of dating her. And I'm petrified at losing all the things I thought I always wanted. I've already lost so much: My job, my paycheck, my routine, my trust in Gabe, his trust in me. You, of course. Mom, now that she has John. And I'm scared of losing even more. Like Sam, when she has her baby. And any idea of what I want and who I want to be. I'm terrified this is making me as nuts as Talia. Only, not in her kooky, whimsical, adorable way. Not in a way that inspires novels and excites celebrities and fills the pages of gossip magazines. No, just plain crazy.**

I stare at what I've written till it goes blurry from the liquid pooling in my eyes. Ironically, admitting how scared I am makes me feel a tiny bit less scared.

That is, until I'm startled by a text. I assume it's Sam again, but it's my brother: **Just walked by waiting room and saw Gabe on TV! Channel 17. Good for him!**

I click the remote, and then there they are on my TV screen: Gabe and Talia, hip to hip on the iconic pink couch of that vapid talk show *The POV*. It's hard to tell whether they're being forced so close together by the bevy of hostesses surrounding them, but it's easy to tell what's going on with Gabe's left hand: It's being clutched by Talia's right hand.

A hostess leans in to Gabe and places her palm on his thigh. I clench my own palms into fists, and yell at the TV, "Can everyone just keep your goddamn hands to yourself?"

The hostess addresses Gabe, her voice honeyed: "So, rewriting this past relationship as fiction is what brought you two back in touch. That's sort of romantic." A whoop rises from the audience. "Did the writing help you work through what went wrong with the two of you so you could move on with a fresh slate?"

"Oh, give me a break," I say, guessing Gabe will respond with a version of the same.

But he sounds earnest when he says, "You could say that. Writing can definitely be cathartic." *What?*

"Well, the fans sure love you guys," the hostess replies. "Let's watch a bit of you in action." She presses a button and a screen descends behind the couch. Suddenly I'm accosted by a montage of Gabe and Talia dancing at the Book Festival gala, then posing on the set of the *People* shoot, then canoodling on a pier bench as the sun sets in the distance. As photos flash up one after the other, Shania Twain croons, "You're still the one." I feel simultaneously nauseous and appalled.

I get another text, and this time it is from Sam: **Did you talk to Gabe yet?!?!** She pings me again a few minutes later: **Hello! Earth to Molly!**

I reply, **PLEASE STOP BOTHERING ME AND BUTT OUT OF MY BUSINESS. FOR YOUR INFO I CAN'T TALK TO GABE BC HE'S BUSY FLIRTING WITH TALIA ON THE POV.** Then I silence my phone and turn back to the TV.

Another hostess chimes in: "*The Charms of Dahlia* has hit the bestseller list, Larissa Laraby has expressed interest in playing Dahlia in a movie adaptation, and now Talia, you say you might pen a book of your own to capture your side of the story." The surprise on Gabe's face is just a flicker, but it's satisfying—he isn't in on this plan of hers.

"I've shopped around the idea," Talia says in a vaguely European accent. "A she-said counterpart to Gabriel's he-said version. There's been interest."

"And Gabe," the hostess says, "I've heard a rumor about a sequel to your book."

"Maybe," says Gabe. "I'm not necessarily convinced that a sequel makes sense for the story's narrative arc or the protagonist's characterization."

The hostess' eyes go dull before the end of his sentence; she clearly doesn't want to discuss literary elements. She cuts in to ask, "And how about a sequel for the two of you, now that you've reunited?" It's the question they've all been dancing around.

Talia's laugh is practiced. "You never know," she says.

Say something, I will Gabe. *Say you have a fucking fiancé*. But he doesn't. He just shrugs. The hostess slaps him on the arm. "Well, aren't you the mysterious silent type."

Gabe's smile is the one I fell in love with: dimpled, charming, at the moment infuriating. I hurl my remote at the TV, and as it plunks against the screen, the camera pans to the cheering audience, eyes alight at the possibility of romance rekindled.

♦ ♦ ♦

"Congrats on your national TV debut." Gabe didn't pick up, so I'm leaving him a voicemail. "You and Talia were *adorable* together. I hear a sequel might be in the works . . . you never know!"

He calls back a half hour later: "Hey, I saw you called." Wherever he is, it's very loud.

"I saw you on *The POV*."

"You did?" The connection is too poor for me to detect his tone; I'd like to say it's panicked, but it might be proud. "It was all really last-minute. The Laraby sisters were supposed to be on promoting their new emoji set, but Liliana got pink-eye, so LaLa suggested they slot me in."

"LaLa, huh?" It's such a ridiculous nickname for a grown woman.

I hear someone congratulate Gabe and Gabe thank them. "Sorry, what?"

"Nothing." I'm silent for a moment, waiting for an apology, an acknowledgment, *something*. "So, um, what the hell?"

"I know, it was sort of trashy. My publicist claimed we'd be talking mostly about the book's themes, but I guess I should've known better."

"With expert literary analysis from Professor Talia, Ph.D.?"

"That was just supposed to be the hook, having Talia there. It was Jonathan's idea. It seemed stupid to me, but my publicist says book sales jump every time there's a press mention of Talia and me and our supposed renewed interest in each other."

"*Supposed* renewed interest, huh?"

"Wait a minute, are you angry?" Gabe sounds incredulous.

I'm incredulous at that. "Yes, Gabe. Of course I'm angry! A photo of you two in a magazine is one thing, but the talk show host asked you directly if you might get back together with Talia, and you didn't even mention that no, you wouldn't, because hello, you're engaged to another woman! What is this, *Jane Eyre?* Am I the crazy crone you keep secretly locked in the attic so you can pursue your true love interest . . . on the set of *The POV*?" Despite everything, it feels good to say these things to Gabe.

His laugh is unkind. "No, Molly, I'm not the one keeping secrets, remember? *The POV* is just a silly talk show. Everyone knows the gossip is all fake."

"Well, here's my POV: Whatever secrets I supposedly kept from you don't even compare to this. And honestly, I'm not sure you do think it's all fake anymore. Next thing I know, you and Talia will be releasing a steamy sequel to your sex tape, and you'll tell me the whole thing's just a publicity stunt to promote your book sequel."

"Don't be ridiculous, Molly-moo."

"Don't 'Molly-moo' me. You're a writer, Gabe, not a movie star or the goddamn president. Although even movie stars and presidents are allowed to admit if they're engaged to be married. Enjoy your half a minute of fame, and be sure to keep me posted on the book sales." I hang up and chuck my phone at the TV. Its plunk isn't nearly as satisfying as the remote's was.

I look around my apartment for more things to throw, but all I see are all of Gabe's and my stuff intermingled. I can't stay in this space any longer. I grab my laptop and flee.

I have three new emails, one each from Sam and Kirsten, both wanting to rehash the TV segment and hear how I'm doing, and one from my mom, weighing the pros and cons of a signature wedding cocktail, so I assume she doesn't yet know about *The POV*. I wonder about Gabe's parents, whom he's flying up to see tonight. They don't even own a television. Probably they'd be more disappointed with their son for appearing on daytime TV than for anything he said on the show. They might even be thrilled, concluding that he's finally renounced his belief in the stuffy institution of marriage in favor of free love. Well, they can all just go practice their hippy-dippy crock of crap under a tree somewhere, far away from me.

I return to my Word document, but writing to my dead father now seems like further evidence of my craziness. So, I toggle back to my email and click "Compose." The blank body is an invitation, and my fingers fly across the keyboard:

My fiancé is busy having romantic reunions with his ex on national TV and hobnobbing with reality stars at VIP parties in L.A. Meanwhile, I'm at home in my PJs, banished from corporate America and desperately waiting for five o'clock so I can uncork a bottle of wine, which, incidentally, I can't even afford. Life is splendid! And how are you?

My finger is twitchy above the mouse. *Oh, what the hell?* I think. I type in Charlie Ashbury's email address and hit "Send."

Chapter 24

IT's JARRING TO see my mother in the passenger seat of a pickup truck. John waves to me from the driver's seat, and I realize I've misremembered his appearance, painting him in my mind as both older and stockier than the reality. He wears a button-down in a fashionable fit, although that could be a coincidence. "Don't worry, John's doing his own thing," my mom says. She's come to the city for a visit—Leo couldn't slip away from work, Lana didn't even return my text, and Gabe has extended his visit with his parents, so it's a mother-daughter day by default.

After hopping out of the truck, my mom pulls me into a viselike hug and sniffs at my unwashed hair. "Are you smelling my hair?" I ask.

"Don't be ridiculous. But have you heard of this fantastic invention called dry shampoo?" She can't see me rolling my eyes. "Say hi and bye to John."

I reach into the truck and awkwardly shake John's hand. "You girls have fun," he says. "Shop till you drop!"

"We will!" My mom blows kisses until he's out of sight.

"I thought we were doing brunch," I say. "I researched the best waffle spot."

"Oh, I'm off waffles," my mom says. "Do you know how much sugar and fat whipped cream has?"

"Yes, Mom, whipped cream is literally only sugar and fat."

"We can grab green juices on the way to our appointment."

"Appointment?"

"To pick out wedding invitations." She sounds impatient, but I'm certain she never mentioned this. My stomach's growls turn from hungry to distressed.

"Mom, I'm really not in the mood."

"Then get yourself in the mood." She tugs at my arm and thrusts us into oncoming traffic.

Our destination is a high-end stationery shop. The back room features a round table filled with couples: The women look dressed for an Upper East Side charity luncheon, the men for a golf outing, and the sole gay couple wears matching head-to-toe Ralph Lauren. It's my worst-nightmare desert island scenario. The store manager looks like a forty-year-old sorority girl, underfed and over-Botoxed. After inviting my mother and me to sit, she launches into a speech about invitations being the *foyer* (French pronunciation) to your wedding experience, your first opportunity to broadcast to loved ones the tone of your marriage-to-be.

I'm anxious to ditch this nonsense even before she passes around cards that I recognize as my old coworker Melinda Lowe's designs. A woman in pearls and a headband coos at the details, and I'm reluctant to admit that they are sort of pretty. My mother raises a hand. "Do you have any beachy patterns?"

"Sure, we have nautical themes, seashells, yachting. Here." She hands us a stack of samples. They're the Mercedes-Benz of invitations, gilded and embossed and embroidered, layered with silk and jewels and velveteen ribbon.

"How much do these cost?" I ask. The woman beside me glares, as if I just demanded that we all go around and state our salaries. As it turns out, the prices could pass for salaries.

"Mom," I whisper, "I can print out my own invitations at Staples. You do remember I'm unemployed, right?"

"Come on, Molly. I'll pay, my treat—it'll be my wedding gift. Feel how thick the paper stock is. They won't even stay up on people's fridges! Imagine what Joe and Barb will say!"

"Is that why you want me to have fancy invitations? To annoy Gabe's parents?"

"Honey, I'm just having fun. Look, they're passing around a bottle of bubbly."

"*Mom,*" I whine. "Please can we get out of here?" This comes out louder than I intended, and I feel people's eyes on me. Everyone here is awful, with their square-tipped manicures and designer watches, exchanging private glances and politely sipping Prosecco. The room's walls seem to be closing in on me, and I start to hyperventilate. I have to bolt. On my way out, I accidentally knock over a tall display of scrapbooks, which I don't bother picking up. With a pit in my stomach, I understand that it's me who's the awful one.

My mother is on my tail. She finds me on the sidewalk. "Molly, honestly. We couldn't even stick around for one glass of wine?"

It's a relief to be back in the fresh air. "How about bagels?"

My mom looks resigned. "Sure, whatever you want."

I feel better after eating. I'm calm enough to politely decline my mom's offer to go gown shopping at Kleinfeld. (The Bella So gown goes unmentioned; I've shoved it to the back of both my closet and my mind.)

"What's Gabe up to today?" It's the second time she's asked.

"He's still in San Francisco, remember?"

"Oh right." It's her very-concerned voice, and she won't stop nodding.

I take a deep breath, attempting to rise above my annoyance. "Let's visit Leo," I say.

* * *

220 • lindsey j. palmer

As we walk through Lenox Hill's double doors and the antiseptic smell hits my nostrils, I realize what a bad idea this is. Leo is at work; I would kill him if he foisted our mom upon me at my job—that is, back when I *had* a job. I decide to stall, whisking us down to the cafeteria.

A funny thing happens when we sit down with our coffees and chocolate-chip cookie to split: I swear I see my father at the next table. It's as if the photo of him that I studied for hours as a child has come to life—the one where he's hunched over and cradling a cup of coffee, contemplative in a way that always made me hope he was thinking of me. It takes me a moment to realize it's actually my brother sitting there, looking like he's aged a decade in the past two months. His eyes hang heavy and his hair is our father's gray-flecked curls.

"Leo?"

"I'm on my break," he says, startling like he's been caught. He doesn't ask why we're there. I notice he's not wearing his white coat, and he notices me noticing.

"We didn't want to disturb you," says my mom, beckoning him to our table. "We just popped in to say hi."

Leo joins us, and our mom pats his back absentmindedly. "How was dinner?" he asks.

"Leo, it's two p.m.," I say.

"Right, sorry. Long shift."

"Refill?" I shake my empty coffee cup.

Leo and I get in line behind a pack of nurses. As my brother broods, I think about how no matter how well you know someone, they're also kind of a stranger. But one thing I know about Leo is that if I just wait patiently, he'll eventually let me in on what's going on. It takes about four minutes.

"Lana's away," he says. "At rehab. It's one of the best facilities in the country."

I nod, feeling my limbs turn to putty. It's a relief, in a way, to get confirmation of what's long been lurking at the edges of my awareness.

Now that Lana's pill problem is a fact, I'm forced to face my feelings. *Poor Lana.* Maybe she was reaching out to me, that day I got fired. Maybe she was trying to ask for help, and instead I played along, treating the afternoon like a debaucherous game, and never speaking a word about it afterward. How shitty of me. My insides thrum as I think of Lana idling alone in their big, empty apartment while Leo's practically been living at the hospital. *Leo.* What must he be going through? I can barely look at his ragged face. "How are you doing?" I ask.

Leo shrugs. "I'm relegated to desk duty, for one. Someone stole my DEA number and used a fake name to fill prescriptions out in Staten Island. Painkillers, naturally." He looks exhausted. His tone goes official: "The hospital is conducting an investigation into my role in the matter."

"Oh, Leo." I place a palm on his shoulder, considering the two bombshells he just dropped—their weight, their seriousness, and hold on . . . *their connection?* Would Lana do that—steal from Leo, deceive him, and jeopardize his whole career?

"It wasn't Lana," Leo says, reading my mind. "You know what kind of saleswoman she is. I'm sure she had no problem charming however many doctors into writing her legit prescriptions, upping her dosage, anything she asked for."

"Good point," I say quickly.

"Anyway, I knew about the OxyContin. I just had no idea it'd gotten so out of hand." Leo shakes his head. "But she was in so much pain. I'm a doctor, for god's sake. I must be the world's biggest dumbass."

Leo looks so distressed. A tempest of fury erupts inside of me. It's one thing for Lana to abuse her own body. But to wreak havoc on her marriage, to deceive and hurt her husband, my brother—how cruel. It suddenly seems obvious: Of course Lana swiped Leo's DEA number. People are selfish and untrustworthy, no matter how well you think you know them. After slaving away for years to become a doctor, Leo's only mistake was getting close enough to Lana to give her the opportunity to take it all away from him.

"How could she betray you like this?" I blurt out. The nurse beside us winces and Leo's eyes go wide, and I realize my volume. I'm upset about more than Lana, of course. I'm picturing Gabe on the talk show couch with Talia; I hear in my question an echo of Gabe's accusation of me.

"Opioids are something fierce, Molly." Leo's voice is reedy and sad.

"So, what'll happen to you?"

"I don't know," Leo says. "For now, I wait. I'm trying to take it one day at a time." I hear how the language of addiction and recovery has already permeated his vocabulary. He might as well add that it'll be a long road ahead.

"Please don't tell Mom, okay? I'll have to share about Lana eventually. But hopefully not the other stuff."

"Of course. Tell me if there's anything I can do."

"Actually, there is something." I'm anticipating an errand, or a letter to the hospital vouching for Leo's integrity. But instead, my brother holds out a card for the rehab clinic. "Lana's allowed to get letters. I'm having trouble writing. She could use a friend right now."

The card feels toxic in my hand. What could I possibly write to Lana—hate mail? "Sure, no problem," I say.

When we return to the table, my mother remarks, "It's about time. I thought you'd been paged for a surgery and brought Molly in to assist."

Leo's laugh is halfhearted; ordinarily he'd make a dig about my lack of fine motor skills, which was apparent even on the softball field two decades ago.

We start chatting about wedding planning, which for once feels like the most innocuous topic. When Leo says he better get back to the floor, my mother pulls him into a hug. "I'm here for you always," she says, holding on tightly. "You know that, right?" It's as if she knows.

"Call me," I tell Leo.

"I'll see you next week, right? At Gabe's book party." *Right*, that.

Chapter 25

GABE APPEARS IN the bedroom holding two beers. He's back from California, and I'm packing for my girls' getaway. "Hi," I say.

"Hi." His smile is sweet, inviting, maybe apologetic.

I can't help it—despite my anger, despite everything, I still feel twinges of love, of lust. Gabe hands me a beer and flops onto the bed. The casualness of the gestures has me choking back tears. "Thanks."

"So, who all's going upstate?" he asks. *Am I going crazy?* I wonder. *Are things somehow fine between us?*

"Sam and Kirsten and me."

"Not Lana?"

I look at him sharply, confused, before it occurs to me that he doesn't know that Lana is in rehab. At one time, it felt like everything I knew was also known by Gabe, all of our thoughts permeable, transferred to each other as if through osmosis. But our boundaries have gone rigid. "No, not Lana," I say, zipping my suitcase shut.

Side by side, Gabe and I brush our teeth and then slip into bed. It's like a shadow dance version of our relationship, flimsy and delicate, our love a low hum, barely discernable. Obviously, we need to talk. But Gabe seems exhausted from his trip; within two minutes, he's snoring.

I, on the other hand, am wired. After much tossing and turning, I get up, thinking maybe I'll write to Lana. I pull out the notebook Kirsten gave me for my birthday, its cover plastered in trite commands: *Be the change you want! Say Namaste all day! Float on the wings of hope! Trust the power of positive thought!* I half-heartedly mine them for inspiration, then sigh and crack the spine.

"Dear Lana," I begin. I try out a casual, breezy approach, but after a few lines, I decide it's all wrong and flip the page. Next, I go for serious, but soon I abandon that version, too. I attempt half a dozen more notes, my tone at first furious, then forgiving, then formal, then flippant, then funny. Each version is genuine, in its way, even as they all sound fake, too.

I think about Lana. I wonder what her room is like in rehab, whether she's homesick, and what withdrawal feels like. I turn to a blank page and dash off a new note. It's simple: just wishing her well and saying I'm thinking of her. Before I can second-guess myself, I tear out the page, seal it in an envelope, and press on two starfish stamps left over from the save-the-date debacle. The design is pretty, Creamsicle-colored creatures sprawled onto sand, which I know Lana will appreciate. For the moment, this feels like enough.

When I slip back into bed, Gabe gravitates toward me in his sleep. I drink in his scent and his warmth and the snug fit of his limbs cocooned around mine. "My Molly-moo," he says, the words thick on his tongue. I've never known Gabe to sleep-talk, but his eyes are still shut when he starts kissing me. Despite all my reservations, I succumb to his touch. How strange it is to be in bed together, our bodies bare, in the most intimate of intertwinings, and yet still to feel so far apart. Maybe this is a détente. Maybe Gabe has let go of his anger at me. Maybe he's forgiven me, and hoped I've forgiven him too. And maybe I have. I sense Gabe climbing toward climax and, setting aside all the maybes, I give in to it, too. For a moment, I feel close again to Gabe.

Then he seizes the covers, his body twitches, and he lets out a loud fart. Soon, he's snoring again. My warm glow dwindles, replaced by an image from *The POV* photo montage: Gabe and Talia on a bench, taking in the sunset. *Wait.* I bolt upright. Gabe said the segment was a last-minute slot-in. *The POV* is taped live, in the morning. Was it a sunrise? No, I distinctly remember the sun bleeding out over the Pacific. Was it a green screen, the golden hour digitally inserted? No, it was definitely the real thing. So, was it a sunset from the night before? How long had Gabe known about the segment? Did he lie about it? And if so, what's the significance? Does it even matter? Suddenly spent, I collapse back into my pillow. Whatever game Gabe and I are playing, I feel like I've forgotten the rules and lost count of the score.

Needing a break from my thoughts, I reach for my phone. I open my email. There in my inbox is the one name I realize I want to see.

He can sometimes feel like a figment of my imagination. Practically living off the grid, like some kind of monk. A flicker from a faraway world. A mirage. When I emailed him last week, part of me felt I may as well have been beaming my message into outer space.

But, of course, Charlie Ashbury is real, flesh and blood. He even gets intermittent Wi-Fi out in the boonies of upstate New York. His reply is just two lines:

Hang in there, pardner. Remember Pizza Palace?
And then an address.

•   •   •

Pizza Palace. All these years later, I can still conjure up the salty tang of the four-cheese pie, and the beeps and bells of the pinball machine. Charlie worked there after school, and even before we were dating, I would go in and order a jumbo Coke just for an excuse to sit there spying on him. Charlie never seemed to notice the commotion or even his customers. He'd just stand around behind the counter in an ill-fitting visor, staring broodingly at something I could never spot, until the manager hollered at him to snap out of it and get back to work.

One day we were down by the lake, halfway through a twelve-pack of beer, when Charlie remembered his shift. We walked back across town, Charlie cracking me up reciting the daily specials, his speech all slurry. I wasn't so surprised when, hours before he was supposed to close up, he appeared at my house. He claimed a customer had gotten in his face about the wrong change, so Charlie pressed a slice into the guy's face. It was meant to be funny. But Charlie hadn't realized how hot the pizza would be, or that it would leave pepperoni-shaped burns on the guy's cheek. Charlie was fired; he was lucky he didn't get sued.

With no job, Charlie was broke, so for weeks afterward, I bought his lunch. I didn't mind, though. The whole Pizza Palace incident seemed absurd to me. Charlie's position was that he'd given that customer a good story to tell, which was worth a few minor burns, and I agreed.

Now, I click on the email reply window. I type, "Should I put in an application at Sandals 'n Such?" That's where Charlie eventually got hired after Pizza Palace, fitting old women's feet into ergonomically correct footwear.

I think about how, half a lifetime later, I too got fired after attacking someone—Summer Rose Lee, a name that still strikes me as fake. Thanks to me, she too has a good story to tell. But now, at age thirty, I find this rationalization much less convincing than I did back at age fifteen. I decide to take Charlie's advice: to hang in there. I erase my response, I put down my phone, and I kiss the cheek of my sleeping fiancé.

I don't fall asleep, though—I'm alert all night.

•   •   •

Sam's honk is right on time, and loud enough to wake the whole block. I assume Gabe is just pretending to sleep through it, but I sneak out without disturbing him, guiltily relieved to skip a goodbye.

Kirsten has made a playlist for the drive, half dedicated to Sam ("O-o-h child," "I got you, babe," "Be my baby"), and half to me ("Chapel of Love," "White wedding," "Wouldn't it be nice"); I can't help noticing the baby songs are better than the marriage ones. Sam's bowling-ball belly doesn't stop her from driving eighty miles per hour and careening between lanes like we're being chased. Still, I find it relaxing to sit back and listen as she describes all the bizarre things going on with her body—the varicose veins dribbling down her calves, the twice-daily nosebleeds, the cystic acne on her butt. This last detail horrifies even Kirsten, who usually speaks of pregnancy as a holy rite.

The rustic cabins sounded charming when Kirsten first described them. But now, in the fading light of a bleak March day, the bunk beds, the lack of electricity, and the diverse array of creepy-crawlers I spot sharing our space are less appealing. The three of us stay silent as the campground manager walks us the quarter-mile to the outhouses, hands us each a roll of biodegradable toilet paper, and claims its scratch-iness is all part of the fun of roughing it. Back in the cabin, I can tell Kirsten is gearing up for a pep talk. Sam plops onto a mattress, which wheezes dramatically under her weight, then Kirsten and I seat our-selves on either side of her, and the bed springs sound like they might give out. Sam emits a noise that's either laughter or the start of a ner-vous breakdown. It gets us all giggling.

"We don't have to stay here, do we?" I whisper.

"Oh, thank god," says Sam, already grabbing her bag. Kirsten shrugs and we return to the car.

I feel like we're the girls in *Troop Beverly Hills,* fleeing nature for a luxury hotel. Every year in college, the three of us watched that movie while gorging on the Girl Scout cookies Kirsten ordered from her nieces. Only this is upstate New York, not Beverly Hills, plus it's off-season. The only lodging we find within a thirty-mile radius is a doll-themed bed-and-breakfast with a single vacancy: the Barbie room, containing one king-sized bed.

In the mildewed lobby, Sam pulls us into a huddle. "We could sleep in the car."

"Let's just pretend it's the American Girl room," Kirsten says. She requests a key.

"Oh joy," Sam says under her breath.

"You mean 'Oh, Felicity!'" Kirsten says, looking thrilled. "Get it?"

"Sam, you should name your daughter Felicity," I say. "Then we'll finally have the missing member of our American Girl crew."

Sam screws up her face. "I'd sooner name her Gloom. Or Woe."

"Or Dolores," Kirsten says. "That's 'sadness' in Spanish."

The innkeeper clears her throat. "Dinner is being served. It's family style." The aroma wafting from the kitchen can best be described as grease, and sitting around the table in the next room are eight deeply lined faces, all rimmed with wisps of gray-white hair, all straining to check out us newcomers. The only sounds are silverware against porcelain. It's chilling.

"Goody, I'm starving," says Kirsten, right as Sam says, "We already ate."

"Maybe we'll catch dessert," I add, motioning my friends toward the stairs. The table's gazes stick to us like glue.

Entering our room, I take in the piles of Barbie dolls and related accessories. "Holy shit," says Sam, "it's a pedophile's paradise."

"I think it's, uh, nice," Kirsten says unconvincingly.

We change into our PJs and climb onto the one bed, where Sam hoards all the pillows to prop up her belly. Kirsten arranges a handful of Barbies into a line: Ballerina Barbie, Equestrian Barbie, Bridal Barbie, Rock Star Barbie. Sam and I watch in awe at our friend's transformation into a glib fashion commentator as she trots each doll across the bedspread, detailing their outfits and personal styles.

Sam grabs a doll, contorts its legs into a spread-eagle, and initiates a series of audible inhales and exhales. "'Help me, help me, I'm in labor!'"

She trots over a Ken doll. "'It's okay, bae, I'm here. I'll be dad of the year to the little twerp. What, you want an epidural? No way, sweets—we're going *au naturel*.'"

"What is this, play therapy?" I ask. Kirsten tosses me Bridal Barbie, and I run my fingers across her dress, a big pouf of taffeta with a gauzy pink overlay. I cover her placid smile with the veil.

"Sorry," Sam says. "Tom's had us on the circuit meeting doulas and midwives, even though I told him I'll be giving birth at a state-of-the-art hospital in Manhattan with all the drugs on offer. He thinks I still might change my mind."

"What's your take on eating the placenta?" Kirsten asks. "I hear it's very nourishing."

"Gross," Sam says. "I'm going Western medicine all the way. I'm trying to get my doctor to advance-prescribe me pills for the baby blues, just in case. And I'm fighting my insurance to cover a post-partum tummy tuck."

"Maybe you should launch a Kickstarter," I suggest.

"Project Eliminate Sam's Belly Jiggle," Kirsten says, laughing. She tries to grab hold of her own belly, but there's nothing to grab.

Sam chucks a Barbie at her. "Oh, don't be jealous of how fat I'm getting."

Kirsten strokes the doll's hair. "So, I have news. I'm moving ahead with adoption."

"Oh good," I say. "I knew Caleb would come around."

"Well, he hasn't yet, not quite. But whatever he decides, I'm going ahead with it." She sounds confident, but her smile is brittle. "If need be, I can always get some fancy firm job, quadruple my salary, and hire an au pair." Sam and I silently take in the weight of this. "It's fine. I'm fine. Or, I will be.

"Anyway," she says, waving a hand to change the subject, "Molly, tell us about wedding planning. You sent around those bridesmaid dresses ages ago. Did you pick one yet?" But I'm distracted, imagining the lucky baby who'll find his way to Kirsten from some faraway land. "Molly?"

"Huh? Oh." Kirsten's confession gives me the courage to voice aloud what I've previously only admitted to myself in private, fleeting moments: "I'm having second thoughts."

"Whatever you choose is fine with me. Any style or color or—"

"Not about the dresses."

I keep my eyes on Bridal Barbie, worrying the lacy hem of her skirt and flexing her stupid arched feet that only allow her to stand upright while in high heels. Kirsten's comfort is instantaneous: "That's totally normal, Molly. The stress is overwhelming, and you and Gabe have so much going on. Before my wedding I was so freaked out, Caleb and I got into a screaming fight over corsages. Corsages!"

"Maybe you're right," I say, although from what I recall, Kirsten and Caleb were more in love than ever in the lead-up to their wedding. Also, it isn't corsages that's stressing me out. Plus, it's only true that Gabe has so much going on; not me.

"It's just a case of nerves. And I'm here to help. Give me tasks, please!"

"Thanks, Kirsten," I say. "Are you guys tired? I'm wiped."

I catch my friends exchanging a look. Only after we turn out the lights do I realize that Sam didn't chime in at all.

◦ ◦ ◦

It's the longest night in memory. Wheezing, whistling snores penetrate the inn's walls, although apparently reaching only my ears; Sam and Kirsten are out cold, unresponsive to my *Pssts*. I'm freaked out by everything: the room's unfamiliar shadows, the distant creak of a door, and the inn's other guests whom I have a sudden suspicion are some kind of elderly coven. According to middle-of-the-night logic, the mass of dolls surrounding me seem like they might spring to life; tinny high-pitched giggles echo through my head like nightmares. My mind darts to Lana, off in another strange room, in some little town with a too-quaint name, experiencing whatever hell withdrawal is. I know I'm lucky to be here with my two best friends, even if they're currently unconscious. I try to imagine the future, when both of them are mothers. When they're busy with their babies, and Leo and Lana are working on repairing their marriage, and my mother is nestled in her love nest with John making waffles or not making waffles, and Gabe is at work on his next novel . . . where will I be and what will I be doing?

My urge to escape is too powerful to resist. I wriggle free from the warmth of the blankets and my friends, grab the first jacket I see, and tiptoe out the door. I soar down the staircase and around the banister, then race toward the lobby. By the front door, I freeze, startled by what looks like a ghost. It takes me a solid minute to realize it's just one of the other guests, in a nightgown, her silver hair streaming behind her like a tail. "Shthph *STOP!*" she hisses. It sends a shiver down my spine, even as I know she must be sleepwalking. I allow her a wide berth as I pass.

It's creepy-beautiful out in the moonlight, the air streaky with mist. I circle the inn a few times, relieved simply to be pumping my legs. I'm invigorated. I feel like my lungs can fit double their usual oxygen. When I shove my hands into front pocket of the borrowed jacket, my fingers touch metal: the keys to the rental car.

I haven't driven in months. It's a rush to gun the gas and zip down the pavement at sixty, seventy, seventy-five miles per hour, to steer myself wherever I want to go. And yet, I also sense I'm being driven by something external. I remember something Gabe said months ago—it feels like a century ago—about the larger forces at work in our lives. Fate. Navigating the dark, empty roads, I feel at once lost and guided, oriented and astray.

Later I will wonder exactly when I realized where I was going, and how I knew how to get there, and if in fact I'd known all along that I would end up there. I park the car and step out into air fragrant with foliage, the moon on maximum wattage, the stars a billion winks. New York City seems like it's on another planet.

It's 2:30 a.m., but Charlie appears at the door moments after I knock. He's in only his boxers, his skin pale with sleep, prickling with goose-bumps in the chill. My own skin is warm and buzzing. Charlie runs a hand through his mess of hair and then yawns with his whole body—arms reached, torso arched, muscles flexed. I feel as if my muscles have all melted. I have to remind myself to breathe.

"Hey, it's Molly," he says, matter-of-factly. "Gee golly."

I follow him into a cabin as cozy and cluttered as the one from earlier today was dreary and bare. I survey his things like they're precious artifacts: pressed leaves tacked to the wall, stack of geology books on the floor, liquor bottles and cans of peanuts on the counter. On the bed in a tangle is the knit red blanket that I recognize from all Charlie's other beds in all our other encounters. I feel outside of time.

Charlie doesn't ask what I'm doing here, or how I've been. He doesn't offer to take my jacket or invite me to take a seat. He just watches me, patient and seemingly uncurious about what will happen next. I, on the other hand, am so curious and so impatient that I think I might hyperventilate. I take off my sneakers and jacket, and have to stop myself from shedding everything else all at once. Charlie's face spreads into a smile as he takes in my outfit: flannel pajamas and fleece socks. I couldn't look less sexy if I tried. As if on cue, he says, "You're stunning no matter what, aren't you?"

I feel like I'm on a balance beam, teetering back and forth, like I have an equal chance of staying upright and stumbling over, of falling toward Charlie and away from him. His fingers against my waist steady me, and music cues up in my head. It's that sweet, slow song from all those years ago, when Charlie and I were teenagers waltzing around his room and then falling asleep in each other's arms, our first night together. I realize I'm humming it, and then I'm moving, sliding and spinning around the small space of Charlie's cabin. Whatever is happening with my arms and hips seems beyond my control, but this strange dance is all mine. I feel utterly myself, in all my versions—a child before I met Charlie, a teenager falling in love with my brother's friend, an adult reunited with my first love, the person I was a few months ago down by the lake on that frozen night, and me right here and now, Charlie's eyes tracking my every movement.

Oddly, my thoughts go to Dahlia, alluring maddening spirit of contradictions. I conjure up her striptease, that party performance and seduction and private expression all at once. Then I feel as though I'm channeling her, like she's alive in me, directing my movements, propelling me toward Charlie's body and into his bed.

Charlie takes me into his arms. It's both familiar and new, welcome and terrifying. The kisses and caresses are little shocks of pleasure, immediate and arresting, even as they also contain memories, and memories of memories. I drop into my body, synapses on high alert, swimming in sensation. Our desire for each other is like quicksand, a thrilling, bottomless acceleration. I feel like I've been holding my breath for months and finally I'm inhaling big, greedy gulps of oxygen. As Charlie moans my name, I flip myself over and press my face into his pillow, taking in his scent. His hands grip my hips, and his body is heavy against mine as he rocks me back and forth. He's kissing the nubs at the back of my neck, and tugging at my hair, and there seems to be no separation between his touch and my sensation. It occurs to me that I could be anyone right now: me, or Dahlia, or who knows who. The thought sends me over my first peak of pleasure. And then I'm falling, deeper and deeper into this space that feels both inconceivable and inevitable, that's at once uncharted and like home. I can't imagine ever climbing my way out again, and what a delicious relief it is to realize I don't even care.

* * *

234 · lindsey j. palmer

The spell of stillness is broken by the breeze tickling leaves against the window and birds announcing the day. Then I feel Charlie's wince against my chest. "This won't end well," he says, before erupting into a hacking cough.

I sit up, defensive, but Charlie points to two birds hopping up on a branch outside. "They didn't migrate this winter. Now they're stealing each other's nests and food and their morning song is off."

"So, it's more like their *mourning* song, with a 'u,'" I say. Charlie doesn't react. Gabe is the one who appreciates wordplay—my throat constricts, and I force the thought from my head.

"All the extra carbon in the atmosphere is mixing them up. They don't recognize the world they're living in. At the rate we're messing with the environment, a few of these species will be gone within a decade."

"That's sad," I say, wondering, *is this really what we're talking about—birds?* Also, *is any of this real? Am I truly here?*

"It's tragic is what it is," Charlie says. "Anyway, I think there's coffee." He gestures vaguely toward the kitchenette, before yawning and dipping back into sleep. Like all of this is perfectly normal, my waking up beside him in bed, both of our clothes strewn about the floor.

As Charlie snoozes, I listen to the birdsong. It sounds sweet to me. I wonder how he could hear these notes as somber. I'm hit with a wave of déjà vu—a memory of the yurt, waking up with Gabe, also nestled among trees, listening to the birds, lying under the same wide sky. A wave of shame rolls through me. Suddenly, Charlie's body feels sweaty and hot at my side, his leg like dead weight on my hip. I wriggle out from under it, catching a whiff of his sour breath, and I feel disgusted— with him, with myself, with humanity in general, and again specifically with myself.

The chilly air is a shock to my skin. I'm still shivering even after I pull on my flannel pajamas, lace up my sneakers, and zip up my jacket. I take one last look at Charlie, slumbering obliviously in his fetal curl. *Hang onto this,* I tell myself, against my better judgment. The screen door makes an ugly screech on my way out, but I swear I hear something else, too. Charlie's voice: *Goodbye*, or, *Don't go*, or, *I love you*. Or maybe just the rustling of the trees. I tell myself it doesn't matter.

But I don't leave right away. Instead, I sit frozen behind the steering wheel, clutching the car keys. I watch the birds do their thing: flitting about, trilling and tweeting, pausing on a branch. To me they seem perfectly fine, happy even. But what do I know? Maybe they can sense they're in peril, and they figure, might as well enjoy themselves while they can. The truth is, I can't muster up much feeling for a bunch of birds. Really, I'm waiting, hyper-aware of the faded green rectangle in the corner of my eye, Charlie's front door, an idle image. Half of me wishes Charlie would burst through it and beg me to stay; the other half dreads the same thing. Everything around me looks peaceful and calm. I probably appear the same way. But inside, I am roiling and turbulent, and I know I don't belong here. I start the ignition and speed off.

Chapter 26

With no cell service, it takes me fifteen minutes of zigzagging to find a breakfast spot. Ravenous, I tear through two bagels before I'm back to the inn.

I pause outside the Barbie room, take a deep breath, and crack the door. "Hey guys," I say, aiming for breezy. "I was up early, so I ran out for bagels and coffee."

Kirsten hops out of bed. "Carbs and caffeine, hurrah!"

"How early?" Sam asks. I feel her eyes on my neck, where I didn't think to check if Charlie's nibbling left evidence. "And why'd you go out in your pajamas?"

I shrug. "You were both snoring like steam engines. I don't know how your guys deal with you."

"I don't know how yours deals with you," Sam says, low enough that I can pretend not to hear.

"Everythings for Sam and me, and sesame for you, Kirsten." As we eat, I tell the story of my middle-of-the-night doll phobia; it's entertaining in the light of day.

* * *

We ask the innkeeper to recommend a hike. "There's a trail down the road," she says, eyeing Sam's stomach. "Mostly flat."

Sam is moodily silent, and I don't have the energy to converse. Luckily, Kirsten can be counted on to keep up a chipper monologue about the plants, the bugs, the view. "I can totally imagine living in a place like this," she says. "I'm starting to feel super-over the city." I murmur a vague acknowledgment.

Half a mile in, we spot two fellow inn guests ahead on the trail. The woman is stooped, taking tentative steps, as the man guides her with a hand on the small of her back.

"How romantic," Kirsten says. "Think of all they must've been through together."

"Sweet," I say, but really I'm eyeing their decrepit figures and mulling over the cruelty of time. I flash on a disturbing thought: The older we get, the more terrible acts we have a chance to commit; maybe aging is just the piling up of so much guilt and shame until our insides can't take it anymore, and then our bones start disintegrating and our skin starts wrinkling and sagging. I hold up my hands to examine them for age spots.

"So, guys, what should we watch next for Netflix-and-Spill?" Kirsten asks.

"I hear some people really like *The Affair*," Sam says. "Or *Big Little Lies*." She's walking behind me, and her words feel like stabs in my back. I pick up my pace.

"Let's do a comedy for once," Kirsten says. "*The Good Place* looks fun."

Her bright suggestion hangs in the air, until Sam sighs and says, "I'm not feeling this. I'm gonna head back." She stalks off, and I think, *Good riddance.*

"Jeez, it was just an idea," Kirsten says. "What's with her?"

"Probably hormones."

The way Kirsten picks the thread back up, it's as if she just finished telling me her adoption plans: "Anyway, once Caleb really, truly understands that I won't give up on motherhood, I know he won't give up on me. Maybe an ultimatum sounds silly and lame"—I shake my head; who am I to judge anything?—"but I've never wanted anything so badly. You know?" I switch to nodding, even though I have no idea. "It's like, *you* would never stand in the way of Gabe writing because you know how important it is to him. That's what it means to be in a committed relationship."

"Uh-huh." A fly buzzes by my ear; my head is all white noise.

"And if I'm wrong—if Caleb feels stronger about *not* adopting than about being with me, then I suppose that's what's meant to be." Kirsten shrugs.

I know I should wrap a comforting arm around my friend, or tell her how brave she is, but her words make me feel like the world's biggest coward, and all I can think to say is, "Let's turn back, too, okay?"

∙ ∙ ∙

I'm almost relieved when, over watery coffee in the inn's dayroom, Sam says in her faux-casual way, "Hey, didn't you say that dude Charlie got a job as a ranger around here?" She was like a ticking time bomb and now I can stop bracing myself, waiting for her to explode.

"No way!" Kirsten says. "That guy you dated, Molly? Leo's friend?"

"I bet he'd give us a tour of the park," Sam says, looking intently interested in the contents of her mug, ignoring my glare. "We could learn about leaves and worm species and all that shit."

"Since when do you care about worm species?" I say, again trying for breezy, but I can hear the edge in my voice. "Anyway, I guess Charlie does work around here, but I'd prefer to hang around with just us. It's a girls' weekend, isn't it?"

"Is it?" Sam says, voice sharp. "Come on, live a little. Let's do it."

So, we do. I make a show of consulting a map. I even send us on a detour, attempting to get us lost, but Sam's sense of direction, like her determination, is keen. Inside the park, she pulls into a spot just a few feet from the one I vacated this morning. We all get out, and Sam locates a ranger. To my disappointment, he doesn't say that Charlie is off-duty, or incapacitated, or un-findable. Instead, he points a firm finger at the information center.

This time Charlie does look surprised to see me. He also looks hungover and exhausted. His ranger uniform hangs on his limbs. I'm suddenly furious at myself. I try to purge the anger from my voice: "Charlie, you remember Sam and Kirsten. Sam suggested we drop by for a tour."

"Ah," Charlie says. I feel him searching me for answers, but I avoid eye contact in favor of a display on the American bison. "Well, as much as I'd like to show you ladies around, I'm on duty until closing. It can get pretty crazy up in here." He gestures around; we're the only ones there. "Someone's gotta reign in the chaos."

Kirsten blinks, maybe waiting for a better punch line. She's never understood the appeal of Charlie, although she's too kind to admit it. But Sam has about-faced into charming flirt mode. With a hand on Charlie's bicep that makes me want to abandon her in the middle of an unmarked forest trail, she interviews him about whatever she can remember from high school biology: food chains, deforestation, the carbon cycle. Charlie is rendered helpless by the attention; pregnant belly notwithstanding, Sam must be an alluring anomaly among the park's usual visitors.

I can't help it: I swat Sam's hand away from Charlie's arm. "He said he's busy. I think we should go."

"Is there a gift shop?" Kirsten asks. "I'm a sucker for a souvenir."

"Fine, we'll leave," Sam says. "But we came all this way, we may as well document it." She whips out her phone and, before I can blink, snaps a selfie of the four of us. "Oh, cute!" There's no way it's cute—we're barely congregated, all looking in different directions. "And look, I have a few bars of cell service. I'm just going to upload this to Instagram, hashtag no filter."

"Sam," I say.

"What?" She looks up, thumbs hovered over keypad, her pose of innocence so convincing that only a best friend would suspect the challenge beneath. Charlie, somehow, has the sense to flee; he produces a pack of cigarettes and slips outside. "What?" she says again.

"Stop it."

"So, you *don't* want me to post a photo of you and Charlie to social media?"

"Cut the crap, Sam. Obviously I don't want that. Why are you being such an asshole?"

"Finally!" She throws her hands up in the air. "I wondered what it was going to take to get you to admit your feelings. After lying through your teeth to us all morning. After months of moping around, throwing yourself a pity party. And why? Because Gabe wrote a book acknowledging that he used his penis before he met you, and *boohoo*, you're sad, but you won't even talk to him about it. After flipping your shit and getting yourself fired, and then embarking on a top-secret life of spending and screwing, of lying to and alienating anyone and everyone who gives a shit about you. Finally!"

"Excuse me, but how is any of this any of your business?" I ask.

"I'm your best friend, Molly! I care about you, believe it or not. But I'm so sick of trying to help you when you keep blowing me off to go fuck up your relationship and everything else in your life!"

I'm seething. "Sam, I never asked you for your help! Also, you are *such* a hypocrite. You're up on your high horse, when meanwhile, you have never once not done whatever and whomever the hell you wanted."

"You're right, I've slept with other guys while I've been with Tom," she says. "But guess what? Tom knows because I tell him! He and I are grown-ups who actually talk about things and make decisions together.

Shit happens. I got pregnant, and we talked about it, and now we're having a baby. I'm sorry, Molly, but when's the last time you said one goddamn honest thing to Gabe, or to me or Kirsten, or to yourself, for that matter?"

I'm too stunned to speak. And Sam isn't done berating me: "No wonder Gabe thinks it's okay to pull some stupid publicity stunt palling around with his ex-girlfriend to sell his book."

I don't know when exactly Kirsten meandered over. "You guys, what's going on?" She's panicky, looking back and forth between the two of us. "Molly? Sam?"

I squeeze her hand. "I'm sorry, Kirsten." And then I take off.

* * *

I've suffered from motion sickness ever since I was a kid. Whenever Leo wants a favor, he brings up the time when I, aged nine, spewed chunks onto his lap on a family road trip. Thankfully, there's no one next to me on this Greyhound, so I can sprawl across both seats while concentrating on not vomiting. That's preferable, anyway, to thinking thoughts of any real substance. Still, I can't stop Sam's taunt from playing on a loop in my head: *When's the last time you said one goddamn honest thing to yourself?* Well, here's an honest thought: If I hadn't come across a bus station a mile from the park visitor center, I'm not sure what I would have done. Actually, scratch that. *Honestly*, if I hadn't come across a bus station a mile from the park visitor center, I would've doubled back to Charlie's cabin, spent another night there, and subsequently despised myself for it. But, luckily, it didn't come to that. So now I'm halfway back to the city, with approximately half a shred of pride intact.

I was supposed to be gone another night, and my clothes and toothbrush and house keys are all still upstate, languishing among the Barbie dolls. So, I take a Lyft from Port Authority to Leo's apartment, praying he has the night off. When he answers the door, I nearly leap into his arms.

"Hey," he says, clearly not as thrilled to see me as I am to see him.

"Can I crash on your couch for the night?"

"Uh, okay, but can I ask what you're doing here?"

"Being here for you. Duh." I again hear Sam's taunt in the back of my head. "Well, that and other stuff I'd prefer not to talk about at the moment."

Leo doesn't push me. "All right. Then let's not talk about anything, okay?"

"Deal."

We settle in to watch whatever's on TV, which turns out to be *The Little Rascals*. A few minutes in, I realize I know what's coming next. A distant memory arises of our hometown movie theater, of splitting a box of Junior Mints with Leo, of making him hold my hand through the whole movie even though it wasn't scary. It must've come out when I was six or seven. I get chilly and ask Leo for a sweater. The one he hands me smells like Lana, and somehow it only makes me chillier. I squeeze my brother's hand.

He squeezes back, and says, "Let's just watch the movie." And we do. But I don't let go of his hand, and he doesn't let go of mine, either.

* * *

Leo's couch is more of a statement piece than a piece of furniture designed for human comfort. I'm fitful for hours, illuminating my phone screen every few minutes only to discover again and again that no one is trying to reach me—not my friends, not Gabe, not Charlie, not even my mother.

I've never been a good sleeper. When I was little, I begged my parents to teach me how to fall asleep. I wanted a real lesson, like the ones I'd had on tying my shoes and reading my ABCs. Counting sheep,

244 · lindsey j. palmer

listening to soothing music, deep breathing—none of it worked. My mom would plead with me, *Aren't you tired?* Of course I was tired— that was the whole problem. Having a problem didn't mean you knew how to solve it.

My father understood. He'd stay up with me, and make us peanut butter toast and mugs of warm apple cider. Then we'd sit at the kitchen table reading—*The Boston Globe* for him, a Ramona book for me. My father taught me the word "insomnia" and told me some of the smartest people suffered from it: Abraham Lincoln, Vincent van Gogh, our president. He made me feel proud of my inability to shut off my thoughts. The hours of the night would stretch out and swirl and slowly slip away, until the sun finally peeked out from the horizon. I remember those nights as some of my happiest.

But then my father got sick, and he started sleeping all the time. Meanwhile, I slept even less. I'd make my own peanut butter toast and keep vigil at his bedside. My mother let me do this during the daytime, but if she caught me lurking by the bed in the middle of the night, she'd toss off the covers and march me back to my room. "Big girls sleep through the night—in their own beds," she'd say, deaf to my pleas to stay. "You're a big girl, aren't you?" For hours, I'd watch the shadows dance across my walls, wondering if one day I'd get sick and then finally be able to sleep, too.

Around that time, I started slipping into Leo's room and tucking myself into his bed. I'd wiggle into his warmth and nuzzle against the scratch of his pajamas. My brother slept deeply; without waking up, he'd lift an arm to accommodate me. There in his bed, I could finally rest.

I do the same thing now, drifting from Leo's couch to his bed. And just like all those years ago, he lifts an arm to let me in beside him. My brother's breathing is a soporific, and when I'm close to drifting off, I whisper, as if something is wresting the words out from inside of me, "I spent the night with Charlie." It's such a relief that tears spring from my eyes. Leo murmurs, maybe in his sleep, and then he flops over and flings his arm around me. In that way we sleep, like little kids.

* * *

After two nights in two different beds with two different men, I'm back in my own bed, waiting nervously for Gabe to return home. The bed is made up with Power Ranger sheets, rough and scratchy against my skin. I gave them to Gabe as a joke after his mother revealed that as a boy he'd slept with all the action figures, throwing a tantrum if one went missing. Only when we haven't done laundry in weeks do we resort to using them.

At one a.m., Gabe texts me that he's crashing at his parents' hotel—they're in town for his book party. After that, I sleep fitfully, splayed out across the bed, waking frequently to the glares of the brightly costumed superheroes. Even through their alien-like helmets, I feel their judgment.

Chapter 27

GABE'S BOOK PARTY is at the bookstore where he took me on one of
our first dates. It was at the height of that early exciting phase of the
relationship, when the two of us felt so full of potential, the air between
us practically fizzing with it. Gabe was my treasure trove, any snippet I
discovered about him gold. As we wandered the bookstore arm in arm,
I loved watching my new boyfriend run his fingers along the spines of
books like they were holy, this space his house of worship. He held up
volumes and shared how each one had affected him. Sheepishly, he confessed his dream: to see his own name displayed in the store window
one day for his own book reading. I dreamed along with him, feeling
proud to be his partner. That's when I came up with my private name
for him: "Scrabe," Scribe + Gabe.

Gabe introduced me that day to E.B. White's book of essays *Here is
New York*. Like me, White was a Maine native transplanted to New
York, and his words felt like they could've originated from inside my
head. Since my first days as an NYU freshman, I'd always felt ambiva-
lent about the city. I was in awe of the noise and the activity, so different
from the hushed, wide-open spaces I was used to. I was equal parts
impressed and intimidated by the throngs of people all doing their own
things, all seeming so sure of themselves, unbothered by the hordes of

neighboring bodies. I understood the ironic magic of New York, that within the crowds was the potential for a person to feel freer, to find one's own place—even if I personally hadn't yet fulfilled that potential. Getting to know Gabe started to change that.

Gabe bought me a copy of *Here is New York* and we read it aloud together. It was a paean to the city and its settlers, those who powered the streets with passion, those who found a deep belonging here precisely because of its constant churn and change. Zipping around the city with Gabe made me feel finally like I too was one of those settlers, an essential part of the place. I was falling in love twice over—with a guy and with a place. I told this to Gabe, and he inscribed my book: "To my favorite New York settler."

Walking to the bookstore now, I reconsider his dedication. Settlers are pioneers, adventurers, seekers of something new. But eventually they settle down, settle disputes, settle for what comes . . . or not, I suppose. One can always *un*-settle. It's exactly how I feel at the moment: unsettled.

Gabe's dream has officially come true. There it is, I see: his name displayed in the bookstore's window. The sidewalk chalkboard is a work of art, no doubt the creation of some vastly overqualified bookseller. The announcement, "Gabriel Dover, *The Charms of Dahlia*, March 15th, 7 p.m.," is drawn into a billow of smoke; it comes from a cigarette that's held by a replica of the woman from the book cover.

I spot him inside the store: Gabe, my Scrabe. E.B. White described New York as a poem whose magic is at once real and elusive. I feel it standing here on the sidewalk, noticing a smudge in the corner of Gabe's chalked name, and watching him through the glass, surrounded by people who've come to celebrate him.

Inside, I find Gabe, peck his cheek, and then withdraw. I don't want to break the spell halo-ing around him, the well wishes of his parents and friends, his coworkers and acquaintances, and a smattering of people I don't recognize. I get a glass of wine and hang around the periphery, revisiting the books from Gabe's show-and-tell years ago, the authors' names stamped in bold lettering across the covers: Carver, Exley, Kesey, Robbins, Salinger, Updike, Vonnegut, Wolff. Now the books strike me not as sacred but stale, a bunch of old men and their tired prose. How arrogant it seems to declare yourself an author, to consider your private thoughts worthy of publication and an audience. At the edge of my hearing is Gabe's full-throated laugh.

I'm two generous glasses of wine in when Kirsten and Caleb arrive. Caleb greets me with a hug. "I hear you girls had a blast upstate," he says. "Kirsten noticed you left a few things behind." My friend wordlessly hands me my duffel bag, her forehead wrinkled with concern.

"That's me, always so forgetful." My cheeks go hot under Kirsten's gaze. "Thank you for coming. It'll mean a lot to Gabe."

"Let's go greet the author," Caleb says. As he leads Kirsten through the crowd, he places a hand on the small of her back, the same gesture of the elderly man on the trail upstate. It's impossible to imagine the two of them splitting up. I return to the wine station for a refill, then weave my way through the store. When I spot Kirsten loitering in the children's book nook, I duck and head the other way.

Each ding of the doorbell draws my eye to the entrance. Every face is a disappointment. Only when the store owner announces that it's time to get started and the rows of seats fill do I realize whom I've been waiting for: Sam. I check my phone—maybe she texted—but the only message is from Leo, saying he's battling epic traffic but on his way. As Gabe is called up to the lectern, I find a spot to stand in the back. When Leo slips in, I see him look around for me, give up, and then hover at the side.

The owner is finishing her introductory remarks, about how Gabe has been a loyal and longtime supporter of the store, and how proud it makes her when members of the community become authors. "With that, I'm thrilled to announce Gabriel Dover, to officially launch his debut novel, *The Charms of Dahlia*."

The applause is generous and resounding. I clap until my palms sting, conjuring up all I've felt about this book over the past six months. At the peak of the acclaim, the doorbell dings again. In walks Talia. It's like slow motion, how she saunters before the crowd in her slinky slip dress and claims a seat front row, center. Surely she planned this late arrival, this opportunity to make an entrance. It's an announcement of her import, her essentialness to the book and to this event and, of course, to Gabe. A moment later, Jonathan slips in, too, looking disgruntled.

I feel the burn of eyes on me, awaiting a reaction. Strangely, anticipating tonight, I forgot to worry about Talia. Scrutinizing her sexy getup makes me feel frumpy in my jeans and t-shirt, even as I know that her outfit, not mine, is the outlier. I notice she's wearing jellies—odd, although not as odd as the fact that I remember them from the first time I met her, at that long-ago reading of Gabe's friend. This can't be a coincidence. *Nothing has changed,* her footwear seems to be implying; *I've still got a hold on him.* I swig back the rest of my wine, deposit the empty cup at my feet, and immediately trip on it, producing an awful plasticky screech; I raise an apologetic palm to the hushed room.

Once again, Talia has distracted me from Gabe—or, I've let her distract me from him. I've missed Gabe's opening remarks. When I tune back in, he's clearing his throat, bending back his book's spine, and starting from the start: "It had been five weeks, six days, and nine hours since Russell had kissed a girl."

The words are an echo of a different time. I first read them half a year ago, I realize, when I felt so proud of Gabe, when I had yet to learn the contents of his book. I can't help it—tears start pooling in my eyes. I retreat once again to the wine station, and when I return with my full, sloshing cup, Gabe is reading about Russell's breakup with his high school girlfriend, and his new college friends ridicule of his heartbreak: "They didn't know what it meant to have a partner and a best friend whom you trusted and respected to the core of your being."

I repress an eye roll. This whole "to the core of your being" business is so juvenile and idealistic, like declaring, "All you need is love." No one should trust anyone else to the core of their being. But maybe that's the point—it's a description of teenage sweethearts, after all. Although maybe this really *is* Gabe's idea of true love. As I'm debating the point, Gabe looks up from the podium and, for the first time—maybe coincidentally, maybe not—he catches my eye. His expression is inscrutable. I realize I have no idea the extent to which he trusts and respects me. Certainly not to the core of his being. Maybe not at all.

"When Russell first laid eyes on Dahlia," Gabe reads on, "he didn't feel trust *or* respect. He felt lust." Talia shifts her position so aggressively that her chair squeaks, a reminder to everyone present that she is the muse for this lust-worthy creature. I watch Jonathan place a hand on her arm, and Talia shrug it off. Kirsten catches my eye, and we both giggle silently. How thankful I feel for my friend.

Gabe's voice has gone misty, describing how Russell fell instantly for Dahlia and her charms, and then their preposterous flirtations, followed by a first kiss. "He was already a little in love, and he knew this was only the beginning."

Look up, I silently beg Gabe, gulping down the rest of my wine. Look up now, smile or wink or acknowledge me in any way at all, and I'll set aside my fury at this fictional bullshit, and at all the ways you've sold us out in favor of your ambitions. I'll own up to my own bullshit and we'll figure it out together. We'll find a way to rebuild our trust and respect for each other, if not to the core of our beings then at least enough to be okay. We'll repair our friendship, our partnership, our love.

Gabe does look up. But—and maybe this, too, is a coincidence, but I suspect not—I watch as he catches Talia's eye. I watch her beam at him, and I watch him reflect the beam right back at her. This is *their* moment. I feel as though I've been hollowed out, my insides evaporated.

The thing about ending up empty is that there's suddenly all this space. And trickling in to fill it is a clarity: There's no way back for the two of us.

I don't care if I'm making a scene. I push through the crowd, whispering "Excuse me," and "Coming through," stepping on people's toes and shoving past their shoulders, all so as not to have to hear another sentence of writing by the man I was supposed to marry. The wine table has been abandoned, so I filch a half-full bottle and secret it into the single-stall restroom. I blink at myself in the mirror—hair dull brown, shoulders broad, complexion blotchy, the opposite of Dahlia in most every way. "Goodbye, Gabe," I say. Then I clear my throat and shout, "And fuck you," adrenaline pumping.

I text Sam, **I know you're mad, but please forgive me. I need you right now.** Then I lose my footing, I hear a loud thud, and, next thing I know, my cheek is resting on cold porcelain. I feel like I could sleep for a week.

Chapter 28

"Molly, I know all this book stuff has been incredibly difficult on you. For the record, I realize Russell is an asshole. He's sort of a younger, stupider version of me, but also sort of not. I know I've been an asshole, too. But I swear, absolutely nothing is going on between Talia and me. A part of me will always love her, it's true, just like I bet a part of you will always love your exes, and that's okay, isn't it? We've both made mistakes. I forgive you for everything. Can you forgive me, too? I love you and I want to marry you and spend our lives together."

I'm drawn to Gabe's body, his scent, his kisses so soft and delicate that I wonder if I'm imagining them. The sex is tender, almost nostalgic, like even in the moment it's more reminiscence than reality.

• • •

I bolt upright, my underwear damp, the dream version of Gabe already fading from my consciousness. My head is sludge, my body a shivery heap. There's a throbbing pain by my left ear. I'm disoriented, alone on a lumpy couch. Only when Sam appears in the room do I realize I'm in her living room.

"Oh good, you're alive," she says, forcing a mug of coffee into my hand.

"Barely." My voice is hoarse. "What happened last night?"

"Do you really want to know?"

I shrug. "A wise friend of mine recommended that I start facing the truth."

Sam smiles tentatively. "Well, by the time I showed up to Gabe's after-party, you were already wasted, with a huge bump on the side of your head." I touch the origin of the throbbing, and wince. "Right, that. Kirsten was trying to take away your drink, and when she finally succeeded, you grabbed the DJ's mic." I have a hazy memory of clinking a knife against a glass and demanding that everyone shut up and pay attention. "You delivered quite the speech. A kind of peace declaration to Talia."

"Well, that doesn't sound so bad."

"Right, until you abruptly changed course. I believe you called Talia 'a brazen bitch and a bully'—a nice turn of phrase considering your level of intoxication. You also blamed her for everything from your job loss to your need to get plastered to make it through Gabe's reading."

"Oh." My stomach churns.

"You did eventually congratulate Gabe . . . before inviting him to come celebrate with you in a bathroom stall."

"No! I said all that, in front of everyone?"

Sam nods. "Luckily, at that point, I was able to drag you away and force us into a Lyft. So, alas, we never found out whether Gabe would've taken you up on your little offer."

"I am so sorry."

Sam starts giggling. "I don't mean to laugh at you, but the whole thing was sort of hilarious. And honestly, I prefer the hot mess version of you to the weird, secretive stoic you've been lately."

"When you suggested I open up to Gabe, that speech is exactly what you had in mind, right?"

"Oh, totally." Sam's smile makes me smile too. It feels like a truce, and a silver lining to last night's debacle.

Sam goes to shower, leaving me alone with a hangover that announces itself again and again in waves of nausea and shame. I have a wish to burrow under the covers and wake up as someone new, someone clear-headed and steady and good. I pull a blanket over my pounding head and slip back into sleep.

* * *

I'm awoken by an alert on my phone: **JUSTICE OF THE PEACE FIANCÉ MEETING.** *Fiancé*—the word looks fake.

Why do I decide to keep the appointment? Out of inertia, I suppose, and because I can't find a phone number to cancel. Gabe must've had the same thought, because when I show up to the office, he's already seated, arms crossed, feet fidgeting. He glances at me with a mix of scorn and impatience. I feel both jittery and sluggish, like I've had several espresso shots on no sleep. I think about apologizing, but I can't even begin to figure out the scope of my sorry.

The justice appears. "Welcome," he says, taking one of each of Gabe's and my hands into his own. His smile is kind and open. It makes my eyes well up.

The justice launches into a little lecture: "Marriage is a rite, even for the nonreligious. As the institution has changed from a social and economic necessity to an optional arrangement, I believe it's become even more meaningful. When you have real, genuine choice, what you choose is more significant." He takes his time looking Gabe and then me in the eye. "Why, for example, would the two of you, who already share a home and a life together, decide to marry?" *Why, indeed,* I think.

The justice continues, his words slow and steady, without the hedging and stammering that litter most people's speech: "Is it to make sure that your partner never again looks at another man or woman in a romantic way? Maybe, but I doubt it. Is it to lock down the versions of each other that sit beside you today? Could be, but you'd be kidding yourselves. Is it to safeguard yourselves against any future loneliness or unhappiness or suffering? Surely, you know better than that. So, what's the point of getting married? Considering all the risk and challenges ahead and, one could argue, the sheer madness of hitching yourself to another fallible human for decades to come, not to mention the knowledge that so many good people have tried and failed at the venture before you—considering all that, why are the two of you here?"

Here, the justice stops, and my stomach starts churning again. The truth, clearly, is that we're *not* supposed to be here, Gabe and I. But it makes me wonder, what was I expecting out of marrying Gabe in the first place? Didn't a part of me hope for all of these things that the justice has just dismissed out of hand?

"For most engaged couples," he continues, "there's a desire for something more, for a new way of being together. There's a powerful drive or even a calling to commit to the bond of partnership, to love and have faith in each other, despite or maybe even because of your flaws and your humanness." Yes, I think, *exactly*. All of that is what I wanted and wished for with Gabe. Here, the justice's smile grows brighter. "A wedding is a declaration of that commitment to yourselves, to each other, and to your whole community. And what a beautiful thing."

Without warning, a powerful wave of nausea surges through me, swelling into my throat. A hand flies to my mouth, and I dart out the door.

I make it to the bathroom just in time to empty the contents of my stomach into the toilet. The purging exhausts me, and I stay crouched on my knees. I run the pads of my fingers along the etchings in the stall wall: a phone number, a heart, a crude sketch of a naked woman, a tiny, solitary "FUCK" without context or punctuation.

The bathroom door swings open, and I recognize Gabe's footsteps. "Molly? Are you okay?"

The swell rises again in my throat. After I'm done, and the toilet finishes flushing, I feel Gabe's presence on the other side of the stall. I open the door. From the look on his face, I know I must look awful. He strokes my hair, tucking a few strands behind my ears. It's so soothing, and already I'm mourning its loss. The tears come hot and fast down my cheeks. Gabe drops his hands to my shoulders. His touch feels like the only thing grounding me, like he's my gravity, and without him I'll just up and float away.

"We're not going to go through with this, are we?" he says.

"No." I want to add something else, knowing that this is its own kind of rite, its own meaningful choice—but my mind has gone quiet, my body numb.

Gabe nods once, efficiently. He doesn't look angry or relieved, only drained. "I just want to say a few things. At first, I was so angry at you for your paranoia that something was going on between Talia and me, when meanwhile I'd just decided to devote the rest of my life to you. I didn't understand why you were reading my fiction as real, and dismissing our real life—our engagement—as some kind of fiction. But the more strained things got between us, the more I started to confuse fact with fiction, too. The more you pulled away, the more appealing this pretend reunion with Talia became, especially since she was bending over backwards to show how much she wanted me. Things got . . . complicated. On one particular occasion, Talia and I—"

"Stop." I hold up a hand. "Please, enough." I appreciate Gabe's attempt at an explanation, but it's too much, and too late; I don't want to hear another word.

"Okay," Gabe says. "I'll go thank the justice for his time."

Walking home, Gabe and I stride side by side, both squinting in the sunlight, both stunned into silence. I'm struck by how alien our neighborhood looks, all the storefronts changed: the old boutique and bar and laundromat now a coffee shop and a bagel place and a bank. Last week's mural ads on the sides of buildings have been plastered over with fresh ones. Even the Gowanus Canal smells different, and I find myself missing its former stink. I think of E.B. White's notion that the city is defined by its constant churn and change. *What will this all be like when . . . ?* I wonder, not bothering to complete the thought.

I think of the justice's words, his point that getting married is a crazy venture by any logic, but that people keep doing it anyway, for reasons that defy reason. I look at Gabe, and I forgive him for not being the exact person I wanted him to be. I forgive myself, too, for loving him in an imperfect way and for hoping, despite my own imperfections, to be loved back. I forgive us both for getting fact and fiction all mixed up, and for ending up at this juncture that seems to be somewhere in between real and fake—I can't quite believe we're breaking up. I suppress a sob, and then I keep going.

Chapter 29

IT'S NEARLY MIDNIGHT when I show up on the doorstep of my child-hood home, disheveled and disgruntled after a six-hour bus ride. My mother opens the door. "Hi," I say. "The wedding's off."

"Oh sweetie." She leads me straight to the kitchen, where she fixes me peanut butter toast and warm apple cider, and then sits across from me, keeping vigil as I eat and drink, asking me no questions. Gratitude fills me, momentarily replacing my sorrow. When I finish my snack, she says, "I'll fetch you fresh sheets and towels."

In my childhood bed, I examine my fingers, newly unadorned. Gabe and I packed at the same time—he for his book tour, I for Maine—and on my way out it occurred to me to remove my engagement ring. I immediately felt lighter, no longer projecting my relationship status to the world, no longer pretending. I left the ring on Gabe's dresser, though I don't know if he saw it before leaving for D.C. I picture him there now, and I wonder if he's thinking of me here.

Canceling a wedding turns out to be surprisingly easy. Especially when you haven't done many of the things the wedding checklists say you should've done by two months out. Also, when you have the world's most capable and organized mother. She greets me at breakfast with a game plan: "I'll reach out to the vendors about refunds. I've already checked with the inn proprietor. After an intense negotiation, I convinced him to return the deposit in full. Your mom's a tough cookie!" She winks, and I conjure up a weak smile; I'm glad things are going well between her and John. "This morning, we'll pick out cancellation cards to send to the guests. The stationery shop in town—"

"How about Walgreens?" I say.

My mom nods. "Walgreens it is. After that's taken care of, we'll reward ourselves with ice cream."

"How about wine?"

"Wine it is. Anything else?"

"Just, thank you, Mom." She waves off this sentimentality. Today is all about practicality.

It takes me all of three minutes to pick out the font, color, and wording for the cards, and within the hour my mom and I are back home stuffing them into envelopes and stamping and addressing them, assembly-line style. "I wish Gabe were here," I say. "He'd enjoy this." I actually mean it, and this makes us both laugh.

We walk the cards to the mailbox. Releasing the bundle into the void drains me. I'm overcome by loss, and shame, too. A cancelled engagement is such an embarrassment—worse than a divorce, it seems to me, since Gabe and I didn't even have the staying power to make it to the wedding. I picture every person in our lives receiving their cancellation cards, trying to read between the lines for the real story of what went wrong, gossiping with glee or shock or disdain about our failure. Imagining this makes me dizzy; I buttress my body against the mailbox.

"It'll be okay, Molly, I promise." My mother's arm against my own is a support beam. "Be kind to yourself."

I nod. I wish I could fast-forward time, skip this whole part. "What next?"

"Wine, right?"

As if on cue, after a glass and a half, my mom starts pulling out the old photo albums. She's intent on finding evidence of the Halloween when Leo and I dressed up as attorneys. I have no memory of what sounds like the lamest costumes in the history of the holiday; I suspect she's invented it as an imagined tribute to my father. "Leo used to dream of working at Daddy's firm," she says, doggedly flipping pages.

"Come on," I say, "Leo wanted to be a doctor since before he could speak." Some of my earliest memories are of my brother checking the vital signs of our stuffed animals with a toy stethoscope. I'm flooded with anxiety before I can identify its source. *Oh, right*: the investigation into Leo and the faked prescriptions.

"I wonder how Lana's doing," my mom says. "I told Leo he should come spend a few nights with us, but he's too busy. Your brother never gets a break, huh?" I don't know how she does this—practically reading my mind. She returns to scrutinizing the album.

"I'll be back in a minute, Mom." I step outside and dial Leo. We haven't really spoken since the broken engagement. He picks up after the first ring and starts in on the smallest of small talk, treating me like I'm as fragile as eggshell.

I interrupt: "Leo, what's going on—with work, I mean?"

"It's all over, thank god." His sigh is audible. "I'm back on the floor this week."

"Seriously? Why didn't you tell me?"

"You had enough of your own crap going on."

"Oh, whatever. So, what happened?"

"It turns out it was some junkie who was getting her stomach pumped last year," he says. "They caught her trying to fill her third Vicodin scrip in a month at the same CVS. She had a slew of stolen DEA numbers. Good riddance."

"That's great, Leo. Congrats."

"Well, it's not like I achieved anything. But the good part is, now I don't have to burden Lana with any of this."

"So, you never even asked her about the prescriptions?" I'm ashamed to recall my own reaction, assuming Lana was to blame.

"No," Leo says. "I didn't want to pile any more stress onto her situation." I marvel at my brother's certainty, to have never doubted his wife.

"What a relief." Relief is the main emotion flooding through me, although it's undercut with a flicker of disappointment. Everyone I care about is coupled up, even my mom. Is it so horrible that a small part of me might wish myself some company in the breakup department—that buried under my relief about Lana's innocence is a tiny pebble of regret that she isn't guilty?

I tune back in to hear Leo say how much he misses his wife. "She'll be home in a week. Then I guess we'll start the long road of rebuilding our marriage."

Oh, right, I think guiltily. Lana doesn't need to commit robbery or fraud or to put Leo's medical license in jeopardy for them to have marital strife. And I don't really want company in my misery; what I want is for Leo and Lana to return to rock-solid. I consider the problems that tore Gabe and me apart, so flimsy in comparison to the ones Leo and Lana will have to work through. And they'll do it, bravely; they're pros. Gabe and I probably never had the foundation they have. Part of me knows there are as many ways to be married as there are marriages. Still, maybe Gabe and I were never cut out for the institution.

"And how are you?" my brother asks.

"Oh, fine, I guess. I'm here drinking with Mom, a reluctant passenger on her trip down memory lane. She's already paraded out the old photos."

"Do you need me to come up there and rescue you?"

"Thanks for the offer, but nah, I could use a bit more hibernation. And Leo, I'm thrilled for you about your job."

"Thanks, sis."

Back inside, my mother has earmarked a shot of me as a toddler barreling down the beach in a frilly pink bikini. "That ridiculous bathing suit was your favorite thing on earth," she says. "You wore it for days on end, throwing a tantrum when I'd force you to take it off to be washed. You were quite a headstrong little girl."

I stare and stare and can sort of conjure up this early attachment. Just as I can sort of remember the bliss of the beach, of splashing in the waves and building sandcastles and being chased down the shore by my dad—memories of a time before that landscape grew shadowy with heartbreak. Now it's happened all over again, the seaside spot where Gabe and I were supposed to be wed transformed to a landmark of loss. If only I had a version of that bikini now—if only a favorite piece of clothing could provide all the joy I needed in the world.

I yawn widely, suddenly exhausted, and my mom seems to read my mind again: "I found your old moccasin slippers. They're next to your bed."

I head upstairs and slip my feet into the well-worn sheepskin. It does nothing to address any of the messes in my life, of course, but my toes are now warm and cozy, and that's something.

Hours later, restless with insomnia, I drift downstairs. Splayed on the kitchen table is the photo album, a Post-it tagging a portrait of Leo and me with our father crouched between us, all of us in matching navy suits and ties, holding buckle briefcases. My mom's note reads, "See?! Daddy taught you to say, 'You've been served!' instead of 'trick-or-treat.'"

I stare at the photo, our three faces lit up like the jack-o-lantern behind us. How could I have forgotten this? I wonder what else I've erased from my memory. I think of my mother, so caring and supportive these past few days. I had no idea she even knew about the special snack I shared with my dad—peanut butter toast and warm apple cider—still my ultimate comfort. I wonder now, was she really so harsh with me after my father died? Did she really demand that I transform into the picture of goodness and decorum? I'm no longer so sure; my memory can't be trusted. It's a little scary to question what previously seemed so certain. But it also opens up a space in me. It feels like the potential start of something, the clearing of a new path.

• • •

Each morning, I chauffeur my mom to work and then use her car to take myself on meandering tours of my childhood, halfheartedly trying to connect the dots of how I got from then to now, from there to here. I drive past my elementary school and my high school and the various parks where I played as a kid and then revisited years later to drink with packs of friends after dark. Other sites I avoid—the lake, Pizza Palace, Sandals 'n Such, Charlie's street. This selective revisiting of my past holds my interest for a few days, before I grow restless. The following morning, I hang a left out of town.

It's a cool day in Ogunquit, mild for late March. The sea glimmers restlessly, drawing my gaze as I trace the lip of the Marginal Way. I'm headed in the direction of John's inn, not sure if I'll actually stop in. But as I approach, I see John squatting in a flowerbed, spotting me. I wave tentatively. He greets me like I was expected five minutes ago: "Molly, come see my tulips. They just came up."

"Your garden is beautiful," I say. The tulips are the hue of churned butter and the midday sun—a pretty palette for a wedding, I think idly.

John stands, his knees cracking one after the other. "What a nice day for a walk. Mind if I join you?"

"Not at all."

It's a little awkward. John is a leisurely stroller, the type I would barrel past on the streets of New York. Also, I can't think of anything to say. The only fact that comes to mind about John is his love of waffles. I want to apologize about the wedding, and thank him for the refund, but it feels funny to bring up.

"Your mother tells me you love the ocean," he says. Right, of course John and I have this in common. He's put down his roots at the edge of the water I grew up worshipping.

"As a kid, I'd play in there till my lips turned blue," I say. Until suddenly I didn't, I don't say.

"We could go for a dip. It'd be invigorating."

"Today? More like hypothermia-inducing."

"I got your mother to swear she'd swim with me on the first day of summer."

"*My mother*, seriously?" I'm shocked. "I've never seen her wade in past her ankles. My dad used to kid her that maybe she'd melt if she got wet."

We walk for a while in silence. "You know," John finally says, "your father was my divorce attorney."

"I didn't know he did divorces." Or, for that matter, that John had been married, or that he knew my dad.

"Just for a little while, according to your mother. This was twenty-five years ago. I guess, in the end, he didn't have the stomach for it: sad sacks like me, the bitter back and forth. Your father struck me as an optimist at heart."

"Huh." I'm so used to hearing and rehearing my mom's stories and replaying my own handful of memories of my dad that my conception of him is like a well-worn photo that's gone smudgy at the edges. It's odd to hear this new perspective: my dad an optimist who didn't have the stomach for breakups. I wonder if he'd be ashamed of me now.

"Anyway," John says, "I was a mess back then, and he really helped me. He was more like a therapist than a lawyer."

"Both kinds of counselor," I say, thinking Gabe would appreciate the observation. "How did he help you?"

"Well, he reminded me that it's easiest to take the path of least resistance, like staying in a situation you know isn't working. He reassured me that it isn't a failure to give up on something that no longer serves you. Leaving can be brave. It takes enormous strength to choose change."

I laugh a little. "You expect me to believe you remember all of that a quarter-century later?"

John shrugs. "What can I say? Your father gave good advice. It stuck with me."

"He was a smart man."

"He had to be to love your mother," John says. I realize it doesn't really matter if my dad told John those things or not. I like this guy, I decide.

John looks suddenly antsy. "I know this is strange timing, but I wanted to ask you something." He clears his throat, and I grow nervous. "I really care about your mother. In fact, I'd like to spend the rest of my life caring about her, and caring for her. I'd like to propose marriage. That is, if I get your blessing, and your brother's."

"So fast! What is this, a shotgun wedding?" It just slips out.

John doesn't miss a beat. "Yep, you guessed it, your mom's knocked up with triplets. Sorry, kiddo. There goes your inheritance." His laugh is full-throated, and contagious.

"Sorry," I say. I consider my next words more carefully: "If my mom wants to marry you, then nothing would make me happier for her. For both of you." It's the truth.

"Thank you, Molly. That means so much." John extends a fist bump, seemingly without irony. Despite my outburst, I actually think this fast track to marriage is a good sign. It speaks less to John's impulsiveness than to his willingness to commit to my mom. And she deserves him.

"Also," John says, "I wanted to mention, I've closed on another inn."

"Ah, so you are expanding! But in property, not in progeny."

John smiles. "Rumor is, you're a pro at hiring and managing business matters. I could really use your talents for the new inn, especially for the summer season. What do you say about becoming my Human Resources Director, salary negotiable. That is, if you want a break from the rat race of the city."

"The rat race?" I've never heard anyone use this expression in earnest. I picture a pack of rats competing to reach a discarded potato chip on the subway tracks. My mood has gone punchy. I throw an arm around John's neck, like we're old pals. "Thank you for being so kind. It's a generous offer."

But I know I won't take him up on it. In fact, the suggestion to stay in Maine makes me realize how ready I am to get back to New York: to pack up the apartment I shared with Gabe and find a new home, to be there for Leo when Lana returns from rehab and for Sam through her third trimester, and to get my career back on track. "Alas, it's much too idyllic here," I say. "I think I'd miss the grime and noise of the city. Not to mention the rats and their races."

John nods. "Suit yourself. Hopefully I can convince your mother of the other offer. In the meantime, I better focus on my other beloveds, my tulips."

John returns to his garden and I'm drawn to the cliff's edge. It's high tide, and the water is making a valiant effort to fly up over the rocks. It's hard to imagine that in just a few hours, the pool beneath me will ebb away, leaving nothing but a stretch of sand. Even harder to imagine is that just a few months ago, I pictured Gabe and me standing in this very spot exchanging vows. So much in my life has since ebbed away— my engagement, my job, my money, my stability, my confidence. It's tempting to focus on all that's gone. But, as a result, here I am now, all potential, like my own blank beach. It's a freeing thought.

Back when Charlie suggested we make New Year's resolutions, I laughed it off. Then when Sam tried to talk some sense into me about my relationship, I fled. Later, when the justice of the peace sermonized on marital commitment, I only half-heard him through my haze of hangover and regret. And throughout the entire saga of Gabe's book publication, I obsessed over how someone else, not me, was worthy of starring in his story. I know I'm long overdue for a shift in focus—from the past to the future, from Gabe's fiction to my real life, and from all the noise and distractions to my own internal voice, however faint it's grown.

It occurs to me that I don't need a new year to make resolutions. I don't need an audience to deliver a speech. I don't need a wedding cer- emony or even a partner to recite vows. I'm finally feeling ready to make promises and to commit to them—to commit to myself. So, I do it. I compose the words in my head and then I announce them to the cliffs: "Starting today, I'll stop doing things just to meet or rebel against other people's expectations. I'll be honest about what I want, and do what's best for me. I'll be good to people, starting with myself."

The ocean's roar and the wind's whoosh form a chorus of "Amens." Among the reverberations, I imagine I hear my father's voice, too, giving me his blessing.

Chapter 30

GABE TEXTS ME a photo of a road sign that reads, NO PARKING. VIOLATERS WILL BE TOED. He and I both love these kinds of errors. I'm on a bus back to New York, and I spend the next half-hour trying to spot an error to send back. But Connecticut's road signs are all woefully accurate in both spelling and grammar. So, I text back, **Fingered too?**

Gabe responds with an open-hand emoji. Up until a few days ago, I might've spent an hour trying to interpret its meaning—fingered? high-five? stop?—but now I don't bother. It no longer matters, I realize with both sadness and relief.

There's a celebrity magazine in the seat pocket in front of me, and the first page I flip to features a giant photo of Larissa "LaLa" Laraby—she's inescapable. The headline reads, "Are wedding bells ringing for LaLa?" I half-expect Gabe's name to appear as the mystery fiancé. But, halfway through the article, I discover a different familiar name: Melinda Lowe, my old coworker. The article refers to her as an "up-and-coming statio-nery designer." Larissa was apparently spotted buying ten dozen of Melinda's "We're tying the knot!" cards, which are pictured in an inset. A month ago, this would've made me livid. Now it strikes me as funny, how person by person this reality star seems to be infiltrating my life.

Perhaps next I'll receive a press release about the binge TV club she's started with her new besties, Sam and Kirsten.

I take another look at Melinda's cards. They're stamped with a simple but elegant logo: meJLow. Before, I was dismissive of Melinda stumbling so easily into entrepreneurship. But now I see how impressive it is that she's struck out on her own. I remember my vow: Be good to people. I decide to email her my congrats.

Her reply comes minutes later, subject MOLLY! followed by a hefty paragraph:

I was planning to write to you this week. You can't imagine what a shit-show Funhouse Branding has become since you left.

I'm struck by the generous phrasing—she could've written, "since you got fired" or "since you were disgracefully ejected from the premises."

They've been hiring people who are pros at branding and styling themselves . . . but not so much our products! It's like a sitcom of a branding company: Everyone looks the part, but no one's doing any actual work! Natalie's on a hire-and-fire tear, so the office is basically a revolving door. Half the staff doesn't even know where the bathroom is!

I'm entertained by Melinda's observations, and touched, too. She's probably exaggerating, but it's kind of her to imply that the place has unraveled without me as its gatekeeper.

Full disclosure: I'm planning my exit, too, to go full-fledged start-up with my stationery (!). I'd love to tell you more. Can I take you to lunch? Somewhere with tablecloths and a decent Cobb salad? Say yes! Cheers, Melinda

I'm surprised by how excited I am by Melinda's offer. I write back immediately. Then I mentally scroll through my business-casual clothing, pumped at the prospect of once again putting on makeup and heels and heading to midtown.

*   *   *

Though it's been unoccupied for less than two weeks, my apartment looks abandoned, everything coated in a layer of dust. My thoughts drift to E.B. White, the change and churn of the city. Most of Gabe's stuff is gone, as is my ring from his dresser; in its place is a check for two months' rent—the full amount, not just Gabe's usual portion. That'll finish out our lease. I notice that the check's memo line is filled with Gabe's tiny print:

> I present the rent, 100 percent. Went to a book event. —the gent.
> P.S. Never meant the torment, the lament, the dissent. I no longer resent. I repent.

I waver between relief and annoyance. For so long, I've wanted this from Gabe, an apology, an admission that his actions have hurt me. But it's too late now. Plus, he's devoted at least as much effort to style as content. And written it on the two-inch memo line of a stupid check that I'll have to deposit into a ATM. I'm working myself up into a fit of anger, until I remember: Gabe is no longer my fiancé, no longer my anything. I force out a loud sigh. I fold the check in half and stuff it into my wallet. I let it go.

The mail is a pile of wedding-related catalogs, flyers for bridal trunk shows, and ads for honeymoon packages; I must be on every mailing list. I'm about to toss it all when, tucked among the junk, I spot a letter from Sam. She's sent back the wedding cancellation announcement like it's an RSVP, and scrawled on the back:

> Bummer that your original plans fell through. But now that you're free on my due date, will you do me the honor of being my plus-one in the delivery room? (I don't want Tom anywhere near my hoo-ha while I'm pushing out a human.) XO, Sam.

Of course I will.

There's also a card from Lana. I scrutinize the envelope's lettering for evidence of tremors or other trauma, but it's Lana's same old loopy half-print, half-cursive. Inside are pages of bridal gown sketches, plus a note:

> I call it the Molly collection. What do you think??? I've had so much time here to draw. I forgot how much I love it. It's like I'm back at FIT again. I might give it a go professionally . . . as soon as they let me out of this god-awful place (really, it's been a life-saver). Thank-you for your letter. I love you! -Lana.

I want to remain angry at her, for all the struggle and stress she's caused Leo. But I can't summon up the negative energy. All I feel is relief. Lana sounds good—breezy even—and so what if it took her as many drafts to get this down as it did for me to write my note to her? I do the math; she'll be home in two days.

At the bottom of the stack is a slim package addressed to me. I open it to find a book on bird migration, no card or signature. From Charlie, obviously. I guess that he's inscribed the book, and I'm right. Printed on the title page are four words: To continue your education . . . My stomach lurches at the ellipses, whatever their implications. Charlie must know that I won't actually read the book and start up an avian-themed correspondence with him. So, what then? I consider my options: I could toss the book and try to forget about it, and Charlie, too. But Charlie might interpret my silence as an enigmatic come-on—and he might be right. I remind myself of my vow to be honest about what I want and do what's best for me. I know what I need to do. I grab my phone and dial the string of digits that are etched forever into my brain.

"Hey, it's Molly," Charlie says. I hear a smile in his voice.

Lurking in my throat is a "Gee golly" response, but I swallow it. "Listen," I say.

But Charlie doesn't listen; he speaks: "I hear the wedding's off."

Of course, he already knows. "That's right."

I'm gathering my thoughts on where to begin, but Charlie barrels ahead: "Okay, so I'll apply for a bigger living space. There are these sweet cabins just above the tree line, reserved for couples. The park's operations department has an opening, and you'd be a shoo-in for the job. On our days off, we can go hiking and biking and I'll show you all the local swimming holes and breweries."

Charlie is persuasive, as always. It sounds like he's been hatching this plan for months. But knowing him, it's all impromptu, ideas he's convincing himself of even as he formulates them aloud, ideas he'll just as easily forget five minutes from now. "It's beautiful here in the summer," he adds. "I love the view."

"I love the view," I repeat to myself, head spinning. It sounds like, *I love you.*

"Charlie, stop." I have to say it twice before he hears me. "I'm sorry, but no. I can't move up there and play house with you. I can't meet up every few years when I feel like escaping whatever's going on in my life. I can't have both of us stringing each other along as our forever back-up plan, pretending that what we have is anything more than a fantasy. To tell you the truth, I can't be in touch with you at all anymore. Let's just acknowledge that we have wonderful memories together—several sets of them—and then both of us put the other in the past. Permanently, for good."

After a long pause, Charlie says, "Are you sure?"

No. I'm thinking of the afternoon a few months ago when I dragged him along on my shopping trip, when he made another grandiose attempt to convince me to be with him. He compared himself to a wildfire, the kind that destroys in order to restore, that clears away the dead muck and overgrown foliage to allow for new growth. I guess Charlie sort of has played that role for me. But now it's time to tamp it out.

Charlie asks me again, "Molly, are you sure?"

I can be my own wildfire, I think, willing myself to believe it. "Yes."

"Okay," he says, simple as that. This is something I love about Charlie. When he knows I'm being serious, he takes it seriously. He doesn't fight me, or demand further explanation, because what would be the point? It's almost enough to make me cave and say, "Scratch that, I'll be up there in a couple of hours." It would be so easy, the path of least resistance.

But I stay strong. "Thank you," I say. "For the book, I mean."

Charlie laughs, and I can admit it's one of my all-time favorite sounds. "You're welcome," he says. "For the book, I mean. Later, Molly."

"Later, Charlie."

Chapter 31

WHEN I ARRIVE at the restaurant, Melinda is already seated, two coffees on the table. "Milk and two sugars, right?" she says.

"Thanks." I'm not sure if I'm impressed or weirded out by her knowing how I take my coffee.

"So, how've you been?"

"Um." I debate how much of the past few months to get into—I settle on a simple "Pretty good."

"Glad to hear it," Melinda says, before pivoting immediately to explain the details of her start-up. She sounds just like I remember, a valley girl with vocal fry. But when I focus on *what* she's saying rather than *how* she's saying it, I realize her business plan is thoughtful and thorough. Melinda spreads a series of cards across the table and describes each one's target bride type. Now that I don't have to pick out invitations for my own wedding, my anxiety around the subject has vanished. Melinda's designs are cute and clever. She has serious talent.

But, I *don't* have talent—at least, not the artistic kind—and Melinda has yet to say why she wants my input on her designs. Does she assume I'm a potential customer? "I should mention I called off my engagement," I say.

"I heard about that," Melinda says. "I'm sorry." Then she's on to telling me about the funding she's secured. At one point, I might've interpreted this as cold, but now I appreciate Melinda's focus. We're former coworkers, not friends, and she's not pretending otherwise.

Finally, she gets to why she's invited me here: "Happily, business has been booming. But I can't keep up with the demand, and I need help with production and sales and marketing, plus the web site, and growth strategy." Melinda presses her index fingers to her temples. "There's so much to do, Molly, and only me to do it. Can I convince you to come on as a consultant and help me hire a team?"

This sounds interesting and refreshing. But, clouding my excitement is my last encounter with Melinda—her front-row seat to my firing. At the time, I was furious at her for her rubbernecking. Now, I feel ashamed at the tantrum I threw. I decide to broach the matter head-on: "Aren't you concerned about me? I mean, you watched me have a total melt-down as I got kicked to the curb."

Melinda shrugs. "I figured you must've had your reasons. I always give people the benefit of the doubt. That's why I wrote to you after you left."

I mentally scroll back through my email. "You did, didn't you? And I never responded. I'm sorry. It was a rough moment—or, a rough few moments."

"Don't worry about it. Though I have to say, I was surprised to hear from you, and that you agreed to meet up."

"You were?"

"Yeah, I always got the sense that you thought I was sort of a joke."

I feel myself go stiff. It occurs to me that focusing so much on how everyone else has wronged me hasn't left much space for considering my own wrongs against others. I think of Summer Rose Lee, that poor interviewee. And Natalie, my former boss, whom I owe an apology to. And Gabe, of course, and his complaints that I wasn't supportive or proud enough of him. I swallow the lump in my throat, knowing that all that's in the past, unchangeable. But now, right here in front of me, is Melinda, her mien earnest and open as she waits for a response. "I'm sorry," I say. "I'd like to think I've changed a lot recently."

"No hard feelings," Melinda says. Those three words, so simple, so casually offered, give me hope. They make me believe that maybe I can repair the other wrongs, be forgiven, and move on.

"So, about the gig," Melinda says. "What do you think?"

I nearly cut her off: "Count me in."

"Yay, this'll be great! I also have all these ideas for expansion: wedding favors, shower decorations, bridal accessories. I can't wait to hear your thoughts."

I think of Lana's gown drawings. "I have someone in mind who could help."

"Cool!" As Melinda packs up her designs, I can't help it: I ask about Jonathan.

"He and Talia broke up," she says, "if that's what you're curious about." I tear at my napkin, sheepish. "I'm pretty sure it happened right after you broke off your engagement. I hear Jonathan's writing a novel based on their relationship."

I snigger. "Jonathan always has to grab a piece of the pie, doesn't he?"

"He certainly has his finger on the pulse." Melinda says, basically echoing my point, only more charitably. I remind myself of my vow: *Be good to people.* Consequently, I don't even consider reaching out to newly-single Talia to say that she doesn't have a chance with Gabe—or, I only consider it for a split-second. I stand to shake hands with Melinda.

"So great to reconnect," she says, "When can you start working?"

"Immediately."

* * *

For our next Netflix-and-Spill meeting, it's my idea to revert to reading an actual book. Sam suggests a Shakespearean tragedy, with a big bloody finale. But I've been craving a happy ending, and Kirsten is as agreeable as ever. We opt for *Pride and Prejudice,* where every character of interest ends up in love, married, and filthy rich to boot.

All three of us have read the book before, in college for our freshman lit seminar, "The Georgian Novel and the Contemporary Feminist." The class featured two dozen girls plus, according to Kirsten and me, the cutest guy at school. Naturally, we nicknamed him Mr. Darcy. We spent hours flopped onto each other's dorm room beds recounting the meaningful eye contact we'd made with him across the room and dreaming about dating him, while Sam sat by rolling her eyes. In class, we debated which of the Bennett sisters were feminists—Lizzy, definitely; Mary, maybe; only Kirsten made the case for Jane. Kirsten's and my contributions were motivated mainly by a desire to impress our real-life Mr. Darcy, and we realized the irony of this, even without Sam pointing it out. But, at least for me, our communal crush was less about an interest in any guy than our own bonding; by the end of the semester, the three of us were inseparable. Months later, Sam confessed that while Kirsten and I had been sitting around swapping fantasies of Mr. Darcy, she'd been hooking up for real with our T.A. She called him Mr. Bingley in bed, she told us with a wink.

"First things first," I say when I meet my friends to discuss the novel again now. "I'm not in the mood to rehash the dissolution of my engagement." Kirsten wrinkles her forehead with concern. "Here's what I would like to do: drink two to three glasses of Pinot Grigio and talk about the fictional lives of Lizzy and Darcy, not my real one without Gabe."

"Fine by me," Sam says, waving over the bartender. "Let's get this woman some wine."

Pretty soon, it's like we've rewound back to freshman year. "Where do you think our Mr. Darcy is now?" Kirsten wonders aloud. A dozen years have passed since she and I last dissected his every gesture in class.

"He's probably leading meditation retreats out in California," I say, thinking of Gabe's parents. For some reason, this makes Kirsten's expression go dark. "Or teaching kindergarten in some super-progressive school in Finland—inspiring children by day, seducing their sexy Nordic moms by night."

"No way." Sam shakes her head. "I bet he's an accountant out in Jersey with a wife and a pair of bratty kids."

Kirsten and I gasp, like it isn't possible that the object of our intense affection and fascination could be leading such an ordinary life. But then we're quiet, pensive, because of course it's possible. That's the strange thing about time, how it swells and contracts, how in the decade-plus since our freshman year nearly anything could've happened, even as it also seems like our lit seminar let out just moments ago, like here we are, the three of us grabbing a drink, same as when we were eighteen, our legitimate IDs notwithstanding.

"Speaking of handsome men," Sam says, "I finally gave in and got a doula. It's a dude named Malcolm."

"Malcolm the dude-la!" I say.

"I'm stealing that," Sam says. "Incidentally, Malcolm the dude-la is H-O-T hot. And Molly, according to Facebook, he's single."

Her words shock me back to the present. The three of us aren't actually teenagers anymore, daydreaming about a crush. We're thirty-year-old women, and I'm the suddenly single one, which I guess makes me subject to set-ups.

"I'm flattered you thought of me while discussing your birth plan," I say. "I'll be sure to wear something alluring to the maternity ward." I finish my wine—one glass is enough—and I make a decision. "Actually, I'm going to try out being on my own for a while."

"That makes sense," Kirsten says, but then she flashes me a conspiratorial look. "But what if our Mr. Darcy appeared, like, right across from you on Q train?"

I raise my right palm, like I'm being sworn in. "I solemnly swear that if I spot Mr. Darcy on the subway, I'll ask him out. Otherwise, I'm officially on a break from men. I even called Charlie and told him we were done—zero future contact."

"What, why would you do that?" Sam asks, slapping my arm. "Just when you're finally free to do whatever you want!"

Kirsten *tsks* her. "I'm proud of you, Molly."

"Well," Sam says, "I'm holding out hope that you do run into Mr. Darcy on the Q train. Or better yet, the R, so you can canoodle through all the local stops, too."

I laugh, until I notice a look of anguish flash across Kirsten's face. Asking her what's wrong opens the floodgates: "It's just, talk of the subway. And this, the three of us here together." She clutches at both Sam's and my hands as tears stream down her cheeks. Sam raises an eyebrow and makes fleeting eye contact with me; the show of emotion is making her squirm. Kirsten inhales sharply: "Caleb and I are moving to Los Angeles."

"What?!" Sam yelps and flings Kirsten's hand aside. But I grip tighter and don't say a word. I think maybe I misheard.

"Caleb got a job offer from a top firm, and you guys know his family is all out there. Plus, we'll be able to have a home with actual space, and a yard." As Kirsten piles on each point in favor of her move out west, it starts to take on the sharp shape of fact. I'm already mourning the loss of my friend.

"So, Caleb agreed to adoption?" Sam asks.

"Well, not quite," Kirsten says. Sam's face twists up with skepticism. I squeeze Kirsten's hand, inviting her to go on. "It's under discussion. I hope he decides it's the right thing. I think he will, ultimately. But, either way, Caleb and I are two peas in a pod. We're meant to be together."

I'm still speechless, trying and failing to imagine my day-to-day life without Kirsten, without this trio that I've been hanging out with for my whole adulthood. I always assumed that if any of us were to break up our little group, abandoning the others for a new life, surely it would be Sam. Not steady, predictable me (although I realize this description is no longer quite accurate), and definitely not sweet, loyal Kirsten.

Kirsten darts her eyes at me in what I recognize as nervous apology, maybe because I've stayed silent. But who am I to judge her decision to stay with Caleb? As if I'm any kind of relationship expert or arbiter of marital relations. Heading west with her husband strikes me not as weak or cowardly, but courageous.

"Kirsten," I say, clutching her hand tighter, both our palms now clammy with sweat, "You'll love L.A. You'll finally meet people as sunny as you."

Sam snorts, like wishing Kirsten well were some kind of a betrayal. But that's not how friendship works. We don't get to stand in the way of our friend's happily ever after, or at least her happily enough for the time being. "Our devastation at losing you is slightly outweighed by our excitement for you." I nudge Sam. "Right?"

Sam shrugs, noncommittal. She turns to Kirsten. "Your terrible news is making the baby kick like crazy. If she has abandonment issues, that's on you."

"I promise to visit her, and her mama, as often as possible. Deal?"

Kirsten clinks glasses with Sam, and Sam takes a small sip. "The next time I can drink more than four measly ounces is, let's see, T minus fifty days." In other words, her due date. "So, when's moving day?"

"T minus one month."

"Ah." Sam finally sounds more sad than mad.

Kirsten looks at her feet. "I put in my notice at work already."

"And now you're putting in your notice with us," I say.

Chapter 32

WHEN THE SUBWAY is packed, I usually buy into the collective illusion that if everyone avoids eye contact with everyone else, we can all pretend we have privacy. But today on the N train, I look around, inspecting bodies and gestures and faces. I'm searching for that liquid brown gaze and that sharp cut of jaw that so dazzled me as a college freshman; I'm trying to imagine how twelve years might've settled into Mr. Darcy's face. I've nearly given up when my eye catches a different familiar silhouette: Dahlia.

It's the first time I've spotted a copy of Gabe's book in the wild. It's being clutched by small hands, the fingers adorned with chunky silver rings and a purple manicure. I look up to see a woman in her mid-twenties, legs crossed, wearing a chambray shirtdress and orange Toms; one flashes like a siren as she fidgets her foot. She's exactly the kind of reader Gabe would want, and I find myself feeling jealous.

I'm mesmerized, watching her scan Gabe's lines. At first, she's engaged, but after a couple of pages, her eyes wander to her phone and she starts swiping. She's startled by a guy sneezing, she looks up to say "Bless you," then she redirects her attention out the window. I watch for another few minutes as she returns to the book, takes in a left-hand page and a right-hand one, and then turns the page, sighs, and closes the book. It takes me a moment to realize that she's just finished it. She tilts her head to the ceiling, her expression inscrutable.

Finally noticing my attention, she catches my eye, half-smiling. I'm desperate to know why: Is it because she's satisfied with what she's just read, or relieved it's over? Or because we're having a rare moment of human connection on the subway? Or some other reason—or no reason at all? There's no way to know. As the conductor informs us of a delay at Thirty-Fourth Street and thanks us for our patience, the woman and I simultaneously look away, back to our respective silos.

It's not like it hasn't occurred to me that I haven't finished Gabe's book—that I don't even know how it ends. But a part of me subscribes to the idea that if I haven't read the whole thing, then it still isn't quite real, and there's still the possibility of a different outcome. Magical thinking, I know. I also know that scrutinizing strangers for their reactions to the ending is no substitute for reading it myself. But the thought of doing so still fills me with dread.

As the train lurches up over the Manhattan Bridge, I shift my attention out the window, to the wide swath of river and the city skyline. I spot the profile of a different woman: Lady Liberty. Her raised arm and golden torch seem to be reaching out to me, as if to shore up my confidence, as if to urge me to face my fear and finally finish the damn book.

* * *

But then, I get really busy. Melinda has given me a list of a dozen positions to fill. Kirsten insists I come over and play drill sergeant as she packs for California, forcing her to downsize so her luggage doesn't bury her. Sam cajoles me into helping her construct a slew of baby contraptions—a crib and a bouncy chair and something that looks like a mini torture device but that Sam claims is for diaper compression. Then my mother calls to say she's headed to the city and Leo and I must drop everything and meet her for cocktails. She has news.

As soon as I'm off the phone, Leo texts me: **Mom's getting hitched to that lumberjack, right?** I assume so.

We tell her to meet us at a bar called Something Blue, our little joke. Leo and I meet up half an hour beforehand. He seems a little jittery. "It's weird, right?" I say. "Here comes the bride, i.e. Mom."

"Kind of weird, yeah. But mostly I'm just excited for her. Plus, ever since she met John, she's been about twenty percent less in my business."

"True. Not to mention she's happy."

"Right."

"So, how's it been with Lana back?" I ask.

Leo angles for the bartender's eye, and waits until he has a whiskey in hand before responding. "Some stuff was expected. I knew it would be a rocky readjustment, that she and I would have to work at it to get back in synch."

I nod. "So, what didn't you expect?"

"Well, that Lana would still be in a lot of pain. Because the drugs only masked it; they didn't make it go away. And now she can't even take Advil." I don't know what to say. Leo shakes his head. "I see trauma every day. But when I send patients home, with prescriptions and instructions for healing, the assumption is they'll get better. That's how I picture them later: better, recovered. You just don't think . . ." He trails off.

"You're a doctor, Leo, not a god. Pain is a part of life."

"I know."

"And you're Lana's husband, not her savior."

Leo tilts the ice in his glass from side to side. I think he might say more, but before he has a chance, our mother swoops into the bar like a force of nature, and plops herself on a barstool between the two of us. She's twenty minutes early.

"My beautiful, beautiful children," she says. "Just look at you. You're both glowing!" She does this, project herself upon us—really, she's the one who's glowing. When she starts in about how much she loves us and always will and how nothing will ever change that, it's clear she's winding up to her announcement.

"So, what, you're splitting up?" Leo asks.

"Excuse me?" she says.

"He means you're giving the wrong speech, Mom," I say. "That's the divorce one, not the marriage one."

She looks conspiratorially between the two of us. "You guys know already?"

"John asked for our blessings," I say.

"He did not!" She slaps at the bar, beaming. "What a gentleman." But then her expression shifts to hesitant. "And you're okay with this? You know it doesn't take away one bit from what I had with Dad."

Leo looks amused. "I think we can all agree than twenty-five years is a sufficient mourning period."

We order Prosecco and share a toast. As sugary bubbles sparkle down my throat, I consider how nice it'll be to expand our little family trio—with Lana back home, and John soon entering the fold. I feel a pang, thinking of Gabe.

My mother squeezes my hand and looks me in the eye, the tilt of her eyebrows conveying a swell of empathy. I can tell she's about to deliver a speech about the sensitive timing of her engagement. I want to prove I'm fine, so I say, "You should get married over Memorial Day, now that the inn's free then."

"Molly," she exclaims, "how dare you suggest such a thing! John and I would never steal your wedding date."

Out of nowhere, she starts giggling like a little girl, in a way I remember from when my father used to play pranks on her; he'd tuck a rubber snake under the laundry or crouch behind her mirrored closet door and pop out while she was carefully applying her lipstick. He was always finding new ways to surprise her.

"What the hell, Mom?" Leo says.

She looks shy as she reaches into her pocket, pulls out a ring, and slips it onto her fourth finger.

I gasp. "You got married without us?" I'm incredulous, and a little angry. Suddenly I'm remembering the aftermath of my dad's pranks. I was always part of the planning, a co-conspirator, and when it came time for the big reveal and my mom's inevitable shock, she'd collapse into fits of giddiness, infecting my dad and me with the giggles, too. But after that, the two of them would drift off behind a closed door, their joy turning private and exclusive. I was shut out. A moment ago, I was dismissive of my mom's delicate reassurances about her relationship with John, embarrassed by her treating Leo and me like fragile children. But here I am remembering exactly how it feels to be a fragile child craving belonging and comfort.

My mom, on the other hand, has adopted my former flippancy: "John and I were free last Saturday, so we said, what the hell, and hopped on over to City Hall."

"Well, good for you," Leo says. "But we still have to celebrate. How about a party?"

The Bella So wedding gown appears like a pop-up in my mind. It's idling in the back of my closet and, even if I did have somewhere to wear it, it would be too tight for me now since my appetite has returned. My mother, on the other hand, is perpetually bird-like. "Mom, I have just the dress for you."

So, then we're back in my disheveled apartment, half of its objects recently vacated and the other half boxed up or on deck to be. My family is gracious, stepping around the detritus without comment as I go retrieve the gown. When I present it to my mother, for a moment we all simply stare. It's like a divine being, it's so beautiful. I see Leo take in that it's a Bella So, an artifact of his and Lana's past, and I feel myself mourning the sensation of it sheathed around me like so much hope and possibility. I see my mom hesitate to even touch it. "Go try it on," I urge her.

A few moments later, she shouts from the other room, "Oh, I look ridiculous!" But I hear the joy in her voice. It takes very little convincing for her to sashay in to show us. She spins around like a top, her white socks flashing from under the layers.

"Mom, it's stunning!" I say.

"It really is," Leo agrees.

"Oh, stop. Maybe if I were twenty-five and getting married at Cinderella's castle. Molly, it's hard to believe you ever bought this. It just doesn't seem like you."

"I know," I say. "It's not."

⁕ ⁕ ⁕

I don't blame Leo for wanting to steer clear of Bella So, but I'm willing to brave the boutique. It'll be my wedding gift to her, I tell my mother; we'll exchange my gown for any one she wants. Unlike me, my mom seems not at all cowed by the model-y clientele and saleswomen. She quickly zeroes in on an elegant silk design with freshwater pearls lining the spine, knee-length, a modest A-line cut. When she tries it on, I can instantly picture the occasion: a backyard clambake with just family and a few close friends.

At the register, my mom's eyes go wide. I tell her not to worry, that it's already paid for. But she writes me a check on the spot for the full amount minus one hundred dollars. "That's a much more appropriate gift," she says. "Thank you, Molly."

As much as I don't want to accept the money, it'll allow me to move to a new apartment—and to move on. "Thanks, Mom. This means a lot."

On our way out, I spot Ingrid. I can tell she recognizes me because she flares her nostrils before averting her gaze. But I figure, what the hell—I walk right up to her and flash a big smile. "Hi, Ingrid. It's so nice to see you. I'll be sure to send Lana your regards." I'm out the door before I can register her reaction.

Back at her car, my mother touches my shoulder. "Molly, I have a confession." I have no idea what's coming, but I'm more curious than wary. "I only made it through twenty pages of Gabe's book. I just couldn't get into it. Reading it felt kind of icky, like I was invading his privacy."

I laugh. "Since when have you ever felt bad about invading someone's privacy?"

"Is that terrible? Chapter One, and I was done." She glides her palms back and forth, like she's washing them clean of the whole book.

How simple, to decide you're done and—*tada!*—be done. My mom's confession gives me the courage to make my own: "I didn't finish it either," I say. "I read maybe two-thirds, in bits and pieces." It's a relief to finally admit it aloud.

My mom's eyes go wide. "Oh, you're bad. Is that why you two broke up?"

"Nah," I say, shrugging. But I wonder, is it, kind of? I wish I could write out a point-by-point explanation of our breakup. I wish I could cite a series of facts that added up precisely and definitively to the end, like a mathematical sum. But the relationship's dissolution, it turns out, is as murky and mysterious to me as the reasons it once worked.

"Even still," my mom says, "I'm happy your father never wrote a novel, and I pray John never decides to write one either. It seems like it could make things complicated."

"That's one way to put it."

"Why not finish it?" my mom says as she settles into the driver's seat and starts the ignition. "What's the harm now?"

Chapter 33

I KEEP PICKING up Gabe's book and putting it down again to do other things—like, pack up my belongings. Then hunt for a new place to live. Then hire Melinda a staff and plan their on-boarding. Then draw up a proposal to work part-time for John—I figure I can manage the setup of his new inn remotely; that plus consulting for Melinda would add up to full-time. Then work up the courage to call Lana and suggest lunch, then pick just the right restaurant when she agrees to it. Then Google "how to support an addict in recovery" and dive down that Internet rabbit hole.

The morning of my lunch with Lana, I change my outfit three times and drink two cups too many of coffee. My nerves make me late, and when I arrive, I'm surprised not to see my always-punctual sister-in-law. Only when the woman idling by the door turns around to face me do I realize it's Lana. She's fleshier, with a bit of a belly and a layer of padding on her upper arms. The new sturdiness suits her, and it feels good to wrap my arms around her torso. "Lana, hi."

"I got fat, I know." She says it matter-of-factly, with no hint of shame, no subtle appeal for me to insist otherwise. She shrugs. "Leo seems to like that I finally have a butt."

Lana holds out a little white capsule to me, and watches my eyes go wide. The addiction web sites offered no guidance for this. "It's a Tic-Tac, silly." She tosses back a handful. I accept one tentatively, holding it on my tongue like it's a communion wafer, wishing I knew some prayer to keep Lana well.

Sitting at the table opposite my sister-in-law, I observe her over the rim of my menu. She's scanning the specials, crunching at another mass of Tic-Tacs. She strikes me as an altered version of her former self, her gestures looser, her voice dropped a key. But I know my memories can't be trusted—the last few times I saw her she was altered, too, high on painkillers. I think back to before the water-skiing accident, to Leo's birthday party, which feels like nine years—not nine months—ago. Lana finessed every detail: the music, the drinks, the food, and of course herself, her dress a combination of fun and fancy, her makeup muted except for a pop of pink lips, her hair twisted into a chic updo. I always admired how Lana seemed to have it all together. Now her hair is gathered into a messy ponytail and her button-down strains across her torso, with little keyholes gaping between the buttons. She tears off a slab of French bread from the basket and stuffs it into her mouth.

"I was so sorry to hear about you and Gabe," she says mid-chew. "I guess if we're both gonna be wrecks, at least we can be wrecks together, right?" Her laugh reveals bits of crust wedged between her teeth.

Despite this, and despite her disheveled appearance, Lana doesn't seem like a wreck. She seems relaxed, and at ease with this new version of herself. Before meeting up, I'd made a mental list of delicate questions to ask her, like a homework assignment. But chatting now, I can't recall any of them. Lana tells me about the women she met at rehab—some who'd been in and out of recovery for years, who'd lost partners and children and whole lives to their addictions, who couldn't manage to get or to stay well. She says it made her realize how lucky she was, how she had everything. I consider this, and my own self-pity over all I've lost, when really I too have so much.

As I catch Lana up on my life, the incidents with Gabe and Talia strike me as like bits out of a sitcom. I explain how surreal it was to watch Gabe on *The POV.* "I kept shouting at the screen, like some chain-smoking daytime-TV addict," I tell her. "I'd call out Gabe for being a moron, and then get angry when he ignored me." I feel lighter, laughing along with my sister-in-law.

I'm about to describe the ridiculous video montage of Gabe and Talia's reunion, when my field of vision is hijacked. The words disappear from my head. My jaw literally drops. When I recover the ability to speak, I blurt out, "Oh my god." I block my face with my menu, peeking out over it like the world's most rattled spy.

"What?!" Lana hisses.

There she is, two tables away. Sitting cross-legged in a faded sundress, her hair spilling down her back like a statement accessory. She's with a guy—not Gabe, not Jonathan, someone new. She's perched forward to flirt, fidgeting a stack of metal bracelets that clink along with her oversized gestures. The tilt of her chin seems perfectly calculated so her lip gloss will catch the light at maximum shine. Her every movement looks like a pose, studied and deliberate, hyperaware of the gazes of both men and women all around.

"It's Talia," I whisper. "Right over there."

"No!" Lana sneaks a look, then leans in to me. "What should we do?"

A dozen possibilities flit through my head, of how to mess with her or give her a piece of my mind or demand an apology for all the ways she's wronged me. I dismiss each one as flimsy, juvenile, lame. When Talia cocks her head in response to something her companion says, I see her snort. I watch as she scratches her leg, then checks her phone, then combs her fingers through her hair. Her meal comes and it's a veggie panini and fries, the same meal I planned to order. I observe her eat, going first for the fries, dipping them one by one into a pool of ketchup, little dabs of which end up in the creases of her mouth. It's all so ordinary. Talia is just a person, like anyone else. It's a revelation. As a result, all the anger and spite and vengeance I've felt toward her vanishes. *Poof!* I can hardly believe it. What's left is a spaciousness that I haven't felt in months. I breathe in, filling my lungs.

"Well?" Lana looks at me expectantly.

I shrug. "Let's just order."

Disappointment flashes across Lana's face, before she settles into a nod; she seems to understand. I'm trying to recall where I left off my story, but the thread is lost. Anyway, I no longer want to talk about Talia or Gabe or Gabe's book, or any of what's happened. I want to discuss the gown designs Lana mailed me, and tell her about Melinda's start-up.

But I'm interrupted again, this time by vibrations in my pocket. At first, I ignore them, but they continue on a loop, starting up again a moment after stopping. "Sorry," I say to Lana, taking out my phone.

Sam's words burst through my earpiece: "Holy shit, this little lady is on her way. Three weeks early and raring to go—already so precocious, am I right?" It takes me a moment to understand what she's talking about. *Oh!* "I hate to interrupt your regularly scheduled afternoon, but can you meet me at the hospital, uh, stat?"

I scramble with my purse and nearly trip over my chair as I apologize to Lana for cutting our lunch short. "No worries—I'll just go eat with them," she says, indicating Talia's table. "Only kidding. I love you, Molly." Her hug is hearty and heartening—it fills me with gratitude that she's back home and on the mend. "Off you go," she says, patting me on the back and nudging me toward the door.

Heart revving, I weave around full tables and dodge waiters bearing heaping plates of food. But when I reach the exit, something slows me, like a speed bump. I spin around and, in a glance, I take in the restaurant, the patrons, and then one in particular: Talia.

I look at her until I catch her eye. I see her see me and flinch, then rearrange her face into a scowl, defensive, on guard. My smile is spontaneous. And to my astonishment, Talia smiles back. It looks utterly un-posed. As the two of us hold each other's gazes, I imagine us also holding an olive branch, each grasping one end, its length spanning the restaurant, leaves hovering decoratively over the tables. I nod, wishing Talia well with my eyes, and then I turn around, duck out the door, and hail a cab.

*   *   *

Sam's shriek is identifiable from across the maternity ward. At her bedside, I'm assigned the task of insisting that the nurse administer the highest authorized dose of epidural. Once that's taken care of, and Sam wiggles her toes and exclaims how fabulous it is to not feel a thing, my job shifts to dodging her ongoing attempts to set me up with Malcolm the dude-la. I admit he's sexy in an unkempt hipster-y way; I can tell there's a handsome face under that scraggly beard. So, when Sam spends ten minutes on the phone with her mother shouting out directions to the hospital, Malcolm and I get into it about our favorite Brooklyn bars. It feels natural when he asks for my number and suggests we meet up at one of them.

At some point, I nod off in a chair. I'm woken by a nurse's gentle tap. "Your friend is about to start pushing," she whispers.

I don't let go of Sam's hand for what feels like hours. As she pants and pushes and nearly breaks my fingers with her grip, I can't help but feel scared for this brand-new person about to leave the safety and security of the womb and emerge into our complicated world. Sam looks me in the eye, beads of sweat dotting her forehead. "Ready?" she says, as if we're doing this together. I suppose we sort of are.

I squeeze her hand. "Ready."

Felicity Smith is born at 2:32 a.m. She's a lumpy, blotchy little thing who writhes and whimpers as a nurse lifts her onto a scale and announces her weight: seven pounds, two ounces. That makes her official, a human being with a name and a size and ten stubby fingers and ten tiny toes, which Sam is currently examining.

"Feel her head," Sam says. So, for the first time, I touch my best friend's daughter; I stroke the soft blonde tufts, marveling at how it's such a sparse covering on such a fragile shell. "You have to help me protect her, okay?"

"I will," I say, another vow I know I'll keep.

Soon, everyone will rush in to the recovery room. Tom, of course, and Sam's parents, plus a whole welcome wagon of loved ones. Each of them will lay claim to a part of this occasion, and to the baby herself— adding to the deep well of love and care she'll need to grow up into her own. But, not quite yet. For a short stretch of the night, the hospital hum hits a lull, and it's just the three of us—Sam, Felicity, and me—as if we're outside of time and space. My friend holds out her daughter, swaddled snugly, and I scoot into bed beside them and take the cozy package into my arms. I rock her side to side as Sam babbles to her in the new language of motherhood. It soothes Felicity and me both.

The day Sam announced she was pregnant was the same day I told her I was engaged. We met at our favorite French restaurant, the classy one that serves baguettes with olive oil and garlic cloves, where sometimes I feel like I'm only playacting at adulthood. Afterward, we walked along the Gowanus Canal, and as we stood on the bridge, peering down at the murky waters, I revealed my big news. Sam and I were both on the brink of new life stages.

And now here we are, eight months later: I've taken a step back, while Sam is forging forward—into the unknown chaos of feedings and diapers and squeaky things meant to delight and pacify. I fast-forward to a year from now: Maybe Felicity utters her first "Mama" or takes her first steps, and Sam calls to tell me about it, maybe while I'm on a weekend getaway with Malcolm. I jump ahead a decade: Maybe Felicity is over for a sleepover, our monthly tradition of movies and manicures, while her mother is out dancing with Tom or who knows who. These scenarios are simultaneously easy and impossible to imagine.

I return to the present. "Baby's first selfie?" I ask, and Sam nods. I grab my phone, extend my arm, and see the three of us framed in the screen, Sam and I wearing wide grins and Felicity placid. I've heard it takes weeks for babies to start smiling, longer still to laugh. It must take that much experience of the world to understand that it's filled with pleasure and joy, despite everything else. I snap the shot.

"Yoo hoo!" Tom appears in the doorway, hugging a teddy bear, eyes large with tears, looking like a little boy. It makes me wonder if I'll ever stop marveling at people my own age being old enough to have kids of their own, if I'll ever stop having to remind myself that I'm a full-blown adult. Tom's arrival is my cue to go. I hand off Felicity, kiss Sam on the forehead, and slip out.

In spite of the early hour, the waiting room is dense with people. Some doze or stare at the television cube mounted high on the wall; others are animated and chatty. Instead of the sober gloom that hangs over most hospital waiting rooms, there's a communal energy here. New people are being born, and we're all a part of it! Being alone among such cheer makes me a little lonely, so I text Kirsten the baby selfie, captioned, **We miss you!**

I imagine her receiving it while driving across some bland stretch of the Midwest, all her belongings loaded up in a U-Haul behind her. When five minutes pass and she still hasn't responded, my stomach knots up. Gone less than a day, and the loss of her feels heavy already.

I buy myself a vending machine coffee and pick at the Styrofoam cup. I halfheartedly play a round of Words with Friends on my phone, and then mindlessly scroll through social media. I think of Gabe. He would want to know that Sam had her baby, that everyone is healthy and happy. I text him the same photo, uncaptioned.

"Molleeee!" The cry originates from Kirsten's gaping mouth. She's employing every possible muscle to barrel herself through the maternity ward's double doors. I think I must be mad, that she must be a mirage, until I spot a harried-looking Caleb following close behind.

"What are you doing here?" My voice cracks. My eyes go blurry with tears.

Kirsten wraps her sweaty self vise-like around me, and it feels as delicious as cradling newborn Felicity felt an hour ago. She's out of breath: "When Tom told me Sam was in labor, I put the brakes on our departure. A one-day delay is worth it to meet the baby! So, where's our friend and our new little friend?"

When we're let back in to see Sam, the room has transformed: It's teeming with relatives and medical professionals, cluttered with flowers and gifts. Sam yelps when she spots Kirsten, and a path clears to the bed.

"Hello, Felicity," Kirsten coos, reaching for the baby, "our fourth American Girl."

Somehow, before she says it, this American Girl connection slipped my mind. I now remember that I was the one to suggest the name in the first place, back at the doll inn upstate. I turn to Sam: "I thought you said you hated the name Felicity."

Sam shrugs. "It grew on me. And Tom loved it."

Caleb places a tentative hand on the baby's belly. "Can I hold her?" he asks. Kirsten hands off Felicity, and as Caleb bounces her gently in the cradle of his arms, she hovers between sleep and waking, eyelids flickering. I watch Kirsten watch her husband.

"You know," Sam says, "they released a bunch more American Girls after the ones we grew up with."

"The next one was Addy," Kirsten says with authority. "Adeline is a pretty name for a baby girl, isn't it?"

"It is," Sam says, and I agree. I imagine Kirsten's future baby and the tiny dress I'll get for her, "Adeline" embroidered across the front.

Time passes in that elastic way of big milestones, stretching out and springing back, an hour feeling like both a full day and an instant. When Caleb consults his watch and says they better hit the road, Kirsten looks stricken. "I can't," she says, flinging herself onto Sam's bed.

"Yes, you can," I say. "And I should probably go, too." I squeeze Sam's arm, knowing I'll be back tomorrow. Sam blows me a kiss while cradling her baby and stroking Kirsten's hair. Kirsten eventually peels herself away and collapses into Caleb. The three of us leave together.

In the hallway, Kirsten looks at me and then at her feet. "I can't handle another goodbye."

"Let's skip it, then," I say. "Anyway, you know I'll be visiting you before you've even unpacked."

"I love you, Molly. Okay, I'm walking away now."

She's halfway down the hall when I call out, "I love you, too. I'll miss you." Caleb holds her steady as they turn out of sight; I feel grateful Kirsten has him.

As I exit the hospital, the snap of morning air takes me by surprise. It's a beautiful spring day. With no baby to care for, no husband to accompany across the country, no plans at all, I'm totally free.

So, I take out Gabe's book, flip to the last chapter, and start reading:

Russell's explanation for his new phone number was that a New York area code would make him feel like an official city dweller. And it did, along with his Brooklyn sublet and his job at the coffee shop while he looked for full-time work. But also, the new digits meant he no longer had to screen calls from unknown numbers at 2 and 3 and 4 a.m. Russell had always assumed drunks were either angry or jolly or quiet, but Dahlia's drunken temperament ran the gamut from sweet and flirtatious to spiteful and furious. He'd stopped listening to the voicemails featuring her slurring monologues lasting the entire allotted two minutes; now he simply deleted them. He considered warning Verizon not to reassign his old number. An unsuspecting stranger didn't deserve Dahlia. No one did.

All this talk of phones prompts me to check my own. I forgot that I texted Gabe back at the hospital. His reply pops up on my screen: **Salutations from Asheville. Everyone looks great! Pass along my congrats to Sam & Tom.**

I type back, **How's the tour going?**

Good good. Next on to Nashville, then Louisville.

So many villes!

Yep, and I'll be in Yorkville in a couple weeks.

As in, Manhattan?

I'm aware of my heart pounding as Gabe's speech bubble fills with bouncing ellipses. In a blink, they're replaced by: **Yeah. Wanna get together?**

Do I want to get together with Gabe? I think about it. We won't have to discuss bills or wedding logistics. We won't have to be each other's support systems. We won't have to reassure one another of our devotion, or doubt that devotion, or bristle at that doubting. I realize that yes, I do want to get together with Gabe.

Okay, I type, and hit send. Then I put away my phone and keep reading.

It was when he went to pay his first phone bill that Russell realized his bank account had been emptied, his credit cards maxed out. Within an hour, his roommate emailed to say his rent check had bounced. It was Dahlia, of course. It was always Dahlia.

Weirdly, Russell wasn't mad. He'd sort of figured this new life—new city, new job, new freedom—was too good to be true. And truthfully, on nights when he had no plans, when he could hear his roommate and the guy's girlfriend through the wall moaning and moving the bed, he was ashamed to find that he missed all the calls from unknown numbers. It was pathetic, but he missed the persistent attentions of Dahlia.

At the end of the week, Russell collected his $214 paycheck, just enough to buy a week's worth of pizza and rent a van to haul his shit back to his dad's place in New Jersey. He promised his roommate he'd make up the rent, and he would, even if the guy had no reason to believe him.

So, then Russell was back to where he'd been before ever laying eyes on Dahlia: sleeping in a shitty twin bed in his childhood bedroom, flat broke, a total loser. His dad had never lamented his empty nest, and he wasn't the type to throw Russell a Welcome Home party. When Russell made the mistake of telling him the details of how he'd ended up in this position, his dad used words like "stalking" and "fraud" and "felony" in reference to Dahlia. Russell supposed he was technically right, although it didn't feel that way. He insisted he didn't want to press charges. His dad called him a pussy and Dahlia a cunt.

This last sentence makes me laugh out loud. I know it's a disgusting, misogynistic word, but if anyone deserves to be called a cunt, it's lying, stealing, life-ruining Dahlia. I'm usually no fan of "pussy," either, but for Russell it seems fitting: How can he remain so meek, letting Dahlia steamroll him once again? It occurs to me that Russell's dad could not be more different from Gabe's own parents. In response to a similar misfortune with their son, Joe and Barb would be nothing but tender, loving, and Gandhi-quoting. I feel like I'm finally grasping Gabe's fiction—the way it's both real and not real, the way Russell is both Gabe and not Gabe.

• • •

Gabe and I volley texts back and forth. After he caps off his book tour, he's taking a break at his parents' house. And then? He's not sure. I tell him he's welcome to ride out the lease in our apartment; I'll be relocating to Kirsten and Caleb's old place to finish out their lease. Gabe politely declines, omitting the obvious truth that he'd rather not return alone to the home we once shared.

Gabe's time in New York will be busy: two readings, an author panel, and meetings with his agent and editor. I ask if he's working on a new book, and he says yes. A sequel to *The Charms of Dahlia?* No. I ask what it's about then, and he says it's an underwater thriller featuring sea zombies, a sort of Jacques Cousteau-meets-*The Walking Dead* mash-up. In other words, he doesn't want to talk about it, which is fine by me. He does mention that the film rights sold for *The Charms of Dahlia*. Will his bestie Larissa Laraby be playing Dahlia? Probably, he responds; he'll ask her at their weekly chill sesh at her Hollywood Hills estate.

I start looking forward to these exchanges. I put time and energy into crafting my half, the way I used to do when Gabe and I were first dating, and it seems like Gabe is doing the same.

For our meet-up, Gabe proposes May 27th, five p.m., Brooklyn Bridge Park—in other words, our wedding date and time, at a different panorama of rocks on the water. Maybe it's a coincidence, maybe not. I RSVP yes.

In the meantime, I pick up his novel again.

Russell was game to sleep with almost all his new co-workers. The Parks Department had launched an initiative to expand the city's public gardens, and for some reason had hired only sumptuous, sylph-like creatures (plus, inexplicably, Russell). Russell liked the actual work, too. It was outdoors and physically demanding and afforded him views not only of his fellow gardeners, but also of stunning cityscapes.

His coworkers flirted, and they invited Russell to happy hours. He tagged along now and then, and went home with a couple of them, too, their respective dirt-lined fingernails grazing each other's sunburned skin. But usually, Russell boarded the PATH train back to New Jersey after work, and he and his dad ate dinner together, a sedate affair with *SportsCenter* subbing in for conversation. Russell pitched in for groceries, but it was cheaper than going out in the city. Soon he'd have enough saved up to move out.

Gardening was a kind of meditation. Russell barely thought of anything while working. Not even Dahlia, not really. Except for one morning, when a friend texted him an image of a flyer featuring a woman's curvy silhouette, stamped with the text, "The Charms of Dahlia, a modern dance solo spectacle. Directed and performed by Dahlia Freid." It listed a Los Angeles venue and three show times.

So she was okay. She was more than okay—she was dancing and performing and sharing it with whoever wished to show up and be charmed by whatever a "modern dance solo spectacle" was. Russell realized Dahlia had probably used his money to fund this endeavor. He tried to drum up some anger about it, but in truth, he was happy for her. And along with that happiness came a realization: Russell finally felt finished with Dahlia, for good.

The movers arrive tomorrow. I've packed up most of my things and set aside a small suitcase for my trip to Maine. John and my mother are throwing a sunset seafood boil for their belated wedding celebration, just family and a few friends; John's nephew's band will play, his fisherman friend will cater, and Leo and I have been instructed to pick up several cases of tax-free booze in New Hampshire on our way up. Lana is on road-trip playlist duty. The event is still a week away, so who knows, but for now the forecast says sunny and warm—my mom's been sending me updates every few hours. It's sweet how giddy she is. I'm excited, too, for both the party and its aftermath: I'll be sticking around to oversee the set-up of John's new inn, then returning to the city to launch a me ɪLow stationery pop-up shop.

I rifle through the smattering of clothing that remains in my closet. What does one wear to a non-date with one's former fiancé? It's unusually hot for late May in New York, the first wave of summer. Tucked between two sundresses, I spot a flash of pale pink and pull out the hanger. It's the dress I bought on the day of Lana's surgery, the one I imagined wearing on my wedding day. As in, today. I try it on now, and it's still beautiful, the flowy silk caressing my skin, making me feel beautiful. *Screw it,* I think, *people get dressed up for no reason at all, and so can I.* I slip on a pair of sandals, and head out to meet Gabe, grabbing his book to finish on the subway.

Russell and the longhaired goddesses spent the morning planting tulips along the path at Brooklyn Bridge Park. Later, he would think of those tulips like lavish versions of breadcrumbs, leading him to Olivia. Although at the moment, they were just a task to be completed.

The girls were doing Mexican for lunch, but Russell wasn't in the mood for tacos or company. So he found a spot on the rocks, away from the couples and the crowds of kids. He'd recently been going through his college stuff, reexamining the syllabi from the courses he'd attended so sporadically, so distractedly. Dahlia had been the one to convince him to enroll in a Jane Austen and Feminism course.

I laugh, no longer surprised to find facts from my past tucked into these pages—I highly doubt Gabe has ever read a Jane Austen novel.

She imagined it would be romantic for him to quote great literature to her in bed. But, in reality, every time Russell had begun an assigned reading, Dahlia grew irritable, pestering him until he paid attention to her instead of his novel. The main thing he'd studied in college was Dahlia. He'd missed so much.

Russell took one of the books out his bag now: *Pride and Prejudice.* The dog-eared page indicated where he'd left off: Chapter 3. He began reading, and little by little, his surroundings dropped away: the glittering river, the shouts of children, the distant dinky tune of the carousel.

If he hadn't been so focused, he would've noticed that he hadn't felt this focused in years.

So, at first, he didn't notice the girl sit down beside him. As she settled onto the next rock, kicked off her sandals, and unwrapped her sandwich, Russell was absorbed in the meeting of Elizabeth Bennett and Mr. Darcy. Only when a border collie bounded up and deposited a tongue's worth of slobber onto his lap did Russell look up from the page.

The girl was laughing at him. Her laugh was unflattering, her mouth flung open to reveal a piece of lettuce wedged between two teeth.

"You're quite a sight," she said to Russell. "Covered in dirt, reading 19th century chick lit."

Russell protested: "What about you, wearing a shirt for a band nobody's listened to in a decade?"

I smile, thinking of the threadbare Matchbox Twenty shirt that's a regular in my pajama rotation; Gabe used to like to stick his fingers through its holes while spooning me in bed.

"Have you never heard of irony?" She arched an eyebrow.

Russell volleyed: "I believe it's also been a decade since wearing ironic t-shirts was cool."

"Is that right?" she asked, but she was smiling. She bit into her sandwich.

"That looks delicious." Russell realized he was ravenous.

"Here." The girl held out the other half of the sandwich, and Russell accepted it—why the hell not?

He took a bite, tasting stale bread and dry turkey. "Actually, this isn't delicious at all."

The girl laughed again and lobbed a potato chip at him. "Ungrateful much? I'm Olivia, by the way."

"Russell."

They ate, watching the river, watching each other. It wasn't love or even lust at first sight. It was lunch. A conversation. A beginning.
The End.

I close *The Charms of Dahlia* just as the subway pulls into the station. As I exit the train and walk the few blocks to the riverside park, I consider what I'll say to Gabe about his book: I loved it, or I hated it. I wish he'd never written it, or I'm so glad he did. It destroyed us, or it saved us from each other, or it brought us back together, or it has nothing to do with us at all. It's trash, or it's a powerful story with characters I cared about. I'm disappointed in him, or I couldn't be prouder.

All of it's true, in a way. I wonder, will I apologize to Gabe, or will he apologize to me? Will we forgive each other, and renew old promises or make new ones? Or will this be a kind of send-off, one last gathering, a final moment of grace before we part ways for good? I remember my vow, to be honest about what I want, and do what's best for me—although right now, honestly, I don't know what that is. But I'm excited to figure it out. As I approach the water's edge and spot the broad back and the chestnut hair that could only belong to Gabe, a paperback clutched in his hand as he slouches against a rock, I feel ready for anything.

Acknowledgments

THANK YOU TO my agent, Joelle Delbourgo, my champion and cheerleader. I am so grateful for your continued faith and confidence in me. Thank you to the wise women of Skyhorse: to Chelsey Emmelhainz for bringing me on and offering strong early insights, to Alex Hess for ferrying me along with thoughtful feedback, to Kirsten Kim for contributing with astute notes and infectious enthusiasm, and to Caroline Russomanno for helping me over the finish line with great skill and attention to detail. You're a quartet of powerhouse editors! Thank you to my teachers, especially Tom DePeter, Max Apple, and John Browne, and to my mentors through magazines, schools, and beyond. How privileged I've been to receive such a rich education, and to continue learning from such brilliant minds throughout my career. Thank you to my early readers: to Paula Derrow for your invaluable feedback, your generosity, and your friendship; and to Amber Bryant for your encouragement and wisdom, and for joining me each week in our shared commitment to the page (as well as to wine). Thank you to Konditori and various other Brooklyn coffee shops for providing the precise amount of caffeine and ambient noise for peak productivity. Thank you to my parents, Nancy and Al, for your bottomless love and support, and to my brothers, Seth and Adam, for being friends of the finest caliber. Thank you to my daughter, Emilia: You were just a glimmer in my mind when I began this thing, you grew inside of me along with a first draft, and during revisions, you were my delicious-smelling good luck charm snuggled against my chest—then eventually toddling around and attempting to add in a few edits of your own. Finally, thank you to Damian for being by my side through draft after draft of novel after novel, for picking up the parenting slack while I work, and for devoting yourself to co-writing a much bigger story with me.